FRIENDS WITH SECRETS

FRIENDS WITH SECRETS

A Novel

CHRISTINE GUNDERSON

LAKE UNION
PUBLISHING

This is a work of fiction. Names, characters, organizations, places, events, and incidents are either products of the author's imagination or are used fictitiously. Any resemblance to actual persons, living or dead, or actual events is purely coincidental.

Published by Lake Union Publishing, Seattle

www.apub.com

ISBN-13: 9781662522710 (paperback)
ISBN-13: 9781662517662 (digital)

Cover design by James Iacobelli
Cover image: © Ekaterina Bedoeva / Getty; © Cosmic_Design, © denisik11 / Shutterstock

Printed in the United States of America

For Mom and Missy, in memory of Dad,
with all my love.

Chapter One

NIKKI

Nikki Lassiter stood in the baby formula aisle at Target, weeping softly into the downy hair of the four-week-old baby strapped to her chest. Her five-year-old twins did not notice this emotional breakdown. They were too busy giving glass baby food jars to their three-year-old brother, who joyfully chucked them to the floor from his seat in the shopping cart when his mother turned her back. None of the jars had broken—yet. But it was only 8:47 a.m. The day was still young and ripe for disaster.

The tears made it hard to focus on the endless varieties of formula on display in the shining aisles of Nikki's vast suburban Target. She scanned the shelves, trying to remember the name of the formula she'd used when her other children were babies, but the words blurred together, shifted, then broke apart again, phonetic clouds drifting across a landscape of extreme fatigue.

She rubbed her forehead and tried to think. Was it Immune Support? Fussiness and Gas? Or Non-GMO DHA? And did DHA make your baby smart? Or was DHA that terrible thing in plastic? No. That was BPA. She'd just read about it in *Perfect Mothering* magazine as she'd waited in her hospital room for the lactation consultant.

The words Pro-Total Comfort caught her eye. She removed the can from the shelf and examined the label. Nikki *was* pro total comfort. She was also pro undisturbed sleep and pro being alone in an empty room without another human being touching her for five minutes at a time, but unfortunately these comforts were not available in a can. Which was probably why people used drugs.

She cast a doleful glance at Baby Joe as a septic smell rose in the air, like porta-potties at high noon at an outdoor festival for people with gastrointestinal problems.

After putting Pro-Total Comfort back on the shelf, she reached for Fussiness and Gas. It sounded like the name of one of those children's musical groups. *Here's another song about dinosaurs from Fussiness and Gas!*

The cart was full, but she managed to wedge two cans into the small space between her three-year-old son, Daniel; a box of diapers; and a mountain of school supplies. Blue folders *with prongs*, red folders *without prongs*, *eight* washable markers (*not* the ten pack), and *four* highlighters when they only came in packages of three. School-supply shopping was a treasure hunt where you paid $100 to participate and the prize at the end was unfocused anger and a gigantic headache.

It was also a test. Would she be the only mother in the school district unable to track down the clear plastic six-inch ruler? Would her children be mocked for their inadequate, nonconformist school supplies?

Probably not.

But then again . . . what if they were?

Baby Joe stirred in the carrier strapped to her chest, moving his tiny starfish fingers and making the mewling noises only babies can make. She stroked his butterfly-soft cheek, and the back of her eyelids began to burn. He deserved breast milk so he could be ten IQ points smarter and get into Harvard or possibly Stanford, like all the other breastfed babies.

She cast a wary eye at the three formula-fed children she'd already brought into this world. They seemed smart enough. Too smart, actually, with their endless creative arguments about bedtime and why the tooth fairy should bring not just cash but Nintendo Switches too.

Formula was perfectly fine.

Right?

Squeezing her eyes shut, she took a deep breath and fought the hormones flooding her body.

Buck up, buttercup.

She'd inherited this phrase from her sister, a personal trainer who ran predawn open-air boot camps for women who enjoyed being yelled at while they exercised. In her previous life, Nikki had embraced this ethos. People who whined and complained blew deadlines. People who made excuses got scooped by the competition, and people who cried ruined their mascara and made extra work for Roxy, the long-suffering cosmetologist who did hair and makeup for the six and ten o'clock news.

Yet here she was, demoralized and leaking because she'd failed at what the La Leche League called the Womanly Art of Breastfeeding.

Again.

Every time she had a baby, the lactation consultants told her the same beautiful lie, and every time, she fell for it.

Maybe it was because they were so earnest, these women in late middle age with unabashedly graying hair and vaguely biblical names like Rachael or Sarah. They flitted across the maternity ward in linen tunics with patient smiles, like the Virgin Mary with a breast pump.

Ruth was the name of the lactation specialist Nikki had worked with before she and Baby Joe were discharged from the hospital. She'd contorted Nikki's swollen breast into the correct position and said, "Give breastfeeding a real chance this time. Your body will naturally produce the amount of milk your baby needs. You'll see."

And once again, Nikki had seen. Seen Baby Joe's tiny mouth flung wide like a baby bird's, screaming with hunger because her recalcitrant breasts refused to supply enough milk.

Now she was back in the Formula Aisle of Shame, celebrating her forty-third birthday with Fussiness and Gas while her children launched baby food grenades at the floor.

She pinched the bridge of her nose as a fresh round of tears trickled down her cheeks.

Stop it.

She was Nikki Lassiter, for God's sake. Or at least she used to be. Tough as nails. Never cried, never got rattled. Not during tornadoes or prison riots. Not when a gubernatorial candidate's bigamist past and predilection for public spankings came to light five minutes before the debate she moderated. Not even when Deeply Disturbed Dominic, her scariest stalker, appeared beside her in an empty parking lot after the ten o'clock news.

Heavyset and hulking, Dominic had just been released from prison. Standing beside her car, keys clenched in her fist, Nikki had repressed the useless urge to flee in high heels. Instead, she flashed her most confident smile.

"Would you like to come inside and have a cup of coffee with me?"

He followed her back into the station, where the janitor called the police. She'd made small talk with Dominic until the cops had led him away in handcuffs, screaming her name.

She wiped her eyes with the tail of her Def Leppard T-shirt. *That's who I really am.* Calm. Tough. Quick thinking. She was *not* an unhinged woman with questionable hygiene and leaking breasts who sobbed in big-box stores.

You can do this. You are one insanely talented badass.

That's what she used to say to the baby anchors, the young rookies who filled in for her on Christmas or Thanksgiving and got nervous when they stared into the teleprompter's black and unblinking eye.

It always made them laugh, because Nikki did not look like the type of person who called other people anything like that. Nikki looked like the kind of person who organized games of touch football in the backyard after Thanksgiving dinner in a Tide commercial.

This had been the secret to her success. Gus, her old station manager, once told her she was exactly the right degree of attractive. "Not supermodel beautiful, but Girl Next Door Pretty, that's what viewers want. Clean and symmetrical, like a Beach Boys song."

But now she was neither and hadn't been for quite some time. Had she even brushed her teeth this morning? Did morning even exist when you never really went to sleep?

A tear rolled down her cheek, splashing the soft spot on Baby Joe's perfect head.

Damn hormones.

She closed her eyes and gripped the cart handle. How she longed to be done with all this. To have the dormant body of her eighty-six-year-old grandmother. Or better yet, to be a man, without flaring cramps, blood, and big feelings.

Instead, her body seemed to be launching a sort of reproductive going-away party, an end-of-days orgy of double egg production as her ovaries insisted on creating as much new life as possible in the little time that remained.

And it had worked. Distracted, with five-year-old twin girls, a three-year-old boy, and a full-time job, Nikki had kept putting off her annual visit to the ob-gyn to refill her birth control prescription because surely, she wasn't going to get pregnant accidentally at age forty-two, right?

She leaned down and nuzzled Baby Joe's head, inhaling his ineffably wonderful newborn scent. *Wrong.*

A shopping cart squeaked rhythmically from the far end of the aisle. Nikki surreptitiously wiped away her tears as a perfectly coiffed woman with snow-white hair and a pink bedazzled jean jacket came toward her. The polish on the woman's nails matched her jacket, which matched her pink earrings and necklace. This woman epitomized clean and symmetrical. She probably had an immaculate house with sheets that she washed every week, plants she remembered to water, and a pantry filled with pliable brown sugar and unexpired baking powder.

An overwhelming desire to trade places with this woman swept over her. Maybe they could swap houses? And cars. And lives. Just for a day. Or maybe a week. Or just until Nikki woke up in the morning and felt like she *wanted* to get out of bed, instead of *had* to get out of bed because human beings would literally starve, hurl themselves down staircases, or eat detergent pods if she did not fling off the blankets and march into battle when the first cry of "Mommy" pierced her dreams before dawn.

The white-haired woman lifted the reading glasses suspended from a beaded chain around her neck and scrutinized the dizzying array of diapers and Pull-Ups stacked beside the formula.

Then she saw Nikki. Her eyes narrowed, and she stared for a long moment.

Nikki tensed. *Please, God. Not today.*

"Aren't you that woman who used to be—"

Clean? Sane? Intelligent? There were so many things Nikki used to be, before becoming a stay-at-home parent against her will and better judgment two months ago. But those weren't the adjectives the woman in pink was looking for, and she knew it.

"On TV?" Nikki supplied.

"Yes!" The bedazzled woman brightened as if Nikki had just given the right answer on a game show and won a new washing machine.

Nikki manufactured a friendly smile, the kind that used to come naturally when she ran into viewers at Target or the grocery store. It was the smile she used when she read the intro to the "kicker," the happy little story at the end of every newscast, featuring goats, puppies, geriatric skydivers, or intrepid fourth graders raising money to cure cancer.

"Yes. I'm Nikki Lassiter. I . . . used to work . . ." She paused. It was so hard to say those words. Past tense. Not now. Never again. "At Channel Nine."

The woman slapped her cart handle in delight. "I *knew* that was you! My husband and I watched you every night at ten o'clock."

"I'm glad to hear that," Nikki said, bracing herself for the inevitable next question.

"But why did you leave? You were so . . ." The woman paused, once again searching for the right word.

Clean and symmetrical?

"Professional," the woman finally said. "And dependable. Always there, every night."

Dependable. Like a car battery. Or a good bra.

"I wanted to spend more time with my family," Nikki said carefully, inclining her head toward the shopping cart teeming with human life. "When Baby Number Four arrived . . . well . . . it's a lot, you know, all these kids, and I just couldn't . . ."

Compete with Fletcher Avery, the woman who'd replaced her, a twenty-four-year-old with a male first name and female last name, which was surely made up and all wrong, like Barbara Walters being Walters Barbara.

The woman laid a manicured hand on Nikki's arm. "But you always looked like you were having so much fun. You and that Christopher Mandell and the weatherman and what's-his-name who did the sports."

That's because they *were* having fun. A decade on set together made the Channel 9 news team close friends rather than mere coworkers.

It all went to hell when the family who'd owned KDAY-TV for fifty-seven years sold it to a corporate media conglomerate. The new owners replaced Gus, the station manager, with Zander, a twenty-eight-year-old Bitcoin enthusiast with an immaculate five o'clock shadow and a cold brew addiction. He decided to take things in a "fresh new direction" by firing everyone but the sports anchor, with whom he played golf.

"I loved my coworkers." Nikki plucked a jar of baby food from Daniel's chubby hand. "We still talk all the time."

"Well, we miss you," the bedazzled woman said. "But we like that new girl too."

Nikki wrestled her face into a mask of polite detachment. "New girl?"

"Yes, the one who replaced you. Although she isn't quite as . . ."

Nikki held her breath as the woman searched for the right word. *Intelligent? Authoritative? Charismatic?*

"Detached," the woman finally said. "I never knew what you thought about politics, but my goodness, this new lady certainly has opinions, doesn't she? And she's very pretty, of course. One of those beauty pageant girls, wasn't she? Miss Montana, I think. Or maybe it was South Dakota? I'm not sure."

Nikki clenched her jaw so hard her molars hurt. "I have to go now. My baby is fussing."

The bedazzled woman looked down at the infant attached to Nikki's chest, his crescent moon eyes closed in a rare episode of deep and contented sleep.

"Oh, a newborn," she cooed, leaning in closer. "He's beautiful."

Nikki's expression softened. "Thank you."

"By the way," the woman said, glancing at the list clutched in her hand, "could you tell me which Pull-Ups I should get for my grandson? My daughter said he likes the kind with race cars, but I can't find any."

Nikki plucked a package of Pull-Ups from an upper shelf.

"Thank you," the woman said.

"Happy to help." Nikki turned her cart around. "Have a good day."

"You too!" the woman called as she walked away. "And enjoy every precious moment of these wonderful years with your little ones! Time goes so fast."

Nikki gathered her fraying remnants of self-control and pushed her cart into an empty checkout lane while her children sang a loud, off-key version of "Wheels on the Bus" with wild arm gestures.

A clerk in her early twenties gave the kids a friendly wave as Nikki stacked her items on the conveyor.

She looked up at Nikki and smiled. "Your grandkids are so cute."

Nikki's head jerked back, as though the checkout lady had just slugged her in the stomach with a bottle of laundry detergent. A sick sensation flooded her body.

"Children," she said softly, her throat suddenly dry. "These are my *children*. Not my grandchildren."

Children, because I didn't get married until I was thirty-six. Children, because I wasn't even sure I wanted kids until Josh came along. Children, because you'd look old, too, if you hadn't slept in five years.

Not grandchildren. Children. You undiplomatic, oblivious, infantile slut.

The checkout clerk's eyes widened, and she covered her mouth with her hand. "Oh, gosh, I'm so sorry. Your kids, I mean. They're really cute."

Nikki jammed her credit card into the machine and didn't answer. Like a boxer who'd been knocked out one too many times, she didn't have the energy for a sassy comeback or even a polite response.

"Can we have a candy bar? And Play-Doh?" The twins looked up at her with angelic expressions. "Please? Please? Please?"

Why in God's name did they stock checkout aisles with candy and toys, something no sane woman on the planet would ever allow? Further evidence that men ran every corporation in America.

Nikki grabbed three chocolate bars and the Play-Doh, then tossed them onto the conveyor belt without saying a word.

Olivia and Isabella exchanged joyful glances. Obviously, their real mother had been abducted by aliens and replaced by a fantastically permissive lizard person in human form.

The clerk handed Nikki a receipt with an apologetic smile. Nikki shoved it into her purse and pushed her cart toward the door and into the parking lot.

It took ten minutes to load the items into the minivan and buckle the twins, the preschooler, and the baby into the car. After putting the cart away like a responsible citizen, and double-checking the bottom for paper towels, something she was inclined to pay for and then forget, she flung herself into the driver's seat, sweat dripping down her back.

A Target receipt fluttered under her windshield wiper.

She groaned. How did she manage to lose *everything*? A Good Samaritan must have seen her drop it and assumed she was the kind of organized person who saved receipts and sorted them into shoeboxes or scanned them with an app or did one of those smart things they suggested in *Simple Life* magazine to eliminate clutter and reduce stress.

She wasn't that kind of person, of course. But maybe she would *become* that kind of person if she bought gel pens and a new planner with stickers that said *Dentist Appointment!* and *Vacay!* in enthusiastic letters shaped like margarita glasses. Or if she created a Family Organization Command Center with rustic chalkboard calendars from Pottery Barn.

She just needed to download an app, or find a planner she actually remembered to use, or read the right book about decluttering and organization, possibly involving color-coded chore charts and sticker incentive systems for the children. But she could change, if she tried hard enough. She *would* change.

Grimly determined, she plucked the receipt off the windshield and crammed it into her purse as the baby began to fuss, making small grunting noises that would escalate into full-blown screams if she didn't find the pacifier in the next seven seconds.

After dumping the contents of the diaper bag into the passenger seat, she finally located the pacifier in the cup holder, just as Baby Joe erupted like a teakettle, filling the air with angry cries.

Behind him in the third row of the minivan, five-year-old Olivia looked at her twin sister, Isabella, who wrinkled her nose in distaste. "OMG. Baby Joe is a *disaster*."

Olivia rolled her eyes. "Total nightmare."

Nikki rested her head on the steering wheel, trying to ignore the fact that her five-year-olds sounded like sixteen-year-olds, thanks to the combined influence of Shelby, the eighth-grade cousin they worshipped, and Zelda, the nineteen-year-old former nanny now taking appointments for sessions as a life coach.

Maybe Nikki should book an appointment. She needed a life coach. Maybe she needed a full life *transplant*, the way other people got a new heart or kidney. Or maybe she just needed four hours of uninterrupted sleep.

Soothing harp music rang out from her phone, a ringtone chosen in an unsuccessful attempt to create an aura of calm in her daily life. She glanced at the name on the screen. Another call from Gus, pestering her about that media training job. She let it go to voicemail. They needed the money, but nothing could be sleazier than teaching the wife of a politician how to evade tough questions from reporters.

Still. She'd called the potential client and left a message. Someone had to pay the mortgage. Josh's new venture hadn't produced a paycheck yet, and the savings account keeping them afloat got smaller every day. She glanced up at the sunroof and mumbled the prayer that had become a mantra over the last two months.

Dear God. Please let me return to the job and the paycheck I loved.

Then she tossed her phone into her purse and started the car. Clearly, she should put this day out of its misery and go back to bed. She glanced at the clock on the dashboard. No chance of that. It was only 9:19 a.m.

Then she swore under her breath. The Kindergarten Jamboree started at nine.

She exhaled, releasing a strange sound from deep in her throat, a combination moan-sigh, like the cry of a Wookiee mixed with the disturbing cackle of a Tickle Me Elmo doll.

In twenty years as a TV anchor and reporter, Nikki had never missed a deadline. Never. Not once.

But this morning she'd be late. Again.

Chapter Two

AINSLEY

Ainsley Bradley riffled through the drawers in her walk-in closet with rising panic. Bigger than her first apartment, the closet resembled a clothing store with a vaguely Scandinavian aesthetic. Neatly folded cashmere sweaters, sorted by color, graced uncrowded blond shelves bathed in the glow of recessed lights. Shoes and handbags sat on display in a glass-enclosed cabinet, the shoes sorted by height, flats on the left, heels on the right.

It wasn't that Ainsley had nothing to wear. The loveliest clothes money could buy filled her closet, but as usual she didn't know which of these beautiful things *should be worn*. Which shoes were appropriate? What shirt most suitable for the occasion? With a jacket? Or a sweater? And what kind of pants? Or maybe jeans? White jeans? Jean jeans? Leggings? A skirt? What about a dress?

She sat down on the window seat, reached under the velvet cushion, and removed a tiny spiral notebook, a pencil, and her cheat sheet.

Time to consult the Oracle at Neiman Marcus.

A personal shopper had created this road map to the wardrobe choices of the upper middle classes last year when Ainsley's daughter started pre-K. Her upbringing in a rural backwater had not prepared her for the Yeti-swilling, Patagonia-clad suburbs of Washington, DC.

She'd fit in perfectly well with the other moms during the early playground years when the kids were really little. Sitting on mulch, or in the sandbox, she managed to make mostly normal small talk with the other mothers who hadn't showered or combed their hair in days, everyone bleary eyed in spit-up-stained T-shirts.

Then her daughter turned four and started pre-K at St. Preston's Preparatory Academy, and everything changed. The mothers of St. Preston's wore $300 yoga pants and wedding rings with stones the size of Easter eggs, and threw catered birthday parties featuring gluten- and lactose-free cupcakes, ponies, bouncy houses, *and* magicians. Ainsley's carefree days sitting in the sandbox in frayed sweatpants ended forever when her mother-in-law called to tell her they'd been accepted at a school she'd never wanted to apply to in the first place.

Part of her wanted to rip up the cheat sheet. *I shouldn't need this anymore. I should be able to figure this out on my own.*

But she couldn't. She ran her finger down the columns to the appropriate category.

Event: School Function

Season: Fall

Outfit: #7

A numbered tag dangled from each hanger. She rummaged through the closet, removing every article of clothing with a number 7 on the tag, then laid each one carefully across the island in the center of the closet.

If there was a 7 on the tag, the articles of clothing could be worn together, a brilliant system, like Garanimals for insecure grown-ups.

From the various options designated with a number 7, she selected a white button-down shirt, a creamy, lightweight leather jacket, dark skinny jeans, brown suede boots, and silver accessories.

She glanced at the full-length mirror at the far end of the closet and adjusted her necklace.

A safe choice. She didn't want to stand out, even though her height and looks often drew unwanted attention. She just wanted to blend in, not make any mistakes. Like last year when she'd worn the same outfit two weeks in a row. Tiffany Hastings had leaned over at a PTA meeting and whispered, "That's so cute. You're wearing your PTA outfit again."

The memory made her cheeks burn. Now she kept track.

She took a deep breath, grabbed a handbag that cost more than the trailer where she'd grown up, and headed downstairs to collect the children.

"Mommy!"

Adam launched himself off the family room couch and grabbed his mother's hand. Grace looked up from the table in the breakfast nook, where she'd used every shade of pink in the crayon box to draw a farewell picture for Emma, their vacation-bound nanny.

"Time to go, chickens," Ainsley called, grabbing the keys to the Mercedes SUV from a row of neatly labeled tags beside the mudroom door, organized by type and model. Jaguar convertible. BMW station wagon. Tesla sedan.

"Mommy," five-year-old Grace said with great dignity. "We're *people*, not chickens."

"All right, people who are not chickens, get in the car." Ainsley straightened her daughter's pink hair bow. "Get your shoes and say goodbye to Emma. She's ready to go."

The children headed for the mudroom, mobbing their nanny as she attempted to pull her giant suitcase through the door and into the garage.

"We'll miss you." Grace handed Emma a picture of a princess holding a dog while riding a unicorn and eating a Krispy Kreme doughnut, a visual representation of everything Grace loved most in the world.

Emma pulled Grace and her little brother into a tight hug. "I'll only be gone two weeks. You won't miss me at all."

"A huge and preposterous lie," Ainsley said, then closed the door behind them and punched in the security code.

The kids piled into the Mercedes while Ainsley walked Emma to her Toyota Camry. She handed the nanny an envelope.

"What's this?" Emma asked.

"Mad money."

She ripped opened the envelope, eyes widening. "Five hundred dollars?"

"It's a bribe, to make sure you come back."

Emma looked up at her from the driver's seat. "Thank you, Mrs. B."

Ainsley handed Emma the sunscreen she'd forgotten on the kitchen table. "Have a wonderful time in Costa Rica."

"I will. And thanks again." She jammed a straw hat onto her head and grinned up at Ainsley. "You guys are too good to me."

"Golden handcuffs. Now get going or you'll spend your hard-earned vacation stuck at home helping Adam make a worm farm."

Emma pulled out of the driveway with a joyful goodbye wave. Ainsley climbed into her own car and pulled out an elegant leather planner with her initials embossed on the cover. She turned to her to-do list, mentally running through her schedule for the rest of the day.

Ainsley loved lists. She loved the feeling of accomplishment and control that washed over her each time she checked off an item.

Take kids to dentist. Talk to housekeeper about groceries for school lunches next week. Finalize menu for Library Gala. Talk to Ben about Disney over Thanksgiving break.

This last item made her grip the steering wheel a little tighter. They needed to talk about something far more important than Mickey Mouse. Now that he'd announced his run for governor, she had to tell him. She had to find time—no, she had to *make* time for a long, private conversation with no interruptions. It couldn't wait a minute longer.

Or could it? She'd kept this secret from her husband for almost a decade. Maybe a few more days. Or weeks. Or months. Or years. Maybe a few more years wouldn't matter?

A knock on the window interrupted her thoughts. She turned to see Lyman, their ancient head gardener, standing beside the car in a faded denim shirt.

She rolled down the window, and he handed her one perfect pink camellia. "Just started blooming," he said with pride. "Keep it in your car, it's a natural air freshener."

"It's beautiful." She buried her nose in the delicate petals and inhaled the honeyed sent.

A surge of gratitude washed over her as Lyman waved to the kids and shuffled away. What could she possibly have done to deserve all this? A husband she adored. Wonderful, healthy children. A house and gardens so lovely that she sometimes spent whole minutes standing in the yard, gazing at the beauty of it all. And servants. Actual servants who guided her in a thousand subtle ways, helping her succeed where she would otherwise fail.

She said a silent prayer for her life to remain exactly as it was right now, forever. Her husband's foray into politics might change a few things, but hopefully the bones of the life they'd built together would remain the same.

"Everyone buckled?" she asked, glancing at the kids in the rearview mirror.

The children answered in the affirmative, and she checked the dashboard clock. They'd be seventeen minutes early, but she wanted to make sure they got a good parking spot.

Unlike her own mother at a similar event many years ago, Ainsley would arrive both on time *and* sober for her daughter's Kindergarten Jamboree.

Chapter Three

NIKKI

As fate would have it, the only available parking spot was three blocks from the school. The close, convenient spots were already taken by those organized families who arrived early.

After giving Baby Joe a bottle of formula, which he eagerly drained, and helping Olivia find her shoe, which she had somehow lost in the bowels of the minivan, they were ready.

Nikki removed the double stroller. Then she turned to unbuckle Daniel from his car seat and gasped.

Using a blue marker found in the seat cushion, he'd drawn vibrant DIY tattoos all over his cheeks and across his forehead. He'd augmented this look by unscrewing the lid of his sippy cup, dipping his hands in apple juice, and then running his fingers through his hair to create a sort of mohawk. He looked like a berserker, or possibly an ancient Celt.

"Oh, Daniel."

He beamed at her. "Mommy, look at the face pictures I made."

She exhaled, silently counting to ten. Then she cleaned his hands with a diaper wipe and lifted him out of the car. After setting him on the sidewalk, she retied the bathrobe that he believed to be a Luke Skywalker–style desert tunic.

His twin sisters each took one of his hands. "C'mon, Daniel. You can come inside the bouncy house with us."

The girls turned to their mother, waiting patiently as she put the baby in the stroller. Nikki glanced at them, and her heart melted like a chocolate bar left in the sun as she took in the chaotic beauty of her children. Red Popsicle-stained lips, legs dotted with Band-Aids and mosquito bites, long lashes and tumbled hair streaked with highlights no woman could ever achieve in a salon.

They were good kids. Sweet kids. And she'd missed so much time with them over the years. Maybe being fired from her job and replaced by someone younger while on maternity leave was actually a *good* thing. A blessing. As her friend Evangelical Heather always said, motherhood was only a short season in a long life. She needed to improve her attitude. Maybe this would be *fun*.

She gave each of them a kiss on the forehead, and they giggled. Then she headed slowly toward the school with her children in a lumbering caravan beside her.

The middle school band welcomed them to the playground with a shaky but enthusiastic rendition of "Ode to Joy." The head of school stood beside a bouncy house shaking hands and greeting parents as plastic pennants fluttered over folding tables laden with cupcakes and the obligatory orange slices. Children ran across the playground, balloons clutched in their hands.

It looked like the *before* segment of an alien invasion movie, right before civilization crumbles into a dystopian hellhole where everyone carries a crossbow.

Nikki's stomach tightened as a wave of guilt washed over her. Every year of her children's preschool lives she'd promised to come to events like this. And every year she'd been called into work at the last minute. The first year it was a prison riot. Then an anhydrous ammonia leak forcing the evacuation of an entire town, then a devastating tornado.

Josh had always come to the rescue in these situations. He'd leave work early or come in late to make sure the kids always had at least one parent at these events. He'd text pictures of himself and the twins wearing bunny ears at the Easter Bunny Buffet or with pinky fingers extended at the Ladybug Tea. The perfect husband. The perfect father.

She squeezed her daughter's hand a little tighter. She'd hit the jackpot when it came to husbands. Well, except in the financial department. Prince Charming usually came with a castle and a pot of gold. Josh came with massive student loans and a passion for making furniture by hand. Instead of a castle, they lived in a split-level ranch with leaking gutters and microscopic closets.

The baby's tiny face began morphing from contented perfection into an angry scrunch, and Nikki popped a preemptive pacifier into his mouth.

"There you go, my angry little bird," she whispered, stroking his downy head.

She shifted her giant diaper bag to the other shoulder, checking to make sure she had at least three spare pacifiers, just in case she lost the others, and herded her ragged little entourage toward the sidewalk.

Teddy Bear Picnics and Kindergarten Jamborees were her territory now. She needed to throw herself into stay-at-home motherhood with the same vigor she'd once directed toward interviews with indicted county commissioners.

Overhead, a banner sparkled in the sunlight, tugging her glance upward. Even her craft-deficient eyes could see that hundreds of woman-hours and a metric ton of glitter glue had gone into the creation of that sign.

She sighed, recognizing the handiwork of Tiffany Hastings. Who else could write "Welcome to the St. Preston's Kindergarten Jamboree" in perfect cursive letters with a bottle of Elmer's glue? Nikki could no longer write in legible cursive even with a pen. She hadn't liked Tiffany when they went to school here together decades ago and, unsurprisingly, still didn't care for her now.

In Nikki's experience, some people didn't change as they aged. They just became *more so*.

A few grains of silver glitter drifted in the air, a silent reproach to Nikki, who had not volunteered to help with any of the kindergarten meet and greet events over the summer.

The rational part of her brain screamed, *But you were on bed rest!*

That's no excuse! her guilty mom brain screamed back.

An enterprising mom would have found a way to contribute, even from bed. She could have stuffed goody bags. Frosted cupcakes. Called around to restaurants seeking the best deal on cheese pizza. In addition to failing to give her baby the nourishing benefits of breast milk, she was also a Kindergarten Jamboree freeloader *who hadn't even signed up to bring paper plates*, the low-hanging fruit of contributions to school events.

She rubbed her hand across the back of her neck and approached the registration table, womaned by three smiling moms behind a sign marked *School Forms*.

Nikki's heart sank. Not only had she forgotten to bring the school forms, but she'd also neglected to print them, because she'd run out of printer paper. And forgotten to buy more at Target.

Just like high school. And elementary school. And college. She'd done the work, but she'd forgotten to bring it to school, neglected to turn it in.

Zero credit for you.

Nikki approached the table. "I didn't bring my forms."

The volunteer mom behind the table beamed. "You used the Google Doc! We're trying to encourage people to go paperless this year."

"No. I just . . . forgot them," Nikki admitted.

"Oh. Well. No big deal." The volunteer mom's determinedly cheerful expression faltered. "Just bring them in tomorrow when you drop your kids off. But you can take your labeled school supplies to the classroom right now. That way your kids won't have to lug them in tomorrow on the first day of school."

Nikki resisted the urge to pat down her pockets and peer inside her purse, pretending to search for nonexistent school supplies, like an underage college student attempting to get into a bar without an ID.

"Um. I don't have those either."

Her daughters would show up on the first day of school looking like tiny Himalayan Sherpas, backs twisted under the weight of pink erasers and composition books she'd neglected to bring in early.

"I mean, I have the school supplies, obviously," Nikki felt compelled to point out. "But they're still in the car . . . and as such, they are currently . . . unlabeled."

A look of deep concern crossed the volunteer mom's face. "Oh. Okay. I mean, the teachers *expected* everyone to bring them in today. But I'm sure it's probably fine. Just . . . bring them in . . . as soon as you can."

Nikki thanked the woman and turned away, cheeks flushed.

Holy hell. She'd seen an email somewhere, at some point, while she and Baby Joe were still in the hospital recovering from her emergency C-section, but how could she possibly be expected to remember such arcane details? And didn't her husband have an email address too? Why were women expected to both give birth *and* remember to buy No. 2 pencils?

Muffled harp notes sounded from inside her purse. She fumbled through the gigantic bag, unearthing diapers in multiple sizes, broken crayons, and a bottle of drops to cure pink eye.

"Hello?" she said, a little breathless from the search for her phone. She'd once made the mistake of setting her phone to mute and then misplaced it for a week. Since then, her ringer was loud, proud, and always on—provided of course, she'd remembered to charge it.

"It's Gus. How are you?"

"So kind of you to ask. I'm having the time of my life eating bonbons and watching *Days of Our Lives* with the other stay-at-home parents in my neighborhood coffee klatch."

"Glad you're making friends," he said.

"I have no friends," Nikki pointed out, holding the phone between her ear and shoulder as she pushed the stroller. "Because all my friends are at work, working. Now I have to make all new friends. It's on my to-do list, along with diaper rash cream and double-A batteries for the Barbie Corvette."

"Maybe you don't need to make new friends," he said briskly. "I have some news."

"Bad? Or good?"

"Good."

"Zander's fresh new direction for the newsroom wilted and died, and they plan to apologize and rehire us?" she asked hopefully.

"No, but almost as good." A dramatic pause filled the air. "I think Colleen Parker is about to leave Channel Four."

Nikki's mouth dropped open. "No way."

"Way."

"When?"

"She's been in contract negotiations for weeks, and it isn't going well. She's got a month left on her current deal, and if they can't come to an agreement, I think she'll walk."

Nikki's eyes widened. Channel 4 had always been the competition, but they were noble adversaries. Some days they emerged victorious with an exclusive interview or tip from the cops, and other days Channel 9 scooped everyone in the market. It felt a little disloyal, to consider working for the competition, but right now she'd work for Satan himself if it got her out of the house and back into a newsroom with a paycheck.

"You think I have a shot?"

"I had lunch with the station manager yesterday, and he mentioned you as a possible replacement if she leaves."

Nikki paused. She and Gus had worked together so long they were practically telepathic. "But?"

"But they want more bang for their buck with the next anchor they hire. Whoever they sign will head up an investigative reporting unit.

He knows you're great on camera, but he's worried you don't have the experience to do the kind of deep-dive reporting they need."

"But I'm a fantastic reporter!" she said indignantly.

"I know that, and you know that, and everyone in our newsroom knows that, but you need to prove it to this guy before they'll consider hiring you."

"But how can I do that without a photographer and editing gear?"

"Dig something up and do all the legwork off camera. When Colleen walks, they'll call you in for an interview, and you'll have a big, juicy blockbuster to drop in their lap. Channel Four gets a new anchor and an award-winning story, and you're back on the air, doing what you love."

Ideas flooded her mind, all of them weak. Bicycle chop shops? Faulty carbon monoxide detectors? Cancer-causing toxins in nonorganic cleaning supplies?

"I'll come up with something."

"I know you will. How's that media training gig working out?"

"I'm not sure yet," she said. "I left her a voicemail last week, but I haven't heard back."

"Keep me posted, and I'll let you know if I hear of anything else."

"Thank you, Gus. I don't know what I'd do without you."

"We've been through worse, kid. Remember the tornado and hailstorm that knocked all the windows out of the news car, while you were driving it?"

Nikki smiled at the memory. "We had so much fun that day."

"And that's why you belong in a newsroom. I'll keep you posted."

As she said goodbye and slipped her phone back into her purse, she suddenly realized why she desperately wanted her job back.

She missed *excelling* at something, at being good at what she did, and the recognition that came with it.

When the ratings book came out, they'd raised glasses of champagne in Gus's office. Number one in the market again! At work, she had empirical evidence, *actual statistics*, proving she did her job well.

But no benchmarks of excellence existed in motherhood, and she received no recognition for surpassing or even meeting these invisible standards. God did not reach down from heaven and mark the worthy.

Instead, judgment rained down from grandparents, education experts, parenting columnists, in-laws, dentists, and strangers on airplanes. But the harshest judgment came from the endless whisper of self-reproach from within. It came on long days when she fell short of the invisible mark in some small or large way, failing the people she loved with a love so pure and primal that it took her breath away.

Nikki sighed as she watched other mothers head to the registration table bearing completed forms and labeled school supplies. She would now be identified as that chronically late mother who never volunteered, rarely showered, and forgot absolutely everything.

Yet through some strange alchemy, these liabilities disappeared when she entered a newsroom. The squawking police scanner, the constant blare of multiple television screens, and the din of voices *improved* her focus. Her disorganized brain flitted seamlessly from one crisis to the next without missing a beat. But away from that environment, her confidence wilted like a plant removed from sunlight.

Nikki squared her shoulders. She *would* find a way back. She just needed to dig deep and unearth a shocking scandal, a blockbuster story exposing injustice, oppression, and the abuse of power. The kind of story that resulted in new laws and televised congressional hearings. A story that made life exponentially better for the marginalized, the voiceless, the planet, for humanity as a whole.

And also—please, God—for herself.

Chapter Four

AINSLEY

Like Jane Goodall among the apes, Ainsley Bradley scanned the scene before her, searching for signals and subtle cues.

She'd used her label maker and lamination machine to affix her daughter's name to all school supplies. She'd delivered Grace's backpack to the proper classroom. She'd filled out the school forms electronically. But just in case, she also gave the volunteers at the registration table hard copies of the same forms in a manila envelope, marked in perfect handwriting with her child's name, birth date, and homeroom.

Now what? She fingered the diamonds on her tennis bracelet like worry beads.

"Mommy, let's *go*." Grace pulled on her mother's hand, tugging her toward the bouncy house.

"I'm right behind you, sweetie."

The heels on her suede boots made it hard to walk quickly. Fortunately, she'd had a lot of practice walking in heels much higher than these. She slid across the basketball court with some semblance of grace as her children raced ahead of her.

Were heels a mistake? She cast a surreptitious glance at the other moms making their way up the sidewalk and immediately felt better when she spotted a woman trudging toward the bouncy house in yoga pants and a stained Def Leppard T-shirt. She had a baby in a stroller, plus a preschooler with a mohawk, and possibly face tattoos, wearing what appeared to be a bathrobe, and twin girls skipping along beside her, ponytails bouncing.

Ainsley wiped the back of her neck. Was she overdressed? Maybe she should have worn a T-shirt too? But no. Surely *stains* weren't appropriate?

If only Ben were here. He'd tuck her hand under his arm, give her a wink, and sweep her into this event along with him, infusing her with confidence by osmosis. But he was giving a speech on economic development to the Kiwanis club. She'd have to get through this alone.

Again.

A gaggle of moms waved to Ainsley from the refreshment table, and she waved back, relieved to see familiar faces. Not people she necessarily enjoyed talking to, but people to talk with, nonetheless.

As she made her way toward them, her daughter let go of her hand and ran toward the bouncy house. A lump formed in Ainsley's throat as she watched Grace skip away, hair streaming behind her. The other little girls shrieked Grace's name, inviting her to join them. Grace melted into the group, fitting like a puzzle piece.

This made it all worthwhile. The climb-out-of-your-skin discomfort. The fear of doing something wrong, saying something stupid. Constantly feeling like a fish out of water in order to raise children who fit in at a school like this, kids who fit in everywhere, like her husband.

"Ainsley!" Tiffany Hastings embraced her in a light hug. Ainsley resisted the urge to wince as the cloying scent of Tiffany's perfume engulfed her.

She extricated herself and exchanged faux cheek kisses with the Three Jennifers standing beside Tiffany. She thought of them as Red Jennifer, who had striking auburn hair; Blonde Jennifer; and Also Blonde Jennifer. Other than hair color, they had few distinguishing characteristics, and she'd given up trying to think of them as individuals. Red Jennifer worked as a lobbyist for TruElle, a newly renamed and vigorously rebranded tobacco company. Blonde Jennifer designed her own high-end resort wear line called Beach Bunny, and Also Blonde Jennifer helped the less fortunate by chairing committees.

The Three Jennifers were Tiffany's posse, and Ainsley assumed she'd been accepted into this group because they'd gone to St. Preston's with her husband. And because her husband's family had more money than God.

If they had any idea . . . Ainsley shut this thought down as soon as it entered her mind and tried to focus on the conversation, such as it was.

"Oh my God, I love those boots! Where did you get them?"

Every conversation started this way, but Ainsley's mind still went blank. She could never remember details like this: where she bought things, what the brands were. "Um. I think they were a gift."

"Lucky lady, I wish my husband had such good taste."

They were actually a gift from her mother-in-law, part of a never-ending campaign to remold Ainsley in her image.

"Listen." Tiffany Hastings laid a manicured hand on her arm. "You aren't going to believe this, but guess who we've snagged to be our new basketball coach and athletic director? He just signed the contract last night, so we can announce it."

Ainsley opened and closed her mouth like a guppy. She had no idea. Tom Brady? Was he basketball? Or football? She followed his ex-wife on Instagram but wasn't entirely sure which sport he belonged to.

"Come on, I'll introduce you."

But before Tiffany Hastings could drag her away, the woman in the Def Leppard T-shirt joined the group. She had deep shadows under her eyes, and the back of her hair stuck up in an odd way, like a rooster tail. But she was still attractive, in a rode-hard-and-put-up-wet sort of way, and she exuded a subtle aura of authority.

"Ladies," she said, nodding at each woman in a confident, almost masculine way.

Tiffany Hastings gave the woman a smile that didn't reach her eyes. "Hello, Nikki."

Also Blonde Jennifer jumped in to make introductions. "Ainsley, do you know Nikki? You probably recognize her. She's an . . ." Also Blonde Jennifer suddenly looked stricken, and her voice faded.

"I *was* a TV anchor at Channel Nine," the woman said, sticking out her hand, "but I got sacked and replaced by someone younger while I was on maternity leave. Nice to meet you."

There was an awkward pause, and then Ainsley realized she did know this woman. "We've met," she said, shaking the offered hand. "You interviewed us once, at the groundbreaking for the library addition. I'm Ainsley Bradley, Ben Bradley's wife."

"Of course. I remember." Nikki pushed her stroller back and forth as her baby drifted into sleep. "I actually left you a message last week, about media training."

Ainsley stiffened. She'd been trying to avoid this. "I'll find you before I leave. We can work out a time to get together."

A bald-faced lie. If she could avoid media training, maybe she could avoid the media altogether. After all, her husband was the one running for governor, not her. In fact, he'd promised she'd never have to give a speech.

Ainsley's lips curved upward at the memory of this conversation. It might turn out to be the only promise Ben had ever broken. Of course, Ainsley had never broken any promises to her husband either. Lies of omission were not the same as promises.

Tiffany deftly put herself back into the conversational spotlight. "I was just about to introduce Ainsley to our new athletic director and coach. Anyone else want to come along and get his autograph?"

"Is it someone famous?" Nikki asked.

"Oh, yes. You'll never guess."

"Then maybe you should just tell us who he is," Nikki said sweetly.

"Actually, he's coming over to say hi right now," Tiffany said, craning her neck.

The women turned to watch as a tall man with a square jaw and palpable swagger approached the group.

When he was within reach, Tiffany put a proprietary hand on his arm and drew him closer.

"Ladies, I'd like to introduce you to the one and only Wyatt Jericho."

A dormant memory stirred at the edge of Ainsley's consciousness; then confusion rattled her mind as time, memory, and people who should never be together in the same place suddenly converged in front of her disbelieving eyes.

She reached for the handle of a nearby stroller, fighting dizziness as she swallowed the urge to vomit.

Chapter Five

NIKKI

He looked like one of those men in a shaving cream commercial. Square jaw. Blue eyes. Smooth skin. His ears were rather prominent, but maybe large ears were like large hands?

"Hello, ladies. Nice to see you."

The words slid from his throat like honey, deep and masculine. Also Blonde Jennifer reflexively batted her eyelashes.

Nikki rummaged through her tired brain, trying to retrieve scraps of information about this man. If only she'd paid more attention during the sports segments.

"His record speaks for itself," Tiffany said, smug with satisfaction. "He won two NCAA championships when he played in college. Then he won three more championships when he coached the university women's team."

He ducked his chin in self-deprecation. "That was a long time ago. Now I'm the old guy on the bench with a clipboard shouting instructions at players who ignore me. But I'll feel like I'm still contributing something if I can build a winning legacy here at St. Preston's."

"It's about time someone did." Tiffany flicked her hair over her shoulder. "We all loved Coach Biggle, but it was time for him to retire.

He wasn't really focused on winning, you know. He gave everyone equal playing time, regardless of skill."

Her voice dropped to a conspiratorial whisper as she discussed Coach Biggle's strange predilection for making junior high sports fun. "That's fine, of course, for the *less talented* kids, but so frustrating for those *real* athletes who want to play in high school and college."

Nikki bit down on the inside of her cheek. Yet another mother convinced that college tuition was for suckers without the foresight to get their child onto the right elite travel soccer team by second grade.

As she recalled, neither she nor Tiffany Hastings had been particularly talented athletes when they'd all played girls basketball for St. Preston's back in the day, but perhaps Tiffany had given birth to children with excellent hand-eye coordination in the interim.

"Are you coaching the girls, or just the boys?" Nikki asked.

"I'll be the athletic director for the elementary, middle, and high school, and I'll coach high school and middle school girls," he said, turning his blue eyes her way. She had to admit, he was a handsome bastard.

"Then you'll meet my niece, Shelby Stewart," Nikki said.

He nodded. "Already have. Met her at tryouts last week. Nice girl, that Shelby. A real baller."

Nikki raised her eyebrows. Admittedly, she wasn't up on her sports lingo.

"She's a good ball handler," he said. "A real strong player. I'm looking forward to working with her, and the older kids too."

Tiffany tightened her grip on his arm. "Sorry to cut things short, but I have some donor types I'd like you to meet. Maybe you can convince them to scuttle the computer lab expansion and get a new scoreboard for the football field instead."

He nodded to the other women. "Excuse me, ladies. Duty calls."

Tiffany led the coach toward the face-painting booth as the Jennifers trailed behind, leaving Nikki standing alone with Ainsley Bradley.

Nikki glanced at the other woman. She had porcelain skin and lush hair, the kind of hair Nikki had always wanted and pretended to have as a child by wearing her mother's harvest gold macramé plant hanger on her head. By design, Nikki's own hair was unremarkable. If viewers were thinking about her hair, they were not thinking about the news she delivered. Rule Number One: Never make the story about you.

Baby Joe stirred, and Nikki reflectively reached for another pacifier, even though he still had one in his mouth. Ainsley stood beside the stroller, gripping the handle so hard her knuckles had turned white.

Nikki touched her arm gently. "Are you all right?"

Ainsley gave a small shudder, as though ridding herself of something unpleasant. "I'm . . . fine. Just tired."

"I hear you, sister." Nikki adjusted the stroller's sunshade. "Listen, I have to head out, but would you like to nail down a time for our media training session before I go?"

Ainsley hesitated for a moment, then said, "Sure."

Nikki picked up on the brittle tone in Ainsley's voice. Another perfect political wife. The type of woman who stood behind her man as he apologized to the world for doing something shameful with someone who wasn't her.

A feeling of pity crept in. That wasn't fair. Maybe this woman guzzled beer, smoked cigars, and swore like a truck driver when no one else was around.

But this seemed unlikely as she took in Ainsley's crisp white shirt, spotless suede boots, and perfect makeup. Good thing they were paying her a ton for these media training sessions. She'd earn every penny attempting to make Ainsley relatable to women who got their wardrobes from T.J.Maxx and their knockoff handbags from entrepreneurial street vendors, like she did.

They settled on Saturday at 10:00 a.m. at Ainsley's house. Nikki had of course forgotten her calendar at home. She scribbled the date, time, and address on the back of the Target receipt she'd stuffed into her purse.

"Lovely to meet you." Ainsley pulled her leather jacket a little tighter. "I look forward to seeing you on Saturday."

Obviously a lie, but Nikki couldn't blame her because she wasn't looking forward to their appointment either.

She shouldered her giant diaper bag as she watched Ainsley head toward a boy and a girl about the same age as Daniel and the twins, clustered around the snack table. Then she scanned the horizon for her own scattered children.

Panic bubbled beneath the surface as her eyes lingered on the swings, then the monkey bars, and then the basketball court without sighting the familiar yellow bathrobe Daniel wore everywhere.

The worry vanished as she spotted her almost fourteen-year-old niece emerging from the bouncy house with the twins and Daniel in tow.

The children raced toward her as Shelby shortened her long strides, allowing her little cousins to pull ahead.

Olivia collapsed against Nikki's legs. "I win!"

Then she and her siblings flopped into a panting heap on the ground.

"You guys are super fast." Shelby folded her gangly legs beneath her to join them in the grass. "You should play on my basketball team."

Tall and thin with long dark hair, Shelby looked so much like her mother that Nikki sometimes felt like she'd gone back in time, suddenly becoming a little girl again, fighting over Barbie furniture with her sister, Leslie, in the basement of their childhood home.

"When I get bigger, I will," Olivia said.

"Me too," Isabella echoed.

"Mom, can Shelby come over and play? Please? Please?" Daniel begged from his perch on his cousin's lap.

Shelby rose from the ground, pulling Daniel up with her. "Sorry, little dudes, but I've got basketball practice in ten minutes."

"What do you think of the new coach?" Nikki asked as they steered the kids toward the minivan.

"Everyone seems to like him." Shelby bent to pick up the lightsaber Daniel dropped. "How are you doing without Zelda? And Mom said Uncle Josh is out of town for two weeks?"

"It's been a little rough," Nikki conceded.

An epic understatement. At 3:00 a.m. when the baby refused to sleep and her mind drifted, she found herself wondering if her life was a hallucination. Surely she wasn't in charge of all these living things? Babies and preschoolers and kindergartners, not to mention a dog, plus houseplants and a goldfish. Even a lawn. How had she acquired all the trappings of adulthood when she did not know all the things adults were supposed to know?

As she nodded off in front of the TV with the baby in her arms, she found herself half expecting her own mother to walk through the door and take charge, because her own mother was obviously the real mom, the adult who knew how to remove stains, hem slacks, make gravy.

"I can come over this weekend and hang out if you want," Shelby said.

Nikki shook her head vehemently. "Only if I can pay you."

She didn't want to take advantage of Shelby's good-natured willingness to play Barbies whenever her little cousins asked.

"Works for me." Shelby twirled a basketball on the tip of her finger. "I need money for the insanely expensive basketball shoes my mom refuses to buy."

"I have a media training gig on Saturday morning. If you could come around nine thirty, it would be a huge help."

Shelby nodded. "No problem."

The girls held Shelby's hand, and Daniel gravely kissed her elbow as she helped strap them into the minivan.

"I'm positive your mother and I were never this helpful when we were teenagers," Nikki said as Shelby handed Daniel his lightsaber.

"You're my favorite aunt."

"I'm your only aunt," Nikki reminded her as she climbed into the driver's seat and lowered the window.

Shelby grinned. "Hey, happy birthday, by the way. Has it been a good one?"

"Oh, it's been . . . something. You have any big plans for your own birthday? It's coming up."

"Not yet," Shelby said as a subtle flush colored her cheeks. "Still . . . planning."

"Well, keep us posted. And good luck tomorrow," Nikki called as she started the engine. "I can't believe it's your last first day of middle school."

"I can't either."

Shelby stood on the sidewalk and waved as they drove away. Dressed in an oversize T-shirt with no makeup, she looked like a ten-year-old girl instead of a teenager starting eighth grade. A protective urge rose up inside Nikki with a force that took her by surprise, making tears well in her eyes.

Damn hormones.

She glanced in the rearview mirror as her niece sauntered toward the school, dribbling the basketball as she walked.

Nikki's gaze returned to the road as uneasiness settled over her like dust.

Chapter Six

AINSLEY

After grabbing a jar of peanut butter and a bowl of celery sticks, Ainsley settled the kids on the sofa in the soaring great room and flipped on *Sesame Street*. As she jabbed at the remote, her mind flashed back to all the times she and her sister had tried to watch TV after school, only to find the black box silent and unresponsive because their mother hadn't paid the utility bill.

Ainsley hauled herself up the broad staircase, fingers gripping the banister. Thank God Mrs. Clayton and Marcella had the afternoon off. She wouldn't encounter anyone putting newly laundered clothes into her closet or hanging fluffy white towels on the heated rack in the bathroom.

She moved robotically through the massive primary bedroom suite, past the marble fireplace and balcony overlooking the pool and the Potomac River beyond. She stumbled into the sanctuary of her closet, locked the door, and sank to her knees, head pounding, stomach sour. Maybe she'd picked up a bug from the kids?

Wishful thinking. No antibiotic could fix this problem. Her hand shook as she pulled out her cell phone and dialed her sister.

Jolene, named after their mother's favorite Dolly Parton song, picked up on the first ring.

"Hey, I can't talk long. One of our clients wants to buy a Chinese satellite company, and it's a huge CFIUS mess with all kinds of weird tax implications. I've got a meeting with State and Treasury in ten minutes."

When Ainsley called Jolene at work, she imagined her sister in an office high above a Soviet-style factory floor, exhorting workers in gray coveralls to work faster.

She couldn't rid herself of this image, even though she knew Jolene actually sat in a glass-enclosed office on K Street, also known as Gucci Gulch, the concrete heart of DC's lobbying world. Her sister worked insane hours, unraveling the mysteries of the tax code for corporate clients desperate to legally shield their earnings from the long arm of the IRS.

"What's up?" Jolene asked in her perpetually raspy undertone. She'd sounded like a three-pack-a-day smoker since she was four years old. Men found it deeply attractive, and female friends were always asking her to record the "Please leave a message" message on their cell phones.

Ainsley closed her eyes and pictured Jolene in one of her crisp bespoke suits.

Ainsley took a deep breath. "I . . . saw someone today. Someone from the club."

"What club? The country club?"

"No," Ainsley whispered. "The other club."

A long pause. "Did he recognize you?"

"I don't know . . . I don't think so."

"Was he a regular?"

"Yes, but not one of mine."

"Where did you meet him?"

"At school," Ainsley whispered, even though she was alone, in her closet, behind a locked door.

"Is he a parent?"

"He's the new girls' basketball coach."

Jolene sucked in a breath. "Are you *serious*?"

"That's what I need to talk to you about. Do you have time?"

She could hear her sister pick up the landline phone on her desk, asking her assistant to shuffle her schedule.

"How about brunch Saturday?" Jolene asked. "I'm catching a flight to London tonight for that presentation I'm giving on the tax implications of new oversight regulations for derivative swaps. But I'll be back Friday night, okay?"

"Okay."

"The usual place?"

"Yes."

"Does Ben know?"

"Of course not." Ainsley reached for an empty shoebox as the urge to vomit rose again.

"You realize that's a huge problem, right?"

"I know." Ainsley rubbed her forehead. "I've just . . . I've been waiting for the right time."

"Tami Darlene." Her sister's gentle voice whispered the name Ainsley's parents had given her at birth, the name she'd abandoned years ago. "You've been waiting for the right time for *eight years* now."

Ainsley bowed her head. "I know . . . it's just . . . anyway. I'll see you Saturday. We can talk about it then."

"Love you." Her sister's sandpaper voice made the words a caress, and Ainsley's eyes began to sting. Did the universe hand out perfect sisters as compensation when it meted out neglectful, drunken mothers?

"Love you too." Ainsley choked out a quick goodbye and hung up, curling herself into a tight ball, knees drawn up to her chest, blinking rapidly to keep the tears at bay.

She'd come so far. They both had. But what if—

A rap on the closet door made her flinch.

"Hey, honey, you in there? I'm home."

Ben.

She sat up and took a heavy breath, sucking air into her lungs as she tried to bleach her voice of tears and terror, secrets and shame. "I'll be right out."

After removing the clothes she'd worn to the Kindergarten Jamboree, she dressed in what she thought of as her "real clothes." A T-shirt from Target, sweatpants from T.J.Maxx. She could relax now, clad in clothing that wouldn't cost a fortune to replace if she spilled coffee or the kids streaked her with finger paint.

Not that it mattered if she ruined her clothes. She could just throw the shirt away and buy another, and another, and another, every day till the sun burned out, and still not run out of money. Ben's family fortune was like a well with no bottom. Even after eight years of marriage, she still couldn't wrap her mind around the fact that her husband was closer to a billionaire than a millionaire.

She pulled her hair into a ponytail and went into Ben's closet to steal a pair of his comfortable wool socks.

When she and Ben met on their first day of work at the Treasury Department, her entire wardrobe, including her shoes and handbag, had come from the Salvation Army Thrift Store. He hadn't known this, of course, because in a perverse way, his extreme wealth made him oblivious to luxury. He coveted nothing because he could have anything. A Rolex was just a watch. Gucci loafers were just shoes. And when Ainsley saw these things on him, she assumed they were the same knockoffs other people wore, because she'd never met anyone who could afford the real thing.

Growing up, she and Jolene believed that teachers and librarians were rich. Anyone with consistently running utilities, a car that started on cold mornings, and a house made from real lumber on a street with sidewalks seemed wealthy to them. She'd fallen deeply in love with Ben before she realized that private-plane wealthy and librarian wealthy were completely different things.

She emerged from the closet to find her husband lying on the bed staring up at the ceiling.

"Tired?" she asked, approaching the bed.

"Exhausted."

"Things go well today?"

He tugged at her hand, pulling her down beside him. "They're going better now," he said, pulling her close.

She snuggled into his neck, inhaling the scent of him. Crisp. Clean. Masculine. He'd grown more handsome since they'd gotten married, not less. A hint of gray around the temples gave his blond hair and good-natured grin an aura of gravitas it hadn't had eight years ago.

"How was the speech," she asked, resting her hand on his chest.

"The speech was good. Everyone likes our economic development plan, and I'm going to keep talking about how we convinced the semi-conductor guys to build a plant here. But it was the meeting after that I'm really excited about."

She kept her voice carefully casual, grateful he couldn't see her face. "The . . . pornography thing?"

"Yeah. It went way better than I'd hoped. They want to talk again next week."

"Who did you meet with again?" Her heart hammered inside her chest. Could he hear it? Feel it through her skin?

"Two groups that have probably never been in the same room together. On one side of the table we had the Feminist Alliance for Change. On the other side we had the Christian Mothers Forum."

"Really?"

"Oh yeah." He smiled at the recollection. "I mean, at first you could cut the tension with a knife. Tattoos and piercings on one side of the table. Homeschool moms and little old ladies with Bibles in their purses on the other. But by the end of the meeting, they were hugging each other goodbye. It was amazing. Other than abolishing daylight saving time, this Antipornography Initiative is the only issue I've ever seen that brings both the left *and* the right together."

"*Women* on the left and the right, you mean."

"True." He sighed. "I'm not finding a whole lot of interest or support among men, but that's not surprising."

"What's the next step?"

"Well, if the next meeting goes well, they're going to combine forces and create a group called Women against Pornography."

Ainsley raised an eyebrow. "WAP?"

"I know." He groaned. "Maybe we can come up with something . . . better."

"Like the Partnership against Pornography?" she asked with a teasing smile.

"PAP?" He shuddered. "That's awful."

"What about CAP? The Coalition against Pornography."

"Better." He kissed the top of her head. "I've always said you were the brains of the operation."

She smirked. "If that's true, we're in big trouble. So, what happens next?"

"If I promise to support the policies they propose, they'll endorse me."

"What kind of . . . policies?"

"Things that make sense," he said. "Like changing laws that criminalize the victims of human trafficking instead of the perpetrators, forcing tech companies and the government to do more to protect minors from porn and predators online, using zoning ordinances to make it harder to open strip clubs near schools, things like that."

She swallowed hard. "That's wonderful."

"We aren't there yet, but if the next meeting is successful, I think they'll endorse me, and we could accomplish some really amazing things together if I get elected."

She could hear it in his voice, the excitement of finding a solution, fixing a problem. "I'm proud of you."

He laid his hand over hers, gently stroking her fingers. "You know what? I'm proud too. Everyone says you can't win an election by appealing to the middle, but we're proving them wrong. We haven't run a single negative ad, and everywhere I go, people tell me how refreshing it is to see a candidate who's just sort of civil and decent and honest, and you know, *normal*."

Her heart twisted. Civil. Decent. Honest. Normal. Her husband was all those things. And he'd married her.

"Listen, next time I meet with them, I'd like you to be there."

"Me?" Her voice rose an octave, and she tried to lower it. "Why?"

"You could add a lot to the discussion. You're an amazing parent. And you're a woman."

"You noticed."

He nuzzled her neck. "Oh, I noticed all right."

Even after eight years of marriage, his touch still made her skin tingle, but she pushed him away gently with the palm of her hand. She had to find a way to tell him the truth about who she used to be . . . what she used to do.

"I don't know, Ben. I'm an economist, not a social worker."

He propped himself up on his elbow and looked down at her, suddenly serious. "We're a team, Ainsley. And I want you in these meetings because I want your opinion on this stuff. You're the smartest person I know."

"You need to get out more."

"I'm serious. I can't win without you. Behind every great man—"

"Is a woman doing all the real work," she finished for him.

He laughed, and the opportunity for a serious conversation evaporated. She couldn't tell him now, with his face glowing, his mind busy with plans. This was who Ben *was*. Everywhere he went, her husband made things better.

He could have taken his vast fortune, bought a yacht, and frittered his life away clubbing with supermodels. Instead, he sent fifty broke but extremely bright local high school seniors to the college of their choice every fall, paying for tuition, room, and board, even books. He read heartbreaking stories in the newspaper and sent anonymous cash donations to victims of fires, floods, and bad luck. He paid medical bills for cancer patients without insurance. He bought new textbooks for low-income schools.

How can I make things better? Every day he woke up asking that question.

And now he genuinely wanted to make the whole state better, making him one of the few sane, moderate, and reasonable people in recent American history willing to run for office for all the right reasons. How could she deny him this?

"I'm on board," she said, forcing herself to look into his eyes. "A thousand percent, you know that. I'm even meeting with that media trainer you guys set me up with."

"Thank you. It's just a precaution. I promise you won't have to give speeches."

She cocked an eyebrow. "Oh really."

"Well, if I have to have my appendix removed and the whole campaign staff has laryngitis—"

"And if your mother is in Aspen or the South of France." Her mother-in-law loved to give speeches, but her grueling vacation schedule sometimes prevented it.

"And if Mom's unavailable—"

"And if Lenny is drunk." The campaign press secretary had been known to find stress relief in a bottle of scotch at the end of a long day on the phone with reporters.

He groaned. "And if Lenny is drunk, and there is absolutely no one else anywhere capable of speaking on my behalf, *then*, and only then, will we send you out to save the day. But otherwise, I promise, you can stay behind the scenes."

He paused. "But I do think your story . . ."

Dear God. No. She had a reoccurring nightmare about this. Standing onstage in a cavernous ballroom, bathed in a blinding light as people in tuxedos and evening gowns calmly tore off her clothes, strip by strip, leaving her naked and shrinking, like an unraveled mummy.

"No." She pressed her hand to his chest, trying to keep the desperation out of her voice. "I do not want to tell my story."

He planted a gentle kiss on her forehead. "I'm sorry. I shouldn't have brought it up. I know you're sensitive about . . . where you came from . . . I just think everyone else would be as impressed as I am if they knew what you've overcome."

"Sorry," she said, infusing her voice with a lighthearted lilt. "I have no desire to share my Horatio Alger tale with the world. You'll just have to tell your own story, about your hardscrabble life as the son of a socialite and the heir to the Bradley Bar candy fortune."

"Your story is much more compelling," he said, smiling.

She couldn't help but smile back. "But yours involves chocolate."

"Bradley Bars *are* better," he conceded, quoting the company motto. "But enough about me and pornography. Tell me about your day. How was the kindergarten whatchamacallit?"

He sank into the artfully arranged bank of throw pillows, and she snuggled into his chest again, relating the minutiae of her day with the kids, leaving out the one detail that threatened to destroy his dreams and the life they shared.

Chapter Seven

AINSLEY

Four days later, Ainsley maneuvered her giant black Suburban through the school's wrought iron gates, wondering again why she'd agreed to organize the annual First Week of School Teacher Appreciation Luncheon.

This event had been a disaster from the get-go.

First, the Wild Rice Mom had to cancel because she and her entire family caught the back-to-school stomach bug already sweeping through the lower grades.

Then the normally dependable Chicken Breast Mom got stuck in Brussels due to ongoing trade talks with the EU and could not get home in time to make the seventy-five chicken cordon bleu breasts she had promised to bring.

The woman's husband, left to solve this crisis in her absence, dropped off two boxes of fried chicken from Popeyes, congratulating himself on this elegant solution to the problem.

This forced Ainsley to get on the phone at 5:00 a.m. and beg Marco, her loyal caterer, to create and deliver seventy-five emergency grilled-shrimp skewers as a substitute.

Glancing in her rearview mirror to avoid a soccer ball that drifted into the parking lot, she wondered again: Why, why, why had she agreed to do this?

Guilt? Hubris? Insecurity? A psychological need to please others in a sad attempt to earn love and approval because she did not believe that she had intrinsic value as a human being?

Probably. She'd heard that on *Oprah* once, and it sounded about right.

Why couldn't she be more like that Nikki Lassiter person? As far as she could tell, Nikki Lassiter *never* volunteered. Probably because unlike her, Nikki Lassiter was a confident woman who didn't need outside validation to feel *whole*.

She parked beside the gym entrance, then opened her SUV up like a butterfly, rear hatch raised, side doors wide open, hoping this would invite others to help unload the mountain of items inside.

Because in addition to organizing the luncheon, Ainsley had also volunteered to make all the table decorations, a job she actually enjoyed but which took way more time than she'd anticipated.

Tiffany Hastings, the overlord of the Special Events committee, had insisted on a Hollywood theme for this luncheon. As a result, Ainsley had been up until 2:00 a.m. spray-painting seventy-five cardboard Oscar statues in her garage and attaching them to a base of popcorn tubs decorated with shiny metallic stars.

Blonde Jennifer propped the gym door open with a chair and a look of smug condescension. She'd chaired the event last year, where they served soba noodle salad with spring rolls, complete with paper lanterns, individualized fortune cookies for each teacher, and chopsticks emblazoned with the school logo.

Ainsley carried her DIY Oscars inside, and then turned with a heavy sigh to the ten cases of plastic water bottles stacked in the back of her SUV. Shoulders hunched, she carried the first case inside and set it down on the table designated for drinks.

Something caught her attention as she bent to cut the plastic wrap covering the bottles.

There. Out of the corner of her eye.

Wyatt Jericho.

She felt like a sandcastle when the tide came in . . . swept away, destabilized.

He stood under the basketball hoop, giving directions to eighth graders setting up chairs. He turned away from the students and then stopped a mom with an armful of tablecloths and asked a question she could not hear.

Suddenly, the mom pointed at *her.*

Ainsley's heart stopped.

Wyatt Jericho began to weave through the chaotic labyrinth of urn coffee pots, folding chairs, and middle schoolers attempting to be helpful.

Her heart pounded like the bass in the speakers at Godiva's all those years ago. She forced herself to take a deep breath.

Calm down calm down calm down.

She felt his hand on her shoulder and jerked away involuntarily. He gave her an easy grin and raised his hands in a gesture of surrender. "Didn't mean to startle you."

She swallowed. "That's okay."

"Is your car unlocked? I can have the kids unload it for you."

That voice. Authoritative with an edge of innuendo. Even after all these years, it made her skin crawl.

"Yes. It's open." She couldn't look at him. Instead, she bent to pick up another case of water.

"Let me help you with that," he said, coming closer.

"It's no problem." Ainsley held up her hand. "I can get it."

"I insist . . . I never miss an opportunity to help a pretty lady."

He sidled in next to her, his hip brushing hers as he lifted the water bottles from the floor to the table.

She took a step to the left, away from him. His presence was a negative force, a magnet that repelled, rather than attracted.

"You know, Mrs. Bradley," he said, turning to face her, "I was just thinking about you this morning when I saw you. In my bedroom."

She gaped at him with an open mouth. What in God's name did *that* mean?

He smiled at her obvious discomposure. "On television. In that campaign ad with you and your husband and kids. Lovely family. Beautiful little girl, just like her mother."

Saliva began to pool under her tongue. Was this some sort of *threat*? She swallowed hard. "Thank you."

"I understand you went to Biltmore."

How did he know that? She'd never shared that with any of the men at the club. But of course, all this information could be found on the campaign website. Or even from asking Tiffany or someone who knew her at school.

"I did."

"Were you a basketball fan?" He pulled a knife from his pocket and ripped open the plastic cover encasing the water bottles. The sight of his hands, and the knife, and the gaping slash . . . her toes curled involuntarily.

She forced a tight smile. "Sorry, I'm not really into sports."

"Hmm. That's surprising, because you have the body of an athlete."

For the briefest moment, his hand grazed her hip. An accident? She glanced at his eyes and read his intentions there.

She shuffled sideways again.

"Do you work out?" He'd begun to remove water bottles from their plastic wrapping, settling in, like he planned to stay awhile.

"Not really." She actually exercised every day, but that was none of his business.

"Tennis? Golf?"

"Kickboxing, actually." She'd love to land a ferocious jab right in his groin.

"Interesting. What about Pilates? Or pole dancing? I hear a lot of women consider that an excellent form of exercise."

A wave of searing heat pulsed across her skin like an atomic burn. She gripped the edge of the table as all the breath left her body.

Tiffany Hastings walked up. "Did I hear someone say pole dancing?"

Like an overloaded circuit, Ainsley's mind split into a million pieces and went completely blank.

Wyatt Jericho turned to Tiffany. "I was just telling Mrs. Bradley that she should take up pole dancing for the exercise."

"Shh. Don't even *joke* about things like that," Tiffany scolded in a whisper as she leaned in closer. "I was just talking to Monica Fredrickson, you know, the library aide? And she told me that Ben's opponent sent an *oppo research person*, right here, *to the school*, just yesterday, pretending to be an alumni. He was looking through old yearbooks to see if Ben said anything inappropriate when he was back in like, fourth grade."

Tiffany crossed her arms, looking smug. "But they figured out right away this guy did *not* graduate from St. Preston's. I mean, he was driving a *Kia*. They tossed him out, but still, can you *imagine*? These people are *ruthless*." Tiffany turned to Ainsley with a look of sympathy. "But don't worry. I just texted Ben and told him all about it."

Ainsley managed to squeak out a weak thank-you.

"Now." Tiffany took Wyatt Jericho's arm. "Can you help me move the popcorn machine? The kids offered, but I really think it should be done by an *adult*." She turned to Ainsley as she pulled him away. "Oh, and someone named Marco just showed up with like, a thousand shrimp skewers, and he wants to know where he should put them."

Exhausted and weak in the knees, Ainsley watched them walk away. If one more person touched, spoke to, or even looked at her, she would shatter like a piece of glass.

Someone tapped her on the shoulder, and a low scream escaped her throat.

Whirling around, she found Marco in his white double-breasted chef's uniform, his forehead wrinkled in concern. "Are you all right, Mrs. Bradley?"

She covered her mouth with her hand, blinking hard. *Pull yourself together. Right now.*

"I'm so sorry, Marco." She rubbed her forehead. "It's been a . . . stressful event. But everything is better, now that you're here. I'll show you where to put the skewers."

Confused volunteers, a crisis with the lemonade dispenser, and the need to mediate a dispute between Red Jennifer and Also Blonde Jennifer over the placement of the flowers on the principal's table allowed her to push her conversation with Jericho to the back of her mind.

But as she stood behind a folding table wearing plastic gloves and handing out shrimp skewers, she found herself struggling to hold back tears as her mind ranged in terrible directions.

She examined the teachers as they went through the line. Hardworking, respectable women and a few men. How would they look at her if they knew she'd once pranced around in a G-string for money? How would they look at her children?

And these other mothers? Dressed to the nines in their "casual" fall finery, suede skirts with matching boots and cashmere sweaters. How would they treat her when they found out she used to sidle up to strange men topless and perform lap dances?

And Ben. When she thought of Ben, she had to retreat to the ladies' room. She sat down on the toilet and cried. Her good and decent husband would become fodder for late-night television comedians. People would mock him, boycott his company, and refuse to vote for him.

And her children. They would be teased, maliciously. She could hear the high-pitched singsong now. *Your mom's a strip-per. Your mom's a strip-per.*

She allowed herself five minutes. Then she fixed her mascara and returned to the gym, glancing at the table where Wyatt Jericho sat, listening politely as the principal blathered on about the school's commitment to excellence. Apparently, Wyatt Jericho was now considered part of the St. Preston's faculty, part of the *school community*.

She'd created a life as fragile as a tower of feathers, and Wyatt Jericho could destroy it all with a single breath.

Chapter Eight

NIKKI

Daniel pushed Thomas the Tank Engine and Percy across the bathroom floor while Nikki tried very hard to make herself presentable for her maiden voyage as a media trainer. She firmly believed this kind of job should not exist, but it *was* a job, and they needed the money.

But she was too skinny for maternity clothes and too . . . rotund . . . for regular clothes. Only a pair of dusty black pants with a missing button and a black turtleneck with tiny holes dotted across the front fit properly. After several attempts, she managed to tuck the shirt in far enough to cover the most egregious holes and part of the safety pin that now secured the top of her pants.

She stood in front of the mirror. Too much black. She looked like Elizabeth Holmes. Or a goth Steve Jobs.

Daniel looked up at her from the bath mat, wide eyed. "Mommy, why do you have a pin in your pants?"

"Because my pants are broken."

"Why?"

"Because the button fell off."

"Why?"

"Because Mommy is too—" She was about to say *fat*. But you couldn't say that anymore. Talking about being fat would give your children anorexia. It was body shaming. Or something. One more thing to feel guilty about.

Like the Barbies. Her daughters never touched the Aeronautical Engineering Barbie she'd given them at Christmas to foster positive female role models with careers in STEM. They instead preferred a doll she and Josh privately called Harlot Barbie, a bottle blonde who tooled around the basement in a pink Corvette wearing stilettos and a tube top.

"Mommy has gotten too big for her clothes," she explained to Daniel as she plunged deeper into the closet's dark recesses in search of black pumps. "The same way you outgrow your clothes and then we get new ones."

"Maybe you need a cubby," he offered helpfully as he watched her dig through the closet. "I have a cubby at preschool."

"Excellent suggestion." She took a step back, surveying the growing pile of clothes on the floor.

"We could put your name on the cubby, and then you wouldn't lose things," he continued. "Or you could be a hedgehog, and we could put a hedgehog sticker on your cubby."

She tossed a twisted wire hanger into the trash can and looked at him closely. Would he seek out chaos as an adult to re-create the familiar dysfunction of his childhood?

"I could make you a cubby," he said thoughtfully. "If I had a million hundred Legos."

Or would he become a neurotic control freak in response to the disorder in his home of origin?

She frowned and kissed the top of his head. "I would love a cubby made from a million hundred Legos. You are very helpful."

Her kids deserved an orderly environment. Now that she was home full time, she'd come up with a *system*. She'd use those tips she'd read about in *Simple Life* magazine when she got her hair highlighted six months ago. She'd buy that Marie Kondo book. She'd get wicker laundry baskets and write things like *mending* on chalk labels. After she put the kids to bed, she'd settle into a chair and sew buttons onto her black pants while having meaningful conversations with her husband in front of a roaring fire. She'd become the kind of person who darned things, like Ma Ingalls in *Little House on the Prairie*, but without the locusts, rabies, and prairie fires, obviously.

The black pumps were still AWOL, but at the very back of the closet she found her black ballet flats and put them on instead. She glanced in the mirror, frowning at herself and everything around her: the unmade bed, the bursting closet, the hamper frothing with dirty laundry.

In the past, she'd blamed the toy-encrusted floors and emergency toilet paper shortages on her long days at work. But she no longer had that excuse.

She'd do better now that she had more time. Time for a clean house. Time for organization. Time for nutritious meals with organic ingredients instead of DayGlo-orange mac and cheese from a box. Time to be the wife her patient husband deserved. Time to be the mom her children needed.

"As God is my witness," she muttered, stuffing everything back into her closet without folding it, "I will never wear pants held together with safety pins again."

The doorbell interrupted any further resolutions. She scooped Daniel into her arms and rushed down the stairs as she glanced at her watch.

Late. Again.

She almost wept with joy when she opened the door and found her sister, Leslie, on the front steps.

"I'm late." She handed Daniel to her sister as they walked toward the minivan parked in the driveway. "The twins are playing Barbies in the family room, and the baby is actually sleeping."

Daniel put his chubby hands on his aunt's cheeks before making his first demand. "Do the shark, Aunt Leslie!"

His aunt made dutiful chomping noises, pretending to gnaw the flesh from her nephew's limbs as he erupted into giggles.

"Are you leaving or escaping?" she asked Nikki between bites.

"I'm retreating from a battle I can't win."

Her sister put Daniel down, and he ran across the front yard, his filthy bathrobe fluttering in the wind as he brandished his lightsaber.

Nikki's shoulders slumped as she watched him. "I was going to wash that thing last night, but he sleeps in it too. He might need to be sedated and have it surgically removed."

Leslie opened the back hatch of her SUV and pulled out a paper bag emblazoned with *TINKER*, the name of a local toy store.

She glanced over at Nikki as she pressed the button to lower the hatch. "I'm sorry I was out of town on your birthday. You look awful, by the way."

Nikki didn't have the energy to roll her eyes. "Thanks for the vote of confidence."

Her sister shrugged. "I meant it in a loving way."

Nikki knew this was true, and it made the back of her throat burn. She blinked into the distance, fighting the sudden urge to cry. What the hell was wrong with her? Why was she always on the verge of tears?

"It's been a rough week," she conceded. "Staying home with four kids is harder than I thought."

Understatement of the millennium.

The low point had come as she crawled around the floor spreading newspaper under the high chair to catch spaghetti shrapnel and suddenly found herself face to face with a glowing, full-page profile of Fletcher Avery, the woman who'd replaced her.

She learned that Fletcher Avery had married the wealthy owner of several local car dealerships and had a lifestyle blog where, as a public service, and with many exclamation points, she breathlessly documented the construction of their new eleven-thousand-square-foot home overlooking the Potomac River. And as an activist committed to every possible form of justice, including the environmental kind,

Fletcher Avery also vacationed in the Galapagos Islands and had six rescue chickens living in a handcrafted coop in her backyard.

"Well, the cavalry is here now," Leslie said, pulling Nikki into a quick hug. "Tell me when to feed the baby and when to put him down, and I'll take care of the rest."

"Where's Shelby?" Nikki asked, after giving her sister instructions. "I told the girls she was coming, and they made a new batch of slime in her honor."

"She couldn't come. She's at weight training."

Nikki hunted through her purse in search of her keys. "For basketball?"

"Yeah."

"Sounds intense."

Leslie sighed. "This new coach is all about winning. He's taking them to the grocery store to show them what they should eat because they need to be on this extra-healthy, high-protein diet. He wants them in bed at a certain time to make sure they're getting enough sleep, and he has access to all their grades to make sure they don't fall behind academically. We had to sign a form promising to reinforce all these healthy habits."

Nikki unzipped every compartment in her purse. "What do you think about all this?"

"I think it's fine if Shelby can balance it with her schoolwork and keep her grades up. But I'm not sure I like all this pressure. I mean, they're only eighth graders. It's not like these girls are going to end up in the WNBA."

"Tell that to Tiffany Hastings." Nikki triumphantly pulled her keys from her pants pocket. No wonder she couldn't find them in her purse.

Her sister grimaced. "Tiffany's daughter will be the exception, of course."

"She's gifted," Nikki said.

"*And* talented," Leslie added.

Nikki glanced over at Daniel, who now sat in the middle of the yard chewing on the end of his lightsaber. "I'm pretty sure my kids are neither. In fact, Daniel's preschool teacher pulled me aside the other day and told me she's concerned because Daniel has trouble 'settling.'"

"Settling?"

Nikki nodded. "He flits from the finger-painting station to the puzzle station to the dress-up station without really settling in one place for more than a minute or two."

Leslie rolled her eyes. "He's a curious three-year-old boy. *Of course* he flits around the classroom."

"I just hope he isn't . . ." Nikki's voice trailed off.

"What? Witty, smart, and successful, like his mom?"

Gratitude welled up inside Nikki. Leslie had always been her biggest cheerleader.

"He is a bright, sweet little boy," Leslie said firmly, laying a hand on her sister's arm. "You have nothing to worry about."

Daniel came over and attached himself to Nikki's leg. Leslie gently pried him free. "Come on, Velcro Man. Your mommy has work to do."

Nikki told her sister where to find extra diapers and provided largely theoretical instructions on nap times since Daniel refused to sleep.

A feeling of liberation washed over her as she got into her car and sank into the driver's seat. It intensified as she backed out of the driveway, making her feel as though she were fleeing a burning building rather than driving away at a respectable speed in a minivan.

Surely this wasn't right?

Good mothers hated to leave their children. Good mothers cherished time with their babies instead of counting the hours until they went to bed.

The face of Laura, her old college roommate, flashed across her mind, shooting another shard of guilt into her heart. Laura had undergone years of failed fertility treatments before adopting a beautiful little girl and becoming the most patient and loving mother Nikki had ever known, grateful for every lost hour of sleep, every cry, every blot of spit-up staining her clothes.

Children were a blessing. And she had been blessed, four times, with beautiful, healthy babies. What was wrong with her? Why couldn't she be more grateful?

After vowing to improve her attitude, she focused her attention on the GPS and turned right onto the George Washington Memorial Parkway. Flanked by trees on one side and the Potomac River on the other, the parkway made for a beautiful drive on a September morning.

The GPS directed her down a winding road that meandered toward the river, leading her to an ornate iron gate with an intercom embedded in a stone pillar.

Leaning out the window, she pressed the intercom button. No one answered, but the gate slid open.

A smooth asphalt road wound through bucolic fields of wildflowers interspersed with mature trees. As she rounded a curve, the trees parted to reveal the largest house she'd ever seen, the Potomac River sparkling behind it like a chain of sapphires.

She pulled into a circular driveway, stopped the car, and leaned back in her seat, staring up at the mansion in front of her.

If Pemberley and Manderley had a baby, it would look like this.

She glanced around. Maybe Colin Firth would suddenly appear, dripping wet, and offer to take her car?

But when she turned off the engine and got out, she heard only birdsong and the screech of a hawk. Mr. Darcy did not make an appearance, so she grabbed her purse and stepped onto a shady veranda supported by broad white pillars. Copper lanterns suspended from the ceiling on chains flickered with real gas flames.

She squared her shoulders and pressed the doorbell. If Ainsley's husband won his race, the governor's mansion would be a real letdown compared to this.

A woman in an actual maid uniform opened the door, and it was *not* the kind of maid uniform she and her girlfriends once wore to a

Halloween bachelorette party. This maid wore a demure green dress with a starched collar and silent white shoes.

Holy hell. She'd fallen through a wormhole and landed at Downton Abbey.

The maid, who she'd started to think of as Mrs. Danvers, led her into a vaulted room with an enormous marble fireplace and stunning views of the Potomac.

An actual drawing room. Perhaps she and Ainsley would retire here for brandy and cigars when the media training ended.

The maid told her Mrs. Bradley would be with her shortly and invited her to take a seat. Nikki evaluated her options. Was the gilded settee functional? Or purely decorative? What about the velvet chairs in a completely different fabric that somehow matched the other furniture, due to some subtle form of interior design voodoo?

In contrast, her own home featured an ancient Pottery Barn sofa stained with red marker, a rug purchased on clearance from one of those perpetually going-out-of-business carpet stores, and two lumpy leather recliners.

Her living room / playroom / family room suddenly seemed not just inadequate but deeply shameful.

She added another item to her mental self-improvement list. *Make my home a soothing oasis of texture and color by carefully selecting furniture and accessories that express my personality.*

And never, ever let Ainsley see the inside of my house.

The maid asked if she wanted something to drink.

Why, yes. Yes, she did. She wanted a vodka tonic, followed by a cappuccino, chased with a pot of chamomile tea, but she didn't want to create extra work for the maid, so she declined graciously and remained standing.

The click of heels on hardwood heralded the approach of Ainsley, who appeared a moment later resplendent in a green cashmere sweater, leather pants, and low-heeled suede mules.

Holy hell. If she dressed like this for a day at home, what did she wear to the grocery store? Or the school auction?

"Thank you for coming," Ainsley said with what appeared to be a forced smile.

"You have a lovely home."

Ainsley's face flushed a shade of pink that made her even more attractive, if that was possible. "My husband's grandfather built this house. We have a dock and a little boathouse down by the river. It's a great place for the kids to play."

"Sounds like paradise."

Nikki's children had a tire swing, the type of trampoline deemed most dangerous by the American Academy of Pediatrics, and a dilapidated treehouse filled with enough rusty nails to supply every child in the neighborhood with tetanus.

Ainsley led her down a paneled corridor as they engaged in the small talk of elementary school mothers everywhere. *Which teacher did you get? Did you sign up for chess on Wednesdays? Are you attending the parent-teacher social?*

Nikki prided herself on being able to talk to anyone, anywhere, but eventually even this meager supply of tiny talk died away as Ainsley led her into a two-story room filled from floor to ceiling with books.

Nikki drew in a sharp breath. "This is incredible."

"Thanks," Ainsley said with a small shrug. "We're big readers, as you can probably tell."

September light flooded through casement windows overlooking a faded autumn garden. Two upholstered chairs flanked a wood-burning fire. An ottoman held French macarons and a silver teapot.

I want to be Ainsley when I grow up.

Ainsley gestured to the chairs. "Please. Sit down and have some tea. Or would you rather have coffee? Soda? Or something stronger?"

"Tea is great. Thank you."

Nikki took the delicate cup Ainsley offered, popped a macaron into her mouth, and settled back into the plush comfort of the upholstered chair. "It must be wonderful to have a quiet place like this to read."

Ainsley looked around as if seeing the room for the first time. "I actually don't spend a lot of time in here. I prefer to be in the family room or the basement, where I can hear the kids."

Nikki repressed a sigh. *While I hide in the bathroom and hope they don't find me.*

Ainsley obviously loved every moment she spent with her children. Either that or they were barbaric pyromaniacs who couldn't be left unattended. But as Nikki gazed around the room, taking in the tasseled throw pillows and silk curtains that billowed like ball gowns, she knew this couldn't be true. Ainsley's organized and perfect womb would never produce uncivilized children who used their mother as a living Kleenex by wiping their noses across her clothes, *while she wore them*, as hers did.

A heavy mantle of inadequacy settled over her as she scrutinized Ainsley's face. They were probably the same age. Yet Ainsley seemed like the real grown-up, with her silver tea tray and furniture that bore no trace of dog hair or glitter glue. She probably owned a chafing dish and one of those plastic cupcake carriers that Nikki always needed but never actually remembered to buy.

These comparisons were too depressing to dwell upon. She may as well get started so she could return to the Shack of Inadequacy and Baby Vomit she called home.

"So," she said, turning to Ainsley with the same bright smile she used when introducing stories about 5K walks to raise awareness about Lyme disease or Fourth of July neighborhood bicycle parades. "Have you ever had media training before?"

"No." Ainsley picked up a silver Cross pen and a pink leather notebook and prepared to take notes.

"Okay. Here's how it works. A reporter can ask any question they want, and you get to answer any question you want."

"Is this what they call 'spinning things'?" Ainsley asked.

"Yes. Now, a tough reporter won't let you get away with it. But most of these reporters will want to know about your clothes or your passion for colonoscopies or preventing heart disease or whatever you decide to focus on as the First Lady of our great state."

Ainsley scribbled furiously in the notebook, taking it all down.

Nikki popped another macaron into her mouth and waited for her to catch up. They would not have been friends in high school. Ainsley had clearly been the kind of student who sat home on weekends reorganizing her notes and doing SAT prep, while Nikki drank beer at bonfire parties at the local gravel pit.

"Some reporters might probe a little and try to find some daylight between you and your husband on policy issues," Nikki continued, "but you can evade these questions by reminding them that you're not the one running for governor. Because you aren't."

Ainsley wrote that down, too, then looked up from her notebook. "Got it."

"All right. Let's do a practice run. Then we'll talk about what worked and what didn't."

Nikki tossed her a few basic questions about her kids, and Ainsley gave brief but articulate answers. Nikki was relieved to see that her client was intelligent but lacked confidence, and that could be fixed with practice.

"How did you meet your husband?" Nikki asked.

Ainsley stretched her legs as a small smile played around the corners of her mouth.

"I was a career economist at Treasury, one of the civil servants. Ben was a political appointee. We started work on the same day and happened to sit next to each other at a mandatory sexual harassment training seminar for new employees."

"What happened next?"

"Nothing happened, for a long time," she said, smiling at the memory. "After that presentation, he was terrified to even look at me, much less ask me out. And we worked in different departments, so we only saw each other occasionally in the hallway. But I happened to live in an apartment up in Northwest DC about a block from Poetry and Paperbacks. You know, the bookstore?"

Nikki nodded. She'd covered many appearances there by prominent authors in her years as a reporter.

"Well, the bookstore was sort of my second home. I liked to go there on Friday nights after work and unwind by looking at books."

Nikki cocked her head. "While all the other twentysomethings were getting drunk in Adams Morgan, you were prowling around a bookstore?"

"I'm kind of a homebody," Ainsley said. "Anyway, one Friday night I ran into Ben there. We got coffee, and, well . . . that was it. We were pretty much inseparable after that."

"Books brought you together."

"I guess you could say that."

"No. You *should* say that," Nikki insisted. "Every time a reporter asks how you met your husband. Leave out the part about the mandatory sexual harassment seminar. We never want the words *sexual harassment* and your husband's name in the same sentence."

Ainsley frowned. "But that seminar *was* mandatory, for both of us. It wasn't because he'd done something wrong."

"I know that, and you know that, but I can see the attack ad now. 'Candy Bar Heir Attends Sex Seminar.'"

"I never thought of that," Ainsley whispered, gripping her silver pen so hard her knuckles turned white.

"They'll take anything, no matter how small and innocent, and try to make it ugly. Unfortunately, that's how campaigns work these days."

"Okay." Ainsley nodded, her face pale. "I understand."

Compassion flooded through Nikki. Good thing this woman was straight as an arrow, because she could not handle a tough campaign. Sensing that her client wasn't ready for hard questions, Nikki threw her a softball. "What's your husband like?"

The color returned to Ainsley's cheeks. "My sister, who's still single, calls him a unicorn. He's kind, smart, thoughtful, funny, interesting, considerate, generous, smart. He's . . ." She paused, seemingly at a loss for adjectives. "He's honestly the best man I've ever known."

"And rich too," Nikki added.

"Yes," she conceded. "All that, and he's rich too. *And* handsome. Or at least I think so."

"He must have some faults?" Nikki asked, probing a little.

Ainsley went silent as she considered the question. "He's a terrible singer. And he leaves all the bathroom drawers open when he gets ready in the morning."

"That's it?"

"It is, actually." Ainsley bit the end of her silver pen, obviously searching for the right words. "He's just, I don't know . . . he's just a truly *good* person. And that's why he'll be a very good governor," she added, looking pleased with herself for including this overtly political nugget.

Nikki shook her head. "You don't have to say that unless they ask. Keep it focused on him as a husband, a father, and a person, not a candidate. Let other people roll around in the mud and deliver the political messages. The candidate's wife is sort of pure and good, and above all that. A benevolent queen."

Ainsley scribbled in her notebook, nodding. "Got it."

"Okay, let's talk about you."

Ainsley's mouth hardened into a grim line, and her body, so relaxed and fluid before, visibly stiffened. "There's nothing interesting about me."

A tingling sensation prickled across Nikki's body, as though a sleeping limb were suddenly coming to life. Like a good detective, she had a sixth sense, honed by years spent interviewing both the innocent and the guilty. It kissed the back of her neck, issuing a subtle warning.

Ainsley had something to hide.

Chapter Nine

AINSLEY

Were reporters like dogs? Could they smell secrets and lies the way dogs scented fear? No. Of course they couldn't. This Nikki woman wasn't supernatural. She wasn't even particularly well groomed.

Ainsley set her pen and notebook on the table. No time like the present to start learning how to talk . . . or not talk . . . about her past.

"Ready?" Nikki asked.

"Of course." She sat up straight, gripping the arms of her chair, like a person at the dentist awaiting a root canal.

"Where did you grow up?" Nikki asked.

Not at home.

"A small town in Maryland."

"Are your parents still alive? Any siblings?"

"I have a sister who lives in the area. My father was a welder. He died when I was eight."

Images flashed through her mind. Her dad's patient good humor and kind blue eyes. Piggyback rides. Fishing trips. Riding in the back of the pickup truck, wind whipping her hair. They weren't rich, but they were happy. When he died, everything fell apart, including her mother.

"And your mom?"

A mosaic of emotions flooded through her. Love. Loss. Shame. Regret. Anger. She clenched her jaw, shutting down memories, vaporizing each feeling before it manifested in the jut of her chin, the narrowing of her eyes. She'd had lots of practice pretending to feel things she didn't. Or pretending not to feel things she did.

"My mom passed away, too, a few years ago."

Passed away by passing out. In the snow outside our trailer.

"Were your parents married? Divorced?" Nikki asked.

"After Dad died, we were . . . raised . . . by my mom."

Except she didn't raise us. She neglected us.

"Did she have an occupation?"

Only if you define drinking as an occupation.

Ainsley lifted the teacup to her lips and swallowed. "She had a number of jobs when we were growing up . . . rather than one occupation."

"Tell me about growing up. Was it a happy childhood?"

Define happy. *We weren't abused or harmed. Mom didn't have the energy for that. Just neglected. And dirt poor. Does that qualify as happy?*

Ainsley could feel her face hardening, like a mask made of clay. She took another sip of tea and forced her eyebrows lower, shifting her expression back into neutral. "We didn't have a lot of money, but we had what we needed."

Thanks to Mrs. Robertson.

Nikki put her pen down. "I get the impression you aren't comfortable talking about this."

How perceptive. "I'm not."

How could she ever be comfortable talking about the mother who slept all day and drank all night? How could she talk about stealing loose change from her mother's wallet and pulling a little red wagon filled with dirty clothes to the laundromat so she and Jolene had clean shirts and underwear for school?

No. She still couldn't talk about where she came from, who she used to be, what she used to do.

"Okay," Nikki said, raising her hands in a gesture of surrender. "I get it. Only narcissists . . . and men . . . enjoy talking about themselves. But these questions will come up, and I want to help you answer them in a way that's both honest and comfortable. And you don't need to be afraid. Interviews are a piece of cake, as long as you don't have anything to hide."

Ainsley's teacup froze in midair. "Why would I have anything to hide?"

Nikki paused. "I'm not saying you do."

Ainsley took an enormous gulp of tea. *Yes, you are. That's exactly what you're saying.* Her hand shook slightly, and the teacup made a tinkling sound as she set it in the saucer.

Nikki cleared her throat. "But if you did . . . have something to hide . . . well, that could be a problem. I mean, there's really only one rule in dealing with reporters."

"What's that?"

"Never, ever, ever lie to the press. Because when they find out, and they will find out, they will rip you apart like a pack of rabid dogs."

Vertigo washed over Ainsley. She felt like she was tumbling down a long tunnel, arms and legs flailing as she reached out for something to hold on to, something to break her fall.

"A pack of rabid dogs. What a charming analogy."

Nikki looked back at her with a strange expression, curiosity mixed with something else . . . sympathy . . . or maybe pity?

"Look." Nikki set her teacup in the saucer with a decisive clink, her voice gentle but firm. "You guys hired me to tell you what you need to know, not what you want to hear."

Silence filled the room, making the cozy library suddenly frigid.

Enough. She couldn't do this. She had to get away from this woman and her awful questions.

Ainsley glanced at her watch, slapped her hands across her knees, and stood. "I'm afraid we're out of time. We're hosting a dinner for a few families who won a five-course tasting menu at the auction last spring, and I really need to check on the caterer. Could we continue this discussion at our next training session?"

Her voice had an edge, and she instantly regretted both her tone and her words. She genuinely liked Nikki. Prior to the discussion about her past, she'd felt almost comfortable with her because Nikki was so . . . real.

These feelings of affection had begun when she noticed a safety pin peeking out from beneath a turtleneck sweater peppered with small holes at the hem. Nikki looked on the *outside* the way Ainsley felt on the *inside.* Disheveled. Exhausted. Imperfect. They could have been friends . . . if Nikki hadn't been probing into her past, pressing a wound that would never heal.

"Sure. No problem." Nikki reached for her purse and stood. "Why don't you give me a call when you'd like to meet again. Or find me at pickup after school. I've been hearing your daughter's name a lot lately, by the way. It's Grace, right?"

"Yes." Ainsley led Nikki into the corridor and toward the front door.

"I think our girls have been playing together at recess."

Ainsley smiled, a genuine smile for the first time since Nikki arrived. "Of course! You're the mom who—" She stopped, embarrassed.

"Who what?" Nikki asked, cocking an eyebrow.

"Who lets her daughter bring Nutella sandwiches to school. Grace keeps begging me for Nutella sandwiches—"

"And you say no because only a terrible mother would let their child eat chocolate for lunch."

"No! Not at all," Ainsley protested. "I think it's great that you are . . ."

"Too tired to care?"

Ainsley laughed, and her shoulders relaxed. "I think it's great that you are too tired to care, and I'm glad Grace has two nice friends to eat lunch with. Maybe your daughters could come over for a playdate after school sometime?"

"That would be great. We could do a media training session while they play."

Ainsley struggled to keep the horror from showing on her face. She wanted Grace to play with her friends, but she did not want to do this ever again.

"I'll send you some dates," Nikki said.

Ainsley tried to look happy about this. "Perfect."

"By the way," Nikki said, "since the girls will be playing together, could I put you down as one of my officially sanctioned emergency contact people allowed to pick up my kids if I can't get there in time?"

Ainsley blushed, surprised at how much this request pleased her. "Of course. And could I put you down for Grace as well?"

"Sure. I've got plenty of room in my glamorous minivan."

It took Nikki a good five minutes to locate her keys, and Ainsley began to question the wisdom of allowing this woman to pick up her kids in an emergency. After an extensive search of her purse, she found them under an industrial-size box of Goldfish crackers in the front seat of her car. She finally drove off in a minivan that had clearly seen better days as Ainsley waved from the veranda.

Maybe she could pay Nikki *not* to give her media training sessions?

No. That would never work. Nikki seemed like the kind of person who would do the job she'd been hired to do, come hell or high water, an honest person who told the truth no matter what.

Unlike her.

She strode back into the unusually silent house. The caterers weren't expected for hours, and Ben had taken the kids to an open house at the fire station to satisfy Adam's obsession with fire trucks. She grabbed her purse and keys and headed off to meet the only person on the planet who knew all her secrets.

Chapter Ten

AINSLEY

She had a hard time finding a parking spot in Old Town, a charming area on the banks of the Potomac filled with antique shops, boutiques, restaurants, and row houses where George Washington once slept. She finally found a spot big enough for her SUV several blocks from the restaurant. She didn't mind the walk. Maybe the fresh air would clear her head and calm her racing mind.

A cool autumn breeze swept in from the river, scattering leaves that had begun to litter the cobblestone streets. She buttoned her coat to ward off the chill as she walked past houses built from handmade bricks when America was still a colony, passing King, Queen, Duke, and Prince Streets. She rounded a corner and arrived at the crumbling brick building that housed the Three Lanterns, eyes adjusting to the dim light as she entered.

The brunch crowd had started to clear out, leaving the normally noisy restaurant relatively quiet. Her sister waved from a tall leather booth along an exposed brick wall in the back room.

Ainsley slid into the booth across from her. "You're early."

"And you're only on time." Jolene handed her a menu. "Which is late, by your standards."

"I've had a rough week."

Jolene's eyes narrowed. "You've been chewing your nails."

Ainsley sat on her hands. "No. I haven't."

"You aren't wearing lipstick either," Jolene observed. "Another sign of the apocalypse. What's going on?"

The waiter arrived with a pot of coffee, and they ordered the same thing they always ordered at the Three Lanterns: hash browns and pancakes with extra butter, plus bacon, sausage, and toast.

It had taken a few years, but together they'd managed to decode the eating habits of the upper middle classes. Ainsley gave her children muesli, turkey bacon, and fresh fruit. She avoided carbs and claimed to enjoy quinoa, avocados, and even cauliflower rice. But at the Three Lanterns, she and her sister ate all the things they'd fantasized about as kids in a house where they were lucky to get cereal without milk.

They thanked their server, then waited for him to leave.

"Okay, what the hell is going on?" Jolene asked.

Ainsley glanced around, then raised her voice slightly. "At Grace's school, they hired this new basketball coach, and he's . . . he's someone who used to come to the club."

"Okay. You mentioned that on the phone."

Ainsley took a deep breath and continued. "I think he recognized me."

Jolene's eyebrows shot up. "Are you sure?"

"Almost positive." Ainsley began to shred her paper napkin into strips with restless fingers as she described her conversation with Wyatt Jericho.

"Is it possible he discusses pole dancing with every woman he talks to?"

"Honestly," Ainsley said, ripping another strip from her napkin, "it *is* possible. He was one of those guys who . . ." Her voice trailed off as a chain of memories unspooled across her mind, flooding it with people and events she'd tried to forget.

"We had this place upstairs," she continued, "called the Boudoir, where men could pay extra for a . . . you know, a more intimate show."

Jolene nodded. "I remember you telling me about it."

Ainsley ripped another strip from the napkin. "Those of us who worked downstairs . . . whet the appetite. The guys who wanted private shows went upstairs."

"And the coach did that?"

"Yeah. He liked to make girls beg for tips, said sick things during lap dances. He was just . . . a complete lech."

Jolene's face puckered in revulsion. "But you didn't have a lot of . . . contact . . . with him at Godiva's?"

"Do you mean was I giving him private shows up in the Boudoir?" Her voice had an unintended edge. "No, I was not. But I was definitely in the club, doing lap dances downstairs for other guys, or onstage, wrapped around the pole wearing nothing but a G-string. And he was there, a lot, from what I remember."

"Okay. Let's assume he does recognize you from your time at Godiva's. Do you think he'd tell anyone?"

Ainsley thought for a long moment. "I've asked myself that question a thousand times since he talked to me at that teacher lunch, and I honestly don't know. But he . . . touched me." She looked down at her plate. "And that thing he said about seeing Grace in the campaign ad . . ." She shuddered, unable to finish this thought.

"Yeah." Jolene frowned. "Mentioning your 'beautiful daughter.' That's creepy."

"Do you think it's some kind of threat?" Ainsley asked. "Like blackmail or something?"

"I don't know, and I don't want to find out," Jolene said, her voice firm. "There's only one solution here."

"What?"

Jolene leaned forward. "We get rid of the bastard."

Tears sprang to her eyes, and Ainsley didn't know whether to laugh or cry as her heart swelled with a surge of love for her sister. Ben could leave her, the kids could disown her, and her so-called friends could abandon her, but she'd never be alone. Jolene would stand by her, no matter what. Like the intense pressure that forms a diamond, the chaos of their childhood had created an unassailable bond.

"You sound like Tony Soprano," Ainsley said, dabbing her eyes with a napkin.

Jolene reached across the table and squeezed her hand. "I don't mean in a feed-the-fishes kind of way. We just need to get him out of that school and out of your life."

"But how do we do that?" Ainsley jabbed her straw into a glass of ice water. "Everyone loves him. Just the other day Tiffany Hastings said the principal is terrified some other school will try to hire him away."

Jolene considered this as she poured cream and sugar into her coffee. "He knows you used to be a stripper, but *you* know he used to hang out in strip clubs. Maybe we just tell the principal you heard he hangs out in unsavory places, and they fire him."

The waiter approached with a circular tray laden with food. Once he was out of earshot, Jolene leaned across the table. "You also have to tell Ben . . . because if he finds out from someone else . . . or if his opponent learns about this . . ."

Ainsley stabbed her fork into her pancakes. "I will tell Ben . . . I just . . . How do you tell your husband . . . your loving, kind, trusting husband . . . that you used to be a stripper?"

"Maybe you should tell his mother instead and give her a heart attack."

Ainsley spread jelly on her toast with a rueful grimace. "We could only hope."

"Look, Ben is one of the nicest guys I've ever met. He'll understand. Just tell him why you did it."

She snapped a piece of bacon in half. "Does it matter?"

"Of course it matters!" Jolene said, raising her voice.

"Shh!" Ainsley hissed, glancing around at the other diners.

"If you hadn't found a way to pay my tuition," Jolene continued in a whisper, "I'd be the knocked-up girlfriend of a drug dealer who beat the shit out of her whenever he happened to be in a bad mood. Remember all that?"

"Yes, but—"

"Tami Darlene Schmidt, you listen to me. That man *beat* me. He slammed my head into walls and choked me. And I thought I loved him. I was so hurt and lonely and terrified after Mrs. Robertson died that I thought a boyfriend who beat me, cheated on me, and sold drugs was the best I could hope for in life. Don't you remember?"

Ainsley closed her eyes. Of course she remembered. She remembered coming home from college to find her sister wearing a turtleneck on an eighty-degree day to cover the bruises on her neck. She remembered her sister's lank hair and ashen skin the day they buried Verna Robertson, the anguish on Jolene's face so raw it hurt to look at her. She remembered all these things, but it didn't help.

"The *reason* I did it doesn't change the *fact* that I did it." Ainsley picked at her pancakes. "I pranced around half-naked in front of strange men four nights a week for almost a year. I can change my name and marry a rich man from an important family. I can drive the right car and wear the right clothes and eat the right food, and live in a gigantic house, but at the end of the day I'm still Tami Darlene Schmidt who grew up dirt poor in the People's Court trailer park, and I'm still a former stripper."

Jolene shook her head. "There's nothing wrong with being a former stripper."

Ainsley barked out a bitter laugh. "You sound like Lady Godiva. She always called us the only performing artists in America adequately compensated for their work."

"It's true."

"I know that, and you know that, but most people don't see it that way."

Jolene puffed out her cheeks, expelling a deep breath. "Look, maybe it's not such a big deal anymore. Times have changed. People have stripper poles in their basements now. The kids at work are all about sex positivity and not slut shaming and stuff like that."

Ainsley gave her a bitter smile. "Are you saying I was a slut?"

"You know what I mean."

"I do." Ainsley sliced her knife through a sausage. "And maybe my sordid past is fine if you're a twenty-two-year-old women's studies major from Berkeley defying the patriarchy. But what if you're a seventy-year-old Baptist lady who goes to church every Sunday? Are you going to vote for the guy who's married to a stripper? What about the moms and dads at school? Are they going to send their kids over to the stripper's house for a playdate? What about the wholesome Bradley Bar candy brand? And what about my mother-in-law? She's never liked me, and this . . . well, this just confirms what she's always suspected . . . that her trailer-trash daughter-in-law is unworthy of her son and the hallowed family name."

Jolene nodded. "Polluting the shades of Pemberley."

"Exactly." Mrs. Robertson had introduced them to Jane Austen the summer they'd turned fourteen and fifteen, in addition to everything else she'd given them.

"But you're a *former* stripper." Jolene spread a second pat of butter on her pancakes. "It's not like you're currently, you know . . ."

"Walking around topless in front of strange men while they tuck dollar bills into my G-string?" Ainsley took a bite of sausage and shook her head. "It doesn't matter. Once a stripper, always a stripper. That's just the way people think. And they want a First Lady who promotes literacy, not lap dances."

"I wish I could remove those memories from your brain," Jolene said, her raspy voice suddenly tender.

"I wish you could too." Ainsley poured more syrup onto her pancakes. "I wish you could remove all our childhood memories."

"Not all. Things were good when Dad was alive."

"True." Ainsley wrapped her hands around her coffee cup, absorbing the warmth. "And after he died, we had each other."

"And Mrs. Robertson."

They went silent for a moment at the mention of her name, each lost in memories tinged with grief.

"Listen." Jolene waved a triangle of toast at her sister. "I've got an idea. What if I called the principal and told him *I* used to be a stripper in the club where the coach got lap dances in the Boudoir. I can give him my name. If anyone at my job hears that I used to be a stripper, it'll just add to my badass reputation."

Ainsley shook her head. "It's dishonest."

"No. Keeping this a secret from Ben is dishonest."

Ainsley lowered her eyes. Jolene was right. But she couldn't bear to see the loving lines on her husband's face harden in shock as he realized the one person he'd finally allowed himself to trust had failed to tell him something this important. And what if that led him to question everything? What if he thought she was like all those other women he'd dated, women more interested in his money and his family name than his big heart and quiet sense of humor?

Jolene took a contemplative sip of coffee. Then she said, "I don't think me talking to the principal is dishonest. It's just me telling your truth to someone who needs to know."

"I guess we could try that," Ainsley said, massaging her forehead. "Although I'm not sure it will work."

"But we have to *try*. Because if he tells people . . ."

"Fine," Ainsley said sharply. "Do it."

"I'll call him first thing Monday morning."

"Okay." Ainsley poked at her scrambled eggs, which were now cold. "Then call me as soon as you talk to him."

"By the way," Jolene said, sprinkling salt on her hash browns. "How *is* St. Preston's? Didn't like, nine Supreme Court justices go there?"

"Only two." Ainsley pushed her plate away. "Plus, a senator. And a secretary of state. It's your basic upper-middle-class nightmare."

"Does Grace like it?"

Ainsley gathered the shredded napkins, crumpled them into a ball, and tossed them onto her plate. "She seems happy, but she's already far behind in the résumé-building contest. Some of these kids are learning Mandarin in their free time." She enclosed *free time* in air quotes. "And that's after piano lessons, dance, Scouts, soccer, lacrosse, tennis, and swimming lessons at the club."

Jolene shook her head. "They should range free in the People's Court for a week. That would be an education."

Ainsley grinned at her sister. "We were badasses, weren't we?"

"We were scrappy. And smart. And really lucky."

Her smile faded, and she became serious again. "I know. Very lucky."

The waiter brought the check, and Ainsley reached out to grab it before her sister could take it.

"Fine." Jolene put her wallet back in her purse. "You're rich. You can pay."

"You're rich too. Didn't you just get another raise? And a promotion?"

"I did." She pushed her plate away. "But you're I-have-a-guest-house rich. I'm just think-I'll-buy-a-Tesla rich."

"Hard to believe, isn't it?"

"God knows we worked for it," Jolene said. "Sometimes I look at these interns we have from fancy schools, well-connected families. They were born on third base but think they've earned what they have because they're smart. I'm smart, too, but when you come from the place we came from, smart isn't enough. Not by a long shot."

"Careful," Ainsley said softly, "your chip is showing."

"I can't help it. It breaks my heart to see you feel shame about what you did for me."

Ainsley snorted. "Fine. When the kids graduate and Ben retires from politics, I'll lobby Congress to create National Exotic Dancer Recognition Day. How's that?"

Jolene grinned. "You can lead the Stripper Pride Parade."

"But until then, I tell Ben and no one else. This must remain a secret."

"Of course. I'm not saying you should tell the ladies on the PTA. Just your husband."

Ainsley signed the credit card receipt, leaving a 100 percent tip because she'd been a waitress as well as a stripper. "Thanks for meeting me."

"Of course." Jolene gathered up her purse. "And please try not to let this bother you. We're gonna get that creepy-ass coach fired, and no one will find out you used to be the Sexy Sheriff at Lady Godiva's Gentleman's Club. Except Ben, because you're going to tell him, tonight."

"Right. Tonight."

They left the restaurant and said goodbye with a farewell hug on the sidewalk.

"You saved me, you know, never forget that," Jolene whispered, blinking back tears.

"I love you," Ainsley said.

"I love you too."

They parted, and Ainsley headed for her car. When she got inside, she put on lipstick, fluffed her hair in the rearview mirror, and glanced at the clock on the dashboard. The caterers would arrive soon, and she'd have to give them instructions. She'd have only a few minutes alone with Ben before their guests arrived for dinner. They'd both be tired by the time everyone finally left.

She couldn't tell him tonight. Maybe tomorrow.

By the time she got home, she had shed Tami Darlene Schmidt like a skin and transformed back into Ainsley, the name she'd picked for herself from a mystery novel about rich people set in Martha's Vineyard.

She'd become Ainsley, and she had to *stay* Ainsley. How could she expect her husband to accept her past when she couldn't accept it herself?

Chapter Eleven

NIKKI

Nikki looked down at Baby Joe as he babbled happy nonsense from his crib. "You've been drinking Red Bull again, haven't you?"

Instead of sleeping, he lay on his back, energetically kicking his legs. Her heart went soft as he cooed at her. Scientists were right when they said babies, kittens, and puppies used adorableness as a survival technique. Otherwise, she and the other female mammals would have abandoned their offspring to the tender mercies of the hyenas thousands of years ago in exchange for sleep.

"You are a pediatric insomniac." She picked him up and carried him to the changing table. "But it's time to get you up anyway. We have a playdate today at the Palace of Perfection."

In addition to the friendship the twins had formed with Ainsley's daughter, Daniel had also become chums with Ainsley's son, Adam, at preschool, and Ainsley had invited them over for a playdate.

It seemed odd that the offspring of the world's most perfect and imperfect mothers should have anything in common, but she worried that Daniel's refusal to remove his Luke Skywalker–style bathrobe would brand him as the weird kid. He needed all the friends he could get, so she graciously accepted the invitation. Plus, she might be able to sneak in a second media training session so she could finally get paid.

After dressing the baby, Nikki considered her own wardrobe options.

She could no longer zip any of her jeans. The black pants that fit *still* did not have a proper button. And everything else sat in a precarious pile on top of the overflowing laundry bin.

She sighed and grabbed a bundle of Lycra from the bottom of a drawer. Yoga pants again for the woman who hadn't done yoga since the Bush administration.

There were no more clothes in her dresser, but in the bottom of a basket of unfolded clean laundry, she found a wrinkled T-shirt commemorating a 5K race she had no recollection of participating in.

Why did people have dressers anyway? Did anyone really have time to wash, dry, fold, *and* put laundry away? Perhaps dressers were aspirational, like high-end appliances. Everyone *wanted* to be like those couples in the Sub-Zero and Viking Range advertisements, laughing as they ate quinoa and asparagus by candlelight at a dinner party in a gleaming stainless steel kitchen. But in reality, didn't most people use their ovens primarily to heat up frozen pizza and Costco lasagna, and bake brownies from a box?

She brushed her teeth, ran a comb through her hair, and declared herself presentable. It was a playdate, after all, not the Oscars.

She and Baby Joe made their way down to the kitchen, where Daniel had taken all the cans and boxes out of the pantry, creating a sort of parkour course for plastic dinosaurs. Stepping over and around him, she attempted to make her third cup of coffee.

A knock on the sliding glass patio door interrupted her before she could add the cream and sugar. She looked up, and Shelby waved to her from the deck.

Nikki unlocked the door and slid it open. "Shouldn't you be in school at nine thirty on a Thursday morning?"

Shelby came inside. "No, Aunt Nikki. It's a TP and D day."

Nikki gave her a blank look.

"You know, teacher planning and development? Like school, but for teachers? So, students get the day off."

"Wish we'd had those when I was in middle school." Nikki put the baby in his bouncy chair, then stirred sugar into her coffee as Shelby took a seat at the tiny, cluttered kitchen island.

Nikki gestured to the toaster. "Pop-Tart? Eggo waffle?"

"No thanks." Shelby sighed wistfully. "Coach won't let us eat that stuff anymore."

Nikki frowned. "What are you supposed to eat instead?"

"Steak and eggs and kale smoothies."

"Well, I guess it's a good thing you don't live here."

"I know. Mom isn't crazy about making me a huge breakfast every day. She says I should go live at an IHOP."

"I can scramble some eggs for you." Nikki opened the fridge. "Actually, I can't. I don't have eggs. Or butter. Or steak. I have milk, though. Would you like a lovely glass of milk?"

"That's okay. I actually came over for craft supplies."

"We have plenty of those. Nothing to eat, but lots of yarn. What are you making?"

"An atom. For science."

"Help yourself. You know where they keep the glitter glue."

Shelby began rummaging through the girls' "craft area" in the corner of the kitchen. A cross between a landfill and a Michaels store, it contained a small paint-splattered table, two child-size chairs, and open bins filled with paint, crayons, markers, tangles of yarn, empty toilet paper rolls, googly eyes, Popsicle sticks, and of course, glitter glue.

Nikki grabbed an empty shoebox to hold Shelby's supplies and a trash bag for the junk she knew she'd find, and sat down in one of the tiny chairs to help sort through the mess.

"So." Nikki summoned her most casual tone. "Any interesting boys in your class this year?"

Shelby rolled her eyes. "Eighth-grade boys are so immature."

Nikki tossed a broken crayon into the trash bag. "You prefer older men?"

"Something like that." Shelby's cheeks flushed a delicate pink. A curtain of dark hair fell over her shoulder, hiding her face.

Her reaction reminded Nikki of the obsessive crush she'd on Mikhail Baryshnikov at Shelby's age. Although she had never met, or spoken to, the famous Soviet-born ballet dancer, she'd known in her heart that his *age* presented the real obstacle to their love.

Nikki tossed a tube of glitter glue into the box. "How's basketball going?"

"Good."

"What's the legendary Wyatt Jericho like?"

"He's tough." Shelby kept her eyes on the twisted mass of pipe cleaners in her lap. "But I mean, he's hard on us because he wants us to win so we can get a basketball scholarship to a really good college."

Nikki narrowed her eyes. She'd heard something similar once when she interviewed a woman who'd escaped from a cult. The woman explained that at the time, she'd truly thought the cult leader loved her and that he made her wear pioneer dresses and live in a house with eleven "sister wives" because he wanted her to achieve a higher level of self-actualization.

"What do you mean?" Nikki asked. "Does he yell a lot?"

"Yeah, he yells. And he has a lot of rules." Shelby pulled the cap off a marker and tested it on a piece of scratch paper. "Like, we can only wear our hair in a ponytail, but it has to be a certain kind of ponytail, like high up, not the low kind, down on your neck."

"That's weird."

Shelby shrugged. "He says it makes us look more professional if we all have the same hair. He says it freaks out the competition."

"Hm." Nikki kept her voice neutral. She wanted Shelby to feel safe confiding in her. "How's it going with your friends? Are you still tight with Tiffany Hastings's daughter?"

"Skylar? Yeah." She paused. "Weren't you in the same class with Mrs. Hastings?"

"I was."

"Did she do anything like . . . scandalous?" Shelby shot her a sly look.

"Like post inappropriate videos on TikTok?"

Shelby's eyes lit up. "Yeah."

"No." Nikki tossed a dried-up glue stick into the garbage bag. "We carved inappropriate messages into stone tablets with a hammer and chisel when I was young because the internet hadn't been invented yet."

"Seriously, Auntie. Do you have any like . . . good stories . . . about Mrs. Hastings?"

"You mean bad stories, and no I do not." Nikki smiled. "Mrs. Hastings was straight as an arrow. I was the troublemaker."

Shelby's eyes went wide. "You?"

"Me." Nikki nodded. "As you probably know, Grandma's a little strict."

"No shit." Shelby clapped a hand over her mouth. "Sorry. But I know, right? If I don't send a thank-you note within two days of getting a birthday present, she calls and asks if the post office burned down."

"Exactly, and I was poor Grandma's worst nightmare. Always late. Horrible penmanship. Terrible math grades. Never on the honor roll." She crumpled a piece of paper in her fist. "School was hard for me, and I hated it."

"Did you get into big trouble?" Shelby asked, leaning closer.

"No," she said ruefully. "But I got into a lot of little trouble. Didn't pay attention. Didn't turn in assignments. I was the class clown, always trying to make people laugh. It didn't go over well with your grandparents, to say the least. And it didn't help that *your* mom was perfect. She made me look even worse, with all her straight As and presidencies of the student council."

"What happened? I mean, you didn't end up in *jail* or anything . . . did you?"

Nikki laughed. "No. I did not end up in jail because television news saved me. I sat down in front of a teleprompter in a broadcast journalism class my freshman year of college, and it changed my life. I was finally good at something. Really good. And that gave me a goal. I got my act together, found a great tutor, and started working really hard."

"Were Grandpa and Grandma happy?"

She snorted. "They were overjoyed. They believed my presence on television showed the world what wonderful parents they were."

"But if you hated school, why are you sending the girls to St. Preston's?"

Nikki tossed another broken crayon into the trash bag. "Because I had some amazing teachers who tried to help me learn even when I didn't think I could, and some of them are still there. We can't really afford it now that I'm not working, but St. Preston's is a good school with good teachers, and I want to give my kids what your mom and I had."

"Are you still friends with Mrs. Hastings?" Shelby asked.

"I was never exactly friends with her, even when we were in school." Nikki unwound a piece of yarn wrapped around a Popsicle stick. "But Skylar sounds nice."

Shelby nodded. "Yeah. She's chill."

Nikki nodded sagely. Shelby had recently taught her that *chill* was the in-vogue expression for the *totally awesome* of her own youth.

"She's kinda stressed out, though," Shelby said as she tried to untangle a hopelessly tangled ball of yarn. "But now that practice has started, everyone is stressed."

"Stressed out why?"

"Practice is long. We start at four and go till seven o'clock with just a short break to eat. And then on weekends he wants us to come in and watch game tapes on Sunday afternoons."

Nikki frowned. "Watch them where?"

"At school," Shelby said. "But that takes two hours. And I have all this homework, and it's just like, hard to find time for it all."

Her thin shoulders drooped forward, and Nikki suddenly wanted to strangle the coach, the middle schools, the high schools, the colleges, U.S. News & World Report, and everyone anywhere responsible for all the pressure on this slender fourteen-year-old girl she loved as much as she loved her own children.

"Come here." She scooted her tiny chair closer and pulled Shelby into a hug. "You are a great kid doing a lot of great things. But if you flunked all your classes and quit all your activities tomorrow, we'd still love you just as much. You know that, right?"

Shelby squeezed her aunt tight before pulling away. "I know that, Aunt Nikki. And I'm totally fine."

"Are you sure?" Nikki asked.

"Positive." Shelby smiled. "'Flunk all your classes and quit your activities' is not exactly a parent-approved message in the DC metro area."

"Your mom and dad feel the same way, and you know it. We love you no matter what. Unless you get an A-minus." Nikki tossed a dried-out marker into the trash bag. "Then, you know, we kick your ass to the curb."

Shelby grinned. "Obviously."

"Keep me posted on how things are going, okay?"

"I will. I promise."

They dropped a few more items into the shoebox, then rose from the tiny chairs.

"You need anything else?" Nikki asked.

"Just construction paper. Do you have any?"

Nikki thought for a minute. "Maybe upstairs in the girls' bedroom? Let me look."

She ran upstairs and found half a tablet of construction paper under Olivia's bed. As she came back down and entered the kitchen, she heard Shelby's phone ping. Her niece pulled it out of her pocket and read a message. A small smile stole across her face. Then she began to type furiously.

Nikki called from the doorway. "Found some."

Shelby startled and stuffed her phone into her pocket. "Oh. Thanks." She grabbed the shoebox of craft supplies and the construction paper. "I better head home. Thanks again, Aunt Nikki."

"Anytime."

Shelby slipped through the deck door. Nikki chewed the inside of her lip as she watched her niece cut across the neighbor's yard. Shelby's home lay two blocks to the east.

Shelby headed west.

Chapter Twelve

AINSLEY

Ainsley put a paper doily on a tray, then removed it. A frill too far? Nikki did not strike her as a doily kind of person. But maybe she would appreciate the effort?

She artfully arranged grapes and six homemade gluten-free blueberry muffins on the doily-free tray and added a small vase of blue hydrangeas. Too much? Not enough?

She never knew how to handle playdates because she never had them as a child. Instead, she and her sister angled for invitations to the homes of their classmates after school, to houses where someone else's mother made peanut butter and jelly sandwiches and chocolate chip cookies.

The mothers were even nicer than the cookies. They often seemed to be cleaning out their closets just before the girls came over and would discover a coat or a pair of shoes that was too big or too small for their own children and send them home with a bag of clothes, or sometimes even toys.

If they didn't have any luck getting invited to someone's house, they'd head to the library. Mrs. Robertson, the head librarian, kept a box in her office with graham crackers and fruit. They'd raid the snack box, then find a quiet corner in the children's section to do their homework or read until the library closed. Then Mrs. Robertson gave them a ride home.

By the time they reached middle school, they lived with their mother only on paper. Mrs. Robertson's tiny two-bedroom house behind the library had become their real home.

Her cell phone rang as she finished arranging the carrot sticks. She glanced down at the caller ID.

Her sister.

She wiped her hands on her Williams Sonoma apron and picked up her phone. "Hi."

"I called him."

No small talk with Jolene. She always cut right to the chase.

"The principal?" Ainsley asked.

"No. The assistant principal. I couldn't even get to the principal."

"And?"

Jolene snorted. "He's a spineless twerp."

Ainsley braced the phone between her ear and shoulder as she carried the tray into the family room. "What did he say?"

"He asked how many years ago this allegedly happened. Then he asked if I could be mistaken. Then he said he'd look into it, thanked me for calling."

Ainsley set the tray on the coffee table with an angry clunk. "They don't believe you."

Jolene sighed. "Look, I probably wouldn't believe me either. I gave him my real name, but he doesn't know me from Adam. Plus, it isn't illegal to go to strip clubs. And you don't have any proof Wyatt Jericho was even there."

"That's not true. He was a big basketball star and coach at Biltmore. Everyone knew who he was."

"Tami," her sister said gently, "that's not the same as proof. It's just one woman making an allegation. And we all know how that usually turns out. Look at all those women who complained about Harvey Weinstein for years and no one cared. You need *evidence*."

"But how can I prove someone was somewhere *twenty* years ago?"

"Hey, don't shoot the messenger," Jolene protested. "Listen, my flight is boarding, but maybe we need to track down one of those Boudoir stripper girls. Maybe they have some kind of . . . I don't know . . . lurid stories they could share."

"Strippers aren't the kind of people who send out change-of-address cards when they move." Ainsley rubbed her forehead. She could feel a headache coming on.

"Look, I'm just telling you what you need. I'll be back from Hong Kong next week, and we can talk then, okay?"

"I just don't understand—" The doorbell interrupted her. "I gotta go. I'll think about what you said. And thanks for trying."

She heard Marcella the maid heading for the front door. She cut her off at the foot of the stairs. "That's okay. I'll get it."

She felt silly, having a maid. Especially when normal people like Nikki came over. But when normal people *weren't* over, she had to admit it was wonderful not to scrub toilets anymore. She'd done enough of that in her job cleaning hotel rooms after she quit dancing at the club.

But Adam beat both her and the maid to the foyer. He careered around the corner in a Stormtrooper helmet and launched himself at the front door. Tossing all lessons about safety and good manners to the wind, he flung the door wide and yelled, "You're here!" in a delighted voice.

Nikki and Daniel stood on the front steps with Baby Joe in the car seat. Daniel craned his neck, gazing up at the twelve-foot ceilings. "Wow. Your house is bigger than the Death Star."

Ainsley flushed. She never thought a house could be too big, but at times like this, it was.

However, Adam seemed touched by this compliment, as any host would be. "I have a worm farm," he said.

"Can I see it?" Daniel asked.

Adam took his hand, and they disappeared into the backyard.

Ainsley frowned. Oh dear. Their fifteen-acre property made helicopter mothers uncomfortable. She turned to Nikki. "Are you okay with a zip line? It's very low, but I can—"

"I'm okay with matches and lighter fluid as long as it gives me ten uninterrupted seconds of peace and quiet." Nikki picked up the baby's car seat and entered the house.

"Well, my nanny isn't here today, so unfortunately there's no one to watch—"

Nikki waved these apologies away. "Your yard is beautiful, and I'm glad they're outside."

Ainsley's shoulders relaxed. If media training didn't come up, this playdate might actually be pleasant for her *and* Adam.

She led Nikki into the cavernous family room with views of the river. But Nikki had eyes only for the muffins. She fell upon them like a starving animal, or a woman on a keto diet. "I haven't eaten anything but chicken nuggets in two days."

"You don't look like you need to be on a diet," Ainsley said diplomatically.

"Oh, it's not that." Nikki tore off a piece of muffin and popped it into her mouth. "I just don't have time to eat. I make food for the kids, then I run out of steam and end up eating the leftovers on their plates as I clear the table instead of making something for myself. Disgusting, I know."

Ainsley nodded. She and Jolene had eaten some pretty disgusting things at the end of the month when the food stamps ran out. Rice Krispies and pickles. Peanut butter and scrambled eggs.

"Your house is so organized," Nikki said between bites. "It's so clean. Mine looks like a landfill right now."

"Do you have any help?" Ainsley slipped into a chair across from Nikki.

"Nope. Unless you count divine intervention. I pray for patience about twenty-seven times a day."

Ainsley took a muffin too. Apparently, they tasted good. "Not even a cleaning lady?"

"I was the primary breadwinner," Nikki said after taking a swig from the gigantic stainless steel travel mug she'd brought with her. "When I got fired, it put a major hole in our budget. Hopefully my husband's business will plug that hole, but it might take a while."

"What does your husband do?" Ainsley asked.

"He makes furniture, by hand."

Ainsley paused. "It isn't Josh Thatcher by any chance, is it?"

Nikki's eyes widened in surprised. "It is. I kept my last name when I got married. You know him?"

Ainsley stood. "Come here."

She led Nikki into a sparkling breakfast nook surrounded by windows. Nikki ran her hand over the kitchen table in the center of the room and beamed. "You have his chairs too."

"I love *everything* he makes," Ainsley said. "This table is the first thing I purchased when we moved in here."

Nikki's face softened as she ran her hands over the smooth wood. "This gives me hope. But unfortunately, it's hard to make a living building furniture by hand for a few people with very good taste and a lot of money. He's in Moldova right now, trying to find carpenters and this special kind of wood he likes to use. Then he plans to scale up, hopefully without sacrificing quality."

They wandered back to the family room, where Nikki settled Baby Joe on her lap as she opened a can of formula.

Ainsley sat down in a plush chair across from her, gazing at the baby. She missed that stage, where they just wanted to snuggle in your arms.

"Could I . . . hold him?" she asked.

Ainsley had loved children since she started babysitting at age twelve. She loved giving them all the things she and Jolene had gotten from their parents in the brief years before their father died, and later, from Mrs. Robertson. Attention. Affection. Reassurance. Love.

Nikki cast a dubious glance at Ainsley's white jeans and pale linen shirt. "He's been known to poop on strangers."

Ainsley laughed. "I'm willing to risk it."

Nikki rose and tucked Baby Joe into Ainsley's arms. She bent her head, inhaling his scent.

"He hasn't had a bath in a while," Nikki warned.

"He still smells delicious."

Ainsley glanced at Nikki as she leaned back in her chair. She had deep circles under her eyes and no makeup. She looked like she hadn't slept in days.

"How's the campaign going?" Nikki asked, helping herself to a third muffin.

"Pretty well, I think." The baby began to fuss, and Ainsley stood, swaying back and forth, gently patting his back. He immediately hushed. "We've started running ads, and that's been very . . . weird."

She hadn't told anyone how jarring it was to turn on the TV and see her family walking through a pile of autumn leaves hand in hand as her husband promised to create jobs, improve schools, and fight for working families.

Or worse, to turn on the TV and see the attack ads with grainy distorted pictures of her husband, accusing him of hating old people, children, education, and the environment.

Harp notes floated from Nikki's purse. She unzipped every pocket, then finally located her phone in the diaper bag just before it stopped ringing.

"Hello?"

A huge smile lit up her face. "Do you mind if I take this?" she whispered to Ainsley. "It's my husband calling from Moldova. He's flying home today."

"Of course. You can use my office. Down the hall. Third door on the left."

Nikki left the room, and Ainsley wandered through the french doors and out to the patio to check on the boys as Baby Joe fell asleep in her arms.

She looked out at the water, replaying the conversation with her sister about Wyatt Jericho. He'd appeared from the past and planted a bomb at the center of her world. She had to figure out how to defuse it before it destroyed her life.

Chapter Thirteen

NIKKI

Nikki entered a blue-and-white room that smelled like one of those stores selling eucalyptus wreaths and seventy-five-dollar scented candles.

She'd seen rooms like this in magazines at the hairdresser, but she'd never been in a room this lovely in an actual person's *home*. A window seat plump with pillows overlooked the pool and a wide green lawn that ran down to the river. She sat carefully on the silk cushion.

"Hi again," she said into her phone. "We can't wait to see you."

She'd woken that morning with a delicious feeling of anticipation, like Christmas and the last day of school all rolled into one. In a few hours, Josh would be home.

He'd listen to her story about the girls staining the countertops blue while making "potions" in the bathroom. She'd tell him how Daniel, aided by his grandmother and YouTube videos, had developed an inexplicable obsession with Torvill and Dean's "Boléro" ice dancing routine from the 1984 Winter Olympics. While she rocked the baby to sleep upstairs, Daniel poured an entire bottle of olive oil across the kitchen floor, then pretended to skate across it in his footed pajamas "like the Olympics people."

Josh would say something witty about this. He'd make her laugh, and it would all be okay again. His mere presence in the parenting lifeboat would make everything better.

"I tried to call earlier this morning," he said, a hint of reproach in his voice.

She felt her cheeks flush. Once again, she'd forgotten to charge her phone before bed and had woken to a dead screen.

"What time do you land?" she asked, changing the subject.

A pause. "I've got good news and bad news."

Stay calm. Stay positive. "What's the good news?" she asked, trying very hard not to sound like a starving and dehydrated woman on a reality survival show unable to make fire on day fifteen of her thirty-day challenge.

"The timber here is incredible. You should see the grain. It's creamy, with this sienna undertone that looks . . ."

She drifted for a moment. Like the fabled people of the tundra with one hundred words for snow, Josh had a thousand words for the texture and color of wood.

". . . and it's cheap. Really cheap, because it's everywhere. People actually burn it in their stoves over here."

"In their stoves. Really."

"Yeah, it's crazy." He spoke quickly, his voice filled with happy optimism. "And the people here are amazing too. There's this whole village filled with carpenters who make these incredible tables, all by hand. And I've been talking with those two guys I interviewed on Zoom a couple years ago, Guzluk and Petru."

"Guzluk and Petru."

What could the bad news possibly be? Had he taken a Moldovan mistress? Maybe he wanted to add this mistress to their family in a sort of *Big Love* sister wife arrangement? She could be talked into this, if the woman was willing to cook and change diapers.

"Yeah, and guess what?" he continued. "Their visas came through, and they've agreed to come over and work with me! We can triple production without sacrificing quality. Can you believe it?"

"I can't." She rubbed her forehead.

"You'll love 'em," he said. "They're young guys, and they don't speak much English, and I know this is a huge ask, but would it be okay if they stayed with us, just for a few weeks, until they get settled?"

Of course. Of course they could turn their home into a flophouse for homeless Moldovan carpenters. After all, they had two whole bedrooms.

"Plenty of room," she said.

If you counted the unfinished attic currently occupied by an aggressive squirrel family, and the empty space beside the washing machine where she stored laundry baskets.

"Anyway, it's going to be a little pricey to ship it all back, so talk to me before you make any major credit card purchases," he said.

"Credit card purchases?"

"Yeah. We talked about this, remember? Until that small business loan comes through, I have to put business expenses on our personal card, and we're getting close . . . you know . . . to maxing out."

Dear God. That card had a $20,000 credit limit.

"No problem."

Perhaps she could scrape up some extra cash by producing DIY internet porn for men aroused by C-section scars.

"Anyway," he said, "it's going better than I dared to hope."

She reached for one of the throw pillows and squeezed, hard. "That's amazing! So, um . . . what's the bad news?"

A long pause. "I need to stay here another week."

A primal scream filled her lungs. She snapped her mouth shut and swallowed it back.

No. No. No. No. No. NO. NO. NO.

She could not do this for another minute. Not another second. And never, ever for another week.

Yes, you can. You can do this. You are one insanely talented badass.

It took every ounce of the self-control she'd developed over two decades on live television to keep her voice from trembling. She dug her fingernails into her palms, an old on-air trick to stay professional when a heartbreaking story scrolled across the teleprompter.

Get a grip, Nikki.

Josh needed this. He'd *earned* this. All these years, he'd put the kids and her career ahead of his own. She'd had her dream job. Now Josh deserved to chase his.

"I understand," she said in an even voice. "Sounds like you're making good progress."

She could do this. She was a grown woman. She had a college degree in eighteenth-century English literature. She'd once interviewed the president of the United States, for God's sake. Surely, she could handle a few more days alone with a baby, a preschooler, and two kindergarteners. This was what stay-at-home moms did. They stayed at home. With their kids.

"I just need a few more days to deal with customs so I can ship it all back," he said.

"Of course."

"How are things on the home front?" he asked. "Is Baby Joe giving you any sleep?"

She swallowed hard and forced a lighthearted note into her voice. "Well, not really, but the girls are in school all day, so that helps."

"What's it like to be back at St. Preston's?"

"Weird. I've already run into a couple former classmates."

His voice grew muffled. She heard "Hold on, Guzluk. I'll be right there."

Then, "Sorry about that," he said, his voice suddenly clear again. "I gotta run. But when I get home, we're sending you to a spa. What's that place called? Canyon Ranch?"

"If I go to Canyon Ranch, our kids can't go to college," she pointed out.

"They can join the circus."

"Circuses aren't a thing anymore. PETA, remember?"

"They can be carnies."

"True. Daniel has *Future Tilt-A-Whirl Operator* written all over him."

"Seriously, Nikki. Thanks for holding down the fort so I can do this."

"Everything is fine." She looked up at the ceiling, blinking back tears. "Really. Take your time."

"I love you, Nikki."

"I love you too."

She hung up and walked down the hall like a ghost, past the boys playing with Matchbox cars on the floor, through the french doors to the patio, where the baby lay asleep in his car seat as Ainsley adjusted the cover to protect him from the sun.

Ainsley's smile froze. "What happened?"

Nikki looked at her with an empty expression. Then she burst into tears.

Chapter Fourteen

AINSLEY

Ainsley stared at Nikki in paralyzed horror.

What did I do? Why is this woman sobbing? Did I offend her? Is my house too big? Did my muffins make her sick? Does she think I'm trying to kidnap her baby?

In fraught situations, Ainsley defaulted to the assumption that she'd caused the other person's distress.

But this . . . she could not possibly be responsible for this shoulder-heaving orgy of uncontrolled sobbing.

She'd only seen a person cry like this one other time, at the cemetery the day they'd buried Mrs. Robertson. Jolene had cried so hard she couldn't see, almost stumbling into the grave when they stepped forward to drop a fistful of dirt onto the casket.

Ainsley rose from her chair, slipped into the house, and returned with tissues, a glass of water, Advil, and a bag of chocolate chips. Ironically, the heirs to the Bradley Bar candy fortune had no Bradley Bars in the house at this moment of crisis, which obviously called for some form of chocolate comfort.

She placed everything on the teak patio table in front of Nikki and put a tentative arm around her shoulder.

Nikki curled toward her, sobbing like a child. The situation was so odd that it somehow ceased to be weird.

Ainsley patted her back. "Everything's going to be okay."

"It seemed like such a good idea at the time."

"What did?"

Nikki burst into a fresh round of sobs. "Having children."

"Shh," Ainsley whispered. "You have wonderful children."

Nikki shook her head. "I can't do it anymore."

"Can't do what?" Ainsley asked, a little alarmed. Was this what a nervous breakdown looked like? Did people even have those anymore? If not, what did people have instead? Psychotic breaks? Mental health episodes?

"It's so hard."

"What's so hard?"

Nikki sobbed harder, her words becoming almost unintelligible. "Being a mom. I'm a terrible mom."

Ainsley's heart cracked down the middle. Motherhood was only easy if you did it the wrong way. She knew that from watching her own mom, who hadn't even bothered to feed them regularly.

"You listen to me," Ainsley said, her voice suddenly fierce. "Motherhood is hard because you're doing it the *right way*, did you know that? It's hard because you are a great mom."

Nikki wiped her nose on her sleeve. "You think so?"

"I *know* so." Ainsley stroked Nikki's bicolored hair. She really needed to get her roots done. "Do you have any help at home?"

Nikki shook her head. Ainsley could feel a damp mixture of tears and snot spreading across her linen shirt.

"Zelda quit last month to be a life coach," Nikki mumbled.

"Is your husband able to pitch in?"

"He's buying trees in Moldova with Guzluk."

Nikki sounded hysterical again. Was she hallucinating? Did Nikki do *drugs*? Ainsley had known women who did.

"How much sleep did you get last night?" Ainsley asked.

Nikki shook her head. "No sleep. When Josh is gone, they sneak in. Like termites."

"Who does?"

"Kids." She wiped her sleeve across her dripping nose. "They start in their own bed, but they always end up in mine. Daniel snores. Isabella hogs the covers. Olivia kicked me in the eye. Like sleeping with a drunk helicopter. And the dog. The dog is there too. And the baby. Crying in the bassinet."

Eventually, Nikki's sobs subsided, and she seemed aware of her surroundings again. She sat up straight, dried her eyes with a tissue instead of her sleeve, and blew her nose with a prolonged honk.

"I'm sorry," she said, shaking her head. "You must think I'm a lunatic."

"I think you're someone with a body full of postpregnancy hormones who hasn't slept in a very long time."

"I just want to go back to work and be good at something again." Nikki blew her nose again. "And I can go back to work . . . if I can prove I'm a good investigative reporter."

Ainsley frowned. "How do you do that?"

"I don't know. Find a blockbuster story. Expose epic malfeasance or wrongdoing." She gave a hopeless shrug. "You know, in my spare time."

A kernel of an idea took root in Ainsley's mind. But no. She couldn't do *that*.

Or could she?

She'd done a lot of things she didn't think she could do. But she needed time to think. And Nikki clearly needed time to rest.

"Listen." She handed Nikki another tissue. "I'll watch the kids while you take a nap."

Nikki gave her a blank stare. Then she shook her head. "I can't do that."

"It's ten forty-five. You go to sleep, and I'll wake you when it's time to pick up the girls at three, okay?"

"No. I can't let you do that," Nikki protested.

"Yes, you can. Follow me."

She led Nikki to a guest room with a bed covered in a snow-white duvet and a mountain of pillows.

Nikki shook her head. "This is crazy. I can't *sleep* during a playdate."

"Just rest your eyes for twenty minutes. A cat nap."

Nikki looked at the bed. Then she looked at Ainsley. "Okay. But just for *ten* minutes."

Ainsley nodded. "Ten minutes." She closed the door and tiptoed down the hall, smiling.

With the baby still sleeping in his car seat, she returned to her chair on the patio as the boys screamed across the yard, chasing each other with lightsabers.

Looking out across the river, she considered her options.

An investigative reporter could figure out how to track down enough salacious information to fire Wyatt Jericho. But confessing her secret would immediately give Nikki two blockbuster stories. Nikki could expose Wyatt Jericho *and* take down Ben's campaign.

She could visualize the attack ads now, the insidious voice, the grainy pictures of her and Ben.

Vote for Ben Bradley if you want a stripper pole in the governor's mansion.

But if Ainsley did nothing, Wyatt Jericho could blackmail her. Or destroy Ben's campaign.

If she wanted to take down Wyatt Jericho, she had to trust Nikki.

Chapter Fifteen

NIKKI

Nikki opened her eyes, taking in the spotless bedroom, the white duvet, the ceiling without water stains.

She froze. *Where the hell am I?*

Certainly not in her own bedroom. She bolted upright.

Where are the kids?

She blinked as everything came rushing back. She'd taken a nap. During a *playdate*.

She glanced at the window. The September light had a strange, late-afternoon quality.

She glanced at her watch.

Holy hell. It was 4:37 p.m. *in the afternoon*. SHE'D FORGOTTEN TO PICK UP THE CHILDREN.

She leaped out of bed, snagged her foot in the duvet, and crashed to the floor.

Nikki was late for everything, but she had never, ever been late for pickup.

She released a string of curse words as pain shot through her knee. Stumbling to the door, she fought to *remain calm* as panic hovered at the edges of her mind.

She had reoccurring nightmares about this. In some dreams, she simply forgot. In other dreams, she *knew* she needed to pick up the kids but couldn't get there because the school had vanished into thin air, or because she had to slog through miles of immobilizing mud. And if she didn't get there in time, a stranger in a white van would offer her children candy, a puppy, and a ride home, and she would never see them again.

All because she was late for pickup.

Obviously, this was crazy. Her rational mind knew that her children would simply wait with a teacher until she arrived. But facts didn't matter. When it came to pickup, her lizard brain took over, and she was controlled by an atavistic fear of being separated from her children by powerful forces like traffic, work, terrorist attacks, or long lines at Costco. Her children would sit alone and forgotten, like unclaimed suitcases on the baggage carousel, condemned to a lifetime of broken relationships due to the abandonment issues she'd created by being late.

She careered around the bedroom, gathering her belongings. Where *the hell* were her shoes? And her keys. Dear God, where did she leave her keys? And Daniel? And the baby?

Where did she leave the baby?

She thundered down the hall, then slid to a stop at the sound of voices. Girl voices. Olivia's and Isabella's voices.

The twins were not forgotten at school. Through some transportation miracle, they were *here*.

They looked up nonchalantly from the floor where they sat with Grace, surrounded by Barbies. "Hi, Mommy. Thanks for letting us have a playdate with Grace."

She opened her mouth, but nothing came out. She swallowed and tried again. "Of course. Where are Daniel and the baby?"

Olivia waved a naked Barbie in the direction of the basement. "Daniel's playing Legos with Adam. Baby Joe is in the kitchen with Mrs. Bradley. She's making dinner. Can we stay? Please? Please? Please?"

"I'll . . . be right back."

Nikki looked at the far end of the open-plan family room and kitchen. Ainsley stood behind a white marble island in an apron, putting something into a wall oven, looking like a cross between Gisele Bündchen and Betty Crocker.

Baby Joe lay on a play mat in the adjacent sunroom, cooing and kicking his legs as a wonderful scent perfumed the air.

She inhaled. *Holy hell.* Ainsley was baking homemade bread.

"Hi!" Ainsley called from the kitchen.

Nikki lumbered over to the island and sat down. "You picked up the girls," she said, her voice soft with wonder.

"You were sleeping so soundly, I couldn't bear to wake you up."

Nikki glanced at the clock on the microwave. "You took care of all my children and let me sleep for *six hours*."

"You were tired."

Nikki's eyes began to sting. "That is the nicest thing anyone has ever done for me. *Ever.*"

Ainsley waved her thanks away with an oven mitt. "Are you hungry? I'm making dinner."

"No. We can't stay." Nikki reluctantly heaved herself out of the chair. "It's a school night. And we haven't done our Math Magic and Spelling Locomotion homework yet."

The fact that her kindergartners had homework continued to appall her.

Ainsley pulled a Le Creuset baking dish out of a cabinet. "But there's no school tomorrow, remember?"

"There's not?"

"It's a teacher planning day. The middle school was off today, and the elementary school is off tomorrow."

"Oh." Nikki sat down again.

The school schedule was an impenetrable riddle made up of half days, early-dismissal days, gym-uniform days, regular-uniform days, out-of-uniform days, and Bring Dental Floss to School to Make Care

Packets for the Homeless days. She suspected it was an elaborate test designed by administrators. Children of good parents who kept it all straight would be given the one legendary teacher everyone wanted, while the children of bad, disorganized parents would get the first-year teacher who had not yet developed classroom-management skills.

"We don't want to intrude on your family time," Nikki said weakly. Dinner smelled fantastic, and she would have to lug all four children through the grocery store to restock her empty pantry before she could make dinner at home.

Ainsley lifted a pot lid and stirred something with a wooden spoon. "It's just me and the kids tonight. Ben has bingo and bowling on Thursdays. He won't be home until ten."

"Bingo and bowling?" She had trouble picturing the heir to the Bradley Bar candy fortune sitting beside little old ladies with blue hair and dot markers frantically searching for B12.

Ainsley pushed a plate of carrot sticks and hummus toward her. "He likes to hang out at bingo and VFW halls, or shift change at the tire factory, talking to people."

"Campaigning?" Nikki ran her hands over the honed marble countertop. Everything here was so *clean*.

"Right."

Nikki dipped a carrot stick into the hummus. "Smart."

"He actually enjoys it. He's good at . . . What do you call it?" She paused, looking to Nikki for the right word.

"Retail politics?"

"Right. Retail politics."

Nikki nodded. "The best politicians genuinely like people. It's not a good business for introverts, especially with reporters digging into every nook and cranny of a candidate's personal life."

Ainsley dropped a spoon on the countertop with a clatter, and her smile seemed to falter. "Well, it's just me and the kids tonight, and we'd love to have you stay for dinner."

Nikki looked at her closely. Did Ainsley *really* want them to stay? And at this point, did she even care? She hadn't eaten anything since those muffins this morning, and whatever Ainsley was roasting in her high-end appliances smelled fantastic.

"Who am I to argue with the woman who gave me the gift of sleep?" Nikki grabbed another carrot stick. "But you have to let me help."

"You can set the table." Ainsley handed her plates and silverware and placed a bouquet of fresh flowers on Josh's handmade table.

Nikki always *intended* to have fresh flowers in her house. It was one of the many tips she picked up from the magazines in the pediatrician's office.

Add life, color, and fragrance to your home with a welcoming bouquet of fresh flowers. But Nikki always forgot to change the water, the stems turned slimy, and the ensuing smell was neither fresh nor welcoming.

They gathered the children and sat down to eat. She looked across the table at Ainsley, a domestic goddess with blonde hair tumbling around her shoulders, smiling lovingly at the children. Her only imperfection lay in the strange stain on her shirt caused by Nikki's tears and other bodily fluids during her emotional breakdown after she got off the phone with Josh.

Why couldn't she be more like Ainsley? More perfect? More calm? More *content*. Ainsley looked like a woman who had everything and also had the decency to be grateful for it.

Nikki glanced at her children, their small perfect teeth flashing with laughter as they ate salmon, couscous, and asparagus, things they would never eat at home in a million years.

Nikki stabbed a piece of salmon with her fork, vowing to do better. "This is amazing."

"Thanks." Ainsley cut her son's asparagus into smaller pieces. "I like to cook."

"Do you like Pap smears and mammograms too?"

Ainsley laughed, and they discussed Nikki's first and only disastrous attempt to make lasagna.

When the children finished eating, Ainsley's daughter turned to her mother. "Mommy, can Isabella and Olivia stay longer? Please?"

The twins turned to Nikki with identical angelic expressions. "Please can we play a little longer. Please?" Isabella asked.

"Please. Please. Please. Please," Olivia pleaded.

Nikki glanced over at Ainsley, who frowned and chewed on her lower lip, as though allowing the kids to play another twenty minutes was a momentous decision with far-reaching consequences.

They had obviously overstayed their welcome. Ainsley probably needed to discuss menus with the housekeeper or carry broth to the serfs on the estate in a wicker basket.

"No." Nikki shook her head firmly. "We have literally been here all day. It's time to go."

Ainsley rose. "Please. I really need to . . . discuss something with you. Something important." A strange undercurrent of emotion ran beneath Ainsley's words.

Nikki looked at her closely. *Oh no.* Was she going to ask Nikki to chair the school auction? Or organize the next teacher appreciation luncheon?

But surely Ainsley had already witnessed her manifest unfitness to organize things? Maybe Ainsley wanted to make a confession? Share a secret? Reveal that she often went to bed *without flossing*?

"Okay," Nikki said. "But you have to let me clean up."

The kids shot out of the kitchen before their mothers could change their minds. Nikki glanced over at Baby Joe, still cooing happily on his play mat.

Ainsley followed her to the sink with a bowl of couscous, deep creases scoring her brow.

Nikki glanced at her. *This is weird.*

Maybe she needed to come clean and admit that she had actually made Grace's Cycle of Life Rainforest Diorama and only allowed Grace to attach the monkeys at the end?

She stifled a yawn. Ainsley had been unbelievably kind to her today. She'd do her best to pretend to be interested in whatever Ainsley wanted to discuss.

Chapter Sixteen

AINSLEY

Ainsley settled the children in the basement with a Disney movie, then returned to the kitchen, where Nikki scraped plates into a garbage can.

Squaring her shoulders, she approached the island. She could do this. *She had to do this.* She couldn't go after Wyatt Jericho alone. Like Obi-Wan Kenobi, or was it Han Solo? Whatever. Nikki was her only hope.

She opened the dishwasher and glanced at Nikki. Now that she'd gotten some rest, Ainsley could actually see the anchorwoman Nikki had once been, with her high cheekbones and authoritative air.

Nikki handed her a dirty plate. "Hey, can I ask you something?"

Ainsley placed it in the first of her two dishwashers. She liked to load the dishwasher herself, because everyone else, including the housekeeper, her husband, and both maids, did it wrong. "Um. Sure."

Nikki handed her another plate. "Your husband was the finance chairman for the school's capital campaign, right? And he's on the St. Preston's governing board?"

"He was." Ainsley slid the plate into the lower rack. "He stepped down a couple months ago. He didn't want to inadvertently drag the school into any campaign issues that might come up."

Nikki handed her a fistful of dirty silverware. "What does he know about Wyatt Jericho?"

Ainsley froze for a moment. Why in the world was *Nikki* asking about Wyatt Jericho? She continued to drop utensils into the silverware basket. "Why do you ask?"

"Oh, no reason." Nikki unscrewed the lid from a sippy cup. "I'm just wondering why a successful college basketball coach would take a job as an athletic director coaching high school and middle school girls."

The hair on the back of Ainsley's neck began to prickle. She fought to keep her voice casual. "He grew up in this area, and his mother has Parkinson's. He wanted a job that would allow more time for his family."

"But it's gotta be a big pay cut, right?" Nikki began to wipe the plastic place mats with a dishrag.

Why was she asking this? Had Wyatt Jericho told everyone where she used to work? Did Nikki already know her secret? Did everyone?

Ainsley cleared her throat. She'd asked the same questions, discreetly, over the last couple of weeks. "St. Preston's increased the pay for the athletic director job substantially, and then a few families agreed to donate the rest, to get his salary closer to where it was before." Ainsley kept her face buried in the dishwasher so Nikki couldn't see her terrified expression. "I think the Hastings family donated twenty-five thousand dollars. Other families with kids in basketball donated as well."

"That's legal?" Nikki asked.

"It's a private school." Ainsley put a sippy cup on the top rack of the dishwasher. "They can do things at St. Preston's that a public school can't."

"But why are they so anxious to have him here?"

"Prestige." Ainsley shook the cloth napkins into the sink, then tossed them into a pile on the counter. "The Crestwood Academy sends a few kids to the Ivies every year for lacrosse. People want St. Preston's to do the same with basketball."

"I see."

Ainsley couldn't stand it anymore. "Why are you asking these questions?" she blurted in a strained voice.

Nikki put a Le Creuset casserole dish down on the counter and turned to face her. Ainsley forced herself to maintain eye contact. After an uncomfortable silence, Nikki finally spoke. "Can you keep something to yourself?"

Ainsley inhaled. "Yes."

"I think Wyatt Jericho is . . . I don't know how to describe it . . . I just don't trust him."

"Do you have any—"

"Specific reason?" Nikki shook her head. "No. It's just a vibe I get from talking to my niece. She's on his basketball team, and he sounds . . . controlling. And I'm worried about her, but I'm not exactly sure why."

Ainsley clutched a dish towel, twisting it into knots as determination settled into her spine. She had to tell Nikki now, because Nikki would believe the truth about Wyatt Jericho.

"Can I get you a drink?" Ainsley asked abruptly. "Coffee? Tea? Sparkling water? Vodka?"

Nikki gave her a puzzled look. "Um. Tea would be nice. Chamomile?"

"I'll be right back."

With trembling hands, Ainsley filled the kettle and ignited the gas flame. Could she trust this woman? Did she really want to do this? Because once she said the words, they could never be unsaid.

She remembered the day she and Jolene had finally told Mrs. Robertson about their homelife. How their mother spent 90 percent of her time asleep, drunk, or at the bar.

Once they told Mrs. Robertson the truth, things got so much better. She took them into her home. Fed them. Helped with homework. Took them to museums and church and restaurants. Loved them.

Mrs. Robertson saved them from God only knew what, because they'd had the courage to share the shameful secret about their mother's drinking, their chaotic home, their hunger.

The screaming kettle shattered these memories. Ainsley made two mugs of tea and led Nikki to the kitchen table. Nikki made a bottle for the baby and sat down to feed him while Ainsley took a seat across from her.

Ainsley said a silent prayer for courage and took a deep breath. Then she looked Nikki in the eye. "I need to tell you something. Something I've never told anyone before."

Nikki looked startled. "Me?"

"Yes. But only if you promise you will never tell another living soul."

"Um. Okay."

"I'm serious." Ainsley leaned forward. "Isn't there some special confidentiality vow journalists take? Aren't you like doctors? Or priests?"

"Kind of," Nikki said. "If you tell me something off the record, I will never report that information and I will never reveal who gave me the information. But if you tell me something on background, I will reveal the information, but I will not identify the person who gave me the information."

"Like Deep Throat in the parking garage during Watergate?"

Nikki nodded. "Exactly."

"Okay." Ainsley gripped her mug with both hands, gathering up every last ounce of courage. "What I'm about to tell you is way, way, way off the record. You can never tell another person on the planet what I am about to tell you. Do you promise?"

"Yes." Nikki nodded solemnly. "I promise."

Ainsley took a deep breath. Nothing would ever be the same once she spoke these words. She would be in Nikki's power forever. Nikki could blackmail her, blackmail her husband. Coerce her into doing anything she wanted.

She stared at Nikki across the table. Did she trust this woman?

Nikki stared back, her eyes filled with humor and intelligence, exuding a quiet dignity, despite her disheveled hair.

Ainsley opened her mouth and released her secret into the world.

"I used to be a stripper."

Chapter Seventeen

NIKKI

Nikki coughed, choked, and sprayed chamomile tea all over the kitchen table. "That isn't possible," she finally managed to rasp out.

Ainsley smiled bitterly. "Oh yes. It is."

For perhaps the first time in her life, Nikki relapsed into wordless silence. She'd been shocked when Princess Diana died, when Brad Pitt left Jennifer Aniston for Angelina Jolie, and when her twins showed an aptitude for math while she herself still did not fully understand fractions, but this . . . this blew all the other shocking events in her life to smithereens.

"But you're so . . . prim and proper. You're even kind of *snooty*."

Ainsley rolled her eyes. "My real name is Tami Darlene Schmidt. I grew up in a trailer park called the People's Court in a tiny town in rural Maryland called Badwater. Because it *literally* had bad water. The whole place smelled like rotten eggs. My dad died when my sister and I were seven and eight years old, and my mom fell apart. She was a complete drunk."

Nikki shook her head as she tried, and failed, to absorb this revelation. "But you're so put together and . . . you have such great hair . . . I mean, this is like learning that Marie Kondo is a hoarder or something."

Ainsley reached across the table and touched her hand. "Come here."

Nikki picked up Baby Joe and followed Ainsley up a broad staircase, through a master suite larger than the first floor of her house, and into a closet bigger than her kitchen, uncrowded and beautifully organized with shelves, shoe racks, and soft lighting.

Holy hell. With a closet like this she'd never lose her black pumps again. Maybe money really could buy happiness.

Ainsley closed the door, then reached under a cushion and pulled out a notebook. "Look at this." She waved it in Nikki's face. "I need a cheat sheet to tell me how to dress. I spend hours agonizing about what to wear. How to act. What to eat. I have no idea how to be a good wife or a good mom. I just do the opposite of what my own mom did and hope it's right. All day long I try to imitate the people around me, trying to learn the secret handshake, terrified I'm going to screw up and embarrass my husband and my children."

Ainsley sat down abruptly on the floor as her face began to crumple. "You have no idea how awful it is to be someone you're not, *someone you don't even want to be*, just to fit in." Tears began to roll over her high cheekbones, splashing onto her linen shirt.

Nikki inserted a bottle into Baby Joe's mouth as she watched this accomplished woman disintegrate before her eyes. Ainsley was right. She didn't understand. At a young age, she'd realized she couldn't be the person her parents wanted her to be, so she'd stopped trying. At the time, she thought her inability to pay attention or understand math was a curse that prevented her from meeting her parents' expectations. But now, as she watched tears stream down Ainsley's lovely face, she understood that her many inadequacies were also a blessing. Perpetually disappointing her parents gave her the freedom to be herself.

Nikki slid down beside Ainsley, shifting Baby Joe to one arm as she attempted to wrap the other around Ainsley's shoulders.

Ainsley immediately pulled away, drying her eyes with the back of her hand. "I'm sorry."

"Don't be." Nikki pulled a crumpled tissue from her pocket and handed it to Ainsley. "I had an emotional breakdown this morning. Now it's your turn."

"My sister and I were raised by other people's mothers." Ainsley dabbed at her eyes with the tissue. "We spent as much time as possible at our friends' houses. Then this librarian named Mrs. Robertson sort of informally adopted us. She's the reason we graduated from high school. Grew up safe. Got out."

"But how did you get from there"—Nikki gestured at the giant closet and all it represented—"to here?"

Ainsley blew her nose. "I had some teachers who really cared, and I was smart. Straight As and good SAT scores. I got a full ride to Biltmore."

"Wow." Nikki's eyes widened as she shifted the baby to a more comfortable position. "My parents made me apply because it's just across the river, but I wasn't even close to getting in."

"It's a good school," Ainsley said with admirable humility. "I had a work-study job that paid for extras. I was living in the dorms, doing really well. Meanwhile, my sister was finishing her last year of high school back in Badwater."

"How old is she?" Nikki asked.

"Thirteen months younger."

"Practically Irish twins."

Ainsley nodded. "The summer before I left for college, we found out Mrs. Robertson had pancreatic cancer. It was diagnosed late, and she died in October of Jolene's senior year. It happened so fast." She began to scratch at a seam in the hardwood with her thumbnail. "When she died, Jolene fell apart. Just . . . lost it. Like our mom, after Dad died. She stopped going to class and started dating the neighborhood drug dealer."

"Didn't social services get involved?"

"No." Ainsley dabbed at her smudged mascara. "Jolene turned eighteen in September, the month before Mrs. Robertson died. Mrs.

Robertson never formally adopted us, so on paper, it looked like Jolene still lived with Mom."

Nikki frowned. "But why didn't she try to adopt you?"

"Because Mrs. Robertson was Black," Ainsley said with a heavy sigh. "She was afraid social services would insist on placing us with a White family instead. So when she died, Jolene had to move back to the trailer, and that made everything worse. Now she had no real adult supervision in a house full of alcohol with her drug dealer boyfriend living next door."

Nikki could almost track Ainsley's mind as it drifted into the past. The faint curl of her lip when she uttered the word *boyfriend*, the almost imperceptible pause before the word *mom*. Hurt and anger radiated from her lovely face, like steam rising from a hot bath. Nikki longed to comfort her in some way but sensed that touching her, or worse yet, offering pity, would make her feel worse. All she could do for Ainsley was listen.

Ainsley took a deep breath and continued. "I was desperate to get her through her senior year, into college, and out of Badwater for good. But Jolene started saying she wasn't smart enough for college, that she just wanted to keep waitressing at the truck stop instead."

"And that was a change?" Nikki asked.

Ainsley nodded. "An enormous change. No one in our family had ever gone to college, but Mrs. Robertson told us we could get there if we worked hard enough. College became our dream, our goal. But when Mrs. Robertson died, Jolene's confidence died too. And that abusive . . . *bastard* . . . of a boyfriend didn't help."

Ainsley's mouth twisted as she spit the word *bastard* into the air, making it sharp with hatred, heavy with anger.

Nikki's eyes widened. She'd never heard Ainsley swear before. This previously perfect woman was becoming more human by the minute. "What did you do?"

Ainsley frowned. "I came home the weekend of the SAT. The morning of the test, I found Jolene sitting in a booth at a convenience store, smoking cigarettes and eating chicken wings. She'd been up all night, doing God knows what. I poured a pot of coffee down her throat and dropped her at the testing site. Then I got back on my Greyhound bus, went back to college, crossed my fingers, and waited for the results."

"And?" Nikki held her breath.

"She aced it."

Nikki's mouth fell open. "She got a perfect score on the SAT. *Hungover?*"

"Not just hungover," Ainsley said. "I think she was still a little bit drunk."

Nikki's eyes widened as she remembered the painful day she got her own SAT scores. The set of her mother's jaw as she crumpled the results and threw them in the trash without saying a word. "She must be insanely smart."

"She's Mensa," Ainsley said. "Fortunately. That test score made all the difference."

"Then what happened?" Baby Joe's eyes fluttered shut as he drifted into sleep. Nikki slowly removed the bottle from his mouth.

"Well, she had this perfect SAT score, but she couldn't get a scholarship anywhere because her transcripts were so ugly. All Ds. Lots of unexcused absences. Zero extracurricular activities. Then, three weeks before I left for my sophomore year of college, something awful happened."

Nikki froze, baby bottle in midair. "What?"

"Her boyfriend threw her down a flight of stairs and beat her so badly she ended up in the hospital."

Nikki gasped. "Oh, Ainsley . . ."

"Seeing her in the hospital . . ." Ainsley's voice quivered as she blinked up at the ceiling. "It was the single most awful moment of my life."

"I'm so sorry," Nikki whispered, suddenly queasy with guilt for her unremarkable childhood, for the rigid parents who kept her safe with their rules, curfews, and critical but vigilant love.

Ainsley dabbed at her eyes with the tissue. "But it turned out to be one of those horrific things that somehow turns into a blessing because for one brief moment, lying there in that hospital bed with cracked ribs, two black eyes, and a broken ankle, she was actually willing to listen."

"She agreed to leave?"

Ainsley nodded. "I was a resident assistant in the dorms my sophomore year, and I didn't have a roommate. She stayed with me in my dorm room, and we talked to my adviser and the dean. They gave her a provisional acceptance, based on her SAT score and a personal interview where she explained everything."

"Wow."

"Yeah, the dean and my adviser really went to bat for her. However, she couldn't get any scholarships her freshman year because of her terrible grades. But they said if she got good grades her first year, and stayed out of trouble, she could get a full ride for the rest."

"That's fantastic."

Ainsley cocked an eyebrow. "That's what we thought, too, until we did the math. Because of her past 'issues,' they said she had to live in the dorms and 'become fully integrated into campus life.' So, in addition to tuition for her freshman year of college, we had to come up with room, board, and books."

"How much was it?" Nikki asked.

"Back then it was twelve thousand dollars. But it could just as well have been twelve million dollars. We had three weeks to come up with the first payment or she'd lose her spot."

"What did you do?" Nikki asked, leaning closer. She felt like she was binge-watching one of those gripping shows on Netflix about ordinary people who start laundering money for a Mexican drug cartel.

Ainsley turned to her, eyes suddenly hard. "I took off my clothes. I grabbed a pole. And I started dancing."

Chapter Eighteen

AINSLEY

Ainsley shot a sideways glance at Nikki as an awkward silence settled over the closet. Most socially adept adults knew how to handle difficult revelations about a cancer diagnosis or the death of a loved one. But even nonjudgmental, Nutella-sandwich Nikki did not appear to know the appropriate social convention for admissions of past employment as a pole dancer.

She did take some comfort from Nikki's shell-shocked expression. Nikki could have raised her index finger in the air and shouted, "Aha! I *told* everyone you looked like a stripper!" That would have been so much worse. But apparently all her anxiety about clothes, hair, and makeup had paid off.

Ainsley felt drained as she slumped on the closet floor beside Nikki, as though her bones had melted, leaving nothing inside to hold her up. She'd never shared the whole story with anyone. She'd told Ben part of the story, years ago, when their relationship started to get serious. He knew about Jolene's abusive boyfriend, and Mrs. Robertson, and their mother. She'd told him everything, except the detail about how they'd paid for Jolene's first year of college. She told him they got scholarships and financial aid and let him think that covered everything. She hadn't lied exactly . . . just omitted . . . one extremely important detail.

"Okay," Nikki said, shrugging with an admirable attempt at nonchalance. "You became a stripper . . . but how did you arrive at this . . . particular solution . . . to your tuition problem?"

"By accident," Ainsley said. "I was walking to the Dillard Hotel to interview for a housekeeping job."

"Ohh," Nikki sighed as she adjusted the sleeping infant in her arms. "I've always wanted to stay there. But isn't it like, five hundred dollars a night?"

"It was then. It's more like a thousand now. Anyway, it's in this historic neighborhood just off campus, with all these beautiful old homes."

"Robber Baron Row?"

"That's right." Ainsley nodded. "On my way to the interview, I walked past this big, old gothic mansion set back from the street, surrounded by trees. It had a wrought iron fence and an immaculate garden with a little gold sign on the gate that said *Lady Godiva's Gentleman's Club*. We had a neighbor at the People's Court who'd been a stripper, and she was always bragging about how much money she made. But I didn't know anything else about it. So, I went inside."

"What was it like?"

Ainsley shrugged. "I'd describe the decorating style as Gilded Age whorehouse."

"Were you scared?"

She thought about it. "No. I was too desperate to be scared. Jolene's entire future, her whole *life* sat on the edge of this cliff, ready to tip one way or the other, and I was willing to do anything to get her into college and keep her there."

"But why didn't your sister start stripping?" Nikki asked.

"First of all, she physically couldn't," Ainsley said. "She had a broken ankle and cracked ribs, and pole dancing is physically demanding. Six-inch platform heels aren't easy to walk in either. And second, she was just . . . broken . . . and there are lots of men willing to take advantage of broken girls. I wouldn't let her anywhere near the club."

"So how long did you . . ." Nikki's voice trailed off.

"Dance? About ten months. I earned enough to pay for Jolene's freshman year. We applied for financial aid, and eventually that kicked in. She got straight As and then got a scholarship for the next three years. Between scholarships, Pell Grants, student loans, waitressing, cleaning hotel rooms, and work-study, we got by, and we both graduated. I got a graduate degree in economics, she went to law school, and I never had to strip again. I thought I'd put it behind me forever, until Wyatt Jericho showed up at the Kindergarten Jamboree."

"My intuition is right?"

"Dead right. He was a fixture at the club. Sleazy is an understatement."

"You're sure he's the same guy?" Nikki asked.

"Positive. He was one of our regulars, like the Sock Man."

Nikki cocked her head. "The Sock Man?"

"Yeah. The Sock Man used to buy our unwashed socks for ten dollars a pair."

"What did he—"

Ainsley lifted a hand to stop further questions. "You don't want to know."

Nikki paused for a moment, then cringed. "Moving on . . . How do you know you aren't confusing him with someone else?" Nikki's enunciation became crisp, and her voice grew deeper. Ainsley could almost see her slipping into reporter mode.

"Because everyone knew Wyatt Jericho. He was a huge deal." Ainsley crumpled her disintegrating tissue into a ball. "He was a college basketball star at the U who got injured and couldn't go pro, so he started coaching. He came in all the time, and he was . . . nasty."

"Nasty how?"

"Bad temper, controlling . . . demeaning." She looked down at the floor. "He wanted girls to beg for tips. He ignored the rules about touching, and got angry if a girl pushed his hands away. And he said really sick things during lap dances."

"He said these things to you?"

"I never did a lap dance or a private show with him, but that's what the other girls said."

"Maybe they were exaggerating, or making things up?"

"No." Ainsley shook her head vehemently. "I loved the girls I danced with, and we looked out for each other. If someone was violent or sick or handsy, or just a bad tipper, we talked about it."

She smiled at the memory. Some girls were crazy. Some were addicts. A couple worked as call girls on the side. But most of them felt like sisters. Tough, smart, and funny, like Jolene. She loved the slumber party atmosphere of the changing room, girls helping other girls with makeup or hair, and the us-against-them sisterhood of the club: *us* being the women, and *them* being the men stupid enough to part with all that cash.

"Did he recognize you?" Nikki asked.

A chill whispered across Ainsley's skin. She'd been asking herself this question since she first saw him at the Kindergarten Jamboree. "I think so."

Nikki listened in silence as she described her conversation with Wyatt Jericho at the teacher appreciation lunch.

"It sounds like he knows exactly who you are," Nikki said gently.

Ainsley hung her head. She didn't want to admit it, but in her heart, she knew it was true. "What do I do?"

"What have you done so far?" Nikki asked as she laid the sleeping baby across her lap.

Ainsley recounted her conversation with Jolene earlier in the day. "And Jolene is right. The assistant principal is right, too, as much as I hate to admit it. I last saw Wyatt Jericho in a strip club *twenty years ago*. I don't have any *proof* he used to visit strip clubs. It's my word against his, and they think he hangs the moon. It's going to take a lot more than an anonymous phone call to get him fired."

"Plus, going to strip clubs isn't illegal," Nikki pointed out.

"That's exactly what my sister said. And I'll bet half the men in America have been dragged into a club at one time or another for a bachelor party."

Baby Joe began to squirm in Nikki's lap. "I need to change him and get a new bottle. Do you mind?"

"Of course not. And maybe it's time to come out of the closet. And sit somewhere a little more comfortable."

Nikki rose from the floor while holding the sleeping baby, exhibiting the cautious grace of a demolition expert defusing a bomb.

They moved downstairs, where Ainsley checked on the children, who remained engrossed in their movie. She brought a pot of chamomile tea to the library, along with a fruit and cheese plate the housekeeper had left in the fridge. Then she lit the logs in the fireplace and curled up in a chair.

Nikki sat on the rug with the baby, who babbled beside the fire while Ainsley poured her a cup of tea.

"Okay, so where were we," Nikki asked once they got settled.

Ainsley blew across the rim of her mug. "The problem is that I have no proof Wyatt Jericho hung around strip clubs twenty years ago, and even if I did, it isn't illegal, as you pointed out, so why would anyone care."

"Right." Nikki nodded. "It isn't illegal. And it isn't exactly a hanging offense to go to a club once or twice when a guy is young and drunk and stupid for a bachelor party. But what if he's none of those things, and he's *still* doing it."

Ainsley cocked her head. "That might be different."

"How old is Wyatt Jericho now?"

"Well." She looked up at the ceiling and tried to calculate his age. "I think he started coming to Godiva's when he was playing ball, in his early twenties. But he was probably in his thirties by the time I got there. He wasn't playing anymore at that point, and he was well into his coaching career. He's probably in his early fifties."

"Now we're getting somewhere." Nikki dangled a toy caterpillar in front of the baby, who gave her a happy, toothless grin in response. "A middle-aged guy with a minivan and a wife and kids at home hanging out at strip clubs? That's not cool."

"But I looked him up on Wikipedia," Ainsley said. "He's never been married. No wife or kids. And definitely no minivan."

Nikki frowned. "As a woman who took more than a decade to find her spouse, I do not want to imply that people of a certain age are single because they have a foot fetish or a thing for whips and chains, but . . ."

Ainsley finished her thought. "But an unmarried fifty-year-old guy hanging out at strip clubs while coaching teenage girls? That's not a good look, for him or for the school."

"Exactly," Nikki said, taking a long sip of tea.

"But what if he isn't doing this stuff anymore?" Ainsley asked. "And even if he is, how do I prove it?"

Nikki nibbled on a slice of cheese. "Follow the money."

Ainsley gave her a blank look. "Like Woodward and Bernstein?"

"Is there an ATM at Godiva's?" Nikki asked.

Ainsley nodded. "There used to be."

"And do they take credit cards at the bar?" Nikki asked.

"Yes"—Ainsley nodded again—"and they also take credit cards in the dining room."

"Then every time he goes into Godiva's, he leaves a paper trail. Credit card receipts. ATM receipts. A paper trail is *proof*. Proof of where he went, when he went, and what he did."

Ainsley's eyes widened. "You're right."

"And *that's* how we prove he's a single middle-aged man who hangs out at strip clubs not for isolated, bachelor-party-type events but because he's a skeevy dude who is now coaching the teenage daughters of their litigious, high-net-worth, tuition-paying parents," she concluded, gesticulating with a grape to make her point.

Ainsley's eyes widened in admiration. "That's brilliant."

"I'm just a humble unemployed television reporter trying to make a difference in the world," she said with a shrug and a smile.

Ainsley took a sip of tea. "But it's not just about getting rid of him for my sake . . . and it's not just that he has a creepy thing for strip clubs. Like I said, he has a nasty temper . . ."

She paused as something niggled at the edge of her mind . . . a memory . . . and a name.

"There was something else about him . . . some story . . . like he assaulted someone at the club . . . a dancer . . . and then he paid her not to press charges."

"Did he pay her with a check?" Nikki asked.

"I have no idea." Ainsley shook her head. "I can't remember the details. But I think her name was Misty."

Nikki rolled her eyes. "Of course it was."

"Misty Dawn!" The girl's face and name came together inside her mind like a puzzle.

"You're joking?"

"I'm not."

"Well," Nikki said as she popped another grape into her mouth, "if he paid Misty Dawn with a check, we'd have another paper trail. And paying hush money to a stripper because he assaulted her? *That* would definitely get him fired, even by the besotted sports boosters at St. Preston's."

"And that could get you *hired* . . . at that TV station. I mean, wouldn't that be a big story?"

Nikki looked up at her with dawning recognition. "It would. Anytime you can put a semifamous person's name in a headline with the words *stripper* and *hush money*, you have a winner."

"But is paper evidence enough? Don't we need more?"

Nikki nibbled thoughtfully on a cracker and considered the question. "Video is damning, especially if it's video of a person describing something they saw firsthand or personally experienced. Do you think we could track down this . . . Misty Dawn . . . and maybe she could make a statement? If she told us what happened in her own words, and we recorded her, that could be very compelling if we can't find paper evidence."

Ainsley frowned. "I'm not sure that would do any good."

"Why not?"

"Because no one believes strippers," Ainsley said, recognizing the bitterness in her own voice. "We once had a DJ who tried to file a fraudulent insurance claim. He claimed one of the dancers stole his equipment. He got the police involved and tried to press charges against this girl who wasn't even working that night. The cops believed him. The insurance company believed him. And no one believed her, because she was a stripper."

"What happened?"

"Our boss got involved and made him drop the charges." She smiled at the memory of Lady Godiva's righteous indignation. "Then she fired the DJ. But it's the same thing in court, with a jury. We had a girl who witnessed a drug deal in the parking lot at a different club, where someone got shot. They trashed her on the witness stand, and the jury didn't believe a word she said. They ultimately sided with the *drug dealer* because the only witness to the crime happened to be a stripper. And a snooty principal at a fancy private school would be even more skeptical of a woman who takes off her clothes for a living."

"I guess I've never heard of someone calling a stripper as a character witness," Nikki conceded.

"Now you know why."

"Then we'll have to be really discreet." Nikki picked up Baby Joe and rose to sit in the wingback chair. "Because if he finds out we're trying to get him fired, and he tells your husband's opponent to look into your past . . ." Her voice trailed off.

"I know. I know." Ainsley rubbed her forehead. "He could humiliate my family, destroy Ben's campaign, ruin my marriage, and damage the wholesome Bradley Bar candy brand."

"Does anyone know your real name?"

"Ben and my sister do. And it's on our marriage license. But we got married at my mother-in-law's villa on the Amalfi Coast, and we did the paperwork in Italy. It would take a lot of digging to connect Ainsley Bradley with Tami Darlene Schmidt, and it would be even harder to connect Tami Darlene Schmidt to Lady Velvet."

Nikki blinked. "Who's Lady Velvet?"

Ainsley looked down at her lap. "*I'm* Lady Velvet. That was my stage name at the club."

"Your husband knows about all this, right?"

Ainsley opened her mouth, then closed it again. It was difficult enough to tell Nikki her secret. She wasn't ready to admit she'd withheld this vital information from her husband.

"I've never told him." Ainsley tightened her grip on her teacup. "I just . . . can't."

"But you have to tell him!" Nikki raised her voice, and Ainsley shrank in her seat. Suddenly she was seven years old again, chastised by her teacher for being late.

"I'm sorry." Nikki lowered her voice. "But if Wyatt Jericho tells anyone at school, or the press, or worse yet, your husband's opponent . . ."

"Stop. Please. *I know*," Ainsley begged. "But if we drive Wyatt Jericho away discreetly, we save me from having to tell Ben something I should have told him years ago. And we rid the school of a man who shouldn't be anywhere near teenage girls."

"Why are you so afraid to tell your husband?" Nikki asked softly. "He seems like a decent guy to me . . . unless it's all an act?"

"It's not an act." Ainsley swallowed the lump forming in her throat. "That's why it's so hard. Every day he looks at me like I'm the most fantastic woman in the world . . . I love him so much . . . and I can't bear to disappoint him."

"Oh, Ainsley." Nikki reached over and took Ainsley's hand.

"I know it's terrible," she said miserably. "And I will tell him, eventually. But no one else can know, not the Associated Press, or Tiffany

Hastings, or the PTA, or God forbid, the public in general and registered voters in particular. But I can't do this by myself. I need your help."

"Of course I'll help." Nikki gave her hand an encouraging squeeze. "Just let me think about this as a reporter for a minute." She took a contemplative sip of tea, then set the cup on the table with a decisive clunk. "Okay. We do two things. We follow the paper trail. And we find the girl Wyatt Jericho assaulted. What was her name again?"

"Misty Dawn." Ainsley said. "Sometimes she also went by Naughty Nikki."

Nikki looked startled. "I have a stripper name?"

"Only when used in conjunction with *Naughty*."

"I'll keep that in mind if this whole handmade furniture thing doesn't pan out. Do you know her real name?"

"We never used our real names at the club." Ainsley took a sip of tea. "It helped to keep things . . . compartmentalized. There were other college girls there too. Some were mothers. Others had day jobs. Boyfriends. Even husbands. It was just better not to use real names, even with each other. But we had W-2 forms and paid taxes like everyone else, and Lady Godiva knew our real names."

Nikki frowned. "Lady Godiva?"

"Lady Godiva owned and ran the club. She's the best boss I ever had."

"I see." Nikki nibbled thoughtfully on her lower lip. "Well then, we talk to this Lady Godiva person and find out if he's still coming to the club. If he is, we nail down a paper trail to prove it. We also track down Naughty Nikki or Misty Dawn or whatever her name is. If she's willing to speak on camera, or give a statement to the police, we might have enough to get him fired."

"Now *that* sounds like a plan." Ainsley leaned forward. "Making one phone call and hoping someone cares is not exactly a battle strategy."

Nikki continued to think out loud. "If we succeed, no one will ever know you were involved. It won't impact the campaign. Jericho can't blackmail you. You won't have to tell your husband, though I still think you should," she added, giving Ainsley a pointed look. "And I'll have a story to take into my job interview when Channel Four calls."

"Right."

"Okay." Nikki crumpled her napkin into a ball and tossed it on the table. "Where do we start?"

"Can you get away for a couple days?" Ainsley asked.

"My husband did promise to send me to Canyon Ranch when he returns from Moldova."

"We could go into DC for a long weekend and stay in our condo at the Watergate while we do our sleuthing."

Nikki lifted an eyebrow. "You have a condo in DC, twenty minutes from the gigantic house you already have here?"

"Well, it's not *mine*." Ainsley felt her face flush. "It belongs to my mother-in-law. She uses it when she's in town for events at the Kennedy Center. You know, the opera. Things like that."

"Of course." Nikki nodded. "I use all my extra houses for *Hamilton* performances."

"This will be fun, like a slumber party." A note of optimism crept into Ainsley's voice. She hadn't realized how heavy the load of fear and guilt had grown since Wyatt Jericho arrived. It was a relief to share this burden, to finally take action. "Give me a list of things you like to eat. The housekeeper will stock the fridge and get everything ready."

"Don't make it too nice." Nikki pushed her plate away. "Since having kids I've found that the difficulty of reentry to normal life is proportional to the quality of the vacation."

"I'll tell the housekeeper to skip the ironed Frette sheets."

"And the fluffy bathrobes. Skip those too," Nikki said.

"Deal," Ainsley said. "I think this is the beginning of a wonderful friendship."

Nikki raised an empty baby bottle. "Here's to us. By the way, where exactly *are* we going?"

Ainsley raised her teacup and clinked it against the baby bottle. "Lady Godiva's Gentleman's Club, the oldest continuously running strip club east of the Mississippi. We start with the Great Lady herself."

Chapter Nineteen

NIKKI

"Do you know what day it is today?" Josh leaned against the kitchen counter in sweatpants and a T-shirt, sipping coffee from a mug emblazoned with the KDAY-TV logo. The upbeat, jazzy music from the *Curious George* soundtrack played in the background as Daniel watched the episode where George takes over a pizza parlor. Meanwhile, Baby Joe slept in his mechanical swing, oblivious to the noise around him.

Nikki's forehead wrinkled. "It's Friday, right? The twenty-eighth?"

"Yes, but what *day* is it, on the calendar?"

"Um. Grandparents' Day?"

"No."

"Indigenous Peoples' Day?"

Josh took a sip of coffee. "No."

A vague feeling of suspicion washed over her, and she felt like a character on *Law and Order*, brought in by the cops to answer "a few simple questions" before being arrested for murder. "Earth Day? Flag Day? Cinco de Mayo?"

"No. No. And no." Josh shook his head. "Something far more important."

A look of horror crossed her face. Did she somehow forget Father's Day? Or a child's *birthday*? No, even she wouldn't forget that. Plus, her children would never allow such a thing to happen. The girls had been planning their April birthday party since last May.

"Um. Your mother's birthday?"

She could not possibly be expected to keep track of her in-laws when she could barely keep track of her own side of the family.

"No. It involves you. And me." He looked at her over the rim of his coffee mug and arched an eyebrow. "And our endless love."

Her stomach plummeted into her ragged bedroom slippers. She slammed her palm into her forehead. "Our anniversary."

"That's right, my beautiful, cognitively challenged bride. Happy anniversary. And here's a bonus question. Do you know how long we've been married?"

She gave him an injured look. "That's not fair and you know it." She began twisting off her wedding ring to look at the date inscribed on the band.

He reached for her hand and clasped her fingers. "No cheating."

She took a deep breath and tried to do the math in her head, starting with the current year, the ages of the children, and her own age, but it was heavy going.

"Carry the one . . . ," Josh whispered.

"Give me a second." Who was president the year they got married? She began to count on her fingers.

He began to hum the *Jeopardy!* theme under his breath.

"If the girls are five, then we've been married seven years," she said triumphantly. But the girls were born in the spring, and they were married in the fall. Was that right?

"But are you *sure* the girls are five?"

"Stop it." She punched him in the arm. "We've ended fat shaming, slut shaming, and elder shaming, yet it is still socially acceptable to make fun of people who can't do math. It's wrong. And I can recite the entire Gettysburg Address, *from memory*. Can you?"

He pulled her close and nuzzled her neck. "I'm sorry. But I knew you'd forgotten again, and I couldn't resist."

"You didn't . . . get me anything . . . did you?" She of course had gotten him nothing. Not even socks, or a tie, or a World's Greatest Dad coffee mug.

"Oh, I've got something for you," he whispered in a low growl, sending a shiver of pleasure across her skin. Then he pulled away and crossed his arms. "But since you've chosen to celebrate our anniversary by going away for an intimate weekend with Ainsley Bradley, I'll save my gift until you get back."

"I could change my plans . . ."

"Absolutely not." He shook his head. "Maybe Shelby can watch the kids when you get back and we can have a romantic anniversary dinner at Five Guys."

"I should have checked my planner." Not that she ever remembered to write things like birthdays and anniversaries in her planner, but still. She appreciated that he did not use this as an opportunity to harangue her about using the electronic family calendar he'd set up on her laptop.

"I just . . ." She stopped. She couldn't tell him why this weekend with Ainsley was so urgent. "I just need to do this."

The corners of his mouth rose in a quizzical expression, like when they watched television shows like *Ozark* or *Game of Thrones*, and he couldn't remember who was related to who or why they were trying to kill each other. He would hit the pause button and ask, "Who is the little girl with the sword again?" or "I thought she was supposed to be Jamie's *sister*?"

"I thought you didn't like Ainsley Bradley," he said and took a sip of coffee. "I thought she was snooty?"

"I was wrong." Nikki tossed a couple of granola bars into a scuffed leather satchel. She couldn't remember the last time she'd had the luxury of packing snacks for herself instead of the kids.

He frowned. "You're normally a pretty good judge of character."

"That's debatable." She put her arms around his waist. "I married you, didn't I?"

He leaned down and gave her a lingering kiss. "But isn't her husband that guy who's running for governor? The antiporn guy all those radical feminist church ladies are supporting?"

"I don't think the radical feminists and the church ladies are necessarily the same people, but yes, that's one of his big issues."

"Well, she looks snooty to me," he said.

"She owns your fifty-five-inch walnut table *and* the matching chairs."

"I retract all negative statements," he said. "She's obviously a good person with impeccable taste."

Nikki snuggled against his chest. It was so good to have him home again. Best of all, Guzluk and Petru had found an apartment near Josh's workshop. Her home would not become a flophouse for homeless Moldovan carpenters.

"I'm sorry I have to leave," she said, running her hands over his wrinkled T-shirt.

He set his coffee mug on the counter and looked into her eyes, his face serious. "You deserve a break, Nikki. You haven't been . . . yourself."

Something inside her chest tightened, and she worked to keep her voice light. "What do you mean?"

"I don't know." He looked up at the ceiling, as though the answer were written in the water stains created by a leak in the shower pan. "You're normally so cheerful and confident. But lately you just seem a little . . . worn down."

"Maybe that's because *I am* worn down." She snapped the words out, face flushing. A quiet resentment had entered her bloodstream the day she was fired, flowing beneath her skin, flaring when she least expected it. It wasn't Josh's fault she'd lost her job. But his career and the four children they'd produced together prevented her from moving to a faraway city in search of a new one. She had to find a way past this inexplicable resentment before it ate away at her marriage the same way mice had eaten away at their camping gear when Daniel left cheese sticks in the tent pockets.

"And that's why I'm glad you're going away for a romantic weekend," he said, kissing her gently on the forehead. "With Ainsley Bradley."

"Are you *sure* you'll be okay back here?"

"Yes. We'll eat Froot Loops for dinner and watch inappropriate television."

"Not *The Simpsons*. Or those Disney shows with the snarky child actors."

"We'll have a blast."

She looked up at him with exasperated affection. She couldn't tell if he really *believed* that working from home while taking care of an infant and three small children would be easy, or if he just wanted her to enjoy her time away without guilt.

"Leslie said she'd be happy to help out. Shelby too."

He waved her concerns away with his coffee mug. "I'm their dad, not their babysitter. I'll be fine."

"I know. It's just . . . four kids is a lot."

"True." He gave her the smile that still melted her heart. "Four is one more than three."

She punched him in the arm. "Smart-ass."

"Go pack. You don't want to keep Ainsley's chauffeur waiting."

Nikki rolled her eyes. "She doesn't have a chauffeur. And she's not like that. She's actually very down to earth."

He raised an eyebrow. "People with a pied-à-terre at the Watergate are rarely down to earth."

"Well, Ainsley is different."

She clamped her lips together to keep herself from saying more. She'd promised not to share Ainsley's secret with anyone, including Josh, but keeping her word was more difficult than she'd expected.

In the past, she'd shared everything with Josh, and their discussions about work used to be the highlight of her day. He'd discuss supply chain problems or share a sketch of a new piece of furniture. She'd share newsroom gossip about which photographer was sleeping with which reporter.

She'd often thought she'd be a very ineffective adulteress because she'd want to come home after each assignation and discuss it with her husband. But now, with the exception of Ainsley's shocking revelation . . . she had no stories. Just trips to the grocery store, dirty diapers, and rhetorical questions about why children felt compelled to write on walls, eat Play-Doh, and stuff foreign objects up their noses.

But if she and Ainsley were successful, that would change. She'd have a job again. She'd be *interesting* again.

She leaned up and kissed him. "I appreciate this."

"Make the most of it," he whispered, pulling her close. "Because it won't happen again till Daniel turns thirty and moves out of our basement."

Chapter Twenty

NIKKI

Half an hour later, Ainsley pulled up in a black Mercedes so clean that it actually *reflected* the soccer balls, Hula-Hoops, and broken shards of sidewalk chalk strewed across Nikki's driveway.

"Damn it," Nikki muttered as she dug through the wicker basket beside the front door, searching for her tall leather boots. "I knew she'd be on time."

But instead of boots, she unearthed spiders, lint, stuffed animals, dried-out markers, and children's shoes in multiple sizes. The boots, as it turned out, had spent the spring and summer shacked up in the upstairs hall closet with the laundry detergent and cleaning supplies. If Nikki were on a first-name basis with her toilet brush, she would have known this. But unfortunately, she had only a nodding acquaintance with Lysol, Pledge, and Mr. Clean.

"Why?" she muttered as she fought to tug the boots over her calves. "Why would I keep my boots with the bleach and paper towels?"

After a considerable struggle, she triumphed over the boots' side zippers, grabbed her bag, and headed out the door while Josh and Daniel waved from the front steps.

Daniel's high-pitched voice called after her. "Goodbye, Mommy! Bring me a toy when you come back!"

Nikki waved, ran down the driveway, and heaved herself into the creamy leather passenger seat in Ainsley's Mercedes. She glanced at the dashboard clock, and her eyes widened. "How do you do that?"

"Do what?" Ainsley asked.

"Show up at exactly the right time? Like *to the minute*."

Ainsley shifted in her seat and glanced at Nikki with a slightly guilty look. "I was actually here fifteen minutes ago, but I parked a block away . . . and waited."

"Why were you fifteen minutes early?" Nikki could only remember being early once in her adult life, back in the days of paper invites and snail mail, when she lost a baby shower invitation and mistakenly thought the party started at three o'clock instead of four. But she had never arrived anywhere fifteen minutes early *on purpose*.

Ainsley shifted the car into reverse, refusing to meet Nikki's eyes. "Well . . . you know . . . because I didn't want to be late."

"But you only live ten minutes away." Nikki buckled her seat belt. "Why would you be late?"

"Well, what if there was an accident?" Ainsley looked carefully in the rearview mirror, then backed into the cul-de-sac, like the teacher's pet at a driving school for anal-retentive truckers.

"But what if there wasn't?"

"Then I'd be early, which is better than being late." Ainsley came to a complete stop at the intersection, diligently looked both ways, then turned left and accelerated slowly. Nikki glanced at the dashboard. The speed limit was twenty-five miles per hour, and the odometer needle stayed at exactly twenty-five miles per hour.

"Why didn't you just pull up to the house and wait in the driveway?"

"I knew it would make you feel rushed." Ainsley kept her eyes fixed on the road.

"Wait a minute," Nikki said, suddenly suspicious. "Did you *know* I would be late?"

"I . . . made an educated guess." Ainsley waved to a fellow driver, inviting them to cut in front of her as they merged onto the George Washington Memorial Parkway.

"You *planned* for me to be late."

"Yes," Ainsley admitted sheepishly.

"Have you ever been late for a flight?" Nikki asked.

Ainsley looked shocked at the mere suggestion. "Of course not."

"Have you ever been late for a doctor's appointment?"

"No." Ainsley frowned in disapproval. "That would be rude."

"Have you ever been late for *anything*?"

Ainsley paused. "Not as an adult."

Nikki's voice softened. "But as a kid?"

"Yeah." Ainsley stared at the road. "As kids we were late. Every. Single. Day. Mom would sleep through the alarm. Or forget to set the alarm. Or the car wouldn't start. In second grade I asked Santa to bring me an alarm clock of my own. I got up early, woke my sister, made our lunches, and we rode our bikes to school. And after that, Mrs. Robertson drove us."

"And this is why you're always on time?"

"This is why my clothes are always perfect, my hair is always brushed, my makeup always done." Ainsley fingered a diamond ear stud. "People treat you the way you look."

Nikki couldn't argue with that. Years on camera had taught her the same lesson.

"What was your family like?" Ainsley asked, abruptly changing the subject.

"My dad was an engineer for NASA." Nikki took a sip of coffee from her giant travel mug. "My mom was a nutritionist."

Ainsley raised an eyebrow. "I imagine your childhood was a little different than mine."

"Yeah, I imagine so." Nikki tightened her grip on the mug. "There was no salt or butter in our house, and my mom was into quinoa and avocados long before they were cool. Everything was organized. Labeled. On time and controlled."

"Too controlled?" Ainsley asked.

"Too controlled for me." Nikki wrinkled her nose in distaste. "I was disorganized. Scattered. Terrible handwriting. But I was homecoming queen, and I excelled at organizing keg parties."

"And this is why you're . . ." Ainsley's voice trailed off.

"Always late and usually disheveled?" Nikki supplied the words Ainsley was obviously too polite to use herself.

"Yes." Ainsley glanced at Nikki with a shy smile. "I wish I was more like you."

Nikki almost spit out her coffee. "Why in the world would you want to be like *me*?"

What sane person would wish for a *reverse* genie-in-a-bottle situation, using their three wishes to become poorer and less attractive with worse hair?

"Because you're so honest," Ainsley said, turning on her blinker and merging smoothly into the other lane. "And comfortable in your own skin. Like you don't care what people think of you, but not because you're arrogant. Because you're confident."

Nikki stared out the window, taking in splashes of autumn color as her conversation with Josh echoed in her mind. Confident? Not anymore. Now she felt lost in a sea of unrealistic expectations.

These expectations had been given to her by someone else—society? Biology? Pinterest? She hadn't asked for them. They weren't *her* expectations. Yet she'd put them on the moment she became pregnant with her first child, never asking if these expectations fit well, or if she liked the style and color, or if she even *wanted* someone else's expectations.

She'd clutched the expectations of motherhood to her heart without examining them. And now she had to raise polite, athletic, popular, empathetic, resilient, interesting, academically gifted children who would one day attend Ivy League schools on fencing scholarships while she created a perfect home and cooked healthy organic meals, all while running the World Bank, and exercising. Anything less was failure.

"I feel like a fraud," Nikki finally said, struggling to explain something she had never admitted to anyone, even Josh or her sister.

"What do you mean?"

"I have this vision of a perfect mother," Nikki said with a helpless shrug, "and I'm nothing like that vision."

Ainsley gave her a sympathetic smile. "You mean June Cleaver?"

"More like Carol Brady, from *The Brady Bunch*." It *did* sound a little ridiculous now that she'd said it out loud. "Never tired. Always fun and encouraging, but wise at the same time. Totally happy and fulfilled at home with Alice and the kids."

"You do realize Carol Brady wasn't real?" Ainsley pointed out. "And she had full-time, live-in help?"

"My point is that great mothers *enjoy* being mothers."

"And how do you know that?" Ainsley asked.

"Because they say so on Facebook."

"Ah." Ainsley lifted an eyebrow. "Then it must be true."

Nikki chewed on her lower lip. Words were her specialty, communication her gift, yet she found it hard to explain the cloud of inadequacy that had settled over her since she stopped working. "I spend every day wishing I could go back to work, and I feel terrible about it, because I know so many women who'd love to stay home with their kids but can't because they need the money. But I'm home right now, and I just feel . . . trapped . . . instead of grateful and joyful, like my friend Evangelical Heather."

Ainsley stopped at a red light and turned to look at her. "Who is Evangelical Heather?"

"A friend from college. She has five kids, and she homeschools them all. They go to the zoo and museums and do science experiments with baking soda and make medieval castles out of Popsicle sticks and she's just . . . great at being a mother. And she loves every minute of it."

"So this is your standard?" Ainsley asked with a sympathetic smirk. "Carol Brady and Evangelical Heather who homeschools five kids? No wonder you feel inadequate."

"Well, you're kind of a model mother too. I mean, you're so organized and you're always volunteering at school. You don't work, but you don't seem to miss it."

"Listen to me, Nikki." The soft lines of Ainsley's face became firm. "I have a nanny, a housekeeper, two gardeners, two maids, and a family office to organize vacations and book plane tickets. Of *course* I'm organized. And before kids, I had a job I liked, but I didn't love it the way you seemed to love your job. Giving it up wasn't a hardship for me."

"It wasn't?"

She shrugged. "I analyzed inflation, durable goods, and GDP numbers. It was interesting, but I'd rather give my kids all the things I never had, like a mom who is there, physically and mentally, every day."

"You don't miss working?" Nikki asked, a little shocked.

"Nope. I love being home with my kids. But that's just *me*. You need to stop comparing yourself to other women."

"Easier said than done."

Ainsley nodded. "Tell me about it."

"I feel guilty going away like this," Nikki admitted.

"You shouldn't," Ainsley said as they passed National Airport. "This isn't a vacation."

"That's true. We're on a mission."

"Exactly." Ainsley nodded. "Like in a war movie."

"We few, we happy few . . . ," Nikki began.

"We band of mothers," Ainsley quoted as she switched lanes to avoid the long line of cars backed up at the entrance to the Fourteenth Street Bridge.

"I used to memorize Shakespeare in algebra class," Nikki confessed as she rummaged in her purse, suddenly hit with a familiar pang of panic. Had she forgotten her phone?

"Was that helpful?" Ainsley asked.

"No, but it brought me comfort." Nikki unzipped the side pockets and unearthed a card for a haircut appointment she'd forgotten about. "And now that I'm an adult, I have this beautiful collection of random phrases embedded in my mind. I have quotations for every occasion."

"Funerals?" Ainsley asked as she switched lanes, speeding past joggers on the bike path beside the parkway.

"We have not come here to bury Insert Name of Dead Person, but to praise him."

"Weddings?" Ainsley asked.

Nikki triumphantly pulled her phone from her coat pocket. "I knew I hadn't forgotten it! And the appropriate quotation is 'Let me not to the marriage of true minds admit impediments,' obviously."

"Times of trouble and disaster?" Ainsley asked, glancing at the Jefferson Memorial in the distance.

"When in disgrace with fortune and men's eyes," Nikki quoted, absently touching her earlobe. Wait. No earrings. Had she been wearing earrings? Or had she put them in her purse because she was running late?

"I all alone beweep my outcast state," Ainsley continued.

Nikki's eyes widened. "You know it?"

"Of course." Ainsley slowed for a yellow light that Nikki would have sped through. "It's one of my favorites."

"And trouble deaf heaven with my bootless cries," Nikki quoted as she tried to organize her purse without dumping everything onto Ainsley's spotless leather seats.

"And look upon myself and curse my fate," Ainsley continued.

A buoyant sense of surprise washed over Nikki as they repeated the rest of the sonnet in unison. "You don't by any chance happen to be an Austenite?" she asked, almost holding her breath. It was too much to hope that this potential new friend could possibly share her love of Jane Austen.

"Darcy or Captain Wentworth?" Ainsley asked.

"Darcy." A feeling of joy, dormant for weeks, suddenly punched through the crust of weariness encasing her heart, followed by a thrill of discovery, like finding some vital item you didn't even know you needed in the dollar bin at Target, but so much better. "For the domestic help. And because of his beautiful grounds at Pemberley, of course."

"Henry Tilney or Mr. Knightley?" Ainsley asked.

"Henry Tilney all day long," she said as she removed tiny tissue particles from the gloves she'd found in the bottom of her bag.

"I absolutely agree." Ainsley accelerated to pass a senior citizen in a Cadillac driving far below the speed limit. "He's so *witty*, but so underrated. Favorite adaptation?"

"The A&E version with Colin Firth." Nikki pulled a fourth ChapStick from her bag. No wonder her purse weighed seventy-five pounds.

Ainsley nodded gravely. "It's seminal."

"Favorite novel?" Nikki asked with a hint of trepidation. This was the true test. Dilettantes always named *Pride and Prejudice*. True fans had other loves as well.

"For those of us who married after the first bloom of youth, the answer is always *Persuasion*," Ainsley said.

Nikki looked at her with new respect. "Are all former strippers Jane Austen fans?"

"You'd be surprised."

"But you weren't an English major?"

"I wanted to be," she said. "But I was terrified of being poor. I took every accounting, economics, finance, and business class I could. I thought learning about money would help me figure out how to earn it and keep it."

"Did you read a lot as a kid?"

Ainsley nodded. "Jolene and I lived at the library. At first, just because it was safe and warm, and the librarians fed us. Then I actually opened the books. And I realized I could crawl inside them and go someplace else."

"I know. Being in Narnia was so much nicer than being in school."

Ainsley paused. "Have you ever been tested?"

"For what? Is there a medical name for disorganization and chronic lateness?"

"Have you ever been screened for something like ADD?" Ainsley asked.

"Me?" Nikki frowned. "Do I look like a seven-year-old boy who can't sit still?"

"No. But you're obviously smart. And when a smart person has trouble in school, there's usually a reason."

"The reason is disorganization," she said, gesturing at the bizarre assortment of items in her lap.

"Have you *tried* to be organized?" Ainsley asked.

"Well, sure, but nothing really seems to work. I just haven't found the right system, I guess."

"If you want . . . I could try to help," Ainsley offered, her voice suddenly timid. "I'm very organized. Too organized, actually," she added hastily.

A warm tingle spread through Nikki's limbs, as though she'd just received a shy invitation to the prom from a boy she really liked. "I would like that very much," she said formally. "You know, even though we're probably the same age, I aspire to be you when I grow up."

Ainsley quirked a wry smile. "You aspire to be a former stripper with a husband running for public office on an antipornography platform who doesn't know she used to take off her clothes and do lap dances for money? I'd take rampant disorganization in exchange for my past any day."

"I'll take your hair," Nikki said wistfully. "You have great hair."

"Fine. I'll make you a wig. You can have all my hair if you take my secrets. You have nice hair too," Ainsley added generously.

"And your closet," Nikki said. "I'll become a former stripper if you throw in your closet."

"Done." Ainsley took her eyes off the road and glanced sideways at Nikki with an infectious grin.

For a moment Nikki felt a little dazzled, like the night of her first date with her husband, when she suddenly realized God had made another human being with the best parts of her own soul and personality stitched inside them.

With Josh, it was the stunning realization that the person she'd been searching for her entire life sat across from her, solid and real in flesh and bone. That this person actually *existed* and was not a mirage created by longing.

And now here in the car with Ainsley, she realized it had been a long time since she'd found a new person she actually *wanted* to add to her life, someone worthy of space in an existence so crowded and busy that it lacked room even for elemental things like sleep and regular showers.

She'd been lonely since unemployment tore her away from her work family in the newsroom. In her cloistered, exhausted life as a mother, she hadn't found a way to replace those friends, hadn't even been aware that she needed to fill the gap.

Now, miraculously, long after college and far outside of work, it was happening again, an event as important and wonderful to her as it had been to the twins on their first day of kindergarten.

She'd made a new friend.

Chapter Twenty-One

AINSLEY

The Lincoln Memorial loomed ahead as they drove across the Memorial Bridge and entered DC. The beauty of the bridge and the monuments beyond never failed to impress Ainsley. They were stunning visual reminders of how far she'd come, how lucky she was to live here, casually driving past monuments other people traveled thousands of miles to visit or only saw in movies.

They drove past tourists, hunched against the autumn wind as they trudged from the Lincoln Monument to the Tomb of the Unknown Soldier at Arlington National Cemetery. Turning right, Ainsley merged onto the Rock Creek Parkway and headed north, toward Biltmore University and the well-heeled neighborhoods that surrounded it.

She turned onto the broad street that ran parallel to campus, then slowed to a stop when snarled traffic made it impossible to move forward. A sea of red taillights reminded her why she so rarely visited her alma mater. Traffic was bad, and parking even worse. She hadn't been here in a long time.

A swarm of memories buzzed through her mind as she maneuvered around a double-parked FedEx truck, drove past the steak house where she'd waitressed, the hotel where she'd worked as a housekeeper, and the dorm where she'd lived her freshman and sophomore year. Images of friends and professors and classes she'd loved flashed through her brain. But as she headed away from the university and toward the mansions of Robber Baron Row, reminders of what she'd done to save her sister stalked her memory as well.

The sky threatened rain as she turned down a wide street lined with trees and sprawling old homes. At the end of the block, she stopped in front of a well-maintained stone mansion bristling with turrets and chimneys, wrapped in verandas, standing tall and dignified against the bruise-dark sky.

Nikki stared up at the house through the passenger window. "*That's* a strip club?"

Ainsley said nothing. She put the car into gear again, bumping along the cobblestone driveway, under the porte cochere extending from the right side of the mansion, and into the empty parking lot in the rear.

"It hasn't changed," she whispered. "It hasn't changed one bit."

"This is not what I expected," Nikki said, peering out the window.

"One of the robber barons built it, back in the 1870s. When he died, he left it to his mistress instead of his wife."

"I'll bet that didn't go over well."

"The mistress called herself Lady Godiva," Ainsley said with a faint smile. "And she immediately did everything the respectable citizens of Washington, DC, feared she might do. She turned her mansion into a saloon and a house of prostitution with burlesque shows in the ballroom. When she died, she left it to her daughter, who left it to her daughter, who left it to her daughter. A Lady Godiva has run this place since 1883. All women, all from the same family."

"Is it still . . ."

"A brothel? No. They went legit when the city cracked down on prostitution in the 1920s. The burlesque shows eventually morphed into stripping. Now it's one of the oldest strip clubs in the country, and probably the only club owned and run by women."

"That's unusual?"

"The adult entertainment industry is run by men, for men." Ainsley tossed her keys into her purse. "The Godivas were an exception. They treated their employees like family. Everyone wanted to work here. Godiva's had the prettiest girls and the best shows. The men running the other clubs in town had no idea that treating dancers like human beings could actually make you rich."

They got out of the car and crossed the parking lot. "Employee entrance or the front door?" Nikki asked.

Ainsley stared at the dented steel door marked with an "Employees Only" sign, with a buzzer beside it and a video camera over the top. She had a strange out-of-body sensation, as though she'd traveled backward in time. She could see herself standing at this door, one shoulder sagging under her bookbag, the other shoulder weighed down with a satchel containing hot rollers, makeup, lingerie, sequined G-strings, and the chaps, fringed vest, and cowboy boots for her Sexy Sheriff costume.

She squared her shoulders. "We go in through the front door."

They climbed the stairs to the veranda, and Ainsley pushed open the heavy mahogany door. Then she stepped inside, squinting as her eyes adjusted to the dim light.

The odor hit her like a punch, a unique combination of cigar smoke, furniture polish, and whiskey, with a faint undertone of something musky and human, a scent she'd always categorized as lust. A river of memories flooded her mind, carrying scraps of music, snatches of conversation, the chill of the brass pole against her bare skin, the bite of the G-string and the scratch of five-, ten-, twenty-, and sometimes hundred-dollar bills scraping her thighs.

These sensations paralyzed her, and she stood frozen in the vestibule, remembering everything she'd tried so hard to forget.

Nothing had changed. Same furniture. Same oil paintings on the walls. Same elaborate coffered ceilings, dark walnut paneling, and tall windows hung with red velvet curtains. Same wide staircase leading to the alcoves where girls performed private shows, and beyond that a smaller staircase to the third-floor changing rooms and living quarters for the Lady Godivas, the only place in the house off limits to men.

Slowly, her rigid body unclenched, and she turned in a circle, taking in the billiard room, the coat check room, the dining room for private dinners and parties, and the elaborate entrance to the ballroom where she'd performed, with its long bar, catwalk, and stage impaled with four brass poles.

As she adjusted to the shock of being back, small details emerged. Scratches on the furniture, worn spots in the velvet curtains, chips in the gilded frames around the oil paintings.

Her affluent eyes now caught details that were invisible to her college self. Zane Grey westerns and erotic novels with scantily clad couples on the cover filled the library, not the serious, leather-bound first editions on the shelves at home. The oil paintings were not valuable works by old masters, and the tables and chairs were not rare European antiques.

A flash of disappointment washed over her, like she was visiting a house she'd loved as a child and finding it smaller than remembered.

Would Lady Godiva, so large and vivid in her memory all these years, be a shrunken disappointment too?

As though conjured by her thoughts, a voice rang out from the darkness at the top of the stairs.

"Can I help you?" The tone implied that even if she *could* help, she was unlikely to do so.

"Lady Godiva?"

"Depends who's asking."

"I used to work here. My name was Velvet."

Lady Godiva descended the stairs in four-inch heels, a kimono layered over multiple satin slips with ropes of pearls hanging to her waist, making her look like a vaguely erotic Miss Havisham, dressed for the wedding night rather than the wedding. Thick white hair fell below her narrow shoulders, framing a wrinkled face, scarlet lips, and heavily made-up eyes. But the overall impression was one of strength and vigor, rather than frailty and old age.

Lady Godiva squinted at them through the gloom. "Lots of Velvets been in here over the years. What's your real name?"

Ainsley took a deep breath. "Tami Darlene Schmidt."

"Ah. Tami Darlene. I remember you."

"You do?"

"Course I do. You're the girl who read them *Masterpiece Theatre* books with dukes and carriages and whatnot, backstage between sets."

"Jane Austen," she said with a smile. "That's me."

"Did it work out, then? Did you get your sister through the U? Did you get your degree in whatever it was? Economic something or other?"

"I did."

She came closer and patted Ainsley's arm as her perfume engulfed them. "I'm proud of you, honey. Now, what can I do for you?"

"I'm looking for someone, one of the girls who was here when I worked here."

"Come have a drink." She raised a thin arm and gestured toward the gilded double doors at the end of the corridor. "It's noon somewhere."

They followed her through the gloom and into the ballroom, to a round table set in an alcove swagged with golden tassels and red velvet curtains.

Lady Godiva beckoned to a girl in a black tank top rubbing down the bar with a rag and a spray bottle that smelled of disinfectant. "Madison, bring us three shots of Goldschläger and a pot of coffee."

The girl gave Lady Godiva a thumbs-up, then disappeared through a paneled door behind the bar.

They scooted into a red leather booth surrounding the circular table. Lady Godiva reached into her bosom, which seemed to have the same magical properties as the carpetbag carried by Mary Poppins, and pulled from her fluttering garments a gilded ashtray, a pack of cigarettes, and a lighter. "Good thing you came back when you did. Six months from now this place will be gone."

Ainsley's mouth dropped open. "You're selling?"

"Yup." She tapped a cigarette from the pack. "They're tearing it down to build a dog spa and one of them Lulu yoga stores. They tried to offer me four million dollars two years ago, but I held out. Then I got the dog people and the yoga people into a bidding war with them historical preservation people."

She slipped the cigarette carton back inside her camisole. "I woulda sold it to them historical people if they'd taken my advice and turned it into the world's only museum of pole dancing. But they wouldn't recognize a good idea if it waved a red flag and bit 'em in the ass. So, I'm taking the dog spa offer instead. Now I'm getting six million."

She let loose a merry cackle, then lit her cigarette with the sequin-studded lighter. "Seems like a fair price. Plus, the business has changed."

"Changed how?" Ainsley asked.

"Damn internet." She blew a cloud of smoke into the air, and Ainsley resisted the urge to cough. "Porn's everywhere now. Sick, hardcore stuff too. Nobody's interested in seein' topless ladies no more. Nobody wants live shows. Strippin's not a growth industry. Lots of overhead. Labor issues. All the money's in internet porn, and I don't want no part of that sick stuff."

The girl in the black tank top brought a pot of coffee, mugs, shot glasses, and a bottle of Goldschläger to the table.

"You remember our toast?" Lady Godiva asked Ainsley as she poured the gold-flecked liquid into three shot glasses.

Ainsley nodded as memories of the end-of-shift ritual came rushing back. When the club closed, the girls would gather in the changing room with Lady Godiva, count their cash, and drink a toast to male stupidity.

Ainsley raised her glass, then recited a limerick so profane it made Nikki blush.

"Screw the past," Lady Godiva responded, raising her glass.

"Here's to the future," Ainsley replied, finishing the toast.

Then, like alcoholic Olympians in some sort of synchronized drinking competition, they opened their mouths, tossed the liquor back, and slammed their empty shot glasses down on the table at the same time.

They looked at Nikki expectantly, like runners waiting for an out-of-shape straggler to catch up.

"Oh. No thank you," Nikki said, pushing the shot glass away.

"You one of them twelve steppers?" Lady Godiva peered into her face. "A friend of Bill's?"

"No. I just don't usually drink Goldschläger—" She was about to say *before noon* when Lady Godiva cut her off.

"Why didn't you say you're an alkie?" She gave Nikki a reproachful look as she repossessed her shot glass. "I don't wanna be the one who knocks you off your wagon." Lady Godiva tossed her head back and downed Nikki's liquor herself.

"But I'm not—" Nikki protested.

Lady Godiva patted her arm. "You just take it one day at a time. Keep goin' to them meetings and have some coffee instead. Now, Tami Darlene, what can I do for you?"

"Do you remember a guy named Wyatt Jericho? One of Misty's regs?"

"Wyatt the Wanker?" She let loose a hoarse cackle. "Remember them twins from Liverpool? Pamela and Portia, who did that Topless Tea Party routine? That's what they used to call him."

"The basketball star who coached at Biltmore, right?" Ainsley asked.

"Yup." She took a drag on her cigarette. "He's been coming in here for years."

"Wasn't there a story about him and Misty . . . he broke her nose or something, up in the Boudoir, and then he offered to pay her a thousand dollars if she didn't press charges?"

"I recall something like that." She exhaled, enveloping them in a cloud of smoke. "But Misty wasn't no angel either," Lady Godiva continued. "I don't think he *offered* that payment. I think she strongly suggested she'd go to the newspapers and show off her broken nose if he didn't."

"Is he still coming to the club?"

"Sure. He comes in every couple months. Just saw him last week, as a matter of fact." She scowled, tapping her cigarette against the ashtray. "Up to his usual tricks."

"What do you mean?"

"Came in with some skinny young thing he picked up at the Depot. Didn't look old enough to order a drink. Told the bartender not to serve her. When he was twenty years old and hittin' on dancers his own age, it was one thing. But he's a geezer now, and it makes my stomach turn." She stubbed her cigarette into the ashtray. "But he always did like his girls young."

A chill fluttered over Ainsley's skin, and she exchanged a glance with Nikki. "How young?"

"He found out Misty Dawn had a younger sister, still in middle school. Used to pester her all the time to bring the little sis over to his place for a private party. She never did, of course. Misty had good sense, for a woman who'd inhaled a lot of hairspray."

"Do you think we could find her?" Ainsley asked.

"That was her real name, believe it or not." Lady Godiva pulled the pack of cigarettes from her garments and tapped out another. "That girl was destined to be a stripper."

"Do you know where she is now?"

She paused to light her cigarette. Then she said, "North Korea."

Ainsley choked on her coffee. "North Korea?"

"Yup." Lady Godiva took a drag and expelled a gray cloud. "She and another girl left here a couple years after you did. Went to Macao together. Lots of money to be made in Macao. She danced for about six months, then she met one of them North Korean potentates. He was recruiting women for something called the Joy Division, like a harem for that chubby little fella who runs their country."

Ainsley's eyes widened. "Kim Jong-Un?"

Lady Godiva waved her cigarette. “That’s right. Kim Jong something or other. They needed some imported poontang in Pyongyang.” She cackled at her own wit, then started coughing.

“Anyway,” she continued when the coughing subsided, “they offered Misty a bag of cash and asked her to go to North Korea, and she said yes. Last I heard she was livin’ it up in some mansion with a hundred rooms by the sea with a bunch of other girls.”

Ainsley shook her head in wonder. “North Korea.”

Lady Godiva nodded solemnly. “My girls go places in life. Unlike them sad skanks workin’ for Dino Johnson down at the Depot.”

“These girls that Wyatt Jericho hangs around with . . . Are they minors?” Nikki asked.

“The girls he brings in *here* are eighteen if they wanna watch, twenty-one if they wanna drink. I know that ’cause we card everyone. But when he’s not here . . . well, I don’t know what he gets up to when he’s not here.” She gave them a look that suggested every imaginable sin, from jaywalking to bestiality. “And there was one girl I always wondered about . . . she came in just about the time you was leaving. Little runaway girl. Made her a dishwasher.”

A face took shape in Ainsley’s mind. “Harmonee Dean.”

“That’s right.” Lady Godiva nodded.

“How old was she?”

“Fifteen,” Lady Godiva said. “Had a bad situation in a foster home. Came here looking for her mom. When she didn’t find her mom, she asked for a job. Told me she wanted to dance ’cause she needed money and a place to live. I told her she was too young, but I could give her a job as a dishwasher.”

“For about five dollars over minimum wage, as I recall,” Ainsley said.

The old woman blushed. “Had to pay her well or she’d be dealin’ drugs or strippin’ down at the Depot, where they believe girls who claim they’re eighteen but can’t find their driver’s license.”

“And you gave her the Hard Luck room upstairs.”

"Well, that's what it's for, ain't it?"

Ainsley smiled. The building had deteriorated, but Lady Godiva hadn't changed one bit.

"You had some connection with her, didn't you?" Lady Godiva frowned in concentration. "She wanted to try her luck on the street, but you convinced her to stay here with us awhile instead."

Ainsley looked down at her empty shot glass. "We grew up in the same trailer park."

"A plucky little thing," Lady Godiva said with a respectful smile. "A real survivor."

Ainsley leaned forward. "Did Wyatt Jericho ever bother her?"

"He tried to, several times. Offered to give her a ride home till I pointed out she lived upstairs with me and didn't need no ride. I told the bouncers to keep an eye out, and he left her alone after that." She raised an eyebrow. "As far as I know. But I think there was somethin' going on between them. She might be worth trackin' down, if she's willing to talk."

"Any idea where she might be?"

Lady Godiva blew out a plume of smoke. "Findin' former strippers is harder than finding a G-string at a quilting bee. One day she packed up her little pink backpack and told me she'd found her mom. Said she was movin' back in with her. But it always made me uneasy, looking back on it. Wish I'd gone with her, to make sure she really was movin' in with her mom and not shackin' up with Wyatt Jericho."

"Does Wyatt Jericho pay with cash when he comes in, or does he use a credit card?" Nikki asked.

"Most customers buy food and drinks with a credit card and use the ATM for cash tips." She gestured toward the bar with her cigarette.

"Do you think you could dig up any of those receipts?"

"It might take me a while, but I could . . . if I wanted to." She exhaled and narrowed her eyes. "But tell me why I'd want to go to all that trouble?"

"I ran into Wyatt Jericho the other day," Ainsley said.

"Where?"

"My daughter's school."

"Holy mother of God." Lady Godiva bolted up in her seat, almost knocking over the bottle of Goldschläger.

"Exactly. He's the basketball coach."

Godiva clenched her birdlike hand into a fist and slammed it on the table. "You gotta get that son of a bitch out of there."

"That's why we're here." Ainsley pushed her coffee mug away and leaned in closer. "Everyone thinks he hung the moon. They won't fire him unless we have some kind of proof . . . proof that he hangs out in strip clubs, or that he's violent, or that he can't be trusted around teenage girls."

"Or all three," Nikki added.

Lady Godiva stubbed out her cigarette. "Did he recognize you?"

"Yes."

"He'll blackmail you," she warned, pointing her lighter at Ainsley. "I wouldn't put it past him. He's one cold bastard."

"That's why we need credit card receipts. That's why we need to find Harmonee and Misty. Because if we can prove any of this"—she gestured at the bar, the catwalk, and the brass poles—"then I can convince the school to fire him before he has a chance to do anything . . . to me . . . or anyone else."

Lady Godiva scratched her chin. "There was some whispering when he left Biltmore, as I recall. Said he wanted to spend more time with his ailing mother, but there was rumors that he was forced to leave, that they didn't renew his contract or some such."

"Okay, we'll check it out."

Ainsley wrote her name and cell phone number on the back of a cocktail napkin featuring a stylized outline of a woman wearing nothing but hair and pushed it across the table to Lady Godiva.

"Can you call me the minute Wyatt Jericho sets foot in this club again, or if you find any of his receipts? Or if you remember anything else, like where we might find Harmonee or Misty?"

"I will do all those things and more if it'll keep him away from you and away from girls who are too young to know better." She stuffed the napkin into the top of her dress along with the cigarettes and the lighter. "So, tell me, what became of you? You look real . . ." She paused. "Expensive-like."

"My sister and I both graduated from college," Ainsley said, pushing her shot glass away. "We got jobs and went to law school and grad school at night. I got married. I have two kids now, and a nice house. I live in the suburbs."

"Well, that's pretty impressive. You're one of my success stories—you and Trixie Malone, who got named Miss February for *Penthouse*," she said reverently. "But is that all you need? We open in an hour. Got a group of fraternity boys that comes in every Friday when they finish class. Poor tippers, but they eat their weight in chicken wings."

"How are you doing?" Ainsley asked. "You look a little thin."

"Got some cancer in my moneymakers."

Nikki looked puzzled, so Ainsley translated. "Breast cancer."

"Did the chemo and cut out the rest six months ago. Doc says I'm fine now, and I got them bastards at the health insurance to build me back better." She cackled and gestured to her cleavage. "My girls is good as new."

Nikki's eyes widened in alarm, as though she expected Lady Godiva to rip off her kimono and give them a guided tour of her new chest.

"I'm glad to hear that," Ainsley said swiftly. "And I wish we could stay longer, but we have a lot of work ahead of us."

Lady Godiva stood, and they followed her out of the ballroom. Ainsley made a detour and left two twenty-dollar bills on the bar for the girl who'd brought them drinks. As they headed for the foyer, Lady Godiva paused in front of a wall filled with framed photos, some sepia toned, some black and white, others in color.

She gestured to a large photo with a gilt frame in the center of the wall. "Remember this?" Lady Godiva asked.

Ainsley leaned in closer, taking in the image of Lou Leffler, the iconic, silk-pajama-wearing publisher of *Plaything* magazine. Lady Godiva stood beside him, grinning and holding a plaque, surrounded by every dancer in the club. Ainsley spotted herself in the second row on the left side, wearing a cowboy hat, a G-string, and her skimpy Sexy Sheriff vest, wedged between two girls in towering headdresses and sequin-encrusted bras.

"Proudest night of my life," Lady Godiva said wistfully.

Ainsley smiled. "He was on tour, right? Visiting the Top Ten Gentleman's Clubs in North America?"

Lady Godiva nodded and brushed the photo gently with her fingertips. "The magazine gave us the Heritage Club Award, seeing as how we've been here since 1883."

Nikki read the plaque hanging beside the picture. "Longest continuously running gentleman's club in the United States."

Lady Godiva lifted her chin. "Damn straight. We're havin' a final party, by the way, before we close the doors for good. Right after Christmas. Everyone's comin' back for it. DJs. Bouncers. Bartenders and the waitresses. And of course the dancers. You'd see lots of old friends."

Ainsley went pale. She could see it now. *Hey, kids, I'm going to be out of town for a few days. My strip club is having a class reunion.*

She gave Lady Godiva a weak smile. "I'll keep that in mind."

When they reached the door, she fought back the urge to hug Lady Godiva, remembering that she did not like to be touched. "Thank you for your help."

"You let me know what happens with Wyatt Jericho," Lady Godiva said. "I got email, and one of the girls made me a webpage site. And I'm on the Twitter. I like to troll them megachurch pastors."

"It was nice to meet you," Nikki said.

"Likewise." Lady Godiva gave her a solemn nod. "And remember, you listen to your sponsor and do all twelve of them steps, and not just the one where you get to make a list of all the people who piss you off."

Nikki nodded obediently. “I’ll do that.”

Lady Godiva turned to Ainsley. “Stay in touch.”

“I will . . . and thank you. You were good to me, Lady Godiva. You were good to us all,” Ainsley said softly.

“I tried my best to take care of you girls. All them feminist ladies think men are exploiting us.” She opened the door and winked. “But I’ve got six million in the bank that says we’re exploiting them.”

Chapter Twenty-Two

AINSLEY

They climbed into the car. Ainsley twisted her sterling silver key fob with nervous fingers as silence descended over the interior.

"It's okay," Ainsley said as she leaned back against the headrest. "I know you want to ask."

Nikki paused. Then she whispered, "What was it like?"

Should she tell Nikki what she expected to hear? Or tell the truth? Shifting in her seat, Ainsley turned to face her. "Honestly, sometimes it was kind of fun."

Nikki's eyes widened. "Fun?"

She nodded. "I mean, the first couple times were terrifying and embarrassing. But after you got over the weirdness of being naked, you felt kind of . . . powerful. I was in great shape. They had strict rules, so no one was allowed to touch us. I liked to dance, and I don't know . . . I didn't like lap dances, but I kind of enjoyed being onstage."

"Really?"

"Yeah. And I think that's where all the shame comes in. I'm ashamed that I didn't feel ashamed when I danced around topless in front of strangers."

"You *liked* it?" Nikki asked.

Ainsley opened her mouth to answer, then snapped it closed again. How could she explain this to someone who'd never done it? "I liked the other girls and Lady Godiva. We were like a family. And of course I loved the money."

"How much did you make?"

Her gaze drifted to the employee door, where a young woman in sweatpants and a shapeless black coat pressed the buzzer to be let inside for her shift. "It depended on the night, but the most I ever made was a thousand dollars in two hours."

Nikki inhaled. "Are you serious?"

"Yeah. Some guy gave me a five-hundred-dollar tip."

"So, if you didn't hate it and the money was great, why did you stop?"

"Because I started to despise men."

"What do you mean?"

Memories tumbled across time. A tall, sweet guy from history class materialized in Ainsley's mind. He'd lived off campus with his twin sister. Really smart, a little shy. They'd flirted the first two or three weeks of class. After the midterm, he worked up the courage to ask her out as they walked across the quad together, discussing the test they'd just taken on the Visigoths. As he stammered something about dinner and a movie, she felt her lip curl into a sneer. Her own voice echoed in her ears as she heard herself saying, "You want way more than dinner and a movie. Get the hell away from me." She'd flicked her hair over her shoulder and walked away, leaving him standing on the quad, red faced and stunned, his backpack slumped on the sidewalk beside him.

He'd dropped the class and she'd never seen him again, but she'd wondered about him so many times over the years. Did he ever get married? Or had she demolished his confidence so thoroughly that he never dared to ask anyone out again?

She expelled a long breath and tried to explain. "I started to assume that deep down, all men were like the men I saw every night in the club, that they were all like Wyatt Jericho. I lost respect for anyone . . . with a penis, really."

"Makes sense," Nikki said.

"They were so easy to manipulate." Ainsley shook her head as she searched for the right words. "So stupid. And some were sick, too, like Jericho. Within two weeks, I wanted nothing to do with any of them. I stopped talking to the guys in my classes. Stopped hanging out with male friends. And that scared me, because eventually I wanted to find a kind and decent guy like my dad and get married and have kids. And I was afraid if I kept stripping, that wouldn't happen."

"So you quit as soon as you had enough money for Jolene's tuition?"

Ainsley nodded. "I went back to cleaning hotel rooms for minimum wage. But I started to see men as human beings worthy of respect again, so it was worth it."

"I just . . ." Nikki paused. "I mean, I used to think you were the dullest, most straitlaced and judgmental mother in that school . . ." Her voice trailed off.

"And I just tossed back a shot of Goldschläger in the strip club where I used to work."

"Well. Yeah." Nikki nodded. "I mean, I have an idea in my mind of what a stripper looks like, and you do not look like the picture in my mind."

"You were expecting a wet shirt, silicone, and stilettos?"

Nikki gave her a rueful smile. "I guess so."

"That's the problem." Ainsley sighed. "No one has an accurate idea of what strippers are really like, so it always seemed easier to hide my past than try and explain it to people."

She rubbed her forehead, trying to massage away the telltale prick of an oncoming headache. Returning to the club had stirred up memories and emotions she'd tried so hard to forget, like dislodging the sediment caked at the bottom of a pond, making clear water murky again. After so many years, she'd almost convinced herself she really *was* Ainsley Bradley, respectable wife, perfect mother, philanthropist in a St. John suit. The smell and sight of the club reminded her of all the other things she was too.

She reached over and squeezed Nikki's hand. "Thank you . . . for coming with me. I don't think I could do this on my own."

"I'm glad I came." Nikki returned her squeeze. "Lady Godiva alone was worth the trip."

Ainsley flipped on the seat heaters to ward off the growing chill. "Okay. What's next?"

Nikki scrolled through her phone. "According to Wyatt Jericho's Wikipedia page, he signed a five-year contract." She looked up at Ainsley. "*Four* years ago."

"Godiva was right. He left a year early."

"It sure looks like it," Nikki said.

"But how do we confirm this?"

Nikki nibbled on her lower lip and considered the problem. "There's no point in going to the HR people. Anything related to his contract or dismissal would be confidential. But the athletic director might be able to tell us something."

Ainsley nodded. "He would have been Wyatt Jericho's boss. If the players had complaints, they'd go to him."

Nikki continued to scan her phone. "The athletic director's name is Sebastian Hampton. He's been there forever, since Wyatt Jericho was a player, before Jericho even started coaching. And listen to this," she said. "He's the one who appointed Wyatt Jericho as head coach of the women's team when Jericho got injured and couldn't go pro."

Ainsley felt a tingle of optimism. "Okay. We talk to him next."

"We can try," Nikki said after a pause. "But he might not be willing to talk to us if they're trying to hush something up."

"Any ideas?"

Nikki stared out the window, and Ainsley could almost see the wheels turning inside her mind. "We could take the truth and stretch it a bit."

Ainsley frowned. "What do you mean?"

"We appeal to his ego and desire for recognition. We tell them I'm a freelance reporter working on a puff piece about the basketball program and Wyatt Jericho."

"You mean they cooperate because it's good publicity?" Ainsley asked.

"Exactly. We tell him I just need to double-check some facts. Even if he refuses to answer my questions, his reaction will tell us something."

Ainsley frowned. "Isn't that lying?"

"Technically, it's true. I *am* a reporter," Nikki said. "And I *am* a freelancer now that I'm unemployed."

"I don't know." Ainsley chewed on her lower lip. "I'm in this position because I wasn't honest with my husband in the first place."

"Look." Nikki sighed. "I'm not comfortable with it either. I've never lied to anyone I've interviewed. But the school will only believe us if we have evidence, and ironically, telling a small lie might be the only way to find the truth. Frankly, I'm willing to lie like a rug if it protects my niece."

"We're just taking the truth and . . . stretching it a bit."

"Yes."

Ainsley considered their limited options. "I'm not sure I can do . . . *this*." She made an expansive gesture with her arm, encompassing the strip club parking lot and everything they were about to attempt.

Nikki turned to face her. "What's the hardest thing you've ever done?"

A difficult question with so many situations contending for the top prize.

Getting her and Jolene to school every day with no help from their mother. Getting Jolene into college. Meeting her terrifying mother-in-law for the first time. Somehow keeping her own mother away from alcohol for three days straight so she couldn't humiliate her in front of Ben's family, the Treasury secretary, the four ambassadors, and three Fortune 500 CEOs who attended her wedding.

The bite of the air conditioning on her bare skin, and the terrible vulnerability of being the only naked person in a room of fully clothed men the first time she danced onstage, every minute fighting the atavistic urge to cover her exposed breasts with her hands.

The hungry stare of men sitting beneath her at the bar, appraising every angle of her body; pretending not to hear the sick things they whispered during lap dances. Forcing herself to smile when she wanted to kick them in the groin with the heeled spike of her shoes.

She shook her head, trying to dispel these memories. "Lap dances are the hardest thing I've ever done." Then she gave Nikki a wry smile. "Wait. I take that back."

"What could be harder than lap dancing?"

"Organizing the preschool book fair. *That* was a total nightmare. Actually, that's the hardest thing I've ever done because Tiffany Hastings was my cochair."

Nikki shuddered. "If you can organize the preschool book fair with Tiffany Hastings, you can do anything."

Ainsley mustered a less than confident smile. "I hope you're right."

Chapter Twenty-Three

NIKKI

They managed to snag the last guest parking spot in the tiny lot behind the university administration building. Orange and scarlet ivy crept up the sides of old stone buildings as students crossed the quad in hoodies emblazoned with the school's name, giving the campus the iconic look of the recruiting brochures they sent to thousands of high school juniors and seniors, including those they planned to reject in order to increase their U.S. News & World Report ranking. Nikki had done a story on this practice years ago, and it made her feel better about her own rejection by this university as a high school senior.

They entered the building, consulted the directory on the wall, and headed for the athletic director's office.

Nikki felt decidedly old as they moved through hallways populated by pierced and tattooed twentysomethings with hair in colors not found in nature, innocent souls who'd not yet learned about mortgages, health insurance deductibles, or gutters and the need to clean them.

Had she ever been this young? And when exactly had she become old? Did it start when she began to beg for permission to skip parties rather than attend them?

They climbed the stairs to the athletic director's spacious suite of offices on the third floor and pushed open a glass door. They entered a hushed yet busy space adorned with *Sports Illustrated* covers going back decades featuring different Biltmore athletes. Toward the back of the room, where the older issues hung, Wyatt Jericho grinned from a cover emblazoned with the headline "Winning Women."

She headed for the receptionist. An older woman with short gray hair sat behind a massive desk like an admiral piloting the flagship in a naval battle. She reminded Nikki of the assignment editor in her old newsroom: harried, weary, and extremely competent with no time to suffer fools.

Nikki squared her shoulders and walked purposefully to the desk. She'd learned a long time ago that if you acted like you had a right to ask questions, people were inclined to give you answers.

The woman removed her reading glasses and greeted her with a smile. "How can I help you?"

Nikki smiled back. "I'm a reporter working on a profile of Wyatt Jericho. I'd like to speak to someone about awards he won, records he set when he was a player here, that sort of thing. I also understand he raised an enormous amount of money for charity while he was here, and I'd like to focus on the good he did, both on and off the court."

The smile disappeared, replaced by a neutral expression. "Let me see if our athletic director is available."

She disappeared down a hallway and came back a couple of minutes later. Nikki stepped away from the desk and conferred with Ainsley in a low voice.

"I think you should wait outside. He might recognize you." The gauzy political ads with Ainsley and Ben strolling through an autumnal landscape holding hands with their kids seemed to pop up every time she turned on the television.

"But you're the one who used to be on TV," Ainsley whispered back.

"As a journalist. If he recognizes me, it validates my story. If he sees you, he might think it's something political and be less willing to talk."

"Okay," Ainsley agreed. "I'll wait for you outside."

She slipped out through the glass door as the receptionist beckoned to Nikki. "Mr. Hampton has about five minutes between meetings. Follow me."

She ushered Nikki into a spacious office. A good-looking man with dark hair and striking blue eyes rose from behind a desk with an athlete's grace.

"Sebastian Hampton." He extended his hand with a wide smile. "How can I help you?"

He had a deep voice, broad shoulders, and snow-white teeth, a cross between an NFL Monday Night Football announcer and a megachurch pastor. The gray hair at his temples probably placed him in his late fifties, but the biceps bulging under the sleeves of his fitted Biltmore University polo shirt showed he still took care of himself.

Nikki scanned his face quickly, drinking in every detail. Smooth skin, nonexistent pores, and an unwrinkled forehead, courtesy of chemical peels and Botox. Nikki had worked in television long enough to recognize expensive skin.

Vain. Trying hard to look younger than his years.

She flicked a glance at his outreached hand before she extended her own and shook it. No wedding ring.

Interesting.

"I'm doing some fact-checking for a profile piece on Wyatt Jericho," she said with a warm smile. "I'd like to get a little more information on the good work he did off the court, fundraising for causes he supported."

He gestured to the chair in front of his desk. "I've only got about five minutes, but I'm happy to help."

A prickle of irritation washed over Nikki as his gaze roamed over her body. Did he recognize her? Or was he just your basic lecherous bastard?

She sat in the uncomfortable seat in front of his desk as he settled into a high-backed, throne-like leather chair across from her.

Pretentious.

She glanced quickly around the room, soaking up other details. Being a reporter was like being a detective. You could find small clues hidden everywhere if you kept your eyes open.

She swallowed her distaste and arranged her face into a mask of pleasant professionalism.

He leaned back in his chair. "Fire away."

Arrogant. Unafraid. He'd probably never had a hostile interview in his life.

Nikki unearthed an old reporter's notebook from the bowels of her purse and flipped it open. She felt a moment of panic as her fingers searched the bottom of her bag for a pen and found only crayons.

She remained calm and unzipped the side pocket. There. A pen. A triumph of professionalism over the brain fog of motherhood.

"I understand you're the man behind Wyatt Jericho's success." *Flattery gets you everywhere.* "Sort of a kingmaker, if you will."

He clasped his hands behind his head, his body visibly relaxing and expanding. An ego sponge accustomed to soaking up praise.

"Not only was I here," he said, "but I'm the one who recruited him to play at Biltmore in the first place. I hired him to coach when his injuries prevented him from going pro. And I eventually promoted him to head coach, so I like to think my ability to recognize his talent played a role in the amazing program we built here, and the three NCAA championships he won with our women's team."

He hid it well, but she heard it in the tone of his voice. "*My* ability to recognize *his* talent."

Just a hint of jealousy. A shard of resentment. He'd created Wyatt Jericho and given him the opportunity to shine. Had Jericho appreciated this, or selfishly taken all the credit for his own success?

Nikki scribbled in her notebook. "You worked together for a long time?"

"Thirty-three years. He became one of my closest friends. Still is."

Nikki nodded. "I'd like to focus on his charity work. I understand he raised a lot of money for good causes."

"He did." The leather chair creaked as he settled into a more comfortable position. "Wyatt had a . . . difficult childhood. Because of that, he started an organization called Safe Haven, a shelter for women escaping domestic violence. He also started Camp Confidence, a summer camp for underprivileged middle school girls. He raised money to buy the land, build the buildings, everything. He has NBA players, other coaches, and school alumni on the board of directors. He built a huge donor network. He also raised a lot of money for after-school basketball programs for girls."

Nikki dutifully took notes. "In other words, he supports women and girls both on and off the court."

"Exactly. He puts his money where his mouth is." He grinned. "Or rather, other people's money. He's a prolific fundraiser for causes he believes in."

"Does he have a family of his own? I didn't see a spouse or children mentioned in my research."

He shook his head. "Basketball is his life, and his players are like his daughters. He truly cares about these young women. I think he has a sister out on the West Coast, and he's devoted to his elderly mother." He shrugged as though unable to find strong enough words to describe Wyatt Jericho's many gifts to humanity. "He's just an all-around good guy."

Nikki looked up from her notebook and smiled. "Which is why we're doing this profile. I just need to double-check a couple dates, and then I'll be on my way."

"Sure." He grabbed a small beanbag shaped like a basketball, tossed it into the air, and caught it, over and over again.

That's right. Get comfortable. People accidentally told the truth when they got comfortable.

She glanced down at her notebook and rattled off the dates she'd found online for his NCAA championship wins, the year he started playing, and the year he began coaching. "Does that sound right?"

"Yup. That's correct."

"Great." Nikki gave him a big smile and closed her notebook. "This is super helpful. Thank you so much." She stood, and he came around the desk and handed her a business card.

"If you need anything else, just give me a call," he said.

She slipped the card into her purse as they walked to the door. When he put his hand on the knob, she turned to him.

"Oh, I almost forgot," she said, her voice carefully casual. "It looks like he still had a year left on his contract when he left. Is there a reason he departed early?"

His shoulder muscles tightened under the fabric of his polo shirt. "His mother is sick," he said, his gaze focused on the door. "He wanted to live closer so he could take care of her, so he moved out to the suburbs. As I said, he's devoted to his mother."

"But that's kind of a step down, isn't it? Going from college athletes to coaching high school and middle school players."

He crossed his arms. "He needed to step away from his demanding schedule here. She requires a lot of care."

"Parkinson's, did you say?" He hadn't said, but she wanted to test him.

"That's right."

She nodded. Maybe Wyatt Jericho's mother really was sick. Or maybe her health was a cover story to disguise the real reason he left the university. The old "stepping down to spend more time with my family" line was the Beltway's oldest and least believable lie. No one with an exciting and prestigious job *really* wanted to spend more time with their family, a fact to which she could attest.

"Do you think he'll return if his mother's health allows? He's obviously a beloved member of this community."

"We'll see what the future holds." His jaw clenched. "Who did you say you work for again?"

"I'm a freelance journalist."

"But who did you say you were writing for?"

She hadn't said, on purpose, because she hadn't wanted to lie outright. Now she had no choice. "*Capitol Magazine*." Which did not exist.

"Here in DC?"

"Yes."

His eyes narrowed. "You look familiar. What did you say your name was again?"

He couldn't remember her name because she hadn't given him one. "Laura Holt."

"Well, Laura. I'm afraid I'm out of time. I'd like to look over the article before it goes into print, if you don't mind."

She would do no such thing, even if she were actually writing an article, but she wanted him to feel comfortable, not suspicious. "Of course. I'd be happy to send it over."

His shoulders relaxed. "Thanks. Not all reporters are so accommodating. Have you talked to Wyatt yet?"

She smiled and headed for the door. "He's next on my list."

Chapter Twenty-Four

AINSLEY

Ainsley leaned against the wall in the hallway, trying to catch up on emails, when Nikki plowed through the door.

"We need to get out of here." Nikki glanced over her shoulder. "Now."

Suddenly the doors burst open on both sides of the hallway, and a river of students flooded the corridor.

"What happened?" Ainsley almost had to shout to make herself heard above the din.

Nikki flattened herself against the wall and grabbed Ainsley's arm, pulling her close. In a low voice, she recounted her conversation with Sebastian Hampton.

"You told him your name was Laura Holt?" Ainsley frowned. "Is that the best you could do?"

"It was an homage to my childhood heroine," Nikki said stiffly.

Ainsley threw up her hands. "Why didn't you just tell him your name is Nancy Drew and he's a suspect in the Mystery of the Seriously Skeevy Basketball Coach?"

"I'm not used to lying to people!" Nikki hissed in a defensive whisper. "I couldn't think of anything else. Plus, I'm confident he did not spend his formative years obsessively watching *Remington Steele* like I did. Trust me, he won't get it."

"Why are we whispering?" Ainsley whispered as the last students melted away, leaving the hallway empty and quiet again.

"Because I feel like we're onto something, and it makes me nervous." They moved out of the building and onto the sidewalk. Nikki glanced over her shoulder at two sorority girls deep in conversation about someone named Madeline who everyone thought was a total bitch because she voted for Ashlyn instead of Emma for chapter president.

"Nervous in a good way?" Ainsley asked after they slowed down and allowed the girls to pass.

"Nervous in a this-story-could-get-me-sued-for-defamation-of-character-and-make-advertisers-jump-ship-and-bankrupt-the-station kind of way."

Oh dear. Ainsley wrapped her fingers around the straps of her Birkin bag and resisted the urge to gnaw on her nails. "Did anyone ever do that?"

"No, but when you uncover bad things, people try to keep them hidden. They threaten to sue the station or scare away advertisers or do something worse . . . and that makes me nervous."

"What do you mean . . . 'do something worse'?"

Nikki grabbed Ainsley's arm and hurried her toward the car. "You know . . . threats."

"What kind of threats?" Ainsley asked as she unlocked the car.

"Threats . . . of physical harm," Nikki said evasively.

"Like . . . Tony Soprano kind of threats?" Ainsley asked in a small voice as she slumped into the driver's seat.

Nikki locked the passenger door, then clipped on her seat belt without answering. Ainsley locked her own door, then turned on the engine as they sat together in silence waiting for the car to explode.

Finally, Ainsley spoke. "Basically, we've managed to establish that he's a champion of battered women and underprivileged girls. Could I somehow be wrong about all this?"

"I don't think so," Nikki said, finally speaking in a normal tone of voice. "Predators will use any excuse, including charity, to gain access to new victims. Plus, Lady Godiva thinks he's a sick bastard, and she strikes me as a pretty good judge of character."

Ainsley leaned her head against the seat rest. "We've got to find Harmonee Dean. She's the only one who can corroborate everything now that Misty Dawn is . . ." Her voice trailed off.

"'Providing poontang in Poon Yang,' in the immortal words of Lady Godiva?"

"Right. Since we can't talk to her, Harmonee is our only hope."

Nikki nodded. "The police can help with that."

"Do we really need to involve the police?" Ainsley asked, rubbing the back of her neck.

Even after all these years, she still had an instinctive aversion to law enforcement. Sheriff's deputies were the people who showed up with eviction notices at the end of the month. They'd served warrants when her neighbors failed to show up for court.

On several occasions, she and her sister had watched from their bedroom window as the police arrested Larry McAllister, the multi-talented man next door who engaged in a variety of illicit activities, from selling stolen televisions to the distribution of drugs stolen from veterinary clinics. His girlfriend had a calendar, a refrigerator magnet, and a collection of black-and-gold ballpoint pens featuring the bail bondsman's telephone number.

She'd also seen Delilah, one of her sister strippers, arrested for distribution of OxyContin pills in the club parking lot. Lady Godiva, who had no tolerance for drug use, refused to take her back when she got out on bail, and Delilah slid down the strip club slope. She ended up dancing for the infamous Dino Johnson down at the Depot, where local ordinances prohibiting contact between strippers and customers were seen as joy-killing guidelines to be ignored, rather than laws to be obeyed.

None of these people were innocent. But still. In her experience, the police were people to be avoided and were not necessarily the benign "community helpers" her own children believed them to be.

Nikki dug in her purse in search of her phone. "We've established that Wyatt Jericho left the university with a year left on his contract, ostensibly to care for his sick mother. We'll see if anyone has made a complaint about him or filed a report over the years. Then we see if law enforcement can help us track down Harmonee Dean. She's the key."

"But do cops even help with things like this?" Ainsley asked.

Nikki smiled. "I have connections, remember?"

She patted down her coat pockets, found her phone, then dove into her purse again and retrieved her notebook and pen. "I've known some of these cops for years. They've helped me out, and I've helped them out, too, when I could."

She dialed a number and asked for someone. After a few minutes on hold, she connected with a person named Jimmy.

Nikki laughed, hard, at something he said; then she got down to business, asking questions and scribbling answers in a notebook. Suddenly her tone changed. "Are you serious?"

Apparently, Jimmy *was* serious because Nikki rubbed her forehead and sighed. "Not your fault. I appreciate the tip."

The rest of the conversation was filled with gossip about the station manager who had fired Nikki and the new police chief, both of whom were, in the words of Nikki, and apparently Jimmy too, "industrial-strength douchebags."

Nikki hung up and stared out the window.

"Um. Hello?" Ainsley called. "Who is Jimmy, and what did he say?"

"Sorry." Nikki turned to face her. "Just thinking."

"Thinking what?" Ainsley asked.

"That we've hit a dead end."

"Already?"

Nikki suddenly looked even more tired than usual. "Harmonee Dean is dead."

Chapter Twenty-Five

AINSLEY

They drove to the Watergate in silence, Ainsley's chest tight with grief. Their so-called investigation had failed before it even got started. And little Harmonee . . . she should have been in her midthirties by now, raising kids, working, building a life. Instead, she was dead.

The need to focus on unfamiliar traffic patterns gave her a reprieve from these depressing thoughts. She glanced up at the Watergate's iconic jagged terraces and tried to remember the way to the parking garage. After circling the building once, she found the entrance, and they descended into the dingy gray light. They parked in her mother-in-law's reserved spot, removed their bags from the trunk, and got in the elevator.

Nikki's gaze darted up and down the hallway as the doors parted to reveal a nondescript corridor. "This is a little disappointing," she said.

"You expected to see Woodward and Bernstein?"

"Or Nixon's burglars. Or something."

"This might impress you," Ainsley said as she unlocked the door to her mother-in-law's apartment.

They stepped inside. Nikki dropped her bag and let out a low whistle. "So *this* is how the one percent lives."

"I know," Ainsley admitted sheepishly. "It's a little over the top."

"Versailles is over the top. This is . . . something else entirely."

Ainsley instantly regretted the decision to stay here. They should have gone to the Four Seasons. Or the Mandarin Oriental. Even a five-star luxury hotel was modest compared to any space occupied by her mother-in-law. But ironically, she didn't want to stay at a hotel because it seemed like a waste of money when they could stay here for free.

Nikki walked over to a painting and frowned. "This looks . . . familiar."

"It's a Degas." Ainsley stood beside her, regarding the painting. "My husband's grandmother lived in Paris and bought some of his paintings before he became famous. My mother-in-law owns two of them. There's also a small Chagall in the master bedroom. That'll be your room."

"Please," Nikki begged. "Do not make me sleep in the Chagall room. I'll wake up in the middle of the night to go to the bathroom, bump into the wall, and knock it down."

"But it's a beautiful bedroom with a lovely view of the Potomac. I want you to have it."

Nikki shook her head vehemently. "No way, sister. Stick me in the broom closet with the vacuum. That's safer."

"If you insist." Ainsley felt oddly disappointed. She was suddenly aware of a desire to *give* Nikki things, like an uninterrupted night's sleep on ironed Frette sheets in a plush bed with a view of the river.

And first, she'd wanted to do these things out of gratitude for Nikki's simple acceptance of who she'd been and what she'd done, and for her willingness to help.

But this urge intensified after she'd pulled up to Nikki's toy-encrusted driveway. Ainsley knew it would be years before Nikki could have nice things. Her floors would be sticky, her walls scribbled, her car a landfill of abandoned sippy cups and melted gummy bears for at least a decade to come.

Yet this didn't make Nikki pathetic or pitiable in any way. Instead, she reminded Ainsley of a statue she'd once seen of a Roman war goddess, broad shouldered with strong arms, heroic in her gritted determination to be a good mother.

"Go unpack and I'll get lunch ready," Ainsley called over her shoulder as she hung Nikki's coat in the hall closet. "The housekeeper left us lunch. We can figure out our next move while we eat."

Ainsley peeked into the dining room overlooking the Potomac to make sure everything was ready. The housekeeper had set the table with a snow-white cloth, china, silver, and fresh flowers. Ainsley laid out the meal she found in the fridge, a quinoa and kale salad with salmon, fresh fruit, and a chocolate torte for dessert.

She cranked up the gas fireplace and put an Ella Fitzgerald record on her mother-in-law's ancient stereo turntable. Her mother-in-law had stubbornly clung to the vinyl of her youth, making her a musical hipster at age seventy-three, as on trend as a bearded tech bro sipping an IPA.

When Nikki finished unpacking, they gazed out at the river and began to eat.

"This is amazing." Nikki heaved a contented sigh. "And this is your mother-in-law's *second* home?"

"Fourth, actually, if you count her places in Aspen, Palm Beach, and Italy."

"I can't even . . ."

"I know." Ainsley drizzled her salmon with a teriyaki glaze. "I can't either. If you sold just one of these paintings, you could buy every family in the People's Court a lifetime supply of groceries. It's hard sometimes . . . to wrap my mind around it."

"What's it like, being able to buy anything you want?" Nikki asked, flaking off a bite of salmon.

"It's weird," Ainsley said. "I've been married to Ben for eight years, and I'm still not used to the fact that this is my life. I keep doing things I don't need to do, like buying things on clearance at T.J.Maxx. It's funny, but *being* rich doesn't make you *feel* rich."

"What does?"

She shrugged. "I think rich is a state of mind. When you've grown up poor, you can never have enough money to make you feel like you have enough money, if that makes any sense."

"Someday you'll get used to it," Nikki said, waving her fork in encouragement.

Ainsley shook her head. "I think I need to get used to the person I am today. Accepting my past and telling my husband about it would probably help. But I'm just not ready."

"I know. But we'll get you there."

Ainsley gave her a shy smile. She liked Nikki's use of the word *we*. She didn't have to do this alone. She had a friend who knew the truth and, miraculously, seemed to like her anyway.

Nikki ran her fingers over the monogram engraved on her water goblet. "What's your mother-in-law's name?"

"Bunny Bradley."

"Wait . . ." Nikki's eyes widened with recognition. "Isn't her name on one of the auditoriums at the Kennedy Center?"

"Yes, among other things."

"Is that her real name?"

"No, her real name is Barbara. But her parents called her Bunny when she was little, and it stuck. Rich people seem to like nicknames. She calls me Lay-Lay instead of Ainsley."

"I wonder what kind of nickname she'd make from Tami Darlene Schmidt?" Nikki mused.

"Schmitty, obviously." Ainsley swallowed a mouthful of salmon and grinned. "As in, 'Hey, Schmitty, wanna go to Bergdorf's?'"

"Schmitty, let's call for the car and go to Costco," Nikki said in her best Park Avenue accent.

Ainsley extended her pinkie finger. "Schmitty, dear, could you take my Monet to Michaels and have it framed? Here's the seventy percent off coupon I clipped from the Sunday paper."

Nikki spit Perrier across the table and burst out laughing. Ainsley started laughing, too, and once she started, she couldn't stop. Nikki almost fell out of her chair, body shaking with silent snorts. Ainsley laughed so hard she began to cry, helplessly dabbing at the mascara running down her cheeks. When she finally stopped, her ribs hurt.

"It wasn't *that* funny," Ainsley said, shaking her head as she wiped her eyes.

"I know." Nikki attempted to pull herself into an upright position. "But I haven't laughed like that in a long time."

"Me either." And she suddenly realized it was true. She had lots of acquaintances among the moms at school, but she had never let herself get close to any of them. Because what would they think when they found out about the pole dancing and the hidden notebook in her closet telling her what to wear? But Nikki knew all of it. And she was still here.

"You're hilarious."

Ainsley smiled. "*We're* hilarious."

"And well fed," Nikki said with a satisfied sigh. "Thank you so much for this fantastic lunch."

"Okay. You finish eating, I'll clean up, and then we need to figure out what we do next."

Nikki gestured to her phone. "I just got a text from Jimmy, my cop friend. He gave me the name of a detective on the Eastern Shore who has more information on Harmonee. The detective's in court right now, but she can talk to us for about fifteen minutes if we get there by one o'clock."

Ainsley felt her spirits rise. "Do you think she knows something?"

"There's only one way to find out."

Chapter Twenty-Six

NIKKI

They got on the Beltway, where the posted speed limit was fifty-five, but everyone, even Ainsley, she noticed, drove seventy miles an hour, and headed for the Eastern Shore of Maryland.

They sped across the Bay Bridge, an event that would have taken at least an hour on a Friday afternoon in the summer with beach traffic, but on a cool overcast autumn afternoon they zipped across with no delays.

Ainsley slowed as they entered a quaint and ancient town called St. Marie, filled with old buildings where George Washington reportedly slept. Nikki knew that if George Washington *had* actually slept in all these places, he would not have been awake long to run the country. But these legends added to the little town's charm.

"You do the talking again, okay?" Ainsley said, interrupting her thoughts. "Cops scare me."

Nikki started to laugh, then realized Ainsley was serious. "Why?"

"They just make me nervous, that's all."

"Okay, I'll do the talking, but you have to chime in when they ask about Harmonee."

"Deal."

The police department shared space with the fire department in an old brick building in the center of town with a faded Coca-Cola advertisement painted on the wall.

Ainsley slid the Mercedes into a parking spot between a cop car and a beat-up pickup truck, and they headed inside.

Nikki gave their names to a young officer with acne-dappled cheeks sitting behind a desk. They took a seat on a hard wooden bench opposite him and across from a vending machine.

They looked up as a woman approached in a pressed polo shirt and khakis with a handgun holstered at her waist, exuding a quiet authority.

"I'm Detective Edna Chavez." She gave them both a firm handshake. "Come on back."

She buzzed them through a door and into a pleasant cubicle-filled room with high ceilings, hardwood floors, and tall windows that infused the space with light even on a gray September afternoon. They followed her into a conference room with exposed brick walls, a long wooden table, and houseplants on the windowsills.

"It looks like Pottery Barn," Ainsley whispered.

"Disappointed?" Nikki asked.

"Kind of, yes."

Detective Chavez took a long look at Ainsley, probably because of the political ads, then gestured for them to sit. "The roof leaks, it's drafty in the winter, and the elevator isn't up to code, but it's a beautiful old building. Kids on field trips are always disappointed too. I guess they're expecting something from *The Wire*."

They sat down at the table, and Detective Chavez glanced at her watch. She clearly didn't have time for this meeting and didn't expect anything useful to come of it.

"Okay," she said, crossing her arms. "What do you want to know?"

"We're interested in anything you can tell us about the death of Harmonee Dean," Nikki said.

Detective Chavez stared out the window. The afternoon sunlight highlighted the planes of her high cheekbones and square jaw. She was attractive in an angular way, handsome rather than pretty.

"Harmonee was my first case." Detective Chavez spoke in a low, tired voice, almost more to herself than them. "I was working patrol on the day shift. Some kids from the high school cross-country team were out running after school, and they came across Harmonee's body in a wooded area near the bay."

"Wait a second." Ainsley leaned forward. "What do you mean by 'came across her body'? Are you saying Harmonee was *murdered*?"

"Officially, no," Detective Chavez said. "No sign of foul play. No drugs or alcohol in her system. No sign of sexual assault. Not a mark on her, anywhere. She was thin, but otherwise as peaceful as an angel sleeping in the woods. Coroner said she died of organ failure due to dehydration."

"How long ago was this?" Ainsley's face had gone pale. Nikki could see her digging her nails into the arms of her wooden chair.

Detective Chavez looked down at the file in front of her. "It'll be twenty years next month. They found her body the week before Halloween."

Ainsley's shoulders crumpled as she sank into her chair.

"You okay?" Nikki asked.

"When you said she was dead . . . I thought . . . cancer or a car accident . . . I assumed she died recently, as an adult. But this means—"

Detective Chavez looked at her with pity. "She was fifteen years old when we found her body."

"Did she have anything with her?" Nikki asked.

"Just this little pink backpack filled with odds and ends, school-books, lip gloss, things like that. But no Social Security card or school ID."

"How did you identify the body?" Nikki asked, glancing at Ainsley's pale face.

"The kids who found the body recognized her," Detective Chavez said. "She was one of their classmates. One of the teachers at the high school came out and confirmed it. She informed us that Harmonee was in the foster care system, and we nailed down the rest of the details from there. Her dad had died in prison three years prior. Her mother was last seen in Montana, and we couldn't track a current address. The mother finally got herself together and surfaced about a year later. Came and talked to me about the case and picked up Harmonee's belongings."

"What do you think happened?" Ainsley asked.

"We'll never know," Detective Chavez said with a world-weary shrug. "We didn't even do a full autopsy because later that same day we had a mass shooting at the Harbor Haven mall. The shooter got away, and we had a giant manhunt on our hands. You remember that?" she asked, turning to Nikki.

"I do. Seven dead."

"That's right. And nineteen wounded. It was all hands on deck for weeks while we searched for that evil asshole and processed the crime scene. Harmonee's case fell by the wayside. I mean, there was no evidence of foul play. There were no parents beating down our door demanding answers. The teacher who helped ID the body seemed to be the only person who knew or cared about the girl. The death was ruled an accident, with dehydration and exposure as the cause, and we closed the case. But it never sat right with me."

"Why?" Ainsley leaned forward, a hint of desperation in her voice.

"Because we found her body eleven miles from town in a secluded area on Park Service land set far back from the main road. The only houses nearby are these palatial, gated Eastern Shore estates, and she certainly wasn't the kind of kid who hobnobbed with the wealthy."

"So, her death was ruled an accident, and no one was ever charged," Nikki said.

"That's right."

"Did you guys know she was living at a strip club before she disappeared?" Ainsley asked.

She frowned. "No, we didn't."

"Did Wyatt Jericho's name ever come up in the course of your investigation?" Nikki asked.

"The basketball coach at Biltmore?" She shook her head. "No, why?"

Nikki gave Ainsley a gentle nudge. Ainsley squared her shoulders and took a deep breath. Then she explained everything as succinctly as possible, about Wyatt Jericho coaching middle school girls at their school, about his behavior at Godiva's and his interest in Harmonee. Ainsley blushed a deep pink when she explained what she had done and seen at the club.

A look of pain settled over the detective's face as Ainsley spoke. When she finished, Detective Chavez slumped in her chair, silent.

Nikki stiffened. Did she think they were lying? That they were hysterical suburban mothers trying to get an innocent man arrested because he didn't give their daughters enough playing time on the middle school basketball team?

"Look," Detective Chavez finally said, "I wish this case weren't twenty years old. I wish I had an unlimited overtime budget. I wish I could hire fifty detectives to help girls like Harmonee. But I can't. These things you're telling me . . . they're disturbing. But I just don't have the resources to reopen this case. I wish I could help you find the evidence you need to kick that bastard out of coaching for good, but we're a tiny police department, and I've got fentanyl and MS-13 kicking my ass every time I turn around. I just don't have the man . . . or should I say *woman*power to help you. I'm really sorry."

Nikki nodded. She'd covered enough city council, school board, and county commission meetings to understand how budgets worked.

Detective Chavez opened the file in front of her, copied something onto a legal pad, then ripped the page out and handed it to Ainsley.

"This is the address I have for Harmonee's mother, and this is the name of the teacher who identified Harmonee's body. As far as I know, she's still at the high school, teaching art. Maybe she can provide you with the evidence you need to get rid of Wyatt Jericho."

"Which high school?" Ainsley asked as they rose from the table.

"Quincey."

Ainsley glanced at the paper, then crumpled it in her fist and slipped it into her purse. "Call me if you find something new," Detective Chavez said, handing Nikki her card. "Sorry I can't do more."

"You've been great, Detective." Nikki extended her hand. "Thank you so much."

They got into the car and looked at each other. Then Ainsley leaned forward and rested her head on the steering wheel.

"Are you okay?" Nikki asked.

"This is all my fault," she mumbled from behind a curtain of blonde hair. "When Harmonee showed up at the club all those years ago, I should have taken her back to her foster home. Or gone to social services. Or done *something*. But she seemed so scared . . . and fragile. So I told her to stay at Godiva's and take the dishwashing job. And that's where she met Wyatt Jericho. And then they found her body. If she hadn't taken my advice, she'd still be alive."

Nikki rested her hand on Ainsley's back. "You're making a lot of crazy assumptions here. We don't even know for certain that she and Wyatt Jericho were seeing each other before she died. And there's no evidence of foul play. Maybe she had a heart condition or something."

Ainsley raised her head from the steering wheel, dark smudges under her eyes. "You mean she just wandered into the middle of nowhere to die all alone, like some kind of sick animal? Does that make sense to you?"

Nikki sighed. "No. It doesn't."

"Do *you* think he killed her?" Ainsley asked.

"I don't know." Nikki shook her head, suddenly unsure of everything. "I mean, we know he hangs out in strip clubs with women thirty years younger than he is, and that he has a mean streak and a violent temper, but *murder*?"

"That day at the teacher luncheon. He knew I didn't want him to touch me . . . I kept trying to move away . . . but he did it anyway. He has this *arrogance*." She clenched her fists around the steering wheel. "He didn't think Misty had a right to say no in the Boudoir, and probably didn't think Harmonee had a right to say no either. He doesn't think any woman, old or young, has a right to say no."

Her voice grew soft as she turned to face Nikki. "I think Wyatt Jericho is capable of murder."

Chapter Twenty-Seven

AINSLEY

They left the antique shops and bed-and-breakfasts of St. Marie and headed deeper into rural Maryland, beyond mast-filled marinas and crab fisherman motoring through the water in long, low-slung boats. The GPS told them to take a right at West Marine, but it wasn't necessary. Ainsley knew the way.

She and Nikki drove another ten miles and took a left, and the landscape changed again. Farther from the water now, with smaller houses.

They entered the western edge of Badwater. Her nose wrinkled as the familiar rotten-egg smell rose from the nearby sulfur spring. The first Americans had gotten it right when they named the town.

The only people who lived here were people who couldn't afford to live anywhere else.

Her soul turned a little gray as she glanced out the window and saw the landscape of her childhood.

The entrance to the gravel pit. The dilapidated chain-link fence that only partially enclosed Skelly Monroe's Salvage Yard. And up ahead, the drunken wrought iron sign announcing the entrance to the People's Court. It had originally been designed as a sort of dignified arch, like those sometimes built at the entrance to a cemetery.

But for geological reasons no one fully understood, the left pillar had for many years been sinking into the ground, while the right pillar remained where it should be, making THE PEOPLE'S almost a foot lower than COURT.

She hadn't been here in almost twenty years, and *still* no one had fixed that . . . *damn* . . . sign. Or maybe they were just waiting for her to come back and do it herself.

Ainsley gripped the steering wheel. Of all the trailer parks in all the world . . . Harmonee's mother had to come back to the People's Court. And drag Ainsley back with her.

She drove under the arch, pulled into an empty lot, and stopped the car.

"Are you okay?" Nikki asked. "You seem a little . . . tense."

"I grew up here."

The quiet whish of warm air pumping through the vents filled the car. Once again, she had managed to render her friend the professional spokeswoman speechless.

"Okay."

Ainsley gripped her keys. "You don't need to say anything."

Because what could her friend possibly say? *Does the rotten-egg smell come with the house, or do you pay extra for that?* Or *It must be so convenient being next to a salvage yard, in case you run out of hubcaps.*

"Okay."

"I'll do the talking," Ainsley said.

"Okay." Nikki nodded.

They got out of the car and walked down the gravel road leading to the center of the trailer court. The deep, frustrated bray of a hound who could smell people approaching without being free to run out and examine them echoed down the street. Other dogs joined his vocal protest, and Ainsley could see curtains twitching as people looked out to see who approached.

Car doors slammed and lights came on inside the trailers as people returned home from work and school. A group of children played on an ancient steel swing set embedded in the center of the community, screaming with joy, pumping their legs as they tried to fly higher and higher still.

Ainsley turned right, heading for the west side of the community, where the homes on the 600 block were located. She turned left again and touched her hand to her lips.

Gone.

The home where she and Jolene had grown up had disappeared. In its place sat a new double-wide that looked more like a real house than a trailer. Someone had built a deck on the south side, with a grill and two rocking chairs.

The tightness in her chest melted away, and she could breathe again. Since arriving, she'd felt like someone at a party worried about running into an ex and his new supermodel girlfriend. She'd been expecting the sight of her childhood home to bring pain. But with the building gone, her fear of unbidden memories faded away.

She glanced at the paper in her hand and headed in the opposite direction.

Though the sign at the entrance remained a disgrace, the place had improved in the years since Ainsley left. She recalled reading an article about how the high cost of housing had made trailer parks attractive to middle-class homeowners. Ceramic garden gnomes watched over tidy flower beds fallow for the winter, and prim white fences edged many yards.

"This is a lot nicer than I expected," Nikki said. "These houses are neater than mine."

Ainsley shaded her eyes from the afternoon sun and looked west. "This is the newer area. Harmonee's mom is farther back, where the older homes are."

They turned down a side street where the houses were clad with sagging aluminum in faded colors. Ainsley headed for a pastel house at the edge of the park.

They opened a squeaking gate, walked up an ancient, pitted sidewalk to the front door, and knocked.

A woman with long blonde hair wearing cranberry-colored scrubs answered the door. Her face had a vulnerable, voluptuous loveliness, like a blown rose two or three days past its prime.

"You here about the rent check? 'Cause I dropped it off yesterday when it was due," she said, her voice breathy with girlish undertones.

"No, ma'am," Ainsley said respectfully. "We aren't here about the rent. We're looking for Lexy Dean."

She frowned, a hint of fear in her eyes. "I'm Lexy."

She'd been rail thin when Ainsley last saw her, probably because of the drug use, and still pretty, but with a hard face and long, lank hair. Now her body held more weight, and it looked appropriate, like her flesh had finally caught up with her bones.

"Do you remember me?" Ainsley asked.

"Tami Darlene?" A small smile broke out across Lexy's face. "I recognize you now. You're all grown up. Come on in."

They entered the trailer. A cinnamon-scented candle glimmered on the kitchen table. A different but equally inviting smell emanated from the oven, while a space heater in the corner gave off heat and a cozy glow.

Lexy gestured toward a small sofa covered with a blue crocheted blanket. Ainsley stared for a moment at a large landscape painting hanging over the sofa. There was something familiar about the soft light peeking through an arrangement of sweet gum trees and tulip poplars.

"Have a seat," Lexy said.

A cat pulled Ainsley's attention away from the painting, rubbing against her legs and purring as she sat down beside Nikki on the couch.

"Can I get you something to drink?" Lexy asked. "I got chamomile tea, or coffee if you want something stronger."

"Tea would be wonderful," Ainsley said.

As the woman filled the kettle, Ainsley looked around the immaculate, cozy trailer. Inspirational quotes covered a bulletin board above the kitchen table. *One day at a time. God grant me the serenity to accept the things I cannot change.*

And everywhere, angels. Ceramic angels on shelves, angel paintings and sketches on the walls. Angels embroidered on pillows and emblazoned on decorative plates.

Lexy returned a few minutes later and handed them steaming mugs of tea. She sat down across from them in a leather recliner carefully patched with duct tape.

There was an awkward pause. Nikki gently nudged her foot, and Ainsley began to speak.

"Did you know I worked at Godiva's too?" Ainsley asked.

Lexy frowned. "I thought you got out and went to college, made something of yourself?"

"We needed money for tuition, and I remembered you saying dancing paid well," Ainsley said with an unintended edge to her voice.

An alternate universe yawned before her. What if this woman hadn't pranced around the People's Court with a bag of cash, extolling the benefits of stripping? Would she have a normal past with nothing to hide? Would Harmonee still be alive, if Ainsley hadn't been at Godiva's that day to give her bad advice?

"You both worked at Godiva's?" Lexy asked with a skeptical glance at Nikki.

Nikki gave her a wry smile. "Not me, just her."

"Still dancing?" Lexy asked, switching her gaze back to Ainsley.

"No. I gave it up a long time ago." She gestured at the woman's uniform. "Looks like you aren't dancing anymore either."

Lexy stared into her mug of tea. "After Harmonee died . . . I got myself together. Got clean and sober, went back to school, became a massage therapist, and learned acupuncture. Been working at the Harmony Day Spa for the last eight years. When I saw the name of the spa, I knew it was a sign."

"How long have you been sober?" Ainsley asked.

"Since the day I got the call from the police. Harmonee's murder was literally a wake-up call."

Ainsley and Nikki exchanged a surreptitious glance. Another person who found Harmonee's death suspicious.

"Can you tell us why you think your daughter was murdered?" Nikki asked.

Lexy leaned forward, suddenly animated. "Because healthy teenage girls don't just lay down in the woods and die, that's why. Harmonee was a *survivor*. But if you're in foster care and your mom's a stripper, nobody cares if you disappear. They have AMBER Alerts for nice girls who go missing from the suburbs, but not girls like Harmonee."

"Were you in touch with her before she died?" Ainsley asked.

A look of shame crossed her face. "I was in Montana, and my life was real bad back then. Drugs. Other . . . things. I was a terrible mom, and if I'd been here, clean and sober like I should have been . . . Harmonee would still be—"

"It's my fault," Ainsley cut in roughly. "I should have marched her over to social services the minute she showed up at Godiva's. But I didn't because she wanted to stay. I let a fifteen-year-old girl live in a strip club where she met the man who killed her."

"You think it's *your* fault?" Lexy's voice rose an octave. "You really think you're the reason Harmonee ended up dead? You're pretty dumb for a smart girl," she added scornfully.

Ainsley's cheeks flushed. "I'm the one who told her to stay at Godiva's. I should have sent her back to foster care, where she'd be safe."

"You think that?" Lexy's expression hardened. "That she was safe in foster care?"

"Safer than being at a strip club," Ainsley said indignantly.

"Let me tell you something." Lexy moved to the edge of her chair and leaned forward until her face was inches from Ainsley's. "Two years after she disappeared, the dad in that foster family . . ." Her voiced trembled and she swallowed hard, trying to compose herself. "The dad in that foster family was arrested for doing terrible things . . . to girls.

So why do you think she ran away after only a week? She was smart as a whip. And a strip club full of women who gave her a job and didn't ask questions felt like the safest place in the world compared to the alternatives."

"I didn't know . . . ," Ainsley whispered, blinking back tears. "I didn't know why she ran away."

Lexy leaned back in her recliner, energy spent. "And now I find out you were there too. A familiar face. Someone from home. Someone she'd known since she was little." She reached out and took Ainsley's hand. "I'm glad you were there for her."

A strange revelation washed over Ainsley, as though the universe suddenly pulled back a curtain, making visible a dimension she hadn't seen before, a place where a benevolent power moved people like chess pawns, placing them on the right square at the right time, in a position to help their fellow humans.

She glanced at Nikki. Was that why Nikki had been fired? To help Ainsley protect the girls at school? If true, her days as a stripper were a necessary part of a puzzle involving more pieces than she could possibly understand. A layer of shame and regret dissolved, filling her with resolve.

Ainsley looked Lexy in the eye. "The man who killed Harmonee is going to pay for what he did."

Chapter Twenty-Eight

AINSLEY

They took a break to sample the banana bread Lexy had just taken from the oven. Ainsley's mouth watered as she spread melting butter across her warm slice.

She took a bite and turned to Lexy. "Harmonee told Lady Godiva she was moving in with you. Now we need to figure out where she really went."

Lexy brushed crumbs into the sink. "She hasn't told me that."

Ainsley exchanged a quick look with Nikki. "Who hasn't?"

"Harmonee," Lexy said in a matter-of-fact tone as she wiped the counter with a dishrag. "She talks to me. She told me she got murdered, but she hasn't told me who did it."

After a stunned pause, Ainsley recovered the ability to speak. "You talk to Harmonee?"

Lexy nodded. "She's an angel now, and she talks to me about lots of stuff. Mostly about heaven and whatnot. But sometimes other stuff too."

Nikki recovered from this admission before Ainsley did. "Do you have any of her possessions? Anything she had with her . . . when she died?"

Lexy nodded. "I kept all her things. You can look through 'em if you want."

She got up and left the room. Ainsley couldn't look at Nikki because she knew if she did, she'd either start crying again, or laughing hysterically, or both.

Lexy returned carrying a cardboard box with angels decoupaged across the removable cover and handed it to Ainsley. Then she moved to the kitchen, where she began to wrap the banana bread in foil. "I'm gonna bring some bread to the old lady next door while it's still warm. I'll be right back, okay?"

"Sure," Ainsley said. "Take your time."

As soon as the front door closed, they exploded into whispers.

"What in the *hell*—" Nikki began.

"It must be grief and guilt and some kind of, I don't know, *psychotropic disassociation*—"

"Thanks, Dr. Phil, but I don't think that's even a thing. That poor woman is just crazy. But I'd be crazy, too, if—"

"Stop," Ainsley said. "It's too awful to think about. I can't even imagine how hard—"

"I know. I'm worried that our questions aren't good for her . . . mental health. She's kind of creeping me out."

"I like her," Ainsley said firmly. "I think she's deep and spiritual. Like Oprah."

"Ainsley, she's a clairvoyant masseuse."

"You say that like it's a bad thing," Ainsley admonished. "Keep an open mind."

They removed the decoupaged angel cover and peered inside.

Nikki gently lifted a piece of cloth covered in sequins. "This must be the pink backpack they found . . . with her body."

Ainsley removed pens, lip gloss, tampons, a textbook, and a spiral-bound notebook.

Nikki flipped through the notebook, searching for writing or loose pieces of paper. "All the pages are blank."

Nikki reached inside and pulled out a small stuffed tiger wearing an orange-and-black jersey. "Look at this."

Ainsley's eyes narrowed. "The Biltmore mascot."

"They sell these at basketball games," Nikki said. "Or they give them out for free—"

"To children."

Nikki pulled out a small beanbag shaped like a basketball. "Sebastian Hampton had one of these in his office when I interviewed him. This is Biltmore basketball swag."

"But they give out thousands of these things every season," Ainsley said. "Adam has one of these tigers in his room. Harmonee could have gotten it anywhere."

"Is there anything else?"

"Just this textbook."

Nikki picked up the algebra book and began to thumb through it, shuddering. "These equations are giving me PTSD."

"What's this?" Ainsley asked, reaching for the book.

"What?"

"Go back to the last page."

Nikki pulled out a small square of blue cloth. "A doily?"

"No," Ainsley said. "It's a hemstitched linen cocktail napkin. It's embroidered with something." She squinted at the fine lettering across the bottom. "Whisper Point."

"Is that a restaurant?" Nikki asked.

Ainsley rubbed the material between her fingers. "I don't think so. Restaurants wouldn't use something this nice. I think it's the name of a house."

"Like Pemberley?"

Ainsley nodded. "Rich people like my mother-in-law name their houses. Every piece of stationery and linen in each of her houses is engraved or embroidered with the name of the place. Her house in Aspen is called Seven Pines. And her place in Palm Beach is called Lilac Hill."

Nikki whipped out her phone and began tapping furiously. "There's nothing on Zillow for a place called Whisper Point."

"Maybe it's never been on the market," Ainsley said. "Maybe they bought it or built it using an LLC to protect their privacy. Rich people do that too."

"Then how do we figure out where this house is?" Nikki asked.

"We ask someone who knows the name of every fancy home on the Eastern Shore." She thought for a moment, then said, "This is a job for—"

"Superman?" Nikki asked as she returned the items to the box.

"No. My interior designer."

They rose as Lexy entered the trailer. Nikki placed the box on the kitchen table while Ainsley carried their mugs to the kitchen and put them in the sink.

"Lexy, where did you get that beautiful painting above your sofa?" Ainsley asked.

Pride and grief mingled in the soft lines of Lexy's face. "Harmonee painted it. She said it was the view from the swing set when you got goin' real high."

That's why it looked so familiar. Ainsley had seen the same view herself a thousand times as a child. But she'd survived to see it again as an adult, and Harmonee hadn't.

She rested her hands on Lexy's shoulder and said the words she should have said earlier. "It isn't your fault, either, you know."

"Of course it's my fault," Lexy whispered. "I'm her mother. And I didn't keep her safe."

"My mother made mistakes, too," Ainsley said softly, "and I'm still here. The man who killed her is responsible for this. You loved your daughter. Anyone can see that."

Tears trickled down Lexy's cheeks. "That's what she says too. All the time."

"Can I give you a hug?" Ainsley asked, respecting Lexy's power to grant or restrict access to her skin, her warmth, her body, a power no dancer took for granted.

Lexy nodded wordlessly, then crumpled into Ainsley's arms. Ainsley embraced her, stroking her hair.

When Lexy's sobs subsided, Ainsley kissed the top of her head and pulled away. "Tell Harmonee I say hello."

Chapter Twenty-Nine

NIKKI

Nikki's purse rang as they left Lexy's trailer and returned to the car.

She found her phone on the first try, in the side compartment where her keys should have been but for some reason were not.

Her finger hovered over the screen. She had to pick up.

Right?

If Josh were on an important mission while she was home washing baby bottles and unloading the dishwasher while taking care of four small children alone for an entire weekend, *he* would answer the phone. An honorable spouse would take this call.

Plus, what if it involved stitches? Or a detached retina or a broken arm? What if Daniel had finally succeeded in his lifelong quest to eat a detergent pod?

"Hello," she said cautiously, her shoulders hitched up around her ears, waiting for the blow of bad news to strike.

"Hey, babe." It sounded like Josh, but it was difficult to tell due to the chorus of little voices in the background, whining for things they could not have, like ice cream. "I hate to tell you this but—"

She opened her mouth and released a silent scream. Why did this always happen?

It happened because this was what always happened to women when they selflessly answered nature's call to propagate the species and prevent the extinction of the human race. Mother Nature, who secretly wanted the planet all for herself, fought back with pandemics, strep throat, pink eye, tonsilitis, and flu, both A and B.

Josh filled her in on the situation. She listened carefully and promised to be there as soon as possible. Then she hung up, scowled at the heavens, and got in the car.

"What's wrong?" Ainsley asked warily after Nikki got inside and slammed the car door shut.

"Vomit," Nikki said stoically.

"Projectile?"

Nikki nodded. "All over the carpet."

"Diarrhea?"

"Explosive." She gazed out the window with a thousand-yard stare. "Coming forth from all my children, except the baby. Which is problematic, because Josh is operating at ten percent power while the baby is at full strength, demanding things."

"Josh has it too?"

"Not yet, but he's having ominous stomach rumblings. He thinks he can hold out for another two or three hours, but doubts he'll still be standing by bedtime."

"You need to go home."

"Yes. I do," she said heavily. "But if you drive like a bat out of hell, we could get to that school by three thirty to try to talk to Harmonee's teacher before we head back to our real lives."

They flew down the road to Ainsley's old high school. A line of buses loaded with kids lumbered out of the parking lot as they drove in.

"Do you think she's still here?" Ainsley asked as they entered the school and wandered through a maze of hallways filled with blue and yellow lockers, past chemistry labs exuding strange smells and bathrooms with signs on the doors warning about the dangers of vaping.

"Does it look the same?" Nikki asked.

Ainsley shook her head. "It was pretty rough when I was here. This is much nicer."

They finally found the art room on the top floor at the end of a long hallway. A sign beside the open door announced that the room belonged to Ms. Lisa Lyle.

Ainsley checked the scrap of paper the detective had given them. "This is the right teacher."

They knocked on the open door and entered the classroom. Windows on three sides filled the room with gray autumn light.

"Hello?" Nikki called.

A petite, middle-aged woman in a blue apron stepped from an adjoining classroom carrying a plastic bucket filled with water and paintbrushes.

"We're looking for Lisa Lyle," Ainsley said.

"You found her. How can I help you?" She set the bucket on a counter in front of the window and began vigorously swishing the dirty brushes through the clean water.

"We're trying to learn more about a former student named Harmonee Dean," Nikki said.

The woman froze, hands still gripping the paintbrushes. "I haven't heard that name in a long time."

"It's a long story." Nikki took a step closer. "But we're trying to find out what happened to her. We believe someone harmed her, and we think that person might be working in our school."

After dropping the brushes, the art teacher wiped her hands on her apron and turned to face them. "Please, sit down. I'll be with you in just a moment."

She disappeared into the room she'd come from as Nikki and Ainsley sat down at a table covered with tubes of watercolor and acrylic paints.

Lisa returned without her apron, carrying a flat black zippered case with handles. "I've been teaching here for twenty-five years. Harmonee was the most talented student I've ever had."

As she spoke, she laid the black case on the table and unzipped it. "I've saved all her artwork. I use it in my classes, both as an example of technique and to inspire other young artists when they get discouraged."

Lisa removed a pile of paintings and sketches from the case, in various media and on different sizes of paper or canvas, and spread them across the table for Nikki and Ainsley to see.

"Her mother doesn't think her death was an accident, and the detective who handled her case has some suspicions as well." Nikki picked up a small acrylic painting of a butterfly. "Did you notice anything unusual before she disappeared?"

The art teacher ran her fingers over a pencil sketch of a sailboat. "I think she had a boyfriend. And he wasn't anyone at this school, as far as I could tell. In fact, I don't think he attended high school at all. I think he was much older."

Nikki exchanged a glance with Ainsley. "An adult?"

"Yes. He gave her things, expensive things." She pulled back her collar to reveal a gold heart-shaped charm hanging from her neck on a gossamer-thin chain. "I got this necklace years ago, from my fiancé, who bought it at Tiffany for my birthday. One day Harmonee came to school with the same one. I knew it was expensive, and I asked where she got it. She made up some story about finding it in a thrift shop, but I knew that wasn't true."

"Who gave it to her?" Ainsley asked.

Lisa shrugged. "I wish I knew. High school boys don't have that kind of money, and they don't have that kind of taste either. Teenage boys give their girlfriends those dreadful mizpah necklaces or stuffed animals or their class ring. They don't shop at Tiffany. It had to be someone older, if you ask me."

"Was there anything else you noticed around the time she disappeared?" Nikki asked.

Lisa nodded. "Her artwork changed."

"What do you mean?" Ainsley asked.

The art teacher began to dig through the pile of paintings and sketches. "I started seeing a lot of *this*."

She pointed to an acrylic painting of a shoreline, a charcoal sketch of sailboats ranged across a body of water, and a watercolor of a sunset with a lighthouse in the distance.

Ainsley shuffled through the pile. "What about these sketches of people?"

Lisa put on her reading glasses and peered down her nose as Ainsley looked through a stack of faces.

"She sketched them in the cafeteria during lunch and sold them. Everyone loved her sketches," she said wistfully, "even teachers."

Ainsley went very still. "Nikki, look at this."

She held up a small black-and-white sketch of Wyatt Jericho.

Chapter Thirty

AINSLEY

The art teacher leaned in closer, looking puzzled. "Who's he?"

"You don't recognize him?" Ainsley asked.

"Nope."

"Are you a sports fan?"

She gave a derisive snort. "I can't tell a hockey puck from a football."

"He used to play and coach at Biltmore." Nikki set the sketch back down on the table. "Now he's the head basketball coach at our daughter's school, and we think he's the man Harmonee was seeing when she disappeared."

"And you're trying to prove this?"

Ainsley nodded. "At first, we thought he was a sleazy guy who hung out in strip clubs . . . and had a thing for underage girls. We never dreamed he might be capable of murder."

"Until now," Nikki added.

Ainsley ran her fingers over the pencil sketch of Wyatt Jericho. Could this really be true? Had Wyatt Jericho actually killed a fifteen-year-old girl? Because if he did, the girls on his basketball team weren't safe. Protecting her own secret suddenly seemed trivial in comparison.

Lisa picked up a delicate watercolor painting of a mother osprey flying back to a nest where a baby osprey waited. "I don't know exactly what you're looking for. But if it has to do with Harmonee, I want to help."

Ainsley looked at Nikki, and Nikki nodded. Ainsley took a deep breath and told Lisa everything they knew, leaving out the part about her firsthand knowledge of Wyatt Jericho's predilection for strip clubs.

"But how do you *know* he hung out in strip clubs?" Lisa asked.

Ainsley cleared her throat. "Someone who worked there . . . told us."

"Are they reliable? I mean, if they worked in a strip club . . ." The teacher's voice trailed off.

Ainsley's stomach clenched. Lisa seemed like a wonderful person. Kind. Generous. Supportive and compassionate. And yet even *she* thought strippers were morally bankrupt and untrustworthy.

And if most people felt the same way and found out about her past? Ben would lose in a landslide.

"This person *can* be trusted." Ainsley struggled to scrub the emotion from her voice. "Just because she used to be a stripper doesn't mean she isn't telling the truth."

Lisa conceded Ainsley's point with an absent nod, wrapping her fingers around the heart-shaped charm around her neck. "The fiancé who gave me this necklace died in a car accident. We never had a chance to start a family . . . and when Harmonee came along . . . I thought of her as the daughter I didn't get to have. Then she stopped coming to school, and I had to go identify her body . . ."

Her eyes reddened. She shook her head slowly and looked up at the ceiling. After a long moment, she spoke. "I want to help you find the person who did this and put him in prison where he belongs."

"We accept your offer," Nikki said, with a tired smile. "We need all the help we can get."

"Would you mind if we took this pencil sketch with us?" Ainsley asked. "And could I take this one too?"

She pointed at the sketch of Wyatt Jericho and the small watercolor of the mother and baby osprey.

Lisa pushed them across the table. "Take anything that might help."

"Could you do something else for us?" Ainsley asked.

"Of course."

"Do you think you could look through all her sketches and paintings of water and sailboats and see if you can figure out where *this* is?" she said, pointing to one of the watercolors. "Her body was found on the Eastern Shore, and we think she visited a home there at one point. We need to figure out where she was hanging out in the weeks before she disappeared."

They exchanged information and promised to keep her informed of anything else they learned, then headed into the parking lot.

Nikki glanced at the charcoal sketch of Wyatt Jericho. "Do you know what this means?"

Ainsley pressed the key fob to unlock the car. "I'm afraid to ask."

"It means my fourteen-year-old niece is spending hours after school every day . . . with a murderer."

Chapter Thirty-One

AINSLEY

"Do you think she's . . . safe?" Ainsley asked as she slumped into the driver's seat.

Nikki stared out the window at a group of boys in pads and helmets headed to football practice. "I don't think he'd try anything, because he needs this job . . . but I need to tell my sister what we've learned. Because if anything happened to Shelby . . ." Her voice trailed off.

Ainsley closed her eyes and nodded in mute agreement. The news about Harmonee was terrible in itself. Anything more was too awful to contemplate.

They stopped at the Watergate to pick up their bags, then merged onto the Memorial Bridge in rush-hour traffic. Going back to Godiva's, seeing the People's Court again, talking to Harmonee's mother. She felt like a wrung-out sponge after revisiting the sights, sounds, and smells of her past.

Beside her, Nikki scrolled through her phone.

"Any new messages from Josh?" Ainsley asked.

"No, but listen to this shocking story in today's paper." Nikki assumed her best anchor voice and read from her phone. "New research finds mothers feel more worried, stressed, and judged than fathers."

"Is that from *The Onion*?"

Nikki shook her head. "Nope, it's a real news bulletin from a legit paper."

"What's the story on the next page?" Ainsley asked. "Survey reveals small children don't like to brush their teeth?"

"Poll finds majority of women would rather read a book than unload the dishwasher?" Nikki asked.

Ainsley gave a short bark of laughter. "Researchers puzzled as to why children will ignore the father sitting next to them reading the newspaper but will wake their mother from a dead sleep to fetch them a glass of water."

Nikki turned to Ainsley with a weary smile. "I have thoroughly enjoyed my short but memorable day-that-should-have-been-a-weekend with you."

"I'm really sorry you didn't get to sleep at the Watergate on ironed Frette sheets." Ainsley turned on her blinker and merged into the exit lane. "I had planned for us to sleep in tomorrow, have brunch, and go shopping."

"That is not the life I am destined to lead, as the gastrointestinal gods have decreed." Nikki sighed. "But I enjoyed hanging out with you."

Ainsley gave her a shy smile. "We make a good team."

"We really do," Nikki said. "The way you handled that conversation with Harmonee's mother. She never would have opened up to me like that."

"But if it weren't for your connections with the police, we never would have found her in the first place. And that fake interview you did with Sebastian Hampton. *That* was brilliant." Ainsley glanced at the car behind her in the rearview mirror.

Nikki stretched in her seat. "This is one of the best almost weekends I've had in a long time."

"It feels good to do something important." Then Ainsley's smile faded. "But did we accomplish anything? Wyatt Jericho is even worse than we suspected, but we still don't have any evidence to show the school."

"I feel like the answers we need are hidden in that house," Nikki said.

"Whisper Point?"

She nodded. "We need to figure out where it is and then find a way to get inside."

"Let me talk to Kenneth," Ainsley said.

"Who's he?"

"My interior designer." Ainsley merged onto the parkway. "He does a lot of gorgeous second homes in the Outer Banks and on the Eastern Shore."

"Sounds snooty."

"He is now, but we actually grew up together." Ainsley slowed as a sea of red taillights announced a traffic backup ahead. "I knew him back when he was Weird Kenneth, and he had a habit of going into other people's trailers when they weren't home and rearranging all their furniture. They were always grateful, once they realized he hadn't stolen anything. He's like the Yoda of interior design."

"That's helpful."

Ainsley grinned. "Who needs Harvard when you have connections from the People's Court? I'll call him as soon as I get home."

"There's something else you should do as soon as you get home."

"No." She'd been thinking the same thing, but she couldn't do it. Not yet.

The art teacher's reaction remained fresh in her mind. What if Ben had the same reaction, but a thousand times worse because the stripper in question wasn't abstract and theoretical? It was the woman he'd married. The woman he thought he knew.

"Ainsley, this could take longer than we thought," Nikki said. "And what if Wyatt Jericho finds out we're investigating him and decides to discredit you before you can discredit him? He could take everything he knows to your husband's opponent, or the press. The deeper we dig, the more dangerous he becomes."

"Let's deal with one crisis at a time." Ainsley tightened her grip on the steering wheel. "First, we get rid of Wyatt Jericho. Then I'll figure out how to tell Ben."

"Fortunately for you, I'm too tired to argue," Nikki said, stifling a yawn.

They made a quick pit stop at Target to pick up the promised toys for the kids and then headed for Nikki's house. Ainsley pulled into the cul-de-sac and parked beside the mailbox. "I'm sorry to drop you down here—"

"But you can't pull into the driveway because of all the toys?" Nikki asked.

"Well, yes."

"I'll pick up the toys as soon as I finish cleaning vomit from the rugs," Nikki said, shouldering her bag.

"I'm here to help," Ainsley reminded her. And she meant it. She'd cleaned toilets before, and she'd happily do so again for Nikki.

"I know. And thank you. I'll call you tomorrow."

Ainsley reached over and gave her an awkward car hug. "Thank you, Nikki. For everything."

Nikki got out of the car and waved. Ainsley drove away, toward her own, very different home. Ben and the kids would be waiting in the family room. He'd texted to say they were watching football and playing Candy Land.

She'd have to breeze in with toys and kisses, pretending she'd spent the day shopping instead of hunting down evidence to protect them from the man who could destroy their lives.

Chapter Thirty-Two

NIKKI

The stomach bug moved through Nikki's house with merciful speed. Josh did not succumb after all, leaving both adults to handle the crisis as a sort of parenting SEAL team. Nikki spent a day catering to subdued but recovering children who only wanted to watch *The Parent Trap* for a fourth time while Mommy plied them with Jell-O and saltine crackers. Josh stocked the house with Pedialyte, Popsicles, and disinfectant wipes, and the following day everyone returned to school, except the baby, who, due to some kind of epidemiological miracle, had never gotten sick at all.

"Breast is best, *my ass*," Nikki cooed to Baby Joe as she rocked him to sleep with a bottle before his morning nap. "You're one of those superior formula-fed babies with a rock-solid immune system thanks to DHA or RNA or whatever they put in those magical cans of powder."

She'd been surprised to find she'd actually missed her family while she was gone, or rather, *aspects* of her family. She'd missed the warm little bodies snuggled beside her in bed as she read *We're Going on a Bear Hunt* for the fifty-seventh time and the cute things they said, like Daniel's declaration that he didn't need to take a nap today because he was "saving it for tomorrow."

But she did not miss the many unpleasant chores necessary to support these tiny, adorable humans. Like scrubbing gastrointestinal shrapnel from the wall between the kitchen and the bathroom. Why, she wondered, as she crouched on her hands and knees with a bucket of soapy water, did children always feel the need to announce they were going to throw up *before they actually did it*, thus wasting valuable seconds that could be more productively spent dashing to the potty?

By the time the doorbell rang, the walls were vomit-free, but Nikki felt sweaty, disheveled, and cranky.

"What fresh hell is this," she muttered as she peeled off her rubber gloves and made her way to the door.

She looked through the peephole. On her doorstep stood Ainsley and a tall, handsome Denzel Washington look-alike impeccably dressed in a camel-colored cashmere coat with a Burberry scarf.

Dear God. This must be Kenneth, interior designer to rich people with many houses. She couldn't let him come inside. Oh, the shame! The horror! The horror!

The doorbell chimed again. Had they seen her? Could she hide behind the sofa and pretend she wasn't home? But if they rang the doorbell again, they'd wake the baby, a scenario even more daunting than exposing her appalling home to the judgment of an interior designer.

She opened the door and pasted a welcoming expression on her face. "Hi! Come on in!"

They exchanged pleasantries and followed her inside. She didn't offer to take their coats because she knew the hall closet was filled with children's boots, diapers, two Costco-size tubs of animal crackers, paper towels, toilet paper, and no hangers.

Channeling her inner Lady Grantham, she invited them to sit in the family room and offered them coffee, because coffee, baby formula, whole milk, and juice boxes were the only refreshments consistently available in her home.

They eagerly consented to coffee, and she hunted through her kitchen cupboard for unchipped mugs that did *not* say things like "Not my circus, not my monkeys" or "This ain't my first rodeo."

She carefully brushed aside the Lego project currently occupying her only wooden tray and carried her sarcastic coffee mugs and the cream and sugar into the family room, then set them on the coffee table beside a violent tableau of plastic dinosaurs at war with Batman and a legion of My Little Ponies.

"I'm sorry it isn't more . . . elegant," she said, slightly out of breath from the effort of assembling all the required ingredients from her less than organized kitchen.

Kenneth put his hand on her arm. "Darling, where in the world did you get this exquisite coffee table?"

She blinked stupidly, taken aback by the compliment. "My husband made it."

"And that fabulous console table behind the sofa?" He pointed with a manicured finger.

Nikki hid her own decidedly unmanicured hands behind her back. "He made that too."

From somewhere on his person, he whipped out a tape measure. "Do you mind?"

"Um, no. Go right ahead."

He rose from the couch and stepped over Baby Joe's Exersaucer and a Barbie camper. He made his way around the room, measuring furniture and scribbling numbers in a leather-bound Gucci notebook with a gold Cross pen.

"Does he do custom pieces?" Kenneth asked.

"Everything is custom," she said. "He and Guzluk and Petru make every piece by hand."

"Where is his workshop?"

"About half an hour away."

"Take me there." He turned to her with a look of dramatic urgency. *"Immediately."*

"Um. Okay." She felt helpless to resist or contradict this man, who seemed to be some kind of interior design prophet on a mission from a higher power, like Moses, or maybe Noah, but with furniture instead of animals. She lacked the good taste to comprehend this noble undertaking, so it seemed best to simply get out of his way and follow orders.

Ainsley rose from the sofa. "Hold on a minute, Kenneth. We came over to discuss something important, remember?"

"Fine." He put his hand on his hip and rolled his eyes. "Here's the skinny. I know all about Whisper Point, and I can get you inside."

"You can?"

"Ainsley will explain," he said, fluttering his hands dismissively, "because I have more important things to do. This family room is *in crisis.*"

He removed his coat, rolled up his cashmere sweater sleeves, and began to unplug Nikki's lamps.

She turned to Ainsley helplessly. "What is he—"

Ainsley put her finger to her lips. "Trust me. You won't recognize your own house when he's done."

"And that's a good thing?"

Ainsley flushed as her gaze darted around the room. "Well, it's not necessarily a *bad* thing."

Nikki pressed herself against the wall as Kenneth moved past carrying her only surviving houseplant, an indestructible Christmas cactus, and placed it on the mantel. "What is he talking about, with Whisper Point?"

Ainsley shuffled in the opposite direction as Kenneth pillaged the bookcase behind her, removing items and dislodging an embarrassing amount of dust. "Whisper Point was built twenty-five years ago. Kenneth was just starting out then, and he worked as an assistant to the designer who did the house. And get this. The owner was a wealthy Biltmore alum, donor, and a huge basketball fan."

"Sofa," Kenneth ordered imperiously as he pointed to the opposite side of the room. "Over there."

Like well-trained dogs, she and Ainsley immediately bent to pick up the couch. "Does he still live there?" Nikki asked.

"The owner died about eight years ago, and it's a second home. No one has ever lived there full time," Ainsley said as they put the sofa down, then moved it a few inches to the left, then right, guided by Kenneth's exacting gestures. "But his widow lives there in the summer."

"Does Kenneth still work with her?" Nikki watched with trepidation as Kenneth rooted through her junk drawer, then removed a hammer and a handful of nails.

Ainsley nodded. "When his boss retired, Kenny opened his own firm and inherited most of his clients. He designed the home in Florida where this lady lives the rest of the year."

Kenneth began to drive a nail into the wall, and Nikki had to raise her voice, almost shouting to make herself heard over the pounding. "Does he have a key?"

"No," Ainsley hollered back. "But the owner has a crew of cleaning ladies who go in every two weeks, mainly to flush the toilets, run water in the faucets and tubs, check the pipes, and dust. Kenneth goes in with them in the spring to get the house ready before she comes up from Florida."

"So how can Kenneth get us inside?" The hammering stopped, and Nikki cocked her ear to the stairs, listening for the cry of an angry baby woken from a nap, but miraculously, she heard only silence. Maybe formula-fed babies were also superior sleepers?

"Excuse me, ladies, *chair*." Kenneth snapped his fingers at the heavy leather recliner in the corner.

Ainsley stooped to grasp the chair from the bottom. "Unfortunately, Kenneth is going out of town. He's overseeing a yacht project in France."

"I'm sorry," Nikki said, straining to carry her end of the chair backward across the room. "Did you say *yacht* project?"

Ainsley grinned as they set the recliner down. "You mean you didn't hire an interior designer to do the cushions and pillows and artwork on your new yacht?"

"I like to do those things *myself*," Nikki said haughtily. "I DIY the interior design on all my yachts using tasteful items I find at garage sales."

"Well, most people don't, so he'll be in France when the cleaning ladies go to the house on Tuesday. But we can show up and pretend to be part of the crew. We'll search the house and check out the view and see if it matches the artwork Lisa Lyle showed us. And maybe we'll find something linking Wyatt Jericho to Harmonee."

"Shoo." Kenneth flapped his hands, herding them into the kitchen. "And don't peek."

He left them in the kitchen and returned to the family room, muttering something under his breath about the shameful nakedness of a home without preserved boxwood topiaries.

Nikki squirted dish soap into the kitchen sink and cranked the faucet to hot. "But there's one problem. Tuesday is Butterfly Day, and I'm the larva-and-pupa mom."

Then she paused, adding uncertainly as she plunged a baby bottle into the steaming water, "Or do I have the date wrong?"

"No, you're right." Ainsley groaned. "And I signed up to make these adorable butterfly cupcakes I saw on Pinterest with these cute little wings made from Fruit Roll-Ups."

"Of course you did." Nikki sighed as she scrubbed the inside of the bottle with a brush created expressly for this purpose. Every time she picked it up, she wanted to nominate the person who'd invented it for a Nobel Prize in Engineering. "And I don't have a sitter."

"And it's a *Tuesday*," Ainsley pointed out, grabbing a dish towel.

"Right." Nikki tossed the clean bottle into the rinsing water. "No Lunch Bunch."

"We might not make it back in time for preschool *or* kindergarten pickup." Ainsley dried the bottle.

"And both my sister and Josh are out of town that day, so they can't watch Daniel and the baby." Nikki wiped her forehead with the back of her hand as steam rose from the hot water.

"And we can't leave them with my nanny because she takes classes on Tuesdays, and Ben is doing a campaign event at a battery factory."

"We could ask another mom to do pickup," Nikki suggested as she started on another bottle.

Ainsley brightened. "Chloe's mom seems nice."

"But even her minivan isn't big enough for all the car seats," Nikki pointed out. "I have four kids. You have two. That's six right there. Plus, her own kid . . . someone would have to ride illegally in the front passenger seat of death."

They looked at each other, perplexed.

Nikki stopped washing bottles and turned to face Ainsley, wet hands resting on her hips. "Are we really going to let this guy get away with murder because we don't have a sitter?"

"Well," Ainsley said hesitantly, "we could ask my sister."

Nikki picked up her bottle brush again. "Is she good with kids?"

"She's good with loopholes," Ainsley said. "She's a tax lobbyist."

"Isn't she a little busy twisting the arms of congresspeople to do her evil corporate bidding?" Nikki asked as she swished another bottle clean.

"Well, yes, she is," Ainsley conceded. "But even though working at Godiva's was my decision, she feels like it's her fault. She remembers my stories about Wyatt Jericho. She'd move heaven and earth to help us get rid of him."

Kenneth entered the kitchen. "You can come in now. Nikki, cover your eyes."

Nikki dried her hands, and then Ainsley blindfolded her with a kitchen towel and led her into the family room. She felt like a homeowner on one of those HGTV shows who goes out for a cup of coffee and comes back to a new kitchen and master bathroom.

Ainsley removed the blindfold, and Nikki opened her eyes. For several seconds she was speechless.

Through some kind of interior design alchemy, Kenneth had transformed her misbegotten family room into a page from a Pottery Barn catalog.

"How did you *do* this?" she asked, stunned. He'd created a cozy reading nook by placing the recliner near the window and moving the floor lamp. By changing the location of the sofa, he made the room seem bigger and also created a better angle for watching television.

Beaming, he pressed her hand to his lips and kissed it. "Darling, you have a lovely old home with beautiful bones and some truly exquisite furniture. But these gorgeous features were *positively smothered* by the detritus of life."

"The detritus of life?"

He pointed to a large, previously empty cardboard box Daniel insisted on calling the Millennium Falcon. The miscellaneous items formerly scattered across the room were now piled inside.

"Detritus. Clutter. Things that spark *horror* instead of joy." He sighed heavily and pointed at a ratty stuffed elephant the children had inexplicably named Kanga Roo.

Then he picked up an abstract sculpture she and Josh had purchased from a street vendor on their honeymoon in Mexico, an object relegated years ago to a dark corner on a bookshelf. Just looking at it brought back happy memories of sun and sex and sand. It did, in fact, spark joy.

"*This* should be displayed." He put it on the table beside a stack of oversize hardcover books and a wooden box carved by Josh's grandfather, effortlessly creating a lovely vignette.

She looked at him in awe, feeling like Dorothy in *The Wizard of Oz*. Everything she needed had been right here in Kansas all along.

"You have a truly lovely home. We just need to *zhuzh* it a bit," he said as he plumped the only throw pillow she owned.

He waved his hand in a deprecating gesture. "I took the liberty of ordering you some ginger jars, a couple boxwood topiaries, and some new lamps."

"But I'm not sure I can afford—"

He silenced her with a wave of his hand. "It's a gift. From Ainsley and me, and if you don't accept, I'll charge you for my time, and trust me, darling, that would be far more expensive."

She looked from one to the other. "You guys are . . . I mean . . . thank you."

"I'll stop by and arrange the lamps and things when they arrive." He brushed off his hands and picked up his coat. "Now, take me to your husband. I'm working on eleven different homes right now that are simply *screaming* for his console table."

Chapter Thirty-Three

AINSLEY

Jolene showed up at Ainsley's house for her babysitting appointment on Tuesday morning in a pinstriped Armani suit and four-inch heels, having just come from a fundraising breakfast at the Capitol Hill Club for the chairman of the Ways and Means Committee.

Ainsley introduced her to Nikki, who waved from the family room as she cursed under her breath and attempted to assemble the Pack 'n Play.

"You look stunning. But you might want to change," Ainsley said, glancing at her sister's spotless cream-colored blouse.

Maybe this hadn't been such a good idea after all. Her kids loved Jolene, who could whoop on the trampoline, pretend to be a horse, and play hide-and-seek all day long, but they usually saw her on the weekends and during holidays. Today she seemed very much in *tax attorney mode*. What if she had a crisis at work? Would the boys wander off and drink poison while she discussed the implications of the alternative minimum tax with one of her corporate clients?

"Don't worry. I've got sweatpants and sneakers in my bag." Jolene kicked off her heels and wandered over to the island, where she glanced at two pieces of notebook paper spread in front of Ainsley. "What the heck is that? Schematics for a nuclear submarine?"

"It's a map of the *preschool* carpool line," Ainsley said as she traced over the words DON'T GO HERE with black Sharpie.

"We made you a different map for the *lower school* carpool line at St. Preston's, where you pick up the girls from kindergarten," Nikki said, joining them in the kitchen after triumphing over the clueless and probably also single and childless male engineers who designed baby gear.

"You can't get in line for preschool pickup *before* eleven fifty a.m.," Ainsley said.

"But you can't get there *later* than twelve oh five," Nikki explained.

"And when you pick up the girls at St. Preston's, you must *not* get in line before two forty-five," Ainsley said.

"But you can't get to school *after* three ten," Nikki added.

"Or they'll send the girls to Extended Day, and they'll be traumatized because they've never been to Extended Day," Ainsley said.

"And don't cut the line by going through the alley behind the dry cleaner's," Nikki warned.

"Can you imagine what they'd do if she cut through the alley?" Ainsley asked.

They burst into hysterical laughter. "Those St. Preston's moms would come for her with *pitchforks*."

"Especially the lacrosse moms," Ainsley added.

They immediately stopped laughing. "You do not want to mess with the lacrosse moms," Nikki said soberly.

"But you'll be fine as long as you get in line by the *green* door." Ainsley drew a dramatic arrow on the map with her black Sharpie.

Jolene rubbed her forehead. "This is more complicated than the tax code."

"And just as efficient," Nikki said.

Ainsley stepped out from behind the island and twirled for her sister. "What do you think of our disguises?"

Jolene fingered the edge of Ainsley's sleeveless smock. "I remember these things from our days cleaning hotel rooms."

"They're so practical." Ainsley put her hands in the large front pockets. "I kind of wish I could wear one every day."

"My grandmother used to wear one of these." Nikki glanced down at her own floral vest. "It's very retro."

"Hair pulled back. No makeup. Totally authentic," Jolene observed, inspecting them both.

"Cleaning hotel rooms was hard work," Ainsley explained to Nikki, "and we'd get really hot. Makeup would just melt off."

She and Jolene exchanged a glance. Nikki could never understand what it felt like to enter a hotel room someone else had trashed, wet towels moldering on the floor, dirty room service dishes stacked up in a ketchup-blotched pile beside the bed, clothes everywhere, makeup smeared across the bathroom counter. And having to make it all spotless again, but in an invisible way, as though fairies had come and done the work. Cleaning one room and then another and then another, and then another still. A truly Sisyphean task because each time she and Jolene finished a room, a new guest checked in somewhere else in the hotel and made the same mess all over again.

Jolene glanced at her watch. "You guys should get going. If I can handle a member of Congress who doesn't understand why we need to preserve the carried interest deduction, I can handle this. Now *go*."

Nikki was still giving last-minute instructions about what to do when Baby Joe woke up from his nap when Ainsley pulled her out of the house and over to her minivan.

"Can't we take your car?" Nikki asked. "It's so clean and mine smells funny and I think we have *mice*."

Ainsley turned pale. "You have rodents in your car?"

"I mean, I don't know that *for sure*, but the girls brought home this library book called *Melvin, the Minivan Mouse*, and they're convinced they've seen a mouse, and now they're starting to convince *me* that we have a mouse living in our minivan."

"Named Melvin."

Nikki shrugged. "It's possible."

Ainsley heaved a deep sigh. "While I, too, would prefer to travel in a car uninhabited by mouse . . . squatters . . . we can't roll up to our job as cleaning ladies in my Porsche. It will blow our cover, or they will 'make us,' or whatever they say in spy movies. Your minivan, on the other hand—"

"Looks like exactly the kind of thing an itinerant house cleaner would drive?"

"Let's just say it's authentic."

Nikki rolled her eyes. "Fine."

They loaded the minivan with the buckets, mops, and bottles of cleaning supplies Ainsley had purchased to add a realistic touch to their story, punched the address Kenneth had given them into the GPS, and took off.

The day had started with the promise of sun, but now clouds rolled in, prematurely dimming the morning light. As they drove, Ainsley gazed out the window at the dying landscape as it surrendered to the inevitability of winter.

This wouldn't be hard. Necessarily. Cleaning ladies were not armed. They weren't doing anything dangerous. Or illegal. Although entering someone's home when you were not supposed to be there probably *was* illegal.

She could see the headline now: "Ben Bradley Stripper Wife Charged with Breaking and Entering."

Stop. Focus. Take a deep breath.

She closed her eyes and inhaled. She'd done all the other hard things. She could do this too.

She turned to Nikki. "Let me do the talking."

"I admit to knowing very little about cleaning," Nikki said humbly.

They rounded the corner and glimpsed a sliver of water; then a house took shape, with so many windows it appeared to be made of glass.

Ainsley caught her breath. "What a beautiful home."

"It's almost as big as yours."

They found a crumbling barn just off the main road and parked behind it. Then they sat on the dying grass under a cool gray sky and watched the main road. At 10:20 a.m., a small SUV carrying three women sped past.

Ainsley reached for Nikki's hand and squeezed hard.

It was time.

Chapter Thirty-Four

AINSLEY

Nikki and Ainsley pulled up just as the cleaning ladies unlocked the front door and disappeared inside.

"Perfect timing," Nikki said.

She tried to get the lay of the land as Nikki parked by a garage designed to look like a carriage house. Cedar shingles covered the roof, and rows of casement windows lined the front of the home. Behind it, the Chesapeake Bay made a spectacular, if sullen, gray backdrop.

Other picturesque buildings sat scattered across the property. Probably a guest house, and a party barn, and a wine-tasting cottage. Ainsley had been to homes with all these amenities over her years with Ben, but a search involving so many buildings would make their job more difficult.

As Nikki opened the back hatch on the minivan, one of the cleaning ladies emerged from the house, a tall, thick woman with orange hair and skin so pale it seemed to glow.

"Who the hell are you?" she called as she strode across the lawn. She put something to her lips, then expelled a cloud into the air around her.

Ainsley's stomach twisted. Just what they needed. An angry, territorial, vaping cleaning lady.

Ainsley squared her shoulders. "Kenny sent us."

"Why the hell would he do that?" The woman raised her voice, her frown deepening into a scowl.

Ainsley swallowed. She should have anticipated this. The vast majority of cleaning people she'd known took pride in their work. Sending in another crew showed a lack of confidence on the part of management.

"We're not here to clean." Ainsley walked quickly across the yard toward the woman, hoping to head her off before she noticed the supplies in the back of the car. "We're taking inventory."

The woman's orange eyebrows rose on her pale forehead. "He thinks we're *stealing*?"

This was not going well.

Ainsley wet her lips and tried again. "No, of course not. But some people are coming to stay over Thanksgiving, and he wants us to check the sheets and dishes and the toaster and the coffeemaker, things like that, to see if anything needs to be replaced. That's all."

The woman's features softened. "Well, that's okay then. I don't have time to do that kind of extra work right now anyway, with Tricia out on bedrest and Yvonne helping at the Cenex till Donny gets back from Orlando." She took another drag on her vape device and explained. "He won at pull-tabs and got a winner with the scratch-off, so he took the grandkids to Disney."

"We can clean the silverware drawers and the kitchen cabinet shelves, if you like," Ainsley offered deferentially. "But we promise to stay out of your way."

Nikki came over, and Ainsley's shoulders relaxed. She needed a rescue from this conversation. "Sorry to interrupt," Nikki said, "but I gotta pick up my kids in a couple hours."

The woman squinted at Nikki. "You look real familiar. Did you grow up around here?"

Nikki chuckled and shook her head. "I grew up in Virginia Beach. But when I moved up here, people kept telling me I look like this anchor lady on TV."

"That's right!" The woman slapped her vape gizmo against her knee. "You look just like her."

"I wish I *was* her," Nikki said wistfully. "'Cause then I'd be sitting in front of a camera instead of cleaning houses."

The woman nodded sagely. "Ain't that the truth."

Truer than she would ever know, Ainsley thought as she clenched and unclenched her fingers.

"Well, I guess I'd better get back to work." The woman popped the hatch on the SUV she'd parked in front of the house and reached for a vacuum. "The house is in pretty good shape today. Not like last month."

"I thought no one lived here," Ainsley said, "except in the summer?"

The woman put the vacuum down and took another draw on her pipe. "No one lives here full time, but the lady who owns it has a nephew who uses it sometimes on weekends. And man, when he gets done with the place, it's *trashed*."

"How trashed?" Ainsley asked.

"Condoms and ladies' underwear all over the place." She shook her head in disapproval. "Champagne bottles, shot glasses and cigars, red Solo cups with warm beer all over the place, sticky floors. Treats it like a frat house."

"Is it always like that?"

"No," she said firmly. "I'd give up the job if it were. It seems almost . . . seasonal. It's bad in the fall and spring, but quiet in the winter. And then of course the old lady is here in the summer, and she don't make much mess."

"Do you . . . know his name, by any chance? The nephew, I mean?" Nikki asked.

"No. His aunt married the heir to a toothpaste fortune, and he died a few years back. That's all I know." She picked up her vacuum again. "Anyway, gotta get back to work. Nice chatting with you ladies."

"Likewise," Ainsley said, shooting a glance at Nikki.

They waited for the woman to drift out of earshot. Once she entered the house, they erupted in whispers.

"Wild parties and ladies' underwear all over the place?" Nikki wrinkled her nose. "What's that all about?"

"Strippers," Ainsley said grimly. "Some girls used to do private parties on the side. The money was great, but I never did it. I worried about . . . security . . . and I heard that sometimes those girls were expected to do more than dance."

Nikki glanced at her watch. "Let's see what we can find in the house. Then we gotta go. I don't want to subject Jolene to the tender mercies of Daniel and Baby Joe any longer than necessary."

They entered the house in silence and headed for the kitchen. "Poke around in the cupboards," Ainsley whispered. "Then sneak upstairs. Pretend you're inspecting the pillowcases or something. I'll take the basement, and we'll meet back here and search the main floor."

Nikki nodded, and they separated.

Ainsley headed to the basement, turning on lights as she descended the stairs. A massive pool table sat in the center of the room, with a full bar at one end and a small stage with a dance floor at the other.

She sniffed. The place didn't have the musty odor of an empty home. Instead, she smelled the bitter musk of cigar smoke.

She walked over to the windows and looked out at the bay. A spectacular view, even from the basement on an overcast day. She crossed to the other side of the room and opened each door, trying to get a feel for the layout. The pool table, bar, and stage anchored the space. But there were other things down here, too, like a wine cellar and three bedrooms with en suite baths.

She finally came to the last door. It looked different from the others, bigger and made of steel, not wood. It stood alone at the end of a long, windowless hallway. She turned the handle and found it unlocked.

She pushed it open, expecting to find a fourth bedroom. Instead, inky darkness enveloped her. Her hands groped along the wall, until she found the switch and turned on the light.

She inhaled sharply and stepped inside.

Chapter Thirty-Five

AINSLEY

A basketball court.

These people had a basketball court in their basement.

Harsh fluorescent lights embedded high in the ceiling bounced off the blond hardwood floor. Although generous in size, it wasn't a full-size court, but definitely big enough to play an actual game.

The buzz of fluorescent lights created the only sound in the spartan room. It contained a hoop mounted at each end of the court and a metal folding chair and table. Otherwise, the room held only silence.

A sixth sense whispered across her skin, raising goose bumps on her flesh. *There's something here.*

But there's nothing here.

What was she looking for? A note? A necklace? A letter? A sketch?

A feeling of hopelessness washed over her like rain. This was stupid. Anything hidden twenty years ago would surely have been found long ago by someone else.

The gym appeared to be original to the house, while everything else in the basement looked recently updated, with trendy tile and rimless shower doors.

But the metal desk and chair looked old, like they'd been installed with the hardwood floors and the scoreboard. Crossing the free throw line and the half court line, her feet echoed in the empty stillness as she approached the only furniture in the room.

One drawer in the desk. Nothing else.

She slid it open.

The Operation and Maintenance of the Net Pro Scoreboard.

A thin four-page booklet with yellowing pages explained how to turn the scoreboard on and off, how to start and stop the clock, and how to reset the board when the game ended.

The backs of her eyelids began to itch. *I am not going to cry.*

But she wanted to. Because Wyatt Jericho had gotten away with murder. Because no one cared whether girls like Harmonee lived or died. Because she couldn't protect the girls at school any more than she could protect Harmonee. And because even with all her money, she still felt trapped: not by poverty, but by her past and the power it gave Jericho.

She grasped the booklet, about to tear it to shreds.

Then she noticed it.

Someone had ripped out the bottom half of the back page.

Why?

Dropping to her hands and knees, she began to search the tiny crack of space where the floor met the wall. She searched the entire perimeter of the room.

Nothing.

She tipped the desk and the chair upside down, ran her finger along every crevice. An old pencil fell from the desk. Nothing else.

She sat down on the floor and looked up at the ceiling. There was nothing else in this room.

Except the basketball hoops.

She lugged the table across the floor and set it under the hoop. Then she stood on the table and examined both sides of the backboard, running her fingers along the inside of the rim and through the net.

Nothing.

She pulled the table to the opposite end of the court. Nothing on that backboard either. She examined the hoop.

Nothing.

She ran her fingers over the net. Then she felt it. Something lumpy inside the net itself. She unhooked it from the rim and took it down.

Part of the net appeared frayed. It looked like someone had poked a hole in the net and shoved something inside.

She grabbed the pencil. Exactly the same size as the hole.

Wiggling the pencil, she made the hole larger, then ripped the rest of the piping open with her teeth. When the opening became big enough, she pulled out the object someone had shoved deep inside.

Paper. A tiny, tight scroll of paper.

Slowly she unrolled it, smoothing it over her thigh. Tiny handwriting floated in the margins of the page ripped from the bottom of the instruction manual.

She scanned the first line.

"I wanted to name the baby after Wyatt. He found out, and now he's killing me."

Chapter Thirty-Six

NIKKI

Nikki stood on a chair trying to reach a scrap of paper on the top shelf in the bedroom closet. She'd found it difficult to make a convincing show of "inspecting pillowcases," but as far as she could tell, she'd managed to search the first floor and bedrooms in the main house without arousing suspicion.

She'd found nothing, but as she'd glanced out an upper-story window, she'd noticed the guest house nestled in a stand of weeping willows at the far edge of the property.

The trailing branches swayed in the October wind, obscuring and revealing windows as they fluttered in the breeze.

After sneaking out of the main house, Nikki dashed across the lawn and tried the front door.

Locked.

She went around the side and tried the sliding glass door on the backside of the house.

Bingo.

It opened without a sound. She stepped inside and glanced around.

Holy hell.

Only a little smaller than her own *primary* home, the guest house featured blue-and-white furniture with a coastal aesthetic and a wall of windows framing a lovely view of the Chesapeake. The whole thing looked very *Kenneth*.

She'd tiptoed around the main floor, opening desk drawers and cupboards and peeking inside decorative boxes and porcelain vases.

Nothing.

She'd entered the only bedroom and opened the closet, where she'd spotted the crumpled scrap of paper. Boosting herself up with a chair, she'd tried to reach it.

Too far back.

Now, with a groan, she stretched her arm just a little farther and finally managed to grasp the paper with the tips of her fingers. Pulling it toward her, she coughed a little as she kicked up a layer of long-undisturbed dust.

This better be worth it. She sneezed again, then unfolded the paper.

Her heart sank as she gazed down at a receipt for a $653 pair of shoes. No wonder someone had hidden it in the back of the closet.

She wiped her dusty hands on her jeans and surveyed the room from her perch atop the chair. A four-poster bed with an elegant bench at the foot. A chaise longue with a reading lamp. Mountains of throw pillows. More windows and another stunning view. Otherwise, nothing.

Nothing. Nothing. Nothing.

This is hopeless. Like looking for a needle in a haystack, except they didn't even know what the needle looked like or where to find the haystack.

She gripped the back of the chair, momentarily distracted by the view. It must be lovely to stay in a place like this. Guests would wake to the sun rising over the water, with a lighthouse in the far distance and an osprey nest closer by. She could see the mother bird and her chicks nestled into a giant bundle of sticks atop a channel marker.

She squinted at the window as a sense of déjà vu tickled her mind.

Osprey nest. Lighthouse.

Suddenly, the bedroom door flew open. Heart pounding, Nikki whirled around, lost her balance, and gripped the shelf.

Ainsley rushed into the room and closed the door behind her.

"You *scared* me," Nikki hissed, heart pounding.

"We have to go." Ainsley tugged at her hand.

Nikki climbed down and pointed out the window. "Ainsley, *look*."

Recognition stole across Ainsley's pale face. She sat down heavily on the bed. "Harmonee's view."

Silence fell across the room as they gazed at the water, lost in thought.

"She left a note," Ainsley said, breaking the silence. Her voice had a strangled quality, like she was trying not to cry. She pulled a tiny scroll from the front of her smock and handed it to Nikki. Then she buried her face in her hands. "I can't read any more. You do it."

Nikki sat down beside her, carefully unrolled the scrap of paper, and began to read aloud. *"I wanted to name the baby after Wyatt. He found out, and now he's killing me."*

She stopped as the words bore into her mind and body. No. Not *this*. This fairy tale where the princess eats the poison apple, and the prince never arrives for the restorative kiss. Where no one arrives, and she sleeps on, for eternity.

"Keep going," Ainsley commanded in a wooden voice.

Nikki ran her tongue over her lips and continued. *"He wasn't mad when he found me, which surprised me. He invited me to come inside and said he wanted to show me the basketball court. I'd seen it before, lots of times. But he said he wanted to show me something special, something I hadn't seen before. Like a dummy, I followed him. Left my purse and phone and wallet in the guest house. Wandered after him in my flannel pajama bottoms and my sweatshirt and flip-flops.*

"He turned on the lights and went into the gym. He pointed to the far end and said, 'It's down there, on the back of the hoop. Go take a look.'

"I took two steps, and then I knew. I knew as soon as I heard the door slam behind me.

"I never should have told him about the baby. I never should have let him find me here. I should have hidden the minute I heard his car pull into

the driveway. That was my first mistake. Actually, that was my 12th or 37th or 734th mistake. My whole life is a mistake. I guess it makes sense that my death will look like a mistake too. No mess, no blood, no weapon. Just silence and a locked room and my body slowly shrinking until I disappear.

"I'm so tired now and it's hard to think straight. There's no food in here. No water. No windows. Just these awful fluorescent lights. I have no idea how long I've been here. 10 days or 10 weeks? I don't know anymore. I sleep a lot now. I don't have the energy to do anything else, not that there's anything else to do in a locked and empty room. That asshole didn't even leave me a basketball.

"I don't feel sorry for myself. But I do feel sorry for the baby. I'm sorry, little embryo baby. I think that's what you are right now. We learned about it in AP bio. Or maybe you're a zygote? Or a gamete? I don't remember, but I'm sorry.

"I think I would have been a good mother, like my mom. All those hours she spent pushing me on the swings, all those extra shifts she worked at the club to buy me art supplies, the way she sang songs and told me stories at night when we snuggled in bed and turned the heat down low to save money.

"She loved me so much, even with all her issues. And even though I hate the father, I would have loved my baby just as much as she loved me.

"I don't have the energy to say more. I don't even know what I'm saying. Or who I'm saying it to. But I'm going to hide this in a place where he can't find it. It will take all the energy I have left, and then I'll lay down and go to sleep. I won't wake up and that's okay. I'm not afraid of what comes next. The angels are here now, and they tell me it's beautiful. Like climbing inside the most beautiful painting I've ever seen, except this time I don't have to climb back out."

Silence settled over the room as Nikki watched a lone sailboat tack through the gray waves beyond the point. Ainsley reached for Nikki's hand, and Nikki pulled her close.

"He killed her," Ainsley whispered, resting her head on Nikki's shoulder.

"That's why there was no sign of foul play." Nikki's voice felt rusty when she finally spoke. "He locked her in a room and let her starve and die of dehydration."

"Because she was fifteen years old and pregnant with his child. And he was over thirty."

"Statutory rape." Nikki shuddered. Her niece was only a year younger than Harmonee had been. Shelby still slept with a teddy bear and begged to go out for ice cream, still called out "Hey, Mom, watch this" while doing handstands in the pool.

"He'd have gone to jail," Ainsley said in a dull voice.

"Ending his career."

Ainsley squeezed her hand so tight it hurt. "So he killed her."

From outside the house, voices sounded. They peeped cautiously through a window beside the front door, watching as the cleaning ladies loaded their car.

"We need to leave before they start asking if we have a key and a plan to lock up," Ainsley said.

When the women went back inside the main house to fetch the rest of their cleaning gear, they darted out the door and jumped in the minivan.

Nikki patted down her pockets. "Oh no."

She began to dig frantically through her purse. "I can't find my —"

"Keys?" Ainsley pulled a large key fob from her pocket. "You left them in the guest house. Now let's *go*."

Nikki gunned the engine. Tires spinning, they took off, leaving the site of Harmonee's last breath.

Chapter Thirty-Seven

NIKKI

They drove directly to Detective Chavez. They gave her the note and the sketches from the art teacher and told her what they'd learned from Lady Godiva and everyone else they'd spoken to. Detective Chavez promised to question Wyatt Jericho and, if possible, seek a warrant for his arrest. And she promised an update when she had more information.

Before heading home, they stopped to see Lady Godiva, who delivered some bad news.

"I did some digging," she said after taking a long drag on her cigarette. "I got no credit card receipts from Wyatt Jericho. I do got receipts from someone named Walter Jelico. But it's a company credit card, not a personal one, for a company called BS Unlimited."

Nikki raised an eyebrow. "Sounds appropriate."

She gave them a shoebox filled with paper. "I'm sorry I don't got more, but I'll keep my ear to the ground."

Then they collected their children from Jolene, fed them, and put them to bed. Now it was after 8:00 p.m., and Nikki was back at Ainsley's house, slumped across the mohair sofa, every bone and muscle in her body exhausted.

Bedtime had been a nightmare. No one wanted to sleep because it had been such an exciting day, thanks to Jolene.

"Is Miss Jolene a Transformer?" Daniel had asked when Nikki tucked him into bed. He then made a series of stiff-arm movements with *ch-ch-ch* sound effects to demonstrate how it looked and sounded when a mild-mannered tax attorney transformed into an alien robot sent to Earth to seek vengeance on behalf of mistreated mothers in school carpool lines.

Everything had gone so well, at first. Jolene had arrived for preschool pickup at the appointed time. But she then brought the entire process to a standstill by informing the preschool director that her ten-minute pickup window was the logistic equivalent of expecting mothers to land an airplane on an aircraft carrier in the middle of a hurricane.

The preschool director, a woman accustomed to being obeyed by three-year-olds and everyone else, did not appreciate this and told Jolene so. The situation deteriorated from there.

Something similar occurred in the afternoon when Jolene went to St. Preston's to pick up the girls from kindergarten. Despite the detailed maps and the instructions and the dire warnings, Jolene *did* make a wrong turn and accidentally cut through the alley behind the dry cleaner's, thereby putting herself ahead of mothers who had been waiting in line for twenty-five minutes.

When one of the dreaded lacrosse moms emerged from a giant black SUV to challenge her, Jolene looked her squarely in the eye, admitted to making a mistake, and then dared the mother to "come over here and do something about it."

The woman got meekly back into her car, and pickup proceeded without further incident.

Now they sat together in Ainsley's family room waiting for an update from Detective Chavez while Jolene looked through the box of receipts from Lady Godiva and recounted her day as the Joan of Arc of the carpool line.

"I wish I could have seen it." Nikki shot a wistful look at Ainsley, who sat across from her clutching what looked like a glass of muddy swamp water. Each woman was dealing with the stress of today's revelations in her own way. Nikki ripped the foil wrapper from her second Dark Chocolate Silken Abyss Bradley Bar, Jolene had turned to hard liquor, and Ainsley sucked on a superantioxidant kale, carrot, and blueberry smoothie. "Do you think anyone recorded it?"

"You're a folk hero now." Ainsley raised her smoothie in salute. "You are the William Wallace of the St. Preston's carpool line."

"We should put up a statue," Nikki suggested, popping another square of dark chocolate into her mouth. "Or erect a teeter-totter in your name."

Jolene grinned and knocked back her glass of scotch. "I am Thelma *and* Louise. But I don't know how you guys do that every day. I mean, how do you get anything done?"

"We *don't* get anything done." Nikki gave a resigned shrug. "We drop them off at preschool, run to the grocery store, buy a few bananas, and then run back to preschool pickup. Then we put everyone down for a nap, wake them up, and then go to kindergarten pickup. It's impossible to accomplish anything."

"Except today." Ainsley's voice had a hoarse, raspy quality, probably because she'd been crying on and off all afternoon. "We accomplished something important today."

"And I accomplished a job interview with Channel Four." Nikki popped a celebratory square of chocolate into her mouth. The news director had left a message on her cell phone while she and Ainsley pretended to be house cleaners, inviting her in for an interview.

She grabbed a third chocolate bar, because dark chocolate was, after all, a *health* food, and pointed it at Ainsley's phone, which sat like a sacred talisman in the center of the coffee table. "Anything new?"

Ainsley picked it up, checked her text messages and her voicemail. "Not since we last checked seven minutes ago."

"I have to leave at eight fifteen to pick up Shelby from basketball practice," Nikki reminded them. "I can't wait much longer."

“Maybe you’ll get to see him led away from the school in handcuffs,” Jolene said hopefully.

“It’s eight eleven now.” Ainsley glanced at the phone. “Do you think you could stay just a few minutes longer?”

“No way.” Nikki grabbed her purse to begin the ritual hunt for her car keys. “If I’m late, Shelby will have to wait alone with Wyatt Jericho.”

Ainsley and Jolene exchanged a horrified glance as Ainsley rose from the couch. “I’ll walk you to your car.”

“I have to head out too.” Jolene grabbed Lady Godiva’s shoebox of receipts, kissed her sister’s cheek, and headed for the door. “Call me as soon as you hear from the detective.”

Nikki finally located her keys in her coat pocket as Ainsley walked her to the minivan.

“Where’s your sister tonight?” Ainsley asked. “How come you’re picking up Shelby?”

“My sister is now offering goat yoga on Tuesday nights in addition to her morning boot camps, and it’s crazy popular, and my brother-in-law can’t pick her up because his craft brew club—”

The phone rang. Detective Chavez’s name danced across the caller ID.

Ainsley took a deep breath and answered the phone.

Chapter Thirty-Eight

AINSLEY

"Can you hold on a second?" Ainsley asked Detective Chavez. Then she held the phone away from her mouth and gestured at Nikki to get in the car. "Drive," she whispered. "Emma, our nanny, is here with the kids. I'll come with you."

Ainsley resisted the urge to check for rodents as they piled into the minivan. Nikki put the car in gear and tore out of the driveway as Ainsley put her phone on speaker.

"Okay," Ainsley said. "Tell us everything."

A huge sigh emanated from the phone, and Ainsley's heart sank.

"There's no doubt in my mind the bastard's guilty," Detective Chavez began.

"But?" Ainsley asked.

"But he refused to speak to me and referred me to his lawyer. And then the DA told me to drop it."

"You're kidding," Nikki said.

"Why would he do that?" Ainsley asked, her voice rising an octave in outrage.

"Look." Another heavy sigh, followed by the crackle of a loudspeaker. "French fries please, a small Sprite, and a fish filet sandwich, with tartar sauce."

Then she continued. "Sorry. Haven't had time to eat today."

A momentary pause as Detective Chavez presumably handed her credit card through the drive-through window, followed by the crinkle of paper as an unseen person handed the detective her meal.

"Hold on. I'm pulling over," the detective said. "Give me a second."

Ainsley felt a surge of compassion. Almost eight thirty at night and Detective Chavez was still working.

Silence filled the car as the detective presumably pulled into a parking spot, followed by the sound of paper crinkling as she unwrapped her dinner.

"Our DA is actually a good guy, but he won't take a case he can't win," she said through a mouthful of food. "And he doesn't think there's enough evidence here to convict. Anyone could have written that note. It doesn't explicitly say 'My name is Harmonee Dean, and Wyatt Jericho killed me.' The case is still twenty years old with no sign of foul play. And the DA plays golf with Sebastian Hampton, the athletic director, who told him Wyatt Jericho is a stand-up guy and there's no way he could have killed anyone. In fact, they last played golf together at a charity tournament to support a domestic violence shelter *founded* by Wyatt Jericho."

Ainsley shook her head in disbelief. "No one believes us."

"I'm afraid not." More rustling paper followed by a pause to swallow. "And the DA does not want to arrest a high-profile figure like Wyatt Jericho who has the money to hire a top-notch lawyer unless he's positive he has the evidence to nail him."

"Great," Ainsley muttered, trying to contain her outrage.

"There's something else," Detective Chavez said.

Something in her tone made Ainsley want to shrink down in her seat and cover her head with her hands, as though heavy objects were about to rain down from the sky. "What?" she asked cautiously.

"I didn't use any names." More crinkling paper followed by the sound of a straw sucking empty air at the bottom of a cup. "But I obviously had to tell the DA where I got this evidence. If Jericho knows you used to work at Godiva's, he'll eventually put two and two together and figure out you're involved in this, if he hasn't already. You need to be careful. Nikki too."

Nikki chimed in from the driver's seat. "What do we do now?"

Detective Chavez sighed. "Keep digging. I'll do what I can on this end by going through cold cases. I'll talk to detectives in other jurisdictions, look into unsolved missing persons cases, runaways, accidental deaths that maybe weren't accidents. If we can find other victims connected to Jericho, it would strengthen our hand and force the DA to take another look."

Nikki pulled in to the school parking lot. "We're going to see this guy in about five minutes. Are you saying we have to pretend like everything's okay? Like we don't know he's a murderer?"

"Yes," Detective Chavez said. "You do."

Ainsley snorted. *Impossible.* Attend school functions with the man who killed Harmonee? "And if we don't?"

"Look. If we prove this, Jericho loses everything." The exhaustion in Detective Chavez's voice filled the car. "His career, his reputation, his freedom. He'll go to prison if we succeed, and he will be desperate to stop us. And desperate people . . ."

Her voice trailed off.

"Desperate people do dangerous things," Nikki said as she parked in front of the gym.

"Exactly. So be really careful. This guy has already killed once to protect his reputation and his career."

Goose bumps broke out across Ainsley's body as her mind finished the thought. *And he'll kill again if necessary.*

Chapter Thirty-Nine

AINSLEY

Sweat-drenched teenage girls in matching ponytails sprawled on the floor at the far end of the gym, making a semicircle around Wyatt Jericho. He crouched on the floor with a clipboard in his hands, his voice low and serious. Ainsley and Nikki leaned against the stage as other parents drifted in to pick up their daughters from basketball practice.

Wyatt Jericho acknowledged the waiting parents with a nod, then continued to speak to the girls. Tiffany Hastings sidled up to Ainsley and Nikki.

"He's so *intense*," she said with a little squirm of pleasure. "And they're undefeated. He's turning them into absolute *killers* on the court."

Ainsley felt the color drain from her cheeks. *If Tiffany had any idea* . . . But no one had any idea. That's why she and Nikki had to expose him.

The girls rose from the floor, gathered in a circle, put their hands together, and yelled "Spartans" in unison.

So young, Ainsley thought, with their jaunty ponytails and thin shoulders.

Her heart ached as they drifted toward their waiting parents. She wanted to gather them into her arms and pour a lifetime of experience into their minds, to protect them from their own unlined faces and yearning to be loved.

Shelby's face lit up as she spotted her aunt. She sauntered toward them and gave Ainsley a shy smile before turning to Nikki. "I gotta grab my atom project from my locker, and it's kinda big. Can you help me carry it?"

Nikki shot Ainsley a questioning look, and Ainsley resisted the urge to roll her eyes. Wyatt Jericho wasn't going to murder her in the school gym surrounded by other parents.

"I'll wait here," Ainsley said.

She turned to Tiffany Hastings, who introduced her daughter, Skylar, a gangly girl with long legs and a surprisingly sweet demeanor. The girl obviously took after her father.

"Mom . . . I have a test tomorrow." Tiffany's daughter tugged on her mother's hand. "Can we go?"

"Of course, darling. You must be *exhausted*." Tiffany waved goodbye as her daughter led her away.

Other families left the gym as Ainsley waited. She glanced around. A prickle of unease brushed her spine as she turned in a half circle and found the gym empty. Her gaze darted from the hoops to the scoreboard to the bleachers, searching for the exit to the parking lot.

Suddenly a series of loud clicks echoed through the cavernous space as an unseen hand turned off the giant fluorescent bulbs overhead. Each click extinguished a swath of light, plunging her into gray half light, then semidarkness.

On the far side of the gym, light glimmered through the glass panels embedded in the heavy metal doors. A sick taste coated the back of her throat.

Just go.

She took a step forward.

A warm breath brushed her neck as a male voice whispered, "Afraid of the dark?"

Chapter Forty

AINSLEY

She stood paralyzed, blinded by sudden darkness, deafened by the heartbeat pounding in her ears, her throat so dry she couldn't utter a sound.

Get away. Get away. Get away.

She lunged forward, desperate to reach the light. A stabbing pain shot up her shoulder as someone grabbed her arm, wrenching her back.

"Everyone's gone." Wyatt Jericho's voice came in an intimate whisper, raising the hairs on the back of her neck. "We're all alone."

Alone in the gym with Wyatt Jericho.

Just like Harmonee.

Her eyes adjusted to the dim light as he took shape beside her. Square jaw, a flash of white teeth, his eyes a wet gleam in the darkness.

"It's closing time." He tightened his grip on her arm, pulling her close. "Like at the club, where you hung up your G-string and went home for the night. Or went home *with* someone for the night."

Heat flashed through her body, anger temporarily displacing fear. *This again.*

The guys at the club always thought dancers wanted to go with them at the end of the night. *What time does your shift end, gorgeous? Come party at my place when the club closes. I know you want me. I'll be waiting in the parking lot.*

Delusional bastards.

Did some dancers sleep with customers? Yes, but she could count those girls on one hand. After an eight-hour shift in six-inch heels, most dancers just wanted cold cash, a hot shower, and sleep. That's it.

"I didn't do that." Her voice was steady. It was a relief to finally have this conversation, to stop guessing about what he knew or didn't know.

"Really? You're sure you didn't do more than dance?" He spoke softly with an undertone of menace, verbal stairs descending to an unlit basement. "Because lots of girls did. Still do."

She felt her lip curl. "The fact that you know so much about it makes you unfit to coach."

"*I'm* unfit?" He spread his fingers across his chest, looking truly offended. "I remained clothed the entire time I was in the club. You, on the other hand—"

"I'm not discussing this with you." She spun around, breaking his grip.

He yanked her arm again, wrenching it behind her back. Pain shot up her shoulder, into her neck, forcing her into stillness.

"Actually, you are discussing this with me." He pressed his cheek against hers, his sandpaper stubble scraping her skin while the spice of his aftershave filled her nostrils. "Because if you don't, I'm going to discuss it with the Associated Press, the *New York Times*, and the *Washington Post*. Basically, with anyone who is interested. And trust me, *everyone* will be interested."

Don't touch me. Don't touch me. Don't touch me.

Memories flooded her mind, making her dizzy with the past. The greedy hands and sly fingers. The furtive swipe across her backside and the look of innocence when she turned to glare at the offending customers, like a pack of naughty schoolboys, triumphant at breaking the rules.

The words imprisoned in her mind finally escaped through her clenched teeth, into the open air. "Don't touch me."

He laughed softly, and her hands balled into fists. She wanted to kill him.

"You're not in the club anymore," he whispered. "Lady Godiva's bouncers aren't here to enforce the rules. I can touch anything I want."

Something wet touched her neck, creating a cold trail across her skin. Her mind went blank for a moment; then a shudder of revulsion rocked her body as he ran his wet tongue down the side of her neck.

Lady Velvet whispered from the past. *Scratch him.*

She raised her free hand and raked her manicured nails down the side of his cheek.

"You bitch," he cried out, his voice pitched high in surprise, and shoved her away. She stumbled but did not fall.

He stared at her in shock, one hand pressed to his cheek. Then he picked up the duffel bag at his feet and unzipped it. He removed something from the bag. "Look what I've got."

Her heart stopped as he held up the picture that had hung on the wall at Lady Godiva's. The picture with Lou Leffner, the night Godiva's won the Heritage Club Award. The picture of all the dancers, including her, in her skimpy Sexy Sheriff costume.

A jumble of incoherent thoughts ransacked her mind. *Lady Godiva is going to kill him for stealing that picture. Girls are so mean; they won't invite Grace to sleepovers. They'll make fun of Adam. No one will vote for Ben. He'll divorce me. He'll take the kids. And I'll deserve it because I'm a liar.*

With great effort, she shut down these thoughts. *Focus on Jericho.*

She managed a shrug. "Nobody cares. It's not a big deal anymore."

"True," he conceded with a nod. "Some people won't care. But all those senior citizens your husband needs to get elected? They'll care. And stripping is just the tip of the iceberg. Wait till they find out you were a prostitute."

She gasped. "But I wasn't—"

"Doesn't matter," he said, shaking his head in mock sadness. "I can *prove* you were a stripper. And when they find out you did that, they'll believe everything else I tell them. Maybe you were also a recreational drug user. Probably cocaine. Maybe heroin."

"I never touched drugs." Her voice was incredulous. She didn't even really *drink*.

"Or maybe you *sold* drugs, in addition to prostitution. There's also straight-up porn, of course. Maybe you made movies."

"I never—" She felt like she'd tumbled into one of those nightmares where someone was chasing her, but she couldn't move, couldn't run away, because her feet were stuck to the ground.

"You'd be amazed at how much you can do with the right editing software."

Dear God. She'd read an article about this. Revenge porn. Deepfakes. The end of truth. She held up her hand. "Stop."

"Remember *Debbie Does Dallas*? That old porn classic?"

"Just *stop*." The truth she'd hidden for so many years would now be suffocated under an avalanche of lies.

"Maybe we need an updated version. We'll call it *Ainsley Does Anaheim*. Or Atlanta. Or Annapolis. Maybe that's better, 'cause it's *local*."

She opened her mouth, then closed it again. There was nothing to say. Wyatt Jericho had won. And she'd lost. *Because no one believes a stripper.*

He could prove she'd danced topless at Godiva's, and that made any rumor he wanted to spread, any salacious story he wanted to tell, plausible—even believable. Because if she'd hidden that one little fact all these years, she could be hiding anything.

If she'd been completely open about it from the start, if she'd given pole dancing lessons in her basement, no one would have cared. But keeping it a secret gave her stint as a dancer a weight and proportion beyond the act itself. Hiding the truth about her past endowed it with magnetic powers capable of attracting darker lies and even dirtier secrets. She could see that *now*. If only she could have seen it a decade ago, when she first met Ben.

"What do you want?" she asked miserably.

"A million dollars and an end to this crusade you have going with Detective Chavez."

"A million dollars," she repeated, numb.

"That's right." He said this casually, as though confirming a take-out order. "I want a one-million-dollar donation from the Bradley Foundation to Camp Confidence, my summer camp for teen girls. I want you and your husband to present me with one of those big card-board checks at a press conference, with reporters and photographers. I want the whole world to know that you and your husband think I'm a fantastic guy."

"When in reality you're a blackmailer and the man who murdered Harmonee Dean."

His face turned white, and he grabbed her arm again. "I never touched that girl."

"We found a note. She was murdered."

He dropped her arm and took a step back. "That's crazy. Why would anyone kill Harmonee?"

"Because she was pregnant and underage, and her baby would send you to jail and end your career."

"I never touched her," he said again. "I *helped* her. I cared about Harmonee."

"You had a funny way of showing it."

"Fine." The angry lines around his mouth deepened. "If you're going to tell lies about me, then I have some whoppers I can tell about you. And unfortunately for you, stories about a stripper who's been lying about her past are much more believable than lies about a beloved basketball coach and supporter of girls and battered women."

"And if we don't stop?"

He held up the photo. "Then I give this picture to the Associated Press and every major news outlet in the country, and I tell them every-thing I know about you, along with a whole bunch of things I don't, just to add color. Do you understand?"

"And I'll tell them everything I know about you," she shot back.

He gave her a patronizing smile. "And what is that exactly?"

"I'll tell about your predilection for strip clubs and underage girls, and about Harmonee."

"And you'll prove this how?" he asked with mocking politeness.

She said nothing. Because she had nothing to say. He was right. They had no proof. No evidence.

He looked smug. "If you so much as utter my name, I'll sue you for slander and defamation of character. I'll tell them you're a crazy former prostitute and stripper and a porn star with a drug problem who grew up in a trailer park and married for money."

She gasped. "How do you know where I come from?"

"Harmonee told me. Years ago," he said. "She told me how nice you and the other girls were, and how you grew up together. She said you and the other girls warned her to stay away from me, but she knew I was a good guy. She knew she could trust me."

Her mouth twisted in disgust. "You're sick."

"And you're trash. And if I don't get a check for one million dollars, everyone else will know it too."

"Blackmail." She spit out the word, her voice thick with contempt. "You must be so proud of yourself."

"What you're doing is worse." He pointed a bony index finger at her chest. "You're telling lies about me and I can't even *pay* you to stop. I never murdered anyone, much less Harmonee Dean. I did everything in my power to help that girl. And If you try to take me down, I'll take you and your husband down with me."

She held his gaze in the semidarkness. She'd never hated any human being as much as she hated this man.

"Do you understand me?" he asked.

"Oh yes. I understand you."

"Good," he said. "You have ten days to make this happen, starting at midnight. If I don't hear from you by noon on day ten, the picture goes out, along with the sickest, craziest stripper stories I can make up. And I assure you, I can make up some pretty sick shit."

“I’m sure you can,” she said bitterly.

He zipped the picture into his bag and slung it over his shoulder. “I look forward to speaking with you soon.”

His words sounded surreal and incongruous, as though they were ending a successful job interview. Then he strode away, leaving her shaking in the darkness.

Chapter Forty-One

AINSLEY

She sat in the back seat of Nikki's minivan, completely numb, unable to think, much less speak. Up front in the passenger seat, Shelby texted someone, thumbs moving furiously, face lit with a sly smile. Probably discussing a crush or a math test with Tiffany's daughter.

A math test. She'd give anything to have such mundane worries, to rewind to the start of the school year, when wearing the right outfit to the Kindergarten Jamboree seemed vitally important.

Now the absolute worst thing that *could* happen *would* happen, and instead of crying, she found herself resisting the urge to laugh.

Dancing topless versus prostitution, porn, and drugs. She'd thought the truth would shock people, so she'd hidden it. Now Wyatt Jericho's lies would be so much worse than the truth could ever be.

She stared out the window at the passing night. What a fool she'd been. She'd created this mess, and Ben and her kids would suffer the consequences. She glanced down at her purse, at the wallet crammed with credit cards. Maybe she should pay Wyatt Jericho to stay quiet.

She had money of her own. Ben had insisted on that when they got married.

"It's mad money," he'd said as he scribbled away at some papers scattered across the big mahogany desk in his home office.

She sat across from him on the velvet Chesterfield sofa, where she'd curled up with a cup of tea and *Persuasion*, her favorite Jane Austen novel. She'd come to read and keep him company while he caught up on post-honeymoon emails.

He held up a document displaying the amount he planned to deposit into her new account. She almost dropped her tea when she saw the zeroes dancing across the paper. "Ben. *No.*"

"What if you want to buy yourself a nice pair of earrings?" he asked, leaning back in his leather desk chair. "Or a painting you really love but I think is ugly?" He gestured toward the open book in her lap. "Or some weird Jane Austen memorabilia?"

"Three million dollars?" The amount looked crazy on paper and sounded even more insane when she said it out loud.

"I want you to have this," he said, his tone serious now. "It's important to me."

Everything about their relationship with money came out backward. She'd argued *for* a prenup, just to make his mother happy, and he'd adamantly refused because he said it seeded doubt about their commitment before they even said their vows.

And now this.

"I don't want you to feel like you have to ask me for things." He shuffled the papers into a neat pile. "This money is *your* money. Not ours. You don't have to justify it or ask permission."

"But Ben. *Three million dollars?*"

"Say yes or I'll make it four."

She searched his face and found the determined expression he always wore when he considered something a matter of principle, like contesting DC parking tickets handed out by aggressive meter readers when the sign clearly designated a spot as legal.

"No." She closed her book with a decisive thump. "I can't let you do this."

"Please, Ainsley. Let me give you this."

The set of his jaw broadcast his stubbornness, and she knew it was hopeless. He wouldn't give in, no matter how long she argued.

"Fine." She raised her hands in surrender. "I guess if you drink your paycheck away, I'll have enough money to pay the utility bill, but I still think this is . . . *rich-person weird* . . . and completely unnecessary."

Ainsley had coined the phrase *rich-person weird* when she first understood how much money Ben actually had and became his emissary from the land of people with student loans, a mortgage, and cars they couldn't afford to repair.

Having not just a private plane but a *favorite* private plane? Rich-person weird. His great-aunt's practice of cloning her dogs? Rich-person weird. Standing at the airport magazine kiosk and seeing your mother-in-law's pool house featured on the front cover of *House Beautiful*? Rich-person weird.

"I don't want our marriage to feel unbalanced." He came over and sat beside her on the sofa. "I've seen wealthy men and women use money to control their spouses. And I don't ever want you to feel like you have to stay with me because you can't afford to leave."

"Leave?" Her mind stuttered at the very idea. *How* could she . . . ? *Why* would she . . . ? She'd rather leave her own arms and legs, would rather leave her own head and body behind, than leave Ben.

She felt frustrated sometimes because as an economist, a numbers person, she couldn't *express* how much she loved this man.

I love you more than a thousand consecutive quarters of double-digit GDP. She'd given him a card that said that once, on Valentine's Day, as a joke. But it still didn't come anywhere close to expressing how she really felt. He was the contentment and happiness she hadn't felt since her father died. She'd found her home inside Ben's soul.

"Why would I ever want to leave?" she whispered, blinking back tears.

"I don't know. Because I leave my socks on the floor?" He stroked her cheek with his thumb. "Or because I'm a terrible singer?"

"And you think the socks and the singing will become more than I can possibly endure, and I'll *leave*?"

"I just . . . I want you to be happy. That's all." He threaded his fingers between hers, and her heart expanded and grew soft, like something on a vine, ripening in the heat and light of the sun.

Ben's love was grace. Undeserved. Unearned. She could only hope to return it as generously as he gave it.

"I want to give you money, security, peace of mind," he said. "All the things you didn't have growing up."

She almost told him then, about her job at Godiva's. But she didn't, because the words *peace of mind* lingered in her ears with a sinister echo.

Would it bother him to know she'd hidden this information since the day they'd met two years earlier? That she'd kept it from him during the days of their engagement and the long, sweet nights of the honeymoon? Would it eat away at him, making him question other things she'd said, or didn't say?

She should have told him when they'd started dating. The right moment had come and gone on their second or third date, at some restaurant she could no longer remember, or in some movie theater while they shared a bucket of popcorn.

She'd missed her window, transforming her past from a fact into a glaring lie of omission.

"Fine. You can open this account if you want, but I only need one thing." She pulled him close. "And it isn't money."

He brushed her lips with a lingering kiss. "A private island?"

"No."

He nuzzled the soft spot behind her ear. "A yacht with solid-gold toilet seats?"

"No."

"A lifetime supply of Birkin bags?" he asked as he laid a trail of kisses down the side of her neck.

She closed her eyes as his mouth moved lower. "All I need is you."

The account did come in handy when she needed to make clandestine purchases for Ben. She used it to buy his birthday and Christmas gifts. It financed the surprise party she threw on his fortieth birthday and the weeklong getaways she planned for them each year without the kids. They always returned from these trips a little more in love than when they'd left, reminded of why they'd chosen each other in the first place.

Thanks to this account, she could pay Wyatt Jericho a million dollars, and Ben would never know. The press conference was a problem, but maybe she could talk Jericho into a discreet wire transfer from her own account.

Then the words from Harmonee's note filled her mind.

No mess, no blood, no weapon. Just silence and a locked room and my body slowly shrinking until I disappear.

Could she really just pay the hush money and sweep the whole thing under the rug? Allow Harmonee's death to remain the quiet accident everyone assumed it was?

Until it happened again.

Nikki pulled into her niece's driveway and Shelby got out of the car, then staggered up the front steps under the weight of her book bag, her basketball, and the unwieldy collection of Styrofoam balls that made up her atom project.

Maybe it already had . . . maybe he was having a relationship with Shelby or Tiffany Hastings's daughter, and then . . .

Shelby opened her front door and waved goodbye to Nikki.

Another girl dies to protect Wyatt Jericho.

Shelby disappeared into the house, and Ainsley moved up front to the passenger seat. Autumn leaves tumbled across the road as the minivan sped down the street. For so long, Ainsley had felt like those leaves, pushed and pulled by forces beyond her control.

But not anymore.

She couldn't let Wyatt Jericho prey on girls like Shelby. And she couldn't let him destroy her marriage, her husband, her family.

All this time, the solution had hovered before her eyes, blinking and flashing like an obnoxious children's toy. But she'd refused to look at it, refused to even contemplate it.

Now the time had come.

No more living in darkness. Time to step into the light.

Chapter Forty-Two

NIKKI

The minivan's tires crunched across the gravel courtyard as Nikki pulled up to Ainsley's vast white home.

"You okay?" Nikki asked. The veranda's flickering gas lanterns cast strange shadows across Ainsley's face.

"Can you come inside?" Ainsley asked.

A queasy feeling rose in Nikki's gut. Ainsley hadn't said a word since they'd left the school.

She parked the car and followed Ainsley into the quiet house.

"Where is everyone?" Nikki asked.

She heard no evidence of the crying baby, the I'm-not-tired, just-one-more-story, why-do-I-have-to-take-a-bath, but-I-brushed-my-teeth-yesterday soundtrack that played on an endless loop in her own home starting at approximately seven o'clock each evening.

"The kids are asleep. Ben's campaigning. The nanny's in bed. She has an early class on Wednesday mornings."

Ainsley's voice had an odd, robotic quality, and Nikki shot her a sharp glance. She grew even more alarmed when instead of going to the hall closet to hang up her coat, Ainsley kicked off her shoes and dropped her purse and coat *on the floor*.

Nikki did this every day because she did not have a "landing station" in her foyer as advised by all the best magazines.

But for *Ainsley* to do this . . . she peered at her friend, who looked unusually pale.

Ainsley entered the kitchen, where, instead of offering Nikki a beverage, like a good hostess, she sank into one of Josh's wooden chairs, slumped forward, and buried her head in her arms.

Nikki knelt beside the chair and rested a tentative hand on Ainsley's shoulder. "What's wrong?"

"Get the vodka," Ainsley muttered in a barely audible whisper from behind her barricaded limbs.

Nikki froze as a series of bizarre scenarios ran through her mind. Had she and Ainsley somehow traded *personalities*? Could they be the victims of some kind of supernatural *Freaky Friday*–style *incident*?

She found a bottle and glasses in the fully stocked bar in the butler's pantry off the dining room.

Ainsley splashed vodka into the tumbler and downed the contents in one gulp. Then she wiped the back of her hand across her mouth and *belched*.

Nikki stared in horror. *Holy hell.*

With slow, careful movements, as though dealing with a fawn, or some similar, skittish woodland creature, Nikki slid into the chair beside Ainsley at the kitchen table.

"You can talk to me, Ainsley. About anything. You know that, right?"

Ainsley raised her ravaged face. Then she nodded.

"But I can't help you if I don't know what's going on," Nikki continued gently.

A look of dawning recognition spread across Ainsley's pale face. "That's it."

"What is?"

"What you just said." Ainsley blinked earnestly. "That's the key."

"The key to . . . what?" Nikki tilted her head like a dog trying to understand human speech.

"To everything."

"Ainsley." She called up reserves of stamina that had not been replenished since last night, when she'd spent two hours standing beside the crib, jiggling her leg and making whooshing noises until the baby fell asleep. "I have absolutely no idea what you're talking about right now."

Ainsley looked at her with great weariness, as though being called upon to explain string theory to a llama.

"People can only *help* if they know what's going *on*." She spoke slowly, enunciating each word with elaborate patience.

"Help with what?"

"With everything."

Nikki inhaled deeply and looked up at the ceiling, where she hoped to find some extra patience taped to the chandelier.

"Maybe you should start at the beginning," she suggested.

Ainsley nodded gravely. "That's a good idea."

She poured more vodka, gulped it down, and slammed the empty tumbler on the table. Then she cocked an eyebrow and gazed past Nikki with a thousand-yard stare.

"Wyatt Jericho is going to tell everyone I'm a drug-dealing porn star prostitute if I don't pay him a million dollars in hush money at a press conference with Ben and a big check made out of cardboard."

Nikki frowned in concentration, trying to follow this torrent of words.

"Then he licked me. With his tongue. And grabbed me. With his hands." She pushed up her sleeve to reveal bruises shaped like fingers.

Nikki's stomach twisted. "Come here," she whispered.

She pulled Ainsley into a tight embrace. Ainsley began to heave with huge, convulsive sobs as Nikki stroked her hair.

That bastard.

This was one game Wyatt Jericho would not win.

Chapter Forty-Three

AINSLEY

They sat like that for a long time, swaying together as Ainsley cried and Nikki held her. Eventually, Ainsley's sobs subsided, and she pulled away, wiping her eyes with the hem of her shirt. She rose from her chair and returned with a box of tissues, two mugs of tea, and an uncut red velvet cake with cream cheese frosting and two forks.

"Here." She handed Nikki a fork.

"Do you just keep whole cakes lying around your house in case of emergencies?"

"Our chef makes them. Ben likes dessert."

"Aren't we going to cut it?" Nikki asked hesitantly.

"No." Ainsley stuck her fork into the cake and pulled off a clump of red velvet and cream cheese frosting.

"Works for me." Nikki took a bite and moaned. "Oh, how I love cream cheese frosting."

"Okay." Ainsley put her mug down on the table with a decisive clink. "What should I do?"

"You mean what should *we* do," Nikki corrected.

Ainsley smiled for the first time since she'd entered the house. "I can't believe I didn't always know you."

"I feel the same way," Nikki mumbled, her mouth full of cake.

"So, what do *we* do?" Ainsley asked.

"Run through the whole conversation again, in detail."

Ainsley repeated everything Jericho had said. Then she took a deep breath and announced, "I want to tell Ben everything."

She'd known the moment she'd heard her husband's name on Jericho's lips. It sounded like a desecration, a curse from the lips of the unclean.

She'd always thought of Ben as her best friend, yet she'd somehow convinced herself it was okay for her sister, and Nikki, and a dirtball like Wyatt Jericho to know things that her best friend did not. She'd been unfaithful in a sense, by failing to trust him with the truth.

"I'm not paying that bastard a single penny."

"Good." Nikki jabbed her fork into the cake. "Paying him is a terrible option, no matter how you do it. If the Bradley Foundation writes him a check, it's like your husband is endorsing him. It forever links him to Wyatt Jericho financially. Even if you paid him privately, he could claim you or your husband are business partners or investors. He would drag you guys into any sordid messes he creates in the future, or any murders we dig up in his past."

"Basically, we'd pay *him* a million dollars, and he'd silence *us* forever."

"Right," Nikki said. "He's a clever bastard."

"Plus, it's wrong. And involving Ben . . ." She shuddered. "The idea of Ben and Wyatt Jericho in the same room together, much less holding up a check at a press conference . . . it's just repugnant."

"But it would be possible to pay Jericho without Ben knowing?" Nikki asked.

"Well, yes." Ainsley toyed with a clump of frosting. "I could pay him myself. I have my own money, and Ben wouldn't need to know."

"Would you be comfortable doing that?"

Ainsley shook her head. "I might have been. Until I saw those girls tonight. Your niece. And Tiffany Hastings's daughter."

"I know," Nikki said soberly. "It was jarring, seeing him with those girls."

Ainsley nodded. "If I paid him off, he'd keep coaching, and even if he left St. Preston's, he could still get a coaching job somewhere else. If we keep the payment hidden, we keep his *behavior* hidden. We have to expose him publicly, so he never coaches again."

"But if you refuse to pay him, he'll twist the truth into a thousand lies, and the media will *savage* you. I've seen it, Ainsley. They won't be able to resist his stories about the porn star room parent."

Ainsley's stomach clenched. But even if the worst happened, she'd still be alive, and Harmonee would still be dead.

"He's a *murderer*, Nikki. And a sick, twisted person. He's with those girls *every day*. I love my husband and my children more than life itself, but if something happened to Shelby or Tiffany's daughter, or any of those girls, I'd never forgive myself. I have to tell the truth about Wyatt Jericho. And that means telling the truth about myself."

Nikki rested her chin on her hand, deep in thought. "You know, there might be a way to neutralize his lies."

"How?"

"Have you ever noticed how people planning to run for president always release an incredibly boring book called *My Vision for America*, or something like that, before they run? Because on page one forty-seven, there's always some revelation they want to get out there first, on their own terms, about how they spent their sophomore year of high school smoking pot, or they were arrested for shoplifting in eighth grade. It's always better to deliver your own bad news, on your terms, with your own timing."

"You want me to write a book?" Ainsley asked, confused.

"No, we skip the book part." Nikki waved her fork dismissively. "But we tell your story proactively. We get it out there first, on your terms. That makes any lies he tells later less believable. Then we go to the school and tell them he's blackmailing you, and why he's blackmailing you. That should be enough to get him fired, and we at least keep

Shelby and the girls at school safe. In the meantime, we keep working with Detective Chavez to find the evidence we need to put him behind bars for good."

Ainsley grabbed Nikki's hand. "Your job interview. When is it?"

"The day after tomorrow at three p.m."

Ainsley slapped the table. "*I'll* be your blockbuster story."

Nikki frowned. "But when we first talked about this, Wyatt Jericho was going to be my story. Having you as the story . . . that would be very different."

"But I'll have a fighting chance of surviving this with my reputation at least somewhat intact if you're the journalist who tells everyone about my past."

"I don't know," Nikki said slowly. "It could still get really ugly for you and Ben."

"Please, Nikki."

Nikki fiddled with the string on her tea bag, deep in thought. After a long pause, she finally spoke. "I *guess* we could try it. It's not like we have a lot of options."

"I'll talk to Ben when he gets home tomorrow. If he's on board, we coordinate with the campaign and move forward. You give them my story, and the campaign will find a way to spin it, or whatever it is campaigns do. I mean, Ben can still win, if we do this the right way? Right?"

Nikki scraped the last of the cream cheese frosting onto her fork and licked it off. "Given our country's recent political history, anything is possible."

"All bets are off. I understand that. But at least he'll have a chance."

"Are you sure you want to do this?" Nikki looked directly into her eyes. "Because once it's out there, it's *out there*."

"It's the only way to protect the girls. I see that now."

"But are you *sure*?" Nikki asked again. "Because I do think the campaign can handle this if they know what's coming, and it will protect the girls, but it's still going to be rough for Ben and really hard on you, at least for a while."

A feeling of peace washed over Ainsley. She'd been vigilant for so long. Controlling the way she dressed and talked, managing what everyone saw and thought. Carefully guarding the borders of her personality to make sure her real self never slipped through.

"I want to be free, Nikki. The truth will protect these girls. And the truth will set me free."

Chapter Forty-Four

AINSLEY

Ainsley sat in her closet, twisting her fingers in her lap. After a sleepless night, the longest morning of her life was finally coming to an end.

Down in the kitchen, Ben opened and closed the refrigerator, removing the meal she'd prepared for him to find when he returned. She'd left a note on the kitchen island. *Be down in a minute* 🙂 A casual note punctuated with a cheerful smile.

But there was nothing casual about the empty house, or the way she listened with the intensity of a safecracker to each noise from downstairs. The beeping microwave, the clatter of silverware, the twist of a bottle cap.

Almost time now.

She'd given everyone the day off to ensure that she and Ben would be uninterrupted. Grace was asleep in her room, home from school with a sore throat, but Adam had gone to Nikki's for a playdate, leaving the house empty and quiet when Ben returned from his trip.

He'd eaten lunch, then clicked on the TV. The sound of ESPN rose from the family room, announcers discussing statistics on pass completions.

She crept out of her closet and peeked over the banister at her husband sitting on the couch with his laptop beside him. He looked tired but relaxed, stretched out on the couch with a Heineken in his hand.

Time to share her secret.

She entered the room in sweatpants and an old Biltmore sweatshirt, hair pulled back in a ponytail, eyes puffy, face naked. She'd been crying on and off all day, and her makeup had long since washed away.

Ben greeted her, his expression cheerful. "Hey, stranger." He patted the couch beside him.

Instead of sitting next to him, she sank down on the padded ottoman in front of the couch, facing him.

He took one look at her face and immediately clicked off the TV. "What's wrong?"

She clasped his hands. She felt so calm now that she'd made her decision.

"Ben, I have something to tell you."

The color drained from his face. "The kids—"

"The kids are fine . . . Grace has a cold, but she's fine."

Relief washed over his face, followed by panic. "Oh my God. You have cancer."

She smiled in spite of herself. "I don't have cancer."

He sank back into the cushions, his forehead smooth. "What is it then?"

She felt a sudden rush of love for this man who defined calamity so narrowly. Everything would be okay as long as his wife and kids were okay.

"I have to tell you something."

Obviously. But her mind went blank, and she had no idea how to begin. She'd rehearsed this speech in her mind so many times, and now those words tumbled away, scattering like dust on an empty plain.

She looked out at the gray ribbon of river behind the house. If he walked away and kicked her out, if he divorced her and took the kids, at least she'd had a family for a little while. A whole, beautiful, loving family. Given the way she'd grown up, she felt lucky to have had one at all.

"Ben." She clenched his fingers a little tighter. "I'm being blackmailed."

His mouth fell open. "What?"

She took a deep breath and expelled the words in a rush of air. "I used to be a stripper."

His look of bewildered shock was almost comical. Then he chuckled. "Right. And I'm one of those Chippendales guys."

Her shoulders slumped. She hadn't expected this. Would she have to stand up and do a lap dance before he'd believe her? "Ben, I'm not joking."

His smile faded. "You're not?"

"I worked at Lady Godiva's Gentleman's Club in DC for almost a year to pay for Jolene's freshman year of college. One of the guys who used to come to the club is now the basketball coach at St. Preston's, and he's going to tell everyone the truth, plus a bunch of terrible lies, if we don't give him a million dollars."

He squinted at her, as though trying to make out the tiny letters at the very bottom of the eye chart. "You're kidding."

She shook her head. "I wish I were."

He remained silent for a whole minute as a variety of expressions flickered across his face: disbelief, betrayal, heartbreak, and shock. His face finally came to rest on an expression of deep hurt.

"Why didn't you tell me this years ago?" he whispered.

"I wanted to. But I just . . . I didn't have the courage. And I love you so much and I was so afraid that you'd . . ."

"What? Leave you? Stop loving you?"

She nodded, unable to speak.

"Oh, Ainsley." He rubbed his face with his hands. Then he looked at her, eyes rimmed with red. "Do you really think so little of me?"

She burst into tears. "I wanted to tell you, but the longer I waited, the worse it got."

"You were a stripper."

"Yes."

"To pay Jolene's college tuition."

"Yes."

"And you're only telling me this now because someone is blackmailing you."

"Yes." She lowered her eyes. "If I had a choice, I'd never tell you at all."

"Why?"

"Because I love you more than I can express . . . and because losing you . . . and losing the kids . . . is more than I can bear."

"Is that it? Is there anything else you want to tell me?"

"No." She hung her head. "That's my only secret."

He slapped his hands on his knees and stood, then moved to the wall of windows on the far side of the room. "Well, it's a humdinger."

She didn't know what to say, didn't know what he wanted or how to give it to him. Silence filled the space, ringing in her ears like a Klaxon. She waited for him to say more. But he remained silent, staring out at the river.

"Ben . . . I . . ."

He held up his hand. "Please, Ainsley. I need . . . to absorb this."

She managed a tight nod, then forced herself to speak. "I . . . understand."

He rubbed his hands over his face, then crossed the room to peer at her intently. "Do you, though? Because it's not about the stripping. It's about the trust, or lack thereof."

"You don't trust me anymore," she echoed in a small voice. Of course he didn't trust her anymore.

"No." He made a weary spinning gesture with his finger. "It's the other way around. You've obviously never trusted me if you were afraid to tell me something this important. And I need to wrap my mind around that."

He rose from the sofa and lumbered down the hallway to his office with the shuffling steps of an old man. The door shut with a click as her soul dissolved into dust.

If he'd screamed at her, or cursed and sworn, or thrown something, she could handle that. But this stunned pain on the face of the only man she'd ever loved . . . pain that she'd caused . . . this was a billion times more awful than anything she'd imagined.

She sat frozen on the sofa, numb with misery, until roused by a small voice. "Mommy, can I have a Popsicle?"

Grace entered the room, cheeks pale, hair wild, clad in her favorite Hello Kitty pajamas. At the sight of her daughter, tears began to fall. What if she lost her children too? What if her secret left Grace as motherless as she herself had been, once upon a time?

She brushed the tears back quickly with the palm of her hand. Then she reached for her daughter, pulled her close.

"Feeling any better?"

"A Popsicle would make me better," Grace said matter-of-factly.

"I'm sure it would." She took Grace's hand and led her into the kitchen.

"Can we snuggle on the couch?" Grace asked when she finished her Popsicle.

"Yes." Ainsley ran her hand over the tangle of hair cascading down her daughter's shoulders. "Can I brush your hair while we snuggle?"

Her daughter considered this, then nodded.

Ainsley grabbed a hairbrush and a bottle of detangler from Grace's room, then pulled a quilt from the antique chest behind the sofa. They settled themselves on the couch.

"Will you tell me a story about a little girl who goes into the forest and meets a family of talking bunnies and a unicorn?" Grace asked.

Ainsley was accustomed to these oddly specific requests. "Of course."

Grace lay down on the sofa, resting her head in her mother's lap. Ainsley squirted a liberal amount of detangler on her daughter's hair. "Once upon a time there was a little girl who went for a walk in the forest."

She made up the story as she went along, patiently working through each tangle. By the time she finished the tale, her daughter's silky hair flowed down her back in a neat braid.

"That was a good story, Mommy," Grace said. "But my throat still hurts."

"I'm sorry, honey."

Grace sighed. "It's no fun to be sick."

"I know, sweetheart, but I'm here."

Grace looked up at her mother with a wan smile. "Of course you're here, Mommy. Where else would you be?"

Ainsley blinked rapidly as tears once again pricked her eyes. Then she pressed a kiss to her daughter's warm forehead.

Grace took it for granted that her mother would always be here when she needed her because Ainsley *had* always been here when her daughter needed her.

Ainsley had accomplished that much. And as much as she loved Ben, this was what mattered in the end.

Her ears pricked as Ben's footsteps echoed on the floorboards, moving down the hallway. He bypassed the family room where she sat with Grace and headed for the mudroom, then the garage. The faint rumble of the garage door and the low hum of his Porsche delivered the news of his departure like a punch.

She felt hollow inside, like one of the Halloween pumpkins decorating the front porch, as she tried to ignore the questions echoing in her mind.

Where was he going? And would he come back?

Chapter Forty-Five

AINSLEY

She spent the rest of the afternoon and evening at home with Grace—and eventually Adam, too, after Nikki's husband dropped him off—ears tuned to the driveway, waiting for the rumble of Ben's car. But even though he'd been gone for hours, she heard nothing but silence and the autumn wind whistling through the naked trees.

After checking Grace's temperature, which was now normal, she read to the kids and tucked them into bed. Then she puttered around the kitchen, restless and unproductive, before settling in front of the TV in the family room, where even an episode of *Poldark* on Masterpiece failed to hold her attention.

A faint sound from outside made her heart race. She turned down the volume, listening with her whole body. Joy and relief burned through her as tires crunched across the gravel driveway.

Ben was home.

She listened to the small sounds of his arrival. The jingle of keys, the soft thunk of shoes, the rustle of his coat. He entered the family room, and she rose to greet him, shy and uncertain. Maybe this didn't mean anything. Maybe he'd come back to pack a suitcase before leaving for good.

"Hi," she said in a small voice.

He looked tired, sad, and sober. "Can we talk?"

She nodded, gnawing on her thumbnail as she looked at him warily from the far side of the sofa.

He took a deep breath and opened his arms. "Ainsley. Come here."

She took a step toward him. He reached out, bridging the distance between them, and pulled her into a tight embrace. She melted into his chest, wishing she could graft herself onto him, become physically part of him, so he could never leave again.

"I'm sorry," she murmured into the soft cotton of his shirt. "I'm so sorry."

"Look at me."

She took a deep breath and tilted her head upward, meeting his eyes.

"You're the only woman I've ever loved. And you're the only woman I've ever trusted. That's why this is so hard."

"Do you love me . . . less . . . because of this?" she asked, then immediately wished she hadn't.

"Of course not." The corners of his mouth turned up, revealing traces of the old Ben. A giant weight tumbled from her chest. For the first time in weeks, she felt like she could breathe again.

"But I have questions," he said.

She nodded. "Of course."

He sank down on the couch, and she sat beside him, keeping her body at a polite distance, like an acquaintance in the stands at one of Adam's T-ball games.

"Tell me again," he said, his voice low and tired. "Who is blackmailing you?"

"Wyatt Jericho, the basketball coach."

"That guy from Biltmore?"

She nodded, words rushing out. "He's a predator. And the girls at school are in danger. Telling everyone is the only way to get rid of him."

"Wait." He spread his arms and gestured at the distance between them. "We need to talk, but not like this."

She scooted closer, and they sat facing each other, arms and legs entwined, leaning against the cushions. Her heart rate slowed the moment his body connected with hers, and the anxiety building inside her over the last few hours slowly melted away.

"That's better," he said, taking her hands in his. "Now, start at the beginning."

She took a deep breath and told him everything.

When she finished, he massaged his temples as though trying to smooth away a massive headache. He said nothing for a long moment. Finally he nodded. "Okay. I think I've got it."

She exhaled, the last traces of tension leaving her body. "But this could destroy the campaign and everything you've worked for."

He nodded. "It could."

"I've destroyed your dream."

He frowned, shaking his head. "Being governor isn't my dream."

"It's not?"

"Did I ever tell you my Disneyland story?" he asked.

"I don't think so."

He stroked her hand with his thumb and settled deeper into the cushions. "I was nine years old when someone at school took a family vacation to Disney. I heard about all the things they did, and I desperately wanted to go. I asked my parents to take me. My dad said he couldn't because he had to tour a Bradley Bar plant in Europe. I asked my mom if she'd take me over spring break."

"And she said yes?" Ainsley asked, hoping for a happy ending, even though she knew there wouldn't be one, based on her experiences with her mother-in-law.

"Are you kidding?" He shook his head. "Long lines in the hot sun with the common people? There's no way in hell my mom was ever setting foot in a place like Disney. She got Mr. and Mrs. Finney to take me."

"Patrick's parents?"

"That's right."

The wheels began to turn in her mind. Ben's best friend was a boy he'd met on the first day of kindergarten. One of six kids and the son of a garbage collector, Patrick Finney had grown up in a tiny house and attended St. Preston's on a scholarship.

"My mom offered to send the whole Finney family to Disney on the private plane. She offered to pay for the hotel, meals, tickets, everything, if they took me along."

His expression softened. "Mrs. Finney is a proud woman, but she'd do anything for her kids, so she said yes. So I went on a family vacation to Disney with my best friend's family instead of my own."

"How was it?"

"Fantastic." A broad grin lit his face. "I'll never forget the moment we walked into our five-star hotel rooms. Mrs. Finney drew back the curtains and looked over this gorgeous view of the swimming pool. Then she burst into tears and hugged me. And that was the moment I realized how much good I could do with my money. That trip changed my life."

"But it wasn't about going to Disney, was it?" Ainsley asked.

"No. I wanted the *family* part of a family vacation. A trip where you get to be with your mom and dad, the whole family together, for an entire week. Disney was beside the point. I just wanted their attention and their time, and of course, those are the only things they never gave me growing up."

"I'm sorry, Ben."

"But that's my point," he said. "*You've* given me the only thing I've ever wanted."

Warmth spread through her chest as she began to understand. "A family?"

"Yes. A family." He picked up a silver picture frame from the table behind the sofa. "*This* is my dream." He pointed at the photo, taken in the Caribbean, kids covered in sand, Ben with a snorkel dangling from his temple, Ainsley laughing, hair a mess under a wide-brimmed hat.

"I didn't have a family, until you. Until *us*. Last weekend when we sat around the kitchen table after dinner and the kids told those ridiculous knock-knock jokes that have no punch lines and make no sense and Adam laughed until milk squirted out of his nose. *That* is my dream."

Her chest tingled as memories washed over her, warm and gentle like the waves at the beach.

"Or when I taught Grace how to ride her bike? *That's* my dream."

She remembered the look of exhilaration on Grace's face as she rode down their long driveway, Ben running beside her, cheering her on.

"And when I share the details of my day, and you listen, and when you care enough to tell me the details of your day, that's my dream too."

She nodded. Of course she understood. A stable, happy place where the adults made everyone feel safe and loved. That's all she'd ever wanted too.

"This life we have . . . this is my dream, and *you* made it possible."

"But don't you want to be governor?" she asked.

He shrugged. "It would be nice to be able to help people on a grand scale. But that's not my dream. You and Adam and Grace are my dream. And frankly, this campaign has gotten in the way of all that. I've been away from you and the kids so much. And if I have to drop out because of this, it won't be the end of the world."

She was almost unable to speak. "But, Ben . . ."

He put his finger to her lips. "I love you. Everything you are. Everything you were. Everything you've become. All of you. Forever."

"You forgive me?" she asked, blinking back tears.

"For working as a stripper to help Jolene get away from a guy who beat the shit out of her, so she could go to college? There's nothing to forgive."

"But I should have told you. I lied to you . . . for years. Can you really forgive that?"

He was silent for a long moment. "I think I understand where the lie came from."

"You do?"

He sighed and ran his hands through his hair. "I live my life for an audience of one, and that one is you. And I know you feel the same way about me. So I understand the impulse to hide something because you're afraid it will make the only person who really matters see you in a different way. It doesn't make it right . . . but I understand it."

"I still should have told you."

"Yes, you should have," he conceded. "And I want you to promise there will be no more secrets. My parents were like two ships passing in the night. They never told each other anything, and I don't want to live like that."

She looked down at her lap. "I've always been so intimidated because of where I came from."

"Ainsley." He put his finger under her chin and lifted her gaze. "You are beautiful and kind and smart. The fact that you turned out this way makes you more amazing, not less."

"How did I get so lucky?" she whispered, voice thick.

"I'm the lucky one." He squeezed her hand. "And I know we still have things to deal with, but we don't have time to go on some kind of marriage-encounter weekend to work on our trust issues in the middle of a campaign."

She grinned. "Fortunately."

He grinned back. "Thank God. I don't think we're marriage-encounter types. But even if we were, we have to focus on managing this situation, because if we lose the election, Wyatt Jericho and guys like him win."

She nodded, then told him about Nikki's job interview.

"It's an interesting idea," he said, stroking his chin. "Let me call the campaign, and we'll talk with Nikki."

"You think it will work?" she asked.

"It could. But if Nikki is going to drop this bombshell, we need to prepare for the fallout."

Chapter Forty-Six

NIKKI

"I blew it."

Nikki sat in her minivan in the 7-Eleven parking lot with a glazed doughnut in her mouth, a bag of cheese balls open in her lap, and a fluorescent blue Slurpee in the cup holder, attempting to drown her sorrows in sugar and trans fats after botching her job interview.

On Bluetooth, from the other end of the line, Gus tried to make her feel better, his voice filling the car with a string of reassuring phrases. But it was no good.

She'd blown her only chance to return to the job she loved. She'd known it the moment she'd uttered the phrase "killer kohlrabi."

She'd done everything else right. She'd actually been *prepared.* She'd gone shopping and found a suit that fit like a glove on clearance at Nordstrom. She got new shoes, a haircut, and highlights, so her roots no longer showed. She'd reached out to Roxy, the makeup artist at her old station, who'd refused to take any form of payment and insisted on doing her hair and makeup for free. She'd spent hours on the *Washington Post* website, getting up to speed on all the news she'd missed in the brain-fogged weeks after Baby Joe's birth.

She'd pulled on her Spanx and walked out the door as a thin-ish, authoritative Once and Future Anchorwoman, empathetic, intelligent, and attractive, able to kick ass and take names without dislodging a single strand of hair.

Ninety-nine percent of the interview was perfect. Nikki actually *enjoyed* job interviews because they were a performance, and she loved to perform. She had charisma to burn, and she knew how to use it: laughing, flirting, and charming the two women and three men arrayed around a long table in a sterile conference room.

Everything went so well, until that last question where they asked for a blockbuster story idea to kick off the investigative reporting unit she would lead as their new anchor.

She'd nodded sagely as they described what they wanted. *She was ready for this.* She'd rehearsed her story pitch in the shower, while folding laundry, and in the car on the way to the interview. Short and sweet and to the point, incorporating vital words like *secret*, and *scandal*, and *exclusive interview*.

But while her mind repeated these words, something entirely different came out of her mouth.

"Kohlrabi," she said instead. "*Killer* kohlrabi."

Silence filled the room. The fluorescent light overhead buzzed like an angry fly.

"Perilous pears," she added dramatically. "Risky rutabagas. *Grievous* grapes."

She gazed at the faces around the table and saw raised eyebrows. Perhaps she needed to spell it out more clearly.

"Pesticides are poisoning our children and damaging our bodies." She leaned forward and lowered her voice to a conspiratorial whisper. "They're killing us. And they're *everywhere*."

They looked startled, and not in a good way.

"Toxic tomatoes," she ventured.

Silence again. The executive producer looked down at her legal pad and began to doodle something that looked like a sphinx.

"Carcinogenic carrots. Polluted pineapples. *Deadly dates*." She tapped the table for dramatic effect. They leaned back in their chairs, exuding an air of skeptical embarrassment, as though she'd suddenly decided to share the more intimate details of her recent alien abduction and medical examination at the hands of curious beings from the Andromeda Galaxy.

"Noxious nectarines," she added with a hint of desperation.

The general manager frowned. The assignment editor closed her notebook with an impatient flip. Clearly this was not the kind of Pulitzer Prize–winning blockbuster they had in mind.

"Lethal legumes?" she asked in a small voice.

She sounded like a moron, and knew this, but she could not stop talking because the more she talked about vegetables, the less likely they were to learn about her *real* blockbuster story, the story she now felt desperate to hide from them.

No one made eye contact.

"Poisonous potatoes?" she offered.

They looked irritated now, offended even. The news director stood to end the interview. In a frosty voice, he informed her they would "be in touch."

She climbed into her minivan and beat her head softly against the steering wheel. She was an idiot.

"But I thought you had a killer story ready to go?" Gus's voice filled the car.

"I *did* have a killer story," Nikki insisted after swallowing her second glazed doughnut. "I still do. But in the end, I just couldn't give it to them."

It came down to the news director, a man named Anthony Pollen, dubbed Just Like Stalin by his coworkers. He was rumored to be a terrible boss and an unscrupulous journalist.

When Nikki looked into his cold gray eyes, she suddenly knew exactly how he'd handle Ainsley's story.

He'd run promos with boom-chicka-bow-wow background music and shadowy images of women in sequined bras with too much lip gloss leering at the camera while hanging from a brass pole.

An exclusive interview with the porn star who wants to be your First Lady . . . tonight, at six.

This man would include the worst of Wyatt Jericho's whispered allegations, without any evidence to back them up. He'd use Ainsley's past life as a whip, and he'd flog her with it. And then he'd destroy Ben.

It would become an international story, thanks to Ben's money and the fact that everyone on the planet ate Bradley Bars. Ainsley, Ben, and their children would be laughingstocks for a generation. Ben Bradley's good works would be lost in a haze of G-strings. And Ainsley would be forever known as the Porn Star Stripper Mom.

The news director's face had faded for a moment as she'd visualized a fork in the road. To the right, a lifetime spent picking spaghetti off the floor as a stay-at-home mom. And to the left, Ainsley, Ben, and their children hounded by paparazzi shouting rude questions whenever they left the safety of their home, Ainsley's beautiful face forever infamous.

Sitting in her hard chair at the end of the conference table, she considered her decision. Anchor jobs were few and far between. Each city had three or maybe four affiliates at most, and each station had only so many shows. There might not be another main anchor opening for ten or fifteen years. She'd be too old then. She was almost too old now.

"Killer kohlrabi," she'd said in a clear voice.

She'd had to make a choice. And she'd chosen Ainsley.

"But why didn't you give them your story?" Gus asked plaintively. She knew he'd wanted this job for her almost as much as she'd wanted it for herself.

"Because it would destroy the person who gave me the story in the first place," Nikki said.

"Is it a good story?" he asked.

"It's a fantastic story." She gesticulated to no one in particular with her Slurpee. "It's a huge and important story. It's a story that *needs* to be told."

"Then find a better way to tell it. Get it out there on your terms, not theirs."

She shook her head. "I really blew it, Gus. I'll never anchor again."

"You don't know that," he said. "And there are other things in life besides work. You've got a beautiful family. You've got Josh. And you've got friends."

She popped a cheese ball into her mouth. True. She had all those things.

"And remember," Gus said. "The *why* is always more compelling than the *what*."

Find a better way to tell it.

An idea floated through her mind, nebulous as a jellyfish, but still, an idea.

Get it out there on your terms, not theirs.

It didn't matter that Ainsley had been a stripper.

The why is always more compelling than the what.

What mattered was *why* Ainsley had been a stripper.

Her caller ID beeped.

"Thanks for listening, Gus. I gotta go. I'll call you later."

She pressed the call waiting button, and Ainsley's voice filled the car.

"Is your interview done?" Ainsley asked. "Did you tell them?"

"No. I didn't," Nikki said.

"Why not?"

"Meet me at the campaign office in fifteen minutes. I have an idea."

Chapter Forty-Seven

AINSLEY

The campaign office occupied a store that once sold tropical fish in a suburban strip mall. The next-door neighbors included a dentist, a coffee shop, and a mattress store. The coffee shop owners were overjoyed when the campaign moved in, because like vampires with blood, campaign staffers needed caffeine to survive.

Ainsley had met most of the staff before, on brief trips to the office to drop something off or pick something up, but for the most part, she tried to avoid them. They intimidated her, the way they talked a hundred miles an hour in what sounded like a foreign language about things she knew nothing about. Crosstabs, benchmarks, and market saturation. They made her nervous.

But up close, they weren't quite so scary. Lenny, the press secretary, had the haunted look of someone held responsible for things beyond his control. The campaign manager was a thin fifty-two-year-old woman named Brenda with a strange addiction to gummy bears and Diet Coke. She'd lost her husband and only child in a car accident two decades earlier.

Since then, she'd poured her heart and soul into managing political campaigns, work so absorbing she didn't have time to dwell on what she'd lost. Her entire wardrobe consisted of a bipartisan collection of vintage campaign swag. Today she wore a Mondale–Ferraro T-shirt with a McCain–Palin baseball cap, topped off with a sleeveless fleece from her last campaign, an Iowa senate race her candidate had won by twenty-five points.

She gave Ainsley a grim nod as she entered the room.

They hate me.

Ainsley didn't know much about campaigns, but she knew that if Ben won, some of these people could move into interesting jobs in the governor's office. And if he lost because voters found out his wife used to be a stripper, they'd all be unemployed and unable to pay their rent.

And it will be my fault.

She sat in a metal folding chair and took the cup of coffee handed to her by Marlene, the scheduler, an otherwise robust woman with pale, thinning hair. Ainsley wondered if she'd pulled it out as she tried to figure out how to get Ben to three events in four different places, all on the same night.

Just as they were about to begin, Nikki arrived. She blew through the door; waved hello to the press secretary, whom she already seemed to know; gave Ainsley a hug; and then introduced herself to Ben. "Nice to finally meet you in person."

"I've heard a lot about you," he said, smiling as he shook her hand.

"Likewise. I'm copresident of the Ainsley fan club."

He shot a fond look at Ainsley. "She's pretty amazing."

"She is," Nikki agreed. "And we're not going to let these bastards destroy her. Or you."

"All right," Ben said. "Let's get started."

The campaign had a perfectly good conference room, but for reasons Ainsley had never fully understood, every important meeting actually seemed to take place amid the coffee cups, pizza boxes, and newspaper-strewed chaos of the campaign manager's cramped office.

Just as they were about to begin, the door swung open again, and Jolene strode in.

"I came as soon as I could," she said breathlessly. Then she raised her phone to her ear. "Do nothing until I talk to you again. And remember, accelerated tax depreciation is *not* your friend." Then she hung up her phone and tossed it into her giant leather handbag.

Ainsley blinked. "Jolene?"

"I asked her to come," Nikki called out from her seat in the corner. "We need her help. I'll explain in a minute."

Ben introduced his sister-in-law, who took a seat on an unopened box of yard signs. Then he sat down in a metal folding chair beside Ainsley and took her hand. "Honey, can you start by telling them everything you told me?"

Could she? Could she actually tell these strangers the same things she'd told Ben?

Ben gave her hand a reassuring squeeze. She looked into his eyes and found courage there. No matter what she said, he'd still love her. Her kids would still love her. Jolene and Nikki would still love her too.

She took a deep breath and let the story spill out.

No one made a sound when she finished speaking. She felt like the White Witch in the Narnia books she'd loved as a kid, with the power to turn people to stone.

Lenny broke the silence. "That was . . . powerful."

"The why is more important than the what," Nikki said cryptically.

The campaign manager chewed on the end of her pen and gazed at Ainsley with a contemplative expression. "This changes things."

"It does?" Ainsley asked.

"It might," the campaign manager said as she began to pace in front of the window.

"It could," the press secretary said as he scribbled furiously on a legal pad.

"It will," Nikki said decisively as she reached into her purse and removed a pink pen and a notebook with unicorns on the cover, which clearly belonged to one of her children.

"I agree. This *can* work." The campaign manager exchanged a look with Nikki. "If we do it right."

They seemed to be engaged in some sort of telepathic conversation. Ainsley sensed an innate understanding between Nikki and the campaign people. They were all cut from the same adrenaline-junkie, I-am-a-crusader-on-behalf-of-democracy-and-humanity kind of cloth, like Avengers, but without the spandex and weird weapons.

Nikki turned to her. "Do you think you could do that again?"

"Do what again?" Ainsley asked.

"Tell your story," Nikki said.

"With television cameras," the press secretary added.

"Onstage in front of a live audience," the campaign manager said.

Ainsley's mouth dropped open. No. No. No. No. No. NO. This single syllable echoed through her mind accompanied by a thousand terrified screams. She could *not* tell this story again in front of television cameras and a live audience. Were they insane?

Ainsley shuddered. "I can't do that."

"What about the library gala?" The campaign manager turned to the scheduler. "It's the night before Wyatt Jericho's blackmail deadline."

"Have we canceled Ben's speech?" the press secretary asked.

"I was about to," the scheduler said, "but I haven't done it yet."

"What if we switch 'em." The campaign manager glanced at Nikki. "He's supposed to give the keynote, but what if she gets up and talks instead?"

"No." Ben rose from his chair, taking command of the conversation. "We are *not* putting Ainsley through that. Plus"—he looked down at her with a wry smile—"I promised my wife she'd never have to give a campaign speech."

His expression melted the icy ball of fear embedded at the center of her heart, and she suddenly knew that she must volunteer for a mission Ben would never ask her to carry out.

Ainsley took his hand and gently pulled him back into his seat. "I appreciate that, Ben. But maybe I can do this." She turned to Nikki. "Tell me what you're thinking."

Nikki leaned forward. "This doesn't contradict the antipornography message. It *enhances* it. You turned to work like this because you didn't have other economic options. It reinforces everything Ben's been saying about the high cost of tuition. Your sister wanted a college education, and this was the only way you guys could pay for it. How many other women and girls find themselves in a similar situation?"

"And what about Jericho?" Ainsley asked.

"We can't denounce him publicly without proof," the press secretary said.

The campaign manager nodded. "We'll double-check with the lawyers, but he'll sue for libel or defamation of character. And that will give the story a whole second life as the press covers every suit and countersuit and court hearing. We don't want that."

"But even if you don't mention his name, this takes the threat of blackmail off the table," Nikki said.

"He can't tell a secret you've already told yourself."

It sounded so simple when the press secretary said it, and Ainsley suddenly realized it was true.

"And if you tell your story in a sympathetic, matter-of-fact way, without shame, and get it out there first, it completely neutralizes any lies he tries to tell about . . . other things," Nikki said.

Ainsley looked her in the eye. "You mean porn, prostitution, and drug dealing."

"Yes." Nikki nodded. "And with the threat of blackmail off the table, we're free to go to the principal privately and tell the school everything we know, and how we know it. And that should be enough to get him fired."

"And in the meantime," Jolene spoke up from the other side of the room, "we keep looking for the evidence we need to put him away for good."

"Which is why I asked Jolene to come," Nikki explained.

"I've been digging into BS Unlimited. It's a slush fund, and I'm going to figure out who it belongs to and why it exists."

Someone cleared their throat from the corner of the room. "Allow me to assist if I can, ma'am."

A muscular guy with a short military-style haircut stepped forward and inclined his head to Jolene. Then he turned to Ainsley. "Caleb Connors, ma'am, head of your husband's opposition research team."

She gazed from Jolene to Caleb. She could almost see the sparks forming in the air between them. Maybe, finally, this guy could be the one who—

"I don't need any help," Jolene said breezily. "But thanks for the offer."

Ainsley's heart sank. And . . . so much for that. She returned her attention to Nikki.

Nikki gave her a confident smile. "I think you can do this, Ainsley, and do it well."

"But what exactly do I do?"

"You tell your story," Nikki said, "to everyone, from the podium, in front of television cameras, at the Library Charity Gala on Thursday night. The public hears your story from *you*, in your words, on your terms. And they hear it from you *first*, not from a vicious attack ad or from a journalist or from Wyatt Jericho."

Ainsley looked over at Ben. He deserved at least a *chance* to realize his dream. She couldn't take that away from him by refusing to face the truth.

Then Harmonee's pale face rose in her mind. She died alone, in silence, without a voice.

Ainsley had a microphone and a podium and television cameras and a captive audience. Didn't she have an obligation to use these things? An obligation to Harmonee and Misty, and all the girls at the club who danced from necessity rather than choice and for all the girls Jericho had already silenced, and might silence again in the future?

She reached for Ben's hand. "I'll do it."

Chapter Forty-Eight

NIKKI

Nikki attempted to descend the stairs in her evening gown and high heels but found it difficult to maneuver around the conclave of My Little Ponies holding some kind of special legislative session on the landing.

Josh offered a hand and managed to steer her down the stairs without tripping. When she arrived at the bottom, he leaned over and kissed her cheek.

"You look ravishingly clean and symmetrical tonight."

"It's because of Ainsley." She patted her elegant chignon. "Without her, I would have shown up at this gala in black pants held together with a safety pin."

"She thought of everything, didn't she?" Josh rubbed his chin sheepishly. "I thought I was going the extra mile by asking Shelby to come early and watch the kids so you could get ready in peace, but this—"

Nikki grinned. "Don't feel bad. Ainsley excels at planning."

A box had arrived a few days earlier containing an evening gown and the phone number for a seamstress who came to Nikki's home to do alterations. Earlier that evening, Nikki had answered the door to find Roxy standing on the steps with a bag full of beauty tools. Ainsley had hired her to do Nikki's hair and makeup for the gala.

"What did you guys decide to do about the ads?" Josh asked, holding up a handful of tux studs. "And can you help me with these?"

She'd been sharing stories with Josh all week about different options to help voters get to know the real Ainsley, before the news about her past life hit the airwaves.

"We ended up cutting two ads, one with Ainsley looking directly at the camera, talking about growing up in a trailer in Badwater, about cleaning hotel rooms and how hard it was to pay for college. It's running statewide."

"I saw it this morning," he said. "It's a great ad. She sounds . . . relatable."

"That's the goal." Nikki squinted at his shirt, searching for the tiny opening in the fabric. "The second ad starts running at midnight, as soon as the speech ends and the story hits the wire. In this one, Ainsley addresses the whole thing head on, with Ben sitting beside her, holding her hand."

"Why a second ad?" Ben asked, handing her a black-and-silver tux stud.

"We want voters to get the story directly from Ainsley and her speech tonight. Because the minute her story hits the air, those outside groups supporting Ben's opponent will start running attack ads."

"Makes sense."

"There's more." Nikki inserted another stud, then smoothed down the front of his shirt. "Direct mail pieces go out Monday morning, connecting everything to Ben's education-and-antipornography platform. The press secretary will send out a transcript of the speech tonight, and we have op-eds ready to go, cowritten by Ainsley and Ben."

"Written by Ainsley and Ben." He cocked his head skeptically. "Really?"

"Okay, written by me," she conceded, "with a lot of input from Ainsley and Ben."

"You sound like Nikki Lassiter again," he said, pulling her close. "And I've always found Nikki Lassiter to be very attractive."

"Just like my many friends who sent fan mail from the penitentiary."

"Say *attack ad* again," he whispered.

She raised an eyebrow seductively. "Attack ad. Oppo research. *Hard money.*"

He grinned. "Don't stop."

"McCain–Feingold. Super PAC. Ranking *member.*"

"Okay." He held up his hand. "That's enough."

She chuckled as she inserted the last stud. "It's been fun, working with the campaign."

She and Ainsley had spent hours crafting the speech that would set everything in motion. Then they'd perfected Ainsley's delivery, working on each gesture, nuance of tone, and facial expression.

By the time they'd finished, Ainsley had the speech completely memorized, her delivery perfect.

Nikki knew most of this training would evaporate when Ainsley took the stage in front of five hundred people. Only experience could dispel those nerves. But she would hopefully retain the basics when she stepped to the podium, and that should be enough . . . could be enough . . . to save Ben's campaign.

Josh rested his hand on Nikki's shoulder. "I'm sorry, Nikki . . . about the anchor job."

Channel 4 had announced it this morning. They'd hired someone else to fill the position.

"It's okay." It wasn't, of course. She'd cried when she'd read the announcement in the paper, even though she knew she'd blown the interview.

"This campaign work . . . I mean . . . I've loved it." She shrugged, trying to convince herself this was irrelevant. "But it's all-consuming, and it isn't sustainable. The kids are subsisting on frozen pizza. We're always running out of toilet paper. The girls turned in their pumpkin project two days late because I wasn't reading the teacher's weekly newsletter. I need to get back to what's important."

Josh looked at her with a bemused smile, then spoke slowly, as though explaining something complex to a child. "Nikki, did it ever occur to you that as the heart and soul of this family, *you* are also important?"

She stood very still. "No. That has never occurred to me."

But now that he forced her to think about it, she realized it might be true. All those T-shirt slogans. "Happy Wife, Happy Life." "If Mama ain't happy, ain't no one happy." Maybe he was right.

Paradoxically, she'd been kinder to Ben, and more patient with the kids, even though she'd been insanely busy, because she'd been happy.

She'd spent this last week *thinking*, as well as planning, plotting, reading, writing, and talking. Her brain had been working the way her brain used to work, constantly, at her kitchen table, in the car between drop-offs and pickups, at Ainsley's house, and at the campaign office, where she and Ainsley and the rest of the team had worked like dogs to manage the unveiling of Ainsley's secret.

"Let's get through tonight," Josh said. "But tomorrow I want us to think through some options for your future." He looked stern and serious, like when he'd attempted to explain the important hygienic role of underwear in human history, disabusing Daniel of the idea that underpants were optional garments imposed on him by whimsical parents.

"You sound like a high school guidance counselor," she said, smiling.

"I'm serious. Maybe you become some kind of consultant. Or start your own business."

"Selling what?" she asked dryly. "Disorganization and chaos?"

"I don't know." He ran his hands through his hair. "We'll think of something. But seeing you like this again . . ."

"Like what?"

"Energized. Engaged. *Happy.* I don't want that to end when Ainsley's speech ends tonight."

"I don't want it to end either. I've enjoyed being both the parent who picks up the kids and the parent who goes to important meetings. But you can't have it all."

"No, but maybe you can have a little bit of both, periodically, and maybe I can help out more, to make that possible."

"Deal." She shook her husband's hand. Then her face turned serious. "I love you, Josh. I hope you know that."

"I love you too," he said, leaning in for a kiss. "And now you have to help me with these cuff links. I haven't worn a tux since my senior prom."

Chapter Forty-Nine

AINSLEY

A rainbow of evening gowns filled the hotel ballroom, punctuated by the somber jackets of men in black tie. People checked the massive seating charts displayed on easels at the back of the room, then found their tables, men clapping each other on the back, women air-kissing as they greeted people they'd seen days, or sometimes just hours, earlier on the tennis court or at the club.

Giant photos of Mrs. Verna Robertson greeted them as they entered. Pictured on banners hanging from the ceiling, she stood beside a pile of books wearing a tweed skirt, sensible shoes, and a high-necked blouse. The laugh lines around her mouth belied her no-nonsense demeanor, and it beamed down on the partygoers, giving the formal event an aura of good humor.

Ainsley and Jolene paused for a moment, looking up at the woman who'd saved their lives. They'd chosen this photo, taken about three years before her death from pancreatic cancer, because it was taken in the library she had loved and managed for almost forty years.

"She always reminded me of Queen Elizabeth," Jolene said wistfully. "At first I thought it was because of her hair and glasses and that black handbag she always carried. But really, it was because of the way she carried *herself*."

"Do you think she'd be proud of us?" Ainsley asked.

"For raising and donating eleven million dollars to expand a library and fill it with books? Hell yes, she'd be proud of us."

Ainsley looked up at the banner. "But she'd be upset that we're naming the new wing after her."

"Oh yeah." Jolene grinned. "She'd hate that, but she's dead, so she'll have to live with it."

Even after all these years, Jolene's voice had a slight edge when she discussed Mrs. Robertson. Jolene still hadn't managed to forgive her for dying unexpectedly at age sixty-three. Ainsley knew that Jolene understood how irrational this was, but she also knew her sister couldn't help the way she felt.

Ainsley's grief was less complicated. She missed Mrs. Robertson every day, but especially at night, when she read stories to Adam and Grace. When Mrs. Robertson had stepped into their lives in her practical, loving way, she'd taught Ainsley everything she knew about how to be a mother, and in those quiet maternal moments, her absence became an ache.

"It's time," Ben said, taking her arm.

Her stomach fluttered as he escorted her and Jolene to their seats at the main table in front of the stage. She attempted to make small talk with the many acquaintances she encountered along the way, parents from school, people from the club, friends of her mother-in-law, women on the planning committee, but it was heavy going conversationally. Every time she ran into someone she knew, the same words echoed through her mind over and over again . . . *And now you will know everything I've ever tried to hide.*

She suddenly wished she were back at Godiva's. Stripping off her clothes just revealed her body. Now she had to stand in front of these people and expose her soul.

When the time finally came, her palms were wet and her mouth dry. They introduced her husband. He took her hand, and they ascended the stage together.

Ben adjusted the microphone for her, then leaned down and spoke into it. “I know I’m scheduled to speak tonight, but we have a special surprise. Please welcome my beautiful wife, Ainsley Bradley, the most courageous person I know.”

A smattering of polite applause greeted this unexpected change in the program.

Ben returned to his seat, leaving her alone and blinded by the spotlight. She brushed her palms up and down her shantung silk thighs. Just like the mummy in her nightmare, she was about to unravel. With one tug, the bandages would fall away, leaving her shriveled and exposed in front of five hundred people.

She looked down at the first page of her speech. And there, peeking under the spotlight’s blinding glare, she saw Nikki seated in front of the podium.

Her advice flooded Ainsley’s mind.

Take a deep breath. Don’t rush. And if you could dance naked in a room full of people, you can talk standing still with your clothes on.

Nikki met her eyes and moved her lips, emphatically mouthing a string of words. *You are one insanely talented badass.*

Ainsley almost laughed. Her shoulders relaxed.

She stepped into the light.

As the words began to flow, she experienced a strange, out-of-body sensation. She remained onstage, while another part of her floated high in the air, watching herself speak from above, both participant and spectator, present and not present.

When she finished, silence echoed through the ballroom, three or four eternal seconds without sound. Then someone, not her husband or Nikki or Jolene, but someone in the back of the room, started clapping. Then everyone rose to their feet, and the applause became a storm of sound, thundering over her body in a flood of love and approval. Then Ben was there, on the stage beside her, engulfing her in a giant hug, his eyes wet with tears.

She descended the stairs on Ben's arm, embraced Jolene and Nikki, then slumped into her seat like a rag doll.

The lights came up, and the rest of the evening passed in a blur. People she didn't know, shaking her hand, telling her their own stories about how they washed dishes to pay for law school, or worked as a janitor to get through undergrad, praising her courage, thanking her for telling her story.

Then they whisked her away, and she and Ben were in the black Suburban, heading home. She held Ben's hand as she leaned against the window, bathed in the light of a harvest moon as the weight of a thousand secrets fell from her shoulders.

Chapter Fifty

NIKKI

The morning after the speech, Nikki and Ainsley sat in uncomfortable wooden chairs outside the head of school's office. The school secretary, Mrs. Pique, typed aggressively at her keyboard while pointedly ignoring them. They did *not* have an appointment.

Halloween loomed on the horizon, unleashing an anticipatory tremor throughout the school as children looked forward to a strangely transgressive holiday in which they were actively encouraged to solicit and accept candy from strangers.

Like the children, Nikki felt vaguely unsettled. She folded her hands in her lap and repeated the phrase *I am a grown-up, damn it* over and over inside her mind, hoping it would make her feel more confident.

Mrs. Pique had been terrifying thirty years ago when she berated Nikki for losing her sixth-grade field trip permission form, and unlike a fine wine, she had not mellowed with age.

As though reading her thoughts, Mrs. Pique suddenly stopped typing and glared at Nikki over the top of her reading glasses.

"You know, the head of school is *very* busy today. I suggest you speak to the vice principal instead. He's available now."

"No," Ainsley spoke up, her voice firm. "This is an issue for the head of school."

Nikki glanced at her friend in admiration. She liked this new, ass-kicking Ainsley. Plus, she would never have dared to use that *tone* with Mrs. Pique.

"We're happy to wait," Nikki said meekly.

Mrs. Pique scowled at Nikki and refused to even acknowledge Ainsley, which concerned her.

She'd sensed a decided coolness toward Ainsley at drop-off that morning from some of the other moms, notably Tiffany Hastings and her posse, but perhaps people just didn't know what to say as all the newspapers and TV and radio stations, including NPR, reported on your past life as a stripper.

They waited for twenty minutes, thumbing through their phones. Finally, Mrs. Pique looked up from her computer screen with an irritated sigh. "He'll see you now, but only for fifteen minutes. I'm squeezing you in between his other . . . appointments." Her pause implied these other appointments were far more important than anything they could possibly wish to discuss.

Nikki's mouth went dry, and she suddenly wished she'd stashed a bottle of water, or possibly vodka, in her purse. Like Mrs. Pique, the head of school was terrifying, a man who'd run St. Preston's since Nikki was in middle school. For reasons she had never fully understood, both children and adults referred to Mr. Rupert Smedley Philpott, the head of school, by his middle and last name, giving him the double-barreled-surname aura of British aristocracy. The younger, hipper parents referred to him privately as Notorious RSP.

He wore bow ties and tweed jackets and had a small mustache, which he actually *waxed*. He looked like a constipated Teddy Roosevelt, or the banker from Monopoly without the mischievous twinkle in his eye.

They rose and headed for his office. Ainsley knocked lightly, and a voice instructed them to enter. Inside, Mr. Smedley Philpott, a rotund man with forbidding eyebrows, frowned at them from behind an enormous desk.

Nikki glanced around nervously. Dark paneled walls. An ornate fireplace glowing with the dying embers of a real fire. Stained glass windows erected in honor of St. Preston's alums killed in World War I, and a large Persian rug covering the oak floor. Exactly the same principal's office she'd been sent to when caught reading romance novels under her desk in math class in seventh grade.

"Ainsley Bradley," Ainsley said firmly, extending her hand. Nikki did the same, but her fingers trembled slightly.

He rose from his seat and nodded toward the high-backed chairs in front of his desk. "Ladies. Please have a seat."

They exchanged pleasantries about the weather, the infinite patience of their daughters' kindergarten teacher, and the upcoming school auction. Then Ainsley took charge.

"We're here today about Coach Jericho."

Mr. Smedley Philpott tented his hands and nodded gravely. "I assumed as much. One of the assistant principals told me that you, or rather your sister, had called about him before."

Ainsley nodded. "We have. I mean we did."

He regarded them with a look Nikki could not read. "In that call, she alleged that he's morally unfit to be our basketball coach. But she offered no evidence to support this."

"I wasn't willing to share what I knew then. But today I am." Ainsley cleared her throat and sat up a little straighter. "Twenty years ago, I worked as a dancer in a gentleman's club in Washington, DC, to pay for my sister's college education. Wyatt Jericho was a regular at this establishment. He was occasionally violent, with a predilection for underage girls, and should not be allowed anywhere near the students he is currently coaching."

To Nikki's satisfaction, the principal's face creased in concern. "I did read the paper this morning . . ." His voice trailed off.

"Then you know I'm telling the truth," Ainsley said briskly. "I had hoped my children and others would never learn about this. But I had to admit everything publicly because Wyatt Jericho attempted to blackmail me. He demanded a million dollars in exchange for silence about my past. I refused to pay him, and my . . . revelation at the gala last night is the result." She leaned forward in her chair. "Now there's nothing to prevent me from telling you what I know about Wyatt Jericho and how I know it. He should not be coaching teenage girls."

Nikki resisted the urge the leap out of her seat and high-five Ainsley. She looked so regal, with her perfect posture, beautifully dressed as usual in a gray suit, like a queen discussing the misdeeds of a once-loyal subject. The school would *have* to fire Jericho now.

Mr. Smedley Philpott gave Ainsley an appraising look. "I appreciate the courage it took for you to come forward, Mrs. Bradley. After reading about your speech, I felt a responsibility to raise your earlier concerns with Mr. and Mrs. Hastings and the other members of our governing board this morning. We also met with Mr. Jericho, who predicted you would come forward and accuse him of blackmail. He tells us these allegations are completely false."

Nikki's heart dropped. She glanced at Ainsley, who'd gone pale.

The principal removed his glasses and began to polish them with a cloth he'd pulled from his desk. "We cannot act on these allegations without evidence. A police report. A photo of him in this establishment with some of the . . . young ladies you describe."

He put his glasses back on and gave them a cool stare. "But right now, all we have is you telling us you saw Mr. Jericho in a place he claims he's never been, twenty years ago. And I'm afraid that is not enough to fire the coach who's helped us win every game our teams have played this year, a coach who is reaching out to college recruiters as we speak, a coach who is giving our high school players a chance to earn scholarships to some of the finest universities in the country."

Nikki bit down on her tongue so hard she thought it might snap off.

"You don't have any evidence, do you, Mrs. Bradley?" He turned to Nikki with a raised eyebrow. "Or you, Mrs. Lassiter?"

"We don't," Nikki answered reluctantly, before Ainsley could say something she'd later regret.

"Then I'm sorry to tell you there's nothing I can do here." He gave an elaborate shrug. "And I am also advised to tell you, on behalf of Mr. and Mrs. Hastings and the other members of the governing board, that if you do not cease these efforts to tarnish Mr. Jericho's reputation, your children will be asked to withdraw from the school."

Ainsley gasped. "But—"

"I know. I know," he said, waving his hand dismissively. "Your husband and his family have been an asset to this school for generations. But we have to look to the future, not the past, and Mr. Jericho's athletic program is an enormous selling point for prospective families. He's putting this school on the map, and we are not willing to jeopardize that over vague twenty-year-old allegations that cannot be proven."

He folded his hands in front of him, closing the meeting. They'd been dismissed like sixth-grade boys chastised for writing bad words on the bathroom wall.

Ainsley's nostrils flared as she rose from her seat. Nikki gripped her arm and tried to send calming telepathic messages.

These words must have gotten through, because Ainsley took a deep breath, then spoke in a clipped voice. "I see. Well. Thank you for your time. Before I go, can I ask you one final question?"

"You can ask," he said, though his tone implied they'd be unlikely to get an answer.

"Have you ever had any complaints from the girls he coaches or from their parents?" Ainsley asked.

Mr. Smedley Philpott flushed. "I'm not authorized to discuss personnel matters, Mrs. Bradley. Thank you for coming in."

She and Ainsley exchanged a look. So, Wyatt Jericho *had* said or done something inappropriate. Otherwise, the principal would have indignantly informed them that no one else had ever complained.

Shelby's face rose in her mind, her lips curved in a secret smile as she texted furiously in the car on the way home from practice. And the morning Shelby had come over for craft supplies. She'd told Nikki she was going home, then headed in the opposite direction.

What if Shelby . . . She shuddered, unable to complete the thought.

He rose and walked them to the door.

"Thank you," Ainsley said stiffly. "You've told us all we need to know."

Chapter Fifty-One

AINSLEY

As they left his office, they swept through a door that hadn't been fully closed. Ainsley glanced at Mrs. Pique, who shot her a triumphant look.

That woman had eavesdropped on their entire conversation. Ainsley raised her chin and strode past.

It didn't matter. They hadn't told the principal anything the world didn't already know, but still. This knowledge made her vaguely nauseous, just like the picture Ben had showed her before she left the house that morning. When it became obvious he wasn't getting any blackmail money, Wyatt Jericho had given her Sexy Sheriff photo to Ben's opponent, who'd helpfully shared it with the world. Now it was trending on social media.

She and Nikki strode through the foyer, out the front doors, and into the parking lot, where an iron-gray sky threatened rain.

Nikki zipped up her coat to ward off the chill. "I'm sorry, Ainsley."

"I can't believe they'd put their precious athletic program ahead of protecting these girls."

"I can." Nikki glanced at the school. "Everyone on the board of governors worked hard to bring Jericho here. They've been trying to bump the athletic program up a notch for years, and if Jericho *weren't* a murderer and predator, it would be a major coup to have him as coach."

"I just thought . . ." Ainsley gripped her car keys, trying to articulate her thoughts. "I just thought if I did the right thing, everything would fall into place. But I feel like I've made everything worse, if that's even possible."

"You didn't make things worse," Nikki said quickly. "But I am worried about Shelby. After our trip to DC, I told my sister everything we know. She initially wanted to tell Shelby everything and pull her off the team, but this would force Shelby to lie about why she's quitting. Plus Shelby is kind of shy and insecure off the court. Basketball is her social life and a source of confidence—it's everything to her right now. In the end, my sister decided it might be more harmful to make her quit."

"I understand," Ainsley said. "Shelby just wants to play the sport she loves."

Nikki dug in her purse, searching for her keys. "My sister and brother-in-law are going out of town this weekend to celebrate their wedding anniversary, and Shelby's supposed to have a sleepover with Tiffany Hastings's daughter tomorrow night. But maybe I can take her out to dinner instead. We can have a conversation, just the two of us, and I can find out what she's seen or heard . . . and just make sure she's . . . okay. And in the meantime, maybe Jolene will come up with some kind of paper trail linking Wyatt Jericho to the club."

Ainsley glanced up as a group of first graders exploded from the building like confetti from a cannon for morning recess. "Are you doing Colonial Day now or coming back this afternoon? Ben's coming after lunch, but I promised Grace I'd zip through this morning while she's at the wool carding station."

"I'm coming later," Nikki said. "I need to run to Target for Halloween candy and a gift for Sophie K.'s party next week."

"Birthday party?"

Nikki paused. "I got the e-vite this morning . . . a birthday party . . . at Jump-n-Germ."

Ainsley frowned. "The trampoline place?"

"It doesn't mean anything," Nikki said quickly. "Check your spam folder."

Ainsley's mind raced. Sophie K. was one of Grace's good friends. She and Grace and Nikki's girls did everything together . . . and now Grace hadn't been invited to Sophie's birthday party?

"Check your spam folder," Nikki repeated, reading her mind.

Ainsley manufactured a smile. "I will."

"By the way, the girls are pestering me about sleepaway camp with Grace. Do you have any ideas? I know it's early, but I hear these camps fill up quickly."

Ainsley groaned. "I totally forgot. I'll do some research this afternoon."

"Thanks. Because you know if we leave the research to me, it will never get done."

"I'll find the camp. You can label the underwear."

"Divide and conquer," Nikki said. "I'll see you at pickup."

Ainsley headed for Grace's classroom, walking down a cheerful yellow hallway to the kindergarten wing. She wedged her way into a classroom filled with parents smiling fondly at adorable kindergartners in paper Pilgrim hats. She spotted Grace in the corner, diligently carding a scrap of wool, while others pounded plastic hammers against anvils or vigorously churned imaginary butter.

Across the room, Tiffany Hastings shot her a malevolent look. Red Jennifer tossed her head and turned her back, while Blonde Jennifer whispered something to Also Blonde Jennifer, and they both snickered.

She broke into a sweat. Suddenly she was back in middle school again, clad in clothes from Goodwill while everyone else wore Guess jeans and Esprit sweatshirts.

She swallowed hard. *It doesn't matter. Who cares what people think.*

Unfortunately, *she* still cared what people thought, even after everything she'd been through. A rush of disappointment washed over her. She felt like someone who'd swallowed some nasty medicine as directed by her doctor but remained uncured.

She forced her attention back to Grace, who beamed at her from across the room, radiating pride at this opportunity to display her colonial housekeeping skills for her mother.

After about ten minutes, the teacher thanked the parents for coming and politely invited them to leave so the children could trade their butter churns for iPads and return to real work.

Ainsley slipped out of the classroom and walked down the hall, past a group of women who became suspiciously silent when she approached, then whispered furiously when she moved past.

A flash of heat consumed her body as she quickened her pace. What did she expect? For the St. Preston's community to embrace her revelation? Did she think people would rush up and ask her for pole dancing lessons?

She clenched her fists. It didn't matter what people thought. She'd done the right thing. Or at least she'd tried. Not that it seemed to be helping anyone, including the girls on Wyatt Jericho's basketball team.

She stopped at the staircase to let a line of first graders go ahead of her. They had their cheeks puffed out, with one finger held to their lips. This must be the sacred Silent Sign her children had demonstrated for her at home.

Someone bumped her from behind. She whirled around.

Tiffany Hastings raised an eyebrow. "Gee. I'm sorry."

"No problem," Ainsley said coolly.

"Actually, Ainsley." Tiffany Hastings stepped closer, engulfing her in a cloud of perfume. "*You* are the problem."

Ainsley heaved an epic sigh. She'd first met Tiffany at the country club a few months before Grace was born, and after five long years of being nice to this person she loathed, she'd finally had enough. "What exactly are you trying to say, Tiffany? Just spit it out."

Tiffany scowled and stepped closer. "We had a meeting about you this morning. And then Mrs. Pique filled me in on your conversation with RSP. I can't believe you actually accused Wyatt of blackmail, just like he said you would. I just . . . I didn't think you'd actually do something that . . . *low*."

She threw up her hands. "Tiffany, *why* would I make any of this up?"

Tiffany shook her head, ignoring the question. "Do you know how hard we worked to bring Wyatt here? Do you know how much money we've all donated to increase his salary, so he'll stay? And then you come along and try to destroy it all, just to save your own skin."

She frowned. "Save my own skin?"

Tiffany's eyes narrowed. "Wyatt explained it. In politics they call it wag the dog. Your husband's opponent found a picture of you in your stripper costume, and your sketchy past has come back to haunt you. So now you want to distract people by spreading rumors about Wyatt instead."

Ainsley's mouth dropped open. "*Wyatt Jericho* was blackmailing *me*."

Two first graders turned and regarded Ainsley with wide eyes. She forced herself to lower her voice. "*He's* the reason I had to reveal my sketchy past. *He* gave the picture to my husband's opponent."

"Oh, c'mon, Ainsley." Tiffany rolled her eyes. "You expect me to believe that a guy who opened a battered women's shelter is actually a violent man with a bad temper who hangs out in strip clubs. *Seriously?*"

Tiffany's voice dripped with contempt. Ainsley said nothing, because now she understood.

The head of school, the governing board, and parents like Tiffany and her husband had invested time, money, and credibility into bringing Wyatt Jericho to the school. If she tore Jericho down, they'd tumble with him. Until she unearthed pictures of Wyatt Jericho with underage strippers on his lap, they'd never believe her.

"You truly think I'm making everything up?" Ainsley asked, incredulous.

Tiffany fluffed her perfect highlights with a manicured hand. "You know, Ainsley, I don't care that you used to be a stripper, or that you grew up on the wrong side of the tracks. But only someone truly trashy would destroy an innocent person's reputation. You disgust me."

Then she turned on her heel and walked away, leaving Ainsley standing in the hallway, too stunned to move.

It got worse as the day wore on.

She was a pariah at afternoon pickup, standing alone in the parking lot while clusters of parents stood apart from her, whispering. She remained alone until Nikki arrived to stand beside her in solidarity. She told Nikki about her conversation with Tiffany Hastings.

Nikki scowled at the groups of snickering parents on the other side of the parking lot. "We're gonna nail that bastard and prove them all wrong. You'll see."

Ainsley rubbed her forehead. "I hope you're right."

She held it together and managed to get Grace into the car. But their conversation on the way home from school was more painful than anything she'd experienced so far.

"Mommy," Grace called from the back seat, "what's a tripper?"

Her heart dropped. *Dear God. Not this.* She would gladly suffer any humiliation if she could just spare her children from the fallout.

"A tripper?" she asked, throat suddenly dry.

"Connor Killington said you used to be a tripper."

Her phone rang. She glanced down at a number she didn't recognize. She let it go to voicemail. This conversation was far more important.

She turned in her seat. "Remember when Daddy's campaign started, and we told you people would say bad things, so people won't vote for him? And if that happened, you should talk to us?"

Grace nodded.

"Well." She tried to think. How to explain her past to a five-year-old? She didn't want to lie, but she also didn't want her daughter to feel afraid or embarrassed. "People are going to say bad things about me too. They might even say bad things to you and Adam, and if they do, I hope you'll tell me, okay?"

"Okay," Grace said with a cheerful shrug. "But what's a tripper?"

"A tripper is someone who stumbles over things when they walk."

Another lie. The words were out of her mouth before she could call them back.

"That's what I thought!" Grace said. "But you aren't a tripper. Even when you wear tall shoes, you don't trip."

"Also, some people might call me a stripper," Ainsley said carefully, trying again. "A stripper is someone who takes off their clothes . . . when they get hot."

"Because if you don't take off your clothes when you get hot, you'll faint like Cicci Livingston did at chapel last week," Grace said in a matter-of-fact voice.

"Correct." Ainsley nodded. "I used to be someone who took off her clothes when she got hot. And there's nothing wrong with that. It's good to be . . . happy about the way you look . . . with or without clothes on your body. But if anyone tries to say it's a bad thing, you tell me, okay?"

"I will," Grace promised.

Ainsley focused on making a left-hand turn. Then she asked, "What did you say, when Connor Killington told you I used to be a . . . tripper?"

"I said I'd rather be a tripper than a nose picker. Connor Killington picks his nose *all the time*."

Ainsley smiled weakly into the rearview mirror. "And what did he say then?"

"Olivia and Isabella came over and he ran away." She made a whooshing arm gesture. "He's afraid of Olivia and Isabella."

"Why?"

"*Because*," Grace said, as though this should be obvious, "they told him that if he ever said anything mean to me, they'd put glue in his water bottle and then his tongue would get stuck to his teeth, and he wouldn't be able to talk anymore."

Ainsley laughed in spite of herself. She'd been so worried about her kids. She still was. But Nikki's girls were loyal and true. Just like their mom.

They came home and sat down at the kitchen table. Adam made dinosaurs out of Play-Doh while Grace did her spelling words.

Ainsley sat beside them with her laptop and checked her email and spam folder again.

No birthday party invitation for Grace.

Damn it. An atavistic rage rose inside her. She wanted to strangle Sophie K.'s mother for excluding Grace from a child's party because of something *she* had done.

Her shoulders slumped as she rubbed her forehead.

If everyone knew the truth about Wyatt Jericho, they'd understand. But until they did, both she and her kids would be pariahs in the school community. And she had to find some way to accept this.

She reached for her leather-bound planner and her to-do list, normally a soothing activity, and wrote down everything she needed to accomplish. Buy Grace a black hat for her Halloween costume. Find a summer camp for the girls, preferably one with no kids from St. Preston's.

She sighed. Researching summer camps would cross one item off her list. She googled "summer camps for girls" and began to scroll through the results. She sat up a little straighter as one caught her eye.

Play like a Girl Sports Camps, owned and operated by former Biltmore women's NCAA basketball champions.

She glanced at the screen, then returned to the home page and typed frantically.

A familiar face popped up under the search bar. Her eyes narrowed as she read the results.

The women who owned the camp had once played basketball for Wyatt Jericho.

Chapter Fifty-Two

NIKKI

A particularly virulent strain of strep throat swept through Nikki's house the following day, while Ainsley was dispatched to do three campaign events with Ben, delaying their trip to Play like a Girl Sports Camp. They finally arrived at 10:00 a.m. a few days later with the boys and the baby strapped into the back of Nikki's minivan.

They were somewhere in semirural Virginia, out past Dulles airport, a bucolic area with rolling hills, lit by a blue and cloudless sky on an unseasonably warm day.

Ainsley opened the minivan doors to release the boys while Nikki removed the baby and his car seat.

"I went to summer camp, and it was *not* like this." Nikki shaded her eyes as she took in acres of manicured soccer and lacrosse fields interspersed with tennis and basketball courts. In the center sat a tranquil lake reflecting the sky like a mirror embedded in the earth.

They entered the main office, where an attractive young woman in a tank top with curly dark hair offered to give them a tour. She grabbed keys and a walkie-talkie. "My name is Angelina Griffin, by the way."

They introduced themselves, describing their daughters, their ages, and their interests. Angelina's gaze grew sharp at the mention of Ainsley's name.

Nikki could see the wheels working in the young woman's mind as she tried to figure out why Ainsley's name and face were so familiar. Nikki repressed a sigh. She'd figure it out soon enough.

"You know our story, right?" Angelina started the tour for prospective parents in a state-of-the-art aquatics center smelling of chlorine.

"Just the basics from your website," Ainsley said. "But we'd love to know more."

Angelina handed them each a brochure as she led them out of the building and onto a soccer field. "I'm one of the founders of Play like a Girl. I have two business partners, one of whom played with me on Biltmore's back-to-back buzzer-buster NCAA championship teams."

Ainsley's face lit up in recognition. "Those games where it came down to a three-pointer at the last second in overtime?"

"That's right." Angelina nodded. "The championship game, two years in a row."

"I remember." Ainsley looked at her more closely. "You shot the game-winning three-pointer."

"I did," Angelina said with admirable humility. "One of my partners scored the winning basket the following year."

Nikki glanced from Ainsley to Angelina. She had no idea what they were talking about. Her knowledge of sports consisted of phrases like "Well, Greg, how about those Nationals" as a transition to the sports segment when they came out of a commercial break.

They followed Angelina through indoor weight rooms and bunkhouses, across tennis and basketball courts, and through a boathouse stocked with canoes. They finished up at a playground, right next to a rope-climbing course. The boys immediately took off, heading for the swings.

"Do you have any questions?" Angelina asked.

Ainsley exchanged a look with Nikki. "We're totally ready to sign our girls up for summer camp, but we have another reason for being here too."

"We have some questions about Wyatt Jericho," Nikki said.

Angelina stiffened. "Are you a reporter?"

"Not anymore," Nikki said.

"Wait a minute . . ." She did a double take, glancing again at Ainsley. "You're that lady . . . the one in the television ads . . . the one who . . ."

"Used to be a stripper?" Ainsley said with a hint of impatience. "Yeah, that's me. Wyatt Jericho used to come into the club where I worked. He tried to blackmail me. That's the reason for the television ads and the stories in the paper."

"I'm sorry," Angelina said, all trace of the cheerful tour guide now gone. "But I think you should leave."

"Listen." Nikki switched into reporter mode. Time to call on decades of experience talking to people who didn't think they wanted to talk. "Wyatt Jericho is coaching middle school girls at our school. And we're trying to get him fired, but we need proof that he's a sick predator."

"Because no one believes us," Ainsley said.

Emotions flitted across Angelina's face like clouds casting shadows across the sky. She regarded them in silence for a long moment. Then she said, "Wait here."

She disappeared into the office and returned with two women she introduced as her business partners: Jillian, a redhead a little older than Nikki and Ainsley, and a lanky blonde in her twenties named Sarah.

They all sat down at a picnic table while the boys climbed the playground's jungle gym.

"We started this camp about four years ago, and we all played at Biltmore for Wyatt Jericho, but at different times. I was on the first team he coached." Jillian had short hair, a clipped voice, and a commanding presence.

Nikki rummaged in her diaper bag, popped a can of formula, and poured it into a bottle as Ainsley explained everything about her experiences with Jericho at the club, about Harmonee, and about the school's stubborn refusal to listen to any negative information about their coach.

"Sounds familiar." Angelina's curly hair undulated gently as she shook her head in disgust.

"No one believed us either," Sarah said.

Nikki lifted Baby Joe from his car seat. "We've never been able to figure out why he left the university with a year left on his contract."

Angelina and Sarah glanced at Jillian, who, in addition to being older, seemed to be first among equals in their partnership.

She gave a terse nod, and Sarah took a deep breath. "Playing time was contingent on sleeping with Wyatt Jericho."

Angelina's lip curled. "We called it 'taking one for the team.'"

"Every year there were a couple girls who caught his eye," Sarah said. "We never knew why. Usually blondes, sometimes not, and always freshmen. He'd target each girl individually. First, he'd single her out for special praise. Then she'd have to stay after practice for special drills. And then he'd seduce her. If she refused, he made her life a living hell."

"Those girls usually quit the team at the end of the season," Angelina said.

"And if they slept with him?" Nikki asked, easing the bottle into Baby Joe's mouth.

"She'd be special for a few weeks," Sarah said. "Then he'd leave her alone and move on to the next one."

Angelina snorted in disgust. "He was all about variety."

"It got to the point where, when you started, the older girls on the team prepared you. They said, if the coach likes you, you sleep with him three or four times, and then he'll leave you alone and you get to play," Sarah said. "Refuse, and you may as well quit now."

"He did this to everyone?" Ainsley asked.

"No." Sarah shook her head. "He had no interest in some girls, and he left most of the team alone. But every year there were two or three freshmen he'd single out for whatever reason, and they were his targets."

"I was one of them." Angelina raised her chin defiantly. "We all were."

"Did he leave you alone as you got older?" Ainsley asked.

"Yeah," Sarah said. "He never messed with sophomores, juniors, or seniors, but we figured out fast that girls who refused him as freshmen didn't have a career after college. He'd do everything he could to sabotage you. We all knew that if you wanna go pro, or play ball in Europe, or coach somewhere cool, then you sleep with the coach like a good girl."

"Did anyone ever complain?" Nikki asked, then withered under Angelina's scowl. Clearly, she'd asked a stupid question.

"Oh, we complained all right," Angelina said. "To the athletic director."

"Of course." Ainsley rolled her eyes in disgust. "The wise and sympathetic Sebastian Hampton."

"Yeah." Jillian's lip curled. "What a dirtbag."

"He told the women who complained that they were misinterpreting things. That they needed to toughen up, get used to his coaching style." Angelina spoke rapidly, each word spiked with indignation. "Then he'd pull other players into his office and ask if the coach had done anything inappropriate with them, and of course they'd say no, because he hadn't. He wasn't screwing the whole team."

"Just a quarter of the team," Sarah said.

"Did he have any favorites, anyone he sort of favored all the way through?" Ainsley asked.

"No." Angelina shook her head. "He just liked the young ones. The freshmen. He had no interest as we got older. But he remembered who said yes and who said no. Playing time your junior and senior year was determined by how talented you were, and if you slept with him as a freshman."

"Would you be willing to come forward and say this publicly?" Nikki asked.

They glanced at each other. "We can't."

"After our final season, we went to Sebastian Hampton and complained, just like all those other players had done before us," Angelina said.

"And of course, he did nothing," Sarah added. "So, we hired a lawyer. A former player who'd gone to law school and knew all about Wyatt Jericho."

Angelina grinned. "That got their attention."

"We cut a deal with the athletic director." Sarah leaned forward. "If they promised to fire Jericho, we promised to sign a nondisclosure agreement and say nothing publicly."

"It wasn't ideal," Angelina said. "But we just wanted him out of there and away from future players, for good."

Sarah narrowed her eyes. "And then they tried to screw us over."

"Even though we signed the NDA, Sebastian Hampton didn't follow through on his promise to fire Jericho," Angelina said.

"He kept coaching. For another *two years*." Sarah pounded the table for emphasis.

"This time we went straight to the president of the university with our lawyer," Angelina explained. "We gave them one week to fire Jericho, and if they didn't, we'd consider the nondisclosure agreement null and void, and we'd go public."

"They finally did it," Sarah said. "They fired him in August."

"And in September, he started at St. Preston's," Ainsley said. "Now he coaches high school and middle school girls."

Angelina's shoulders slumped. "Look, we've worked really hard to build what we have here. He ruined our basketball careers, but we've succeeded in spite of him."

"I was one of the players who refused to sleep with him," Jillian said. "He made my life so miserable that I gave up my scholarship and left the team."

Angelina rested a supportive hand on her shoulder.

Jillian took a breath and continued. "But it forced me to imagine a life beyond basketball. I went to Wharton. Got my MBA. Worked in venture capital. Made a ton of money. And when these young ladies were looking for an investor . . ." She shrugged and grinned. "Our partnership was meant to be. I've done a lot of things in my life, but I've never had as much fun as I'm having right now."

"It's an amazing place," Ainsley said.

"Everyone here is a woman or a girl. Our coaches, admins, and campers, even the cooks and janitorial staff. Everyone is female," Jillian said, gesturing at the vast facility spread around them.

"It's a safe place for girls to play the sports they love," Angelina added quietly.

After a pause, Nikki turned to Jillian. "Would *you* be willing to speak publicly about what you know?"

"I would, but I haven't seen or spoken to the guy in decades, and again, I didn't sleep with him, so all I have to report are some really unpleasant conversations, but with no evidence to prove they ever took place," Jillian said.

"What about other girls on the team?" Nikki asked. "Players who never signed a nondisclosure agreement. Do you think they'd be willing to speak out, especially now that he's no longer coaching?"

"We could ask," Angelina said.

"We'd come forward ourselves, if we could," Sarah added.

They ended the meeting with hugs and promises to see each other in June if not before, when they dropped the girls off for summer camp.

Nikki put the minivan in gear. "We're getting closer."

"But we still have a long way to go," Ainsley said grimly as they headed home.

Chapter Fifty-Three

NIKKI

Nikki dropped Ainsley off at home, and then offered to pick up the girls from school.

"You're doing this so the mom with the scarlet *S* on her cashmere sweater won't have to face the pitchfork-wielding townsparents at pickup, aren't you?" Ainsley asked.

"No," Nikki lied. "I'm doing this so you have time to whip up a cheesecake or a pavlova or a baked Alaska and feed me dessert after I drop them off."

"Well, regardless of your motives, I appreciate it. And I'll see what I can do about dessert."

By the time Nikki returned, she found Ainsley and Jolene seated at the kitchen table with a freshly baked apple pie.

Ainsley gave the kids a snack and then sent them outside to play. Then she made Nikki a cappuccino in a very expensive-looking device in her walk-in pantry and handed Ainsley a cup with a heart swirled through the foam on top.

"If Ben loses the election, you can support the family with your work as a barista." Nikki took a sip. "This is *excellent*."

She and Ainsley sat down at the kitchen table, where Jolene scrolled through her phone. "It might not be necessary," Ainsley said. "We got some new poll numbers this morning, and Ben is actually *ahead*."

Nikki's mouth dropped open. "No way."

"We're up four points since my speech." Ainsley sat back in her chair, and for the first time all day, she looked happy. "I mean, he was up by eleven before my revelation, but the fact that he's still ahead is sort of breathtaking."

"That's fantastic news, Ainsley."

"I know." She gazed into her cappuccino. "Everyone hates me, no one is inviting Grace to their birthday parties, you're still unemployed, and Wyatt Jericho is still coaching, but if Ben wins his race, at least something good will have come from all this."

"I have more good news," Jolene said. "Or at least, moderately decent news." She took a bite of apple pie, then leaned forward. "You know that mansion on the Eastern Shore where you found Harmonee's note?"

They nodded.

"Guess who owns it?" Jolene sat back and crossed her arms, looking smug.

"Who?" they asked in unison.

"Sebastian Hampton's *aunt*."

Nikki cast her tired mind backward in time, trying to remember what the cleaning ladies had told them when they visited the house. "Remind me again? I can't even remember what I had for lunch today."

"That's because we didn't have time for lunch today," Ainsley said. "The cleaning ladies told us the aunt lives there in the summer, remember? But when she's not there, her nephew uses it for wild parties."

"With condoms and ladies' underwear and empty beer bottles all over the place," Nikki added, waving her fork in the air as the entire conversation came back to her in a rush.

"That means Sebastian Hampton is the nephew who throws wild parties at his aunt's mansion?" Ainsley asked.

Jolene nodded. "And it gets better. Guess what BS Unlimited stands for."

Ainsley looked confused. "Wait. What?"

"BS Unlimited," Jolene repeated.

Nikki was also having trouble following Jolene's rapid train of thought. "Could you back up a bit, for those of us who aren't Mensa?"

Jolene heaved the impatient sigh of a brilliant person forced to explain things to people who were inevitably three steps behind. "The credit card Wyatt Jericho uses when he comes into the club. It's issued to someone named Walter Jelico, an on-purpose spelling error that allows him to deny it's his. And it's a corporate card, issued to an entity called BS Unlimited, which we believe is an abbreviation for Bedroom Sports Unlimited."

"Sounds like an X-rated mattress store," Nikki said.

"It's essentially a slush fund for donations from wealthy Biltmore alums, former athletes, and sports boosters," Jolene explained.

Nikki helped herself to a second slice of pie. "What do they use the money for?"

"Off-the-books recruiting expenses," Jolene said. "Alcohol for sure, possibly drugs. Most withdrawals are in cash, and we suspect the money is used to hire strippers and purchase other 'services,' if you catch my drift. We're still digging, but this is what we've learned so far."

"This is fantastic." Nikki sank her fork into her apple pie. It sounded like an enormous amount of solving for *x*. Just the thought of all that math made her head hurt.

"There's still a lot we don't know," Jolene said humbly, "but we're getting closer."

"'We'?" Ainsley lifted an eyebrow.

Jolene actually blushed. "I've had a little help. From Caleb Connors. The opposition research guy, from the campaign."

"Oh really," Ainsley said, arching a brow.

"Stop that." Jolene slugged her sister in the arm. "He's just . . . he's very smart and he has a lot of friends in the FBI and law enforcement, cybersecurity guys who go after drug dealers and Russian oligarchs, really complex stuff, and they know a few tricks I don't, so between my knowledge of how to *legally* evade paying taxes, and his knowledge of how to dig up information about people who *don't* pay their taxes at all, we've done pretty well together."

"I'll bet you have," Ainsley said with a lascivious grin.

"Stop it. There's nothing going on—"

"Yet," Ainsley said.

"Yet," Jolene admitted, blushing furiously once again.

Ainsley took a sip of her cappuccino. "We have some news too." She brought Jolene up to speed on their conversation at the camp for girls.

Nikki glanced at her watch. "I've gotta get home. I have to turn sixty doughnut holes into Halloween spiders using nothing but frosting, edible googly eyes, and my bare hands."

As she rose to leave, her phone rang. She found it, battery almost dead, in the bottom of the diaper bag on the fourth ring.

She listened, said a few words. Then hung up, her face white.

"Shelby is missing."

Chapter Fifty-Four

NIKKI

She left the kids with Ainsley, treated the speed limit like bad advice and ignored it, and careened into her driveway five minutes later. Josh waited on the front steps, his brow creased with deep lines. She jumped out of the car and raced across the lawn. He pulled her into a hug, then told her everything he knew.

"Your sister stopped by as they were leaving town to drop off Shelby's antibiotics," he began.

She nodded impatiently. Shelby had come down with strep throat earlier in the week and had to take antibiotics twice a day.

"Your sister left them in our mailbox," Josh continued. "Then she called from the road and asked me to drop the pills at Tiffany Hastings's house so Shelby could take a dose before bed."

Nikki knew why her sister had called Josh, why she always called Josh to schedule the annual family beach rental in the Outer Banks or discuss logistics for their mother's birthday party. Because Josh would actually *remember* to take the antibiotics over to Tiffany Hastings's house. Nikki would have forgotten.

She screwed up her face as she tried to recall the labyrinth of arrangements they'd made for Shelby that weekend, hoping Shelby's current location lay hidden in the Rubik's Cube of child-activity logistics.

"Shelby has a sleepover with Tiffany's daughter tonight. Tiffany takes them to basketball practice in the morning. Another mom brings Shelby to me at Isabella's soccer game. Then you drop Daniel at that birthday party and take Olivia to dance while I bring Shelby, Isabella, and the baby home. Right?"

Looking back through the mists of time, she recalled an era when she spent weekends brunching with friends as they parsed the obscure motives of men they were dating, or perhaps not dating, deconstructing why someone had called or not called, followed by shopping, and a nap. Now those memories felt like they belonged to a different person.

Josh frowned. "Your sister told me basketball practice is canceled tonight and tomorrow because the coach is going out of town for the weekend, so Shelby was going straight to Tiffany's house after school to spend the night."

Nikki felt the color drain from her face. Shelby was missing, and Wyatt Jericho was out of town for the weekend.

Coincidence?

It couldn't be, given everything she knew about Jericho. And Harmonee.

She pressed her hand against her abdomen to quell the sick feeling in her gut.

"I finished up at work," Josh continued, "and then drove over to Tiffany's with the antibiotics. I knocked on the door, and the housekeeper answered. She told me no one was home. Tiffany and her husband are in Key West for the weekend, and she said the daughter is spending the night with a friend."

Nikki slammed her palm into her forehead. The old sleeping-over-at-my-friend's-house-while-the-parents-are-away trick. And all the adults fell for it, including her.

"So where is Shelby *right now*?"

"That's what I'm trying to tell you." He shook his head, his face haggard. "*I don't know where Shelby is.* That's when I called you."

Nikki pulled out her phone, then raised her face to the sky, releasing a long moan. "It's dead."

"Do you know Shelby's number?" he asked, turning pale.

She hung her head. Asking if she remembered Shelby's phone number was like asking if she knew her children's Social Security numbers, or the Netflix password, or the square root of pi.

"Have you called my sister?" she asked, trying to keep a lid on her mounting panic. Losing her keys and cell phone were bad enough, but losing her *niece* was beyond the pale.

"I tried, but she's on a plane." Josh held up his phone, displaying an airline flight app. "She lands in five minutes."

Nikki ran into the house. Through some organizational miracle, she found the school directory where she'd left it on the kitchen counter. Using Josh's fully charged phone, she called both Tiffany Hastings and her husband, but got voicemail, probably because they were also on a plane. She hung up without leaving a message. As much as she disliked Tiffany, she didn't want to worry her until she knew more.

"Should we call the police?" Josh asked.

Nikki chewed on her lower lip and glanced at the app on Josh's phone. "Let's talk to my sister first. She'll be on the ground in three minutes. Maybe the plan changed again, and she forgot to tell us."

It was a futile hope, but she clung to it anyway, while images from the guest house on the Eastern Shore filled her mind: the bed facing the window, the lighthouse, and the mother osprey protecting her nest.

The longest three minutes of Nikki's life ticked by. She called her sister the moment the plane touched the runway and told her everything. In the background, Nikki could hear her brother-in-law calling Shelby's phone and leaving messages.

No answer.

In a carefully controlled voice with just a hint of hysteria, her sister tracked Shelby using Find My Phone. "She's at a hotel," her sister said. "In Manassas, Virginia."

Nikki paused. Manassas? Not exactly a secluded, romantic getaway. Still. She didn't want Shelby anywhere near Wyatt Jericho and a hotel room.

"I'll call the police," Nikki said tersely.

"Wait," her sister said. "I'm tracking Apple Pay. She just bought fries and a chicken sandwich at Chick-fil-A. And fifteen minutes ago, she texted to ask if I can take her to the mall to buy new jeans when we get back on Sunday."

She could hear her sister tapping furiously on her phone. "She isn't responding to my texts, but let me check Instagram."

A pause, then, "She just posted a picture of her chicken sandwich. And she just liked a photo of waffle fries posted by Skylar Hastings. They appear to be together."

Nikki exhaled. At least Shelby wasn't *alone* with Wyatt Jericho. But if they were at a hotel with him . . . she shuddered, her mind refusing to pursue this thought.

Her sister sighed. "I don't know what's going on, but I don't think she's in peril if she's Instagramming chicken sandwiches. Can you drive out there and get her. Like right now?"

She decided to keep her worries about Wyatt Jericho to herself until she knew more.

"On my way," she said.

"Do you want me to come along?" Josh asked as she hung up the phone.

"Get the kids from Ainsley and put them to bed. I'll be back as soon as I can."

She kissed her husband, jumped back in her minivan, punched the hotel into the GPS, and stomped on the accelerator.

Thirty-five minutes later, she pulled up to a high-rise hotel connected to a sprawling convention center. She marched up to the front desk and demanded the room number for Wyatt Jericho.

The clerk typed on her keyboard. "We don't have a guest named Wyatt Jericho registered here."

"Walter Jelico?" she asked, spelling the name on the credit card Jericho had used at Godiva's.

The clerk scrutinized her computer screen, then shook her head. "Sorry. No one under that name either."

Behind her in the lobby, a group of teenage boys gathered around a Nintendo Switch. She glanced around, noticing a lot of teenagers. "Is there an event at the hotel today?"

"It's the eighteenth annual Tri-State Mathlete Olympiad," the clerk said. "The opening round begins in an hour."

Nikki's chest expanded. For the first time since Josh's phone call an hour ago, she felt like she could breathe. "Do you happen to have a Chick-fil-A nearby?"

The woman pointed to a wall map of the hotel and convention center, with a star marking the food court. Nikki thanked her and headed through carpeted corridors with multiple banners welcoming mathletes. Weaving her way through crowds of what appeared to be high school kids, she followed the scent of fried chicken to the food court.

At a table near the center, Shelby and Skylar Hastings sat with two skinny boys wearing glasses and Star Wars T-shirts. Shelby gazed adoringly at the freckled boy beside her. He laughed at something she said, smiling into her eyes.

Nerd love.

Nikki sank into a plastic chair at the edge of the food court, next to a bald man wolfing down a taco, and observed the two couples from afar. She texted her sister, All is well. Details to come. Then she uttered a prayer of gratitude and allowed the stress of the last hour to ebb away.

The boys left about five minutes later, while the girls remained at the table, heads close together, giggling and whispering.

Nikki approached and sat down. "Hello, ladies."

Shelby's mouth dropped open. "Aunt Nikki?"

She nodded gravely. "Indeed. It is I, Aunt Nikki. Now please tell me *what the hell* is going on here."

"We can explain," Shelby said.

"Great." Nikki grabbed a waffle fry from Skylar's tray. "You should do that."

The girls looked at each other. Neither spoke.

"Like *right now*," Nikki said, waving a ketchup packet for emphasis.

"Okay." Shelby looked pale. "Am I in really big trouble?"

The last of Nikki's patience drained away, making her voice sharper than she intended. "Listen here, young lady, your trouble increases in direct proportion to the amount of time it takes you to explain why you are eating Chick-fil-A at a mathlete convention in Manassas, Virginia, with Skylar and some guy who looks like Ron Weasley from the Harry Potter movies without telling any of us *where you are*."

Shelby's eyes expanded at Nikki's use of the words *young lady*. Nikki realized she had uttered one of those magical phrases that transported her across an invisible border, officially turning her into her own mother.

"We got a ride out here with Myrtle," Shelby said sheepishly.

"Winston's grandma," Skylar explained. "She has this really cool car called a *Cadillac*."

"We rode with her because she wanted to watch Winston and Calvin compete," Shelby said. "And then we were going to ask Calvin's mom to give us a ride home before you figured out we were gone and got worried."

Nikki rubbed her forehead in exasperation. "Why didn't you just *ask* me or your mom for a ride?"

The girls exchanged a look. "Because the boys are like . . . *old*," Shelby said.

"How old?" Nikki asked, dipping a waffle fry into ketchup.

"They're fourteen," Shelby said.

"But Shelby . . ." Nikki paused. *Numbers again.* She had to concentrate every time the pediatrician asked her to recite the year her own children were born, so she was admittedly a little foggy on the year of her niece's birth. "Aren't you fourteen years old too?"

"Well, I am, but—" Shelby began.

"But they skipped third grade," Skylar explained.

Shelby's face wore a stricken expression. "So even though we're the same age, we're still in middle school, but Winston and Calvin are *freshmen*."

"In *high school*," Skylar said.

"Ah." Nikki nodded slowly, eating another waffle fry as she absorbed this confession. "Older men."

Just like Mikhail Baryshnikov. She understood the allure.

The girls nodded sadly.

"Our moms would *freak out*," Skylar said.

"How long have you been . . . hanging out . . . with these guys?" Nikki asked, opening another ketchup packet.

She wasn't sure what lingo kids used now. Friends with benefits? Dating? Hooking up? Hanging out? Snogging? Shagging? She also wasn't sure what those words denoted. Just texting? Actually talking? Hanging out in person? Making out? Having sex? She suddenly felt a wave of sympathy for the girls in front of her and the complicated world they'd inherited. She wished they could all go back to 1950 and do the twist at a sock hop with guys who looked like James Dean.

"We started hanging out last year, when they were eighth graders and we were in seventh," Shelby said.

"I see. And now they're in high school, in a whole different building. A whole different world." Nikki gave them a sympathetic look. "That must be hard."

"Long-distance relationships suck," Shelby said mournfully.

Nikki allowed a moment of silence to honor the truth of this statement. Then, marshaling her willpower, she pushed the fries away. *Enough.* This was turning into a ten-thousand-calorie conversation.

She wiped her fingers on a paper napkin. "I'm taking you guys home after you watch Winston and Calvin compete in the opening round. And you will both stay at our place until everyone's parents return on Sunday. No staying home alone or with housekeepers who may or may not be there all weekend." She glanced at Skylar, who looked down at her lap. "But in exchange for a ride and room and board, I need you guys to answer some questions."

"You'll let us stay and watch?" Shelby asked, a huge smile stealing over her face.

Nikki shrugged. "Call me sentimental."

The idea of sitting here for another hour and then driving all the way home made her tired down to the marrow of her bones. But she was so relieved to find Shelby safe that she would have granted far more outrageous wishes if her niece had asked. "But first I need some honest answers to a few questions," Nikki said sternly.

Shelby nodded. "Okay. No problem."

The waffle fries began to emit a faint buzzing sound, calling to Nikki from across the table. She found herself unable to resist their siren song and pulled the tray closer.

"Has Wyatt Jericho ever done or said anything to make you uncomfortable?" she asked, opening yet another packet of ketchup.

The girls exchanged a look.

"Yeah," Shelby said. "He's kinda . . ."

"Skeevy," Skylar said.

"Skeevy in what way?" Nikki dipped another fry into the ketchup.

"Like, when he's showing you how to shoot a free throw. He comes up behind you," Skylar explained.

"And he stands like, really close," Shelby said.

Skylar nodded. "Like, way too close."

"And he brushes against you sometimes," Shelby said.

"And he pretends like it's an accident," Skylar added.

Shelby nodded. "But you also wonder if it's like, *on purpose*."

"And he says things." Skylar glanced at Shelby.

Nikki pushed the fries away. She'd lost her appetite. "What kinds of things?"

"Like . . . he makes everything sort of . . . dirty." Shelby's face flushed.

Nikki fought to keep her expression neutral as her stomach tightened in disgust. "What do you mean?"

"Like, if we're down on our hands and knees doing burpees, he'll say something like, 'You love it on all fours, don't you, girls.'" Skylar pitched her voice low in imitation of Jericho.

"Stuff that doesn't even make sense." Shelby scowled. "Like, what does that even *mean*?"

"Is there anything else you can tell me?" Nikki asked, grateful that Shelby did not understand Jericho's double entendre.

The girls glanced at each other again.

"There are some, like, rumors," Shelby said slowly. "About the older girls. That a couple of the seniors are like . . . his girlfriends or something."

"Do you have any names?" Nikki asked.

They shook their heads.

"Okay." Nikki crumpled her napkin into a ball, wishing it were Wyatt Jericho's head. "I really appreciate you being honest with me."

Skylar Hastings looked at Nikki. "Are you going to tell my mom about Coach Jericho?"

"Do you want me to tell her?" Nikki asked gently.

The girl nodded. "I don't think she'd believe us, but she might believe a grown-up."

She reached across the table and squeezed Skylar's hand. "Sunday night when we take you home, I'll talk to her."

Not that it would do any good, but she could at least try.

They spent the next ninety minutes watching Winston and Calvin answer the kind of complex math questions that gave her PTSD. Her phone rang just as they were preparing to leave.

She sighed. It must be her mother, calling yet again to demand a list of Christmas presents for the grandkids. Nikki refused to give in to this kind of organizational terrorism. No one could force her to think that far ahead. She would text her mother a list on Black Friday, and not a day sooner.

She plucked the phone from her purse and found Ainsley's name displayed on the caller ID.

Ainsley's voice came through rushed and breathless. "Godiva just called. We finally have the break we need to nail Jericho."

Chapter Fifty-Five

AINSLEY

Ainsley steered her Mercedes through Saturday-morning traffic as they drove across the Biltmore campus, headed for Godiva's. Nikki sat beside her in the passenger seat, sipping from her stainless steel travel mug.

On the sidewalk, bleary-eyed students slouched toward coffee shops and breakfast joints, some of them already wearing Halloween costumes. Frankenstein and the Bride of Frankenstein held hands as they walked down the sidewalk with SpongeBob, a pirate, and a woman in a suit with pages of paper taped to her arms, legs, and torso.

Nikki pointed to the apparition encased in paper. "I don't get it."

"She's a lawsuit," Ainsley explained.

"Ah, clever. No wonder I didn't get into Biltmore."

Ainsley slowed to let a Prius pull in front of her. She didn't want to get her hopes up, but if Lady Godiva was right, their prayers had been answered. According to Godiva, Wyatt Jericho planned to attend a party chock full of strippers—and possibly underage girls—tonight at the mansion on the Eastern Shore.

"Can I confess something?" Nikki asked.

"By all means." Ainsley steered around a UPS truck parked in the middle of the street. "Why should I be the only one to harbor disturbing secrets?"

"Okay, here it is." Nikki took another swig of coffee, then blurted, "I *loathe* Halloween."

Ainsley's mouth twitched. "Why?"

"Because it's like New Year's Eve for five-year-olds. Kids put on a cool outfit, get drunk on sugar, and stay up way too late. The next day they're hungover and exhausted and have to wake up early and go to *school.* It makes no sense. The day after Halloween should be a federal holiday. I mean, think of the poor teachers."

"Let me guess," Ainsley said. "Evangelical Heather loves trick-or-treating with her family."

Nikki nodded. "Evangelical Heather sews all the costumes. The whole family dresses up, and they have a *theme.* Last year they were all characters from *The Wizard of Oz.* The baby played Toto. She carried him in a basket. And he wore a little baby headband with Toto ears."

Ainsley paused in concentration as a Lycra-clad cyclist wove in front of her. Then she said, "If you made Baby Joe wear Toto ears and carried him in a basket, we wouldn't be friends."

"Why not?" Nikki asked.

"Because if you did that, you wouldn't be Nikki. And I love you *because* you are Nikki."

A look of gratitude lit up Nikki's tired face. "That is quite possibly the nicest thing anyone has ever said to me."

"It's true." Ainsley pulled into Godiva's cobblestone parking lot. "Your flaws make you perfect. And you're a great mother. With great kids."

"Thanks, Ainsley." Nikki's gratitude washed away the tension settling into Ainsley's neck and shoulders as they approached Godiva's. This would work or it wouldn't work, but either way, she'd still have Nikki, Jolene, Ben, and her kids.

She turned off the car and grabbed her purse. "If it's any consolation, this Halloween could be very different than any you've experienced before. Now, shall we?"

Nikki nodded. They climbed the porch and entered the club through the front door.

It took a few moments for Ainsley's eyes to adjust to the dim light, but once they did, everything looked the same as it had on their last visit. She'd expected the club to be quiet and empty at 10:00 a.m. on a Saturday, but "Monster Mash" floated through the air from the ballroom along with raucous laughter.

They wandered inside to find a cluster of fraternity boys eating bacon and chicken wings while three mummies strolled up and down the catwalk, energetically stripping away their bandages to reveal nothing but G-strings. The bouncer, a muscular bald man with a striking resemblance to Mr. Clean, sat in a chair near the stage, scowling at the customers with his arms crossed over his broad chest.

Lady Godiva emerged from behind the bar.

"New girls," she said with a hopeless shake of her head as she glanced at the girls on the stage. "Clumsy as hell. Can't let them anywhere near the pole or they'll break their damn legs. But they gotta start somewhere, so I like to put 'em on the Saturday-morning Bloody-Mary-and-bacon shift."

She led them up the stairs as she spoke, to the club's inner sanctum, where only dancers and the Godivas were allowed. "The girls I told you about is up here."

Light flooded through dormer windows as they entered a wide attic on the house's third floor. Two women sat on a worn velvet sofa beside a giant mahogany desk covered with ledgers, pens, and a retro calculator with a spool of paper attached.

"Ladies, this here's Amber and Lacey." Godiva gestured at two young women sitting on the sofa in T-shirts and yoga pants. "Girls, this here is Ainsley, who used to be Velvet, and Nikki, who wasn't never a dancer, but you could probably tell that from how she looks."

Ainsley glanced at Nikki, who rolled her eyes.

Godiva settled herself in the leather chair behind the desk as Nikki and Ainsley sat down in battered wingback chairs beside the sofa.

Godiva jutted her chin toward the young women on the sofa. "Tell 'em everything you told me."

Both girls were lovely in their own way, but Amber was objectively gorgeous, with delicate cheekbones, curving lips, and tumbled blonde hair. Both were so young it made Ainsley's heart ache, though they appeared to be roughly the same age she'd been when she started dancing at nineteen.

A sewing box sat open on the coffee table, and each girl had a needle, thread, and a bundle of sequined G-strings and bikini tops in her lap. It gave the whole scene an incongruously domestic appearance, like an adult version of *Little Women* where Jo writes erotica and Beth plays the piano for Meg and Amy, who dance the can-can in Marmee's House of Ill Repute.

"We stopped by to get our costumes 'cause we're doing a big private party tonight." Amber gestured at the scraps of fabric in her lap.

Lacey nodded. "On the Eastern Shore in this big mansion, and it pays like, *beaucoup* bucks."

"Who's throwing the party?" Nikki asked.

"This guy named Sebastian." Amber held up a G-string and examined it in the light.

"He's like a recruiter or a coach or something. For a basketball team." Lacey moved her needle through the fabric, attaching a new sequin to a bikini top. "And he throws these like, massive parties for guys he wants for his team."

"And most of the guys are our age. Like, Biltmore players or guys from different colleges. It's not a geezer party where all the guys are like, you know, *forty* or something." She wrinkled her nose in distaste.

Lacey rifled through the buttons and sequins spread across the coffee table. "These parties are *epic*. Tons of really cool dudes, lots of weed. Coke, too, if you're into that."

"And tons of booze if you're not," Amber added with a quick glance at Lady Godiva, whose antidrug stance was well known.

"And it pays like, major coin," Lacey said.

Amber nodded. "Five hundred dollars for the night, and all you have to do is walk around in lingerie. But tonight, everyone's wearing a costume."

"And if you want tips, you can dance and be part of the show." Lacey used small scissors to snip a loose thread.

"They have a dance floor in the basement and this, like, *legit* basketball court." Amber drew a sort of diagram in the air with her needle.

Ainsley nodded. "I've seen it."

Amber's eyes widened. "Have you worked one of these parties before?"

"No," Ainsley said, flattered at the assumption that a suburban mother wearing a Talbots cardigan could still dance. "But I've seen the basement."

"This party is like, *end of days*," Lacey said. "Girls strolling around in lingerie, or stripping onstage, and some—" She snapped her mouth shut and stopped speaking.

"Some girls are doing more than dancing?" Ainsley asked quietly.

"Yeah." Amber nodded, her lovely face suddenly sober. "Upstairs. There's always a few girls willing to do the deed for extra Benjamins."

Lacey turned to Ainsley. "Can I ask you a question?"

"Sure." She had nothing to hide, not anymore.

She cast a glance over Ainsley's body. "Like, how *old* are you, 'cause you're still in like, really good shape."

"I'm thirty-nine," Ainsley said. All those hours in the gym had apparently paid off.

"And how old are you?" she asked, turning to Nikki.

"I'm the cautionary tale." Nikki gestured toward her heavily C-sectioned self. "Avoid carbs, ladies. And use sunscreen. And do Pilates. Or goat yoga. Or *something*. And have two kids instead of four. And don't have the last baby *after* you turn forty. That'll wreck your body for good."

"How old are you guys?" Ainsley asked.

They giggled and exchanged a look.

"You don't wanna know," Lacey said.

"Actually, we do," Nikki said firmly.

"We're both Geminis. We turned eighteen in June." Amber added some feathers to the bikini top she'd been working on. "We graduated from high school last spring."

Ainsley's heart fell. She didn't want these girls to be under eighteen, but at the same time, how were they ever going to catch Jericho if they only hung around girls a few days over the legal limit?

"But there are some girls who hang out at this house who are still in high school," Amber said.

"How do you know that for sure?" Nikki asked.

"Because we went to high school *with* them," Amber said. "They were juniors and sophomores when we were seniors."

"And we went to camp with a couple of them, when we were younger," Lacey added.

"How old are these girls now?" Ainsley asked.

"It depends when their birthday is. I mean, it's only October, so a lot of them won't turn eighteen until later in the school year. So even if they're seniors, most of them are still seventeen," Amber said.

"That's one reason why Sebastian likes them to come." Lacey picked up another sequin. "Some of the guys he's trying to recruit are still in high school. So, he hires dancers about the same age. Makes them feel more comfortable. Or so he says."

"Have you ever seen a guy named Wyatt Jericho at these parties?" Nikki asked.

"Sure." Lacey shrugged. "He's at all the parties."

"Does he do anything . . . memorable . . . when he's there?" Ainsley asked.

Lacey gave her friend a sly look. "She dated him for a while."

Amber punched her friend in the arm. "I did not."

"Yes, you did," Lacey insisted.

Amber rolled her eyes and huffed a sigh. "We went out a couple times last summer. Or stayed in. Mostly at his place."

"How did you meet him?" Nikki asked.

Amber pursed her lips and thought a moment. "We first met him at Camp Confidence when we were in middle school. And he kinda stayed in touch, sending us texts, stuff like that. He's the one who suggested we try dancing. He hooked us up with Dino Johnson down at the Depot, and we started working there. After we had some experience and got better, we upgraded to Godiva's."

"You were eighteen when you dated him?" Ainsley asked.

"Barely." Amber nodded. "But yeah."

"You should come with us tonight," Lacey said impulsively. "It's going to be super fun."

"I appreciate the invitation," Ainsley said. "But I think I'm a little old."

They did not argue this point. Then Amber brightened. "It's Halloween. You could wear a *mask*."

Lacey clapped her hands. "OMG! That's brilliant. I mean, we're *all* wearing costumes."

"You could be the Naughty Ninja," Amber said. "I make *bank* when I'm the Naughty Ninja."

"Or the Jeannie in a Bottle? You know, like, the Harem Hussy routine? Major coin. You could do that whole dance of the seven veils thing. Dudes *dig* that," Lacey said.

"Or Batgirl," Amber said.

Lacey pointed at Nikki. "And she could be Robin."

Amber glanced at her phone. "We gotta run. Time to get our gels done."

When Ainsley and Nikki looked confused, they waggled their fingers. "Our *nails*. At the salon. We have an appointment in ten minutes. Tips are bigger if you have long nails," Lacey explained.

"But it makes it really hard to put in your contacts," Amber added.

"You gotta spend money to make money," Lacey said. "That's why I'm saving up for silicone."

Amber nodded gravely. "Invest in *yourself*. That's our motto."

They began to stuff their costumes into shopping bags. "You should totally come tonight," Lacey said as she gathered up her purse and a Hello Kitty sewing basket.

"You girls wearing the hair ties I gave you for good luck?" Godiva asked.

Amber rolled her eyes. "Yes, Lady Godiva. We'll wear them. We promise."

Godiva nodded, apparently satisfied. "Good. You girls have fun."

"Bye!" Lacey called with one last wave as they disappeared down the stairs.

Godiva leaned back in her chair. The room suddenly seemed empty, like a street after the parade has gone by. "This could be your only chance to catch that bastard in the act."

"But even if we're there and see it ourselves, no one will believe us," Ainsley said.

"So, we record it." Nikki held up her phone. "The camera doesn't lie."

Ainsley thought about her conversation with Tiffany Hastings. *They won't believe me unless I have pictures of Wyatt Jericho with an underage stripper in his lap.*

"If we want this evidence, we have to get it ourselves," Nikki said.

"But we can't just show up at this party *uninvited*."

"Ainsley." Nikki rolled her eyes. "This is not one of your five-course-tasting-menu dinners. I highly doubt guests are expected to RSVP."

"What I mean is, how do we get inside and record the whole thing without being recognized?"

"The girls told you how." Lady Godiva gestured at Ainsley with her lighter. "You're still a looker. Still Lady Velvet with a dancer's body. You can pull this off."

Then she lit her cigarette and glanced at Nikki. "Her, I'm not so sure about . . ."

"But he'd recognize us both," Ainsley said.

"Then pick an outfit with a mask like the girls said. I got all the costumes right here." Lady Godiva spread her arms wide. "Sexy Zorro, the Lone Ranger in Lingerie, Naughty Ninja, Harem Hussy, Catwoman. The disguise is not a problem. And I can help you get inside. I'll drive you there myself in the Strippermobile."

Nikki almost spit out her coffee. "The what?"

"It's like the popemobile," Ainsley explained. "But different."

"It's a big panel van we use to drive dancers to group events like bachelor parties. It'll lend a look of"—Lady Godiva gestured airily with her cigarette—"*authenticity* . . . to your arrival."

"But it's Halloween," Ainsley said. "We have to take the kids trick-or-treating tonight."

Nikki sighed. "Ainsley, how many parents do our children have?"

"Two," she conceded.

"Their *dads* can take them trick-or-treating. Because tonight we're riding the Strippermobile to an epic party."

Ainsley pressed a hand to her fluttering stomach. This plan sounded both sane and insane. Could they really sneak into a party filled with strippers and basketball players, secretly tape Wyatt Jericho with underage girls, and slink away without getting caught?

Her mind flashed to Grace and the birthday party invitation that never came, the principal who wanted to kick her kids out of school, the parents who wouldn't speak to her. She'd risked everything to take down Wyatt Jericho, yet he remained untouched. She had nothing left to lose.

She tossed Nikki a sequined G-string. "Fire up the Strippermobile."

Chapter Fifty-Six

NIKKI

The Strippermobile bounced over potholes, launching the passengers up to the ceiling and back down again on inadequately padded seats. Lady Godiva was not a gentle driver.

In the end, they'd been able to go trick-or-treating *and* embark on their mission to take down Wyatt Jericho. They set out with the kids just before sunset. By seven thirty their buckets were full, and they were happy to go home and examine the loot.

They left Josh and Ben in charge of the epic candy swap taking place on Nikki's kitchen floor and climbed into Nikki's minivan for the rendezvous with Godiva.

She waited in the driver's seat as Ainsley spoke to Ben through the passenger window. She and Josh had engaged in an almost identical conversation minutes earlier as she searched for her purse.

Ben grasped Ainsley's hand through the window. "I'm really worried about this."

"Detective Chavez knows what we're doing. She's standing by if we run into trouble. All we have to do is call."

"I still don't understand why she can't go in with you."

"We talked about this," Ainsley said patiently. "The police can't record a private citizen without a warrant. But Nikki and I can. When we have the video, we call, and she swoops in and makes the arrests."

"But Wyatt Jericho *killed* someone. He's dangerous."

"Ben, this man is destroying our lives. I need to do this."

He nodded. "I know you do. Just, please, please be careful."

Josh approached the driver's side door with Baby Joe perched on his hip. Nikki lowered the window.

"Is there any point in asking you again not to do this?" he asked.

"No."

He kissed her. "I figured as much. I'm proud of you. Please be careful."

They waved goodbye and headed for Godiva's, where they changed into their costumes and met up with Jolene.

After trying several options, Ainsley decided to be the Harem Hussy, because the veil hid her lower face, and because the ornate, sequined bra top provided an excellent place to hide the tiny camera and microphone system Jolene had purchased earlier that day at a big-box store with help from Caleb Connors and the campaign's opposition research team.

Nikki had decided on the Naughty Ninja costume, primarily because black was thinning and because she couldn't fit into anything else. And it had a cape, something she'd always secretly wanted to wear. In a just world, women driving minivans and cleaning up vomit would have capes, while Marvel superheroes wore yoga pants and spit-up-stained T-shirts. Because the world was not just, this might be her only opportunity.

"The camera will feed directly into Nikki's phone," Jolene said, reading the instructions. "But Nikki needs to be nearby if we want to record. Nikki also needs to turn it on and off. Ainsley is wearing the camera, but she can't control it. If Ainsley is out of range, Nikki's phone will revert to recording ambient audio and video, just like a regular phone."

"I'll hide in the closet in an upstairs bedroom," Nikki said. "And record the feed from Ainsley's camera."

"And I'll walk around the party and point my chest at anything incriminating. Once we have the evidence we need, I'll give Nikki the signal, and we'll head out the back door."

"What's the signal?" Nikki asked.

They looked at each other blankly.

"Harmonee," Ainsley said. "The code is 'Harmonee.'"

"Okay, when you say 'Harmonee,' I leave the bedroom, Godiva starts the car, Jolene calls Detective Chavez, and we get the hell out of here. Then she swoops in and makes the arrests."

Ainsley nodded. "Let's do this."

"Wait a minute," Lady Godiva interrupted. "You need to wear this too. For good luck."

She handed Ainsley and Nikki a small rectangle of leather with a hole in each end and a pair of wooden sticks that resembled knitting needles, the kind of natural, retro-feminine hair gear Nikki had worn during her Take Back the Night / Lilith Fair phase her senior year of college.

"Hairpins?" Nikki asked, pricking her finger on the sharp sticks.

"All my girls wear their hair up for private parties," Lady Godiva said as she piled Ainsley's hair into an elegant updo and secured it with the wooden sticks, making her look exactly like Barbara Eden in the *I Dream of Jeannie* reruns Nikki had watched as a kid.

Nikki shoved Godiva's contraption into her purse. Hair was the least of her worries.

They piled into the Strippermobile and headed into the night.

Chapter Fifty-Seven

AINSLEY

Songs from the golden age of stripping drifted on the night air as they parked the Strippermobile in the shadows at the edge of the yard. Aerosmith, Def Leppard, and ZZ Top blended with the odor of Aqua Net hair spray, thrusting Ainsley mentally and emotionally backward in time to the catwalk at Godiva's.

Physically, she was skulking in the bushes outside the Eastern Shore mansion, near the back door. As she waited for Nikki to sprint across the yard, she closed her eyes and chanted to herself, trying to overcome the discomfort she felt as sequins once again bit into her skin, and the crisp October air raised goose bumps on her mostly naked flesh.

You've done this before, and you can do this again. You've done this before, and you can do this again.

She had to make a mental shift and make it fast, or she'd never be able to pull this off.

Suddenly, Nikki's voice whispered in her ear. "You can do this. You're one insanely talented badass."

She exhaled. "Thanks, Nikki."

Nikki gave a curt nod. "Ready?"

"Yes."

Nikki opened the back door, and they slipped inside. Nikki disappeared up the back stairs to the bedrooms.

Ainsley adjusted her veil one last time and moved out of the mudroom; into the throngs of people clustered around the kitchen table smoking weed and playing beer pong; through the living room, where someone snorted cocaine from a mirror on the coffee table; and down to the basement, where pounding bass music thundered through speakers embedded in the ceiling while girls in lingerie pranced around the dance floor on the far side of the room.

She rotated her body as she scanned the room. If the equipment worked, if Nikki had turned on her phone, if there was enough light, then the camera in her bra should be recording everything she saw.

"I've got three wishes, baby." She repressed a shudder as a tall man wrapped one arm around her waist and pulled her close. "Bet you can figure out what they are."

She forced herself to gaze into his eyes, trailing her hand along his shoulder as she swiveled away. "Be right back."

Projecting confidence she did not feel, she moved through the room, searching for her target. But instead of Wyatt Jericho, she saw an endless crowd of abnormally tall young men and scantily clad young women. A few of the men were really just boys with acne and long legs. Could these be the high school seniors Sebastian Hampton wanted to recruit?

But they weren't all children. Some were well-groomed men in late middle age with golf-tournament tans and fat cigars, arms flung around seminaked women half their age. Alumni. Donor types.

She moved through the crowd, closer to the dance floor.

And then she found him.

There.

In the middle of a giant sectional sofa, gazing up at four young strippers gyrating onstage, sat Wyatt Jericho. An almost-naked Cleopatra lounged on his lap, stroking his hair, while a Marie Antoinette with anachronistically large silicone breast implants danced lasciviously in front of him.

Ainsley threw her shoulders back and forced herself to move closer. She sidled up to Marie Antoinette and started dancing beside her.

"It's Jeannie with the light-brown hair. Except you're a blonde," Wyatt Jericho called out over the music. "I like blondes."

"I like blondes too." She pitched her voice an octave higher, making it airy and empty, like a balloon.

He held a drink in one hand. He'd inserted the other down the front of Cleopatra's see-through dress, where he fondled her breast.

He looked up at Ainsley with a drunken leer. "What's your name, baby?"

"Misty Dawn."

"Of course it is. I haven't seen you here before."

"I'm on the circuit." She bent at the waist, thrusting her chest closer to capture the image of Wyatt Jericho fondling Cleopatra. "I just flew in from Vegas."

"Vegas?" His face flushed, and his mellow mood disappeared. "How much did that cost?"

The man who'd punched the original Misty Dawn all those years ago in the Boudoir materialized before her eyes.

Keep going. Get him angry.

"A bunch of us flew in on a private plane. I don't know how much it cost." She shrugged. "They put us up at some five-star hotel downtown. Lots of champagne. Super luxe."

He removed his hand from the girl's dress. "How come I didn't know about this?"

She shrugged again, then giggled, channeling Amber and Lacey. "You should've been there last night. We were in somebody's penthouse. Free coke. Dozens of girls. I mean, it was like *end of days*."

He muttered to himself, "Typical Sebastian. Selfish bastard."

He rose from his seat, unceremoniously dumping Cleopatra. He ran his hand across Ainsley's backside, making her toes curl in her six-inch heels.

"Don't go anywhere, Jeannie with the bright-blonde hair. I'll be right back." Then he strode out of the room.

She was about to follow him when Cleopatra looked up at her from the couch with bleary eyes. "Did you really fly in from Vegas?"

Ainsley glanced at the girl's unlined, heavily painted face. She looked like a child playing with her mother's makeup. She had to be under eighteen.

An ache settled into Ainsley's chest as she leaned in closer to record the girl's words. She'd been drinking . . . or smoking something . . . or worse.

She sat down beside her and tried not to lie directly. "Vegas is great."

"Could you, like, give me some *career advice*?" Her words came out thick, the edges slurred.

"Sure," Ainsley said.

"I'd love to work in Vegas." The girl tucked her legs beneath her, and the gesture broke Ainsley's heart. She should be at a slumber party, not an orgy.

"I want to be a *showgirl*," Cleopatra continued, making an extravagant gesture with her hands, "like in the movies. How did you do it?"

"It's kind of a long story," Ainsley said vaguely. "How long have you been dancing?"

The girl squinted up at the ceiling as she attempted to calculate the passage of time. "Like three months, I guess?"

"How old are you?"

Cleopatra paused and glanced over her shoulder. "I'm sixteen." She raised her hand and made a sluggish gesture toward two girls, one dressed as a mostly naked nurse, the other wearing Little Red Riding Hood's cape and little else. "Cadence and Kayleigh are sixteen too."

Ainsley repressed a shudder. Cleopatra raised a finger to her lips and made an exaggerated shushing sound. "But don't tell anybody, okay?"

"Don't worry." Ainsley winked, feeling guilty even though she knew her lies served a higher purpose. "So how'd you end up here?"

Cleopatra's expression brightened. "Camp Confidence. We were junior counselors last summer, making like, minimum wage. Then Wyatt told us if we wanted to make real money, we should come to these parties and start dancing at the Depot. But I want to be a *real* dancer, like the showgirls in Vegas. Not a stripper."

"You're beautiful," Ainsley said and meant it. "Any show in Vegas would be lucky to have you. Are you stripping now?"

"Just on Thursday nights down at the Depot. Godiva wouldn't hire me." She rolled her eyes. "She's a total bitch."

Ainsley nodded. "Lady Godiva is . . . something. So are you and Jericho . . ." She let her voice trail off.

"You mean have I screwed him?"

Ainsley nodded, stomach twisting as Cleopatra's girlish voice uttered these harsh, adult words.

"Yeah," Cleopatra admitted with a shrug. "A couple times. He's been with Kayleigh and Cadence too."

"So you're telling me . . ." Ainsley fought to keep the repugnance from showing on her face. "You're sixteen years old. And Kayleigh and Cadence are sixteen years old, and you've all . . . had sex . . . with Wyatt Jericho . . . more than once?"

"Yeah." She sighed. "He's like, one star. Do not recommend."

"Why?"

Cleopatra shrugged again. "Bad temper. And he's like, *super* old."

Ainsley nodded. "Bad juju. I get it. But you're young and gorgeous. You don't need geezers like Jericho. So why are you doing this?"

She gave Ainsley an odd look. "Same reason you're doing it. For the money."

"But you're still . . . in high school." She spoke carefully, bleaching her voice of any judgment. "I'm a lot older than you are."

The girl looked down at her lap. "My mom's boyfriend moved in, and it turns out he's a real asshole. Big surprise. So, I ran away. I've been couch surfing for a while, but people are tired of my mooching, and I don't have anywhere else to go. I need money for an apartment."

Ainsley stared at the girl beside her, anxious about things no child should ever have to worry about. Then she thought about her eight-bedroom house, and her guest house and her pool house, and her mother-in-law's houses. She couldn't fix everything, but she could fix this. She leaned in closer. "What if I could find you a place to live, for free."

"Nothing is free." Cleopatra's eyes went hard. "What's the catch?"

"No catch," Ainsley said. "And no skeevy guys."

"Why would you do that?" Cleopatra squinted up at her, looking genuinely puzzled by the nontransactional nature of this proposal.

Ainsley swallowed the lump forming in her throat. "Because a long time ago I needed a safe place to stay, and someone took me in, free of charge, and it changed my life."

Cleopatra went quiet for a long moment. Then she finally spoke. "If this place actually exists, and it's really free, I'd go there. Maybe."

"What's your name?" Ainsley asked.

"Jade."

Ainsley raised a disbelieving eyebrow.

The girl rolled her eyes. "Fine. It's Maddie. Maddie Raskin."

"Okay. I'm going to find you later, Maddie," Ainsley promised. "And you can come home with me. Same with Cadence and Kayleigh."

Cleopatra frowned. "But don't you live in Vegas?"

"I have a place here too."

Her eyes widened. "You must be like, really rich."

"Actually, I *am* like, really rich."

Cleopatra scrutinized Ainsley's face. "I'll think about it," she said, still wary.

Ainsley wanted to kick herself for pushing too hard. "Totally up to you." She raised her hands in a gesture of surrender. "You guys talk it over, and I'll find you later."

She rose from the couch and headed for a relatively quiet corner of the basement. Then she whispered "Harmonee" into her cleavage.

Chapter Fifty-Eight

NIKKI

Nikki couldn't believe her ears.

They'd finally done it. They had video of Wyatt Jericho casually fondling a sixteen-year-old girl whom he'd lured into working as a stripper, a girl who admitted to sleeping with him, along with two of her underage friends. They'd give this video to the *Washington Post* and every television station in the country. Once the media finished with him, Wyatt Jericho would never work at St. Preston's again, or anywhere else for that matter.

She'd been monitoring everything from beneath the massive canopied bed in the master bedroom, just in case someone came in unexpectedly. The bed sat high off the floor, with an elaborate dust ruffle, creating a perfect, if somewhat uncomfortable, hiding place. She crawled out from under the bed, set her phone on the nightstand, and began to search her pockets for her keys.

Male voices drifted up from the main staircase. She frantically patted herself down, then remembered that she'd arrived in the Strippermobile, so she didn't *have* keys.

Time to get the hell out of Dodge and let Detective Chavez take over.

She slipped out of the bedroom, squeezed down the narrow back stairs, and tiptoed out the back door. She skulked through the trees to the place where Jolene and Lady Godiva waited.

Ainsley greeted her with a broad grin as Jolene removed the tiny camera from her sister's chest and turned it off. Ainsley removed her veil and pillbox hat and tugged a sweatshirt and sweatpants over her sequined bra top and harem pants.

Ainsley pulled Nikki into a tight hug. "We did it."

"I just talked to Detective Chavez," Jolene said as she placed the tiny camera back in its padded box. "She's on another call, but she'll be here as soon as she's done."

"Lemme see that video," Godiva said. "I wanna find out which girls he's got in there."

They all crowded around Nikki. She reached into her back pocket and found—

Nothing.

She put her hands in the front pocket of her ninja costume. She slapped her hands over her entire body, even her hair, like a crazed woman engulfed in a cloud of mosquitos.

Not there. Not there. NOT THERE.

She tipped her face to the sky and released a long, low moan of despair.

She'd left the phone containing videotaped evidence of Wyatt Jericho's every sin on the nightstand. Worse yet, she'd forgotten to turn it off. The phone was unlocked and still recording. Anyone who picked it up could see who it belonged to and what was on it.

Ainsley looked like she wanted to cry. Jolene ran her hands through her hair and emitted a string of curse words.

Godiva scowled at Nikki. "I'm forgetful, but I'm *old*."

"We could come back later," Ainsley said tentatively. "After the police go in."

Nikki shook her head. "It's sitting right there on the nightstand. If anyone goes into the bedroom, they'll find it. And destroy it."

Ainsley began to remove her sweatshirt. "I'll go back inside."

"No, I'll do it," Nikki insisted.

"But they'll catch you," Ainsley argued.

Nikki shook her head. "I know exactly where I left it. I'll run up the back stairs, grab it, and be back in five minutes."

"Are you sure you can do this without getting caught?" Jolene asked.

Godiva cocked her head and observed Nikki skeptically. "You're more Mary Tyler Moore than Catwoman."

"Look." She pointed to her black-clad body. "I'm a *ninja*, remember?"

And before anyone could stop her, Nikki crept toward the house with all the stealth and skill her costume implied. Dodging behind bushes and cars, she stole up to the back door, entered the mudroom, and scrambled up the back staircase to the master bedroom.

She stopped in the long second-floor gallery and flattened herself against the wall. Her heart dropped into her shoes as she heard voices coming from the bedroom.

Someone was already inside. She'd ruined everything because she couldn't remember *anything*.

She crept along the hallway to the bedroom door, which remained open. Inside, a basketball game played on a silent television screen as Sebastian Hampton and Wyatt Jericho argued in the bedroom's sitting area.

On the opposite side of the room beside the canopied bed, Nikki's phone sat on the nightstand where she'd left it. It was only a matter of time until the men turned around. And when they did, they'd see her phone, bold as brass and plain as day, red button prominently displayed as it recorded every word they said.

Holy hell.

She had to sneak in and snatch it before they noticed. And she could do it, if they continued to engage in what sounded like a very nasty argument.

She took a cleansing breath. This mission required the exacting movements of a ninja. Or an exhausted woman who would only be rewarded with sleep if she could remove a napping baby from a car seat, carry that baby up a staircase mined with Legos and loud, battery-operated fire trucks, and place that baby in a crib, all without waking the sleeping infant.

She had the skills. She had the training. She'd had four colicky babies to provide the necessary years of practice. She could do this.

She was, after all, one talented mother.

She lowered herself to all fours and crawled across the hardwood floor, trying not to look at the men arguing on the other side of the room. She'd read something once—or had she seen it on a wilderness-survival program about people hunting antelope? Anyway, if you didn't *look* at people, they wouldn't *feel* you looking at them. Or something.

It sounded logical while watching TV in the family room with Josh and the children. It made much less sense now.

"What the hell are you doing flying strippers in from Vegas and putting them up in five-star hotels without talking to me first? And why wasn't I invited?" Wyatt Jericho stood inches from Sebastian Hampton, his fists clenched.

She grabbed the phone and slid her body under the bed as it continued to record.

From under the dust ruffle, she watched as Sebastian stood his ground. "I have no idea what you're talking about."

"Oh really," Wyatt scoffed. "One of those skanks just told me so herself, downstairs."

"Seriously, Wyatt. You're getting paranoid in your old age, and it's not a good look."

Wyatt's anger seemed to ebb, and he turned to face the television again. "You'd be paranoid, too, if someone accused you of murdering a girl you never laid a finger on."

"Oh, come on." Sebastian rolled his eyes. "You never laid a finger on Harmonee Dean? You expect anyone to believe that?"

Wyatt spun to face him again, eyes narrowed. "I was trying to *help* her. I put her up in the guest house till she could find her mom and move back in with her."

"Right." Sebastian snorted. "Then how'd she end up pregnant? Immaculate conception?"

"The baby wasn't mine." Wyatt's fists clenched again. "She got pregnant in foster care."

Silence filled the room.

"What do you mean?" Sebastian croaked in a hoarse whisper.

Wyatt gave him a quizzical look. "It was the foster dad. He ended up going to jail for it. Harmonee wasn't the only one, from what I read in the paper."

Sebastian continued to stare at him. Finally, he whispered, "So that baby—"

"Wasn't mine," Wyatt said with a shrug.

Sebastian sat down heavily on the sofa.

"What the hell is wrong with you?" Wyatt asked.

Sebastian rubbed his hands over his face. "I can't believe this."

"Can't believe what?"

He looked up at Wyatt with hollow eyes. "I . . . I took care of it."

There was another long pause. Nikki watched a range of expressions flicker over Wyatt's face, like a time-lapse video. Confusion, stunned shock, then revulsion.

"You mean you *killed* her?" he whispered, incredulous.

"I was trying to protect you." Sebastian gazed up at him with a dazed look. "I showed up here one day to retrieve some cocaine I left behind, and Harmonee wandered out of the guest house. She told me she was pregnant and wanted to name the baby after you . . ." His voice trailed off.

Wyatt's lip curled. "So you assumed I was the father."

"Oh, come on." Sebastian's voice turned savage. "I can't count all the underage girls you've screwed. I'll bet you can't either."

"True. But Harmonee was . . . different. She was an artist, like my mom . . . I wanted to protect her. I never touched her."

Sebastian hung his head. "You'd just won us our first championship. Things were going so well . . . and I was afraid that if people found out you'd fathered a child with a fifteen-year-old runaway, you'd go to jail and your career would be over."

"So, you killed her." Wyatt's eyes were hard.

"I did. I killed her," he repeated in a hollow voice. "I still . . . some days I still can't believe I *did* that."

Wyatt's lip curled. "You're an animal."

"She didn't suffer." Sebastian turned to him, his voice pleading, as though his method of killing somehow absolved him.

"You *murdered* her," Wyatt pointed out, his voice dripping with scorn.

"I didn't hurt her," he protested, like a child who thinks everything can be forgiven if he just apologizes. "And I regret it, okay? I've regretted it every day of my life. But at the time, I didn't think I had a choice. My aunt was due back in the house for Thanksgiving, and here's this fifteen-year-old runaway living in the guest house, carrying what I thought was your child, and I just . . . I panicked."

Wyatt exhaled deeply, then sank down on the sofa beside Sebastian. "I cared about her, you know? She was tough but sweet. I wanted to help her. I *was* helping her."

Sebastian ran his hands through his hair. "I didn't want to do it. I just . . . I slammed the door and locked her inside, and then . . . I canceled the cleaning people and stayed away for a couple weeks . . . and then it was done. I left her body in the woods a few miles away . . . and that was it."

"And you never told me," Wyatt said, shaking his head in disbelief.

"I didn't think you needed to know. And I didn't *want* anyone to know. It's not exactly my finest hour."

"But now someone *does* know," Wyatt said. "So, what do we do?"

Sebastian thought for a moment. Then he stood. "Nothing. No one's gonna believe a former stripper."

"But she's more than a former stripper," Wyatt argued. "Her husband's rich and he's probably gonna be governor. And that other one used to be a TV anchor. She's got connections."

Sebastian rolled his eyes. "No one's gonna believe a couple hysterical moms."

Wyatt stroked his chin, deep in thought. "Maybe we need to lay low for a while. No more parties. Maybe we liquidate the fund and move the cash into something respectable."

"Like Camp Confidence?" Sebastian suggested, and they both snickered.

"I don't know." Jericho stood. "Maybe we do a legit scholarship fund, until things settle down."

"But I still need to recruit, and raise money," Sebastian pointed out. "And I don't have you as coach anymore. You were a major inducement."

Wyatt shrugged. "Maybe we do what all the other schools do for a season. Play by the rules like everyone else."

"You mean campus tours and pizza parties with some Nikes gifted under the table?" Sebastian gave a derisive snort. "Like *that's* going to entice anyone. Plus, that guy we hired to replace you is a total nimrod. The program is gonna be a hard sell without you and our other . . . inducements."

"We'll figure something out."

"We always have," Sebastian said. "I hope you can forgive me, man."

Wyatt Jericho clapped him on the shoulder. "You did it for me, and that says a lot."

Sebastian picked up the remote and turned off the TV. "Let's try to forget about it for tonight. We'll deal with the whole mess tomorrow."

Jericho ran his hand through his hair and sighed. "We do have a lot of coke and naked women downstairs. Might be a while before we can do this again. No point in letting it all go to waste."

Nikki sucked in a breath. These men shrugged off murder the way other people discarded a sweater on a warm day.

"I'll meet you down there," Sebastian said. "I gotta hit the head first."

Wyatt left the room, but every muscle in Nikki's body tensed as Sebastian headed for the bathroom suite to the right of the bed. She stared up at the box spring, not daring to breathe.

And then, as his shoes moved across the carpet and crossed the threshold into the bathroom, Nikki's phone rang.

Harp music spilled from her phone, filling the room.

She stared in frozen horror at the caller ID. Once again, her mother was calling.

"What the hell?" Sebastian Hampton crossed the room in two giant steps and grabbed Nikki's feet.

Chapter Fifty-Nine

NIKKI

He wrapped his giant hands around her shoes and tugged her out from under the bed. As he pulled her from her hiding place, she lunged for the red button on her phone, trying to pick up the most important call of her life, the call that would allow her to scream for help, if only she could answer.

With a hard slap, Sebastian knocked the phone from her hands. It flew across the room and skidded under a massive armoire, where it stopped ringing.

"What in the hell—" he began again, panting.

Nikki scrambled to her feet and lunged for the door. He grabbed her cape and yanked her backward.

Don't jog with a ponytail. An assailant can grab your hair and use it to control you.

Random scraps of advice careened through her mind, gleaned from the self-defense classes Gus had provided for all female station employees after the incident with Deeply Disturbed Dominic in the parking lot.

Assailants can also grab capes, she observed from some numb place inside her mind. *So why do superheroes wear capes when they are clearly so impractical?*

She struggled with the knot at her throat, trying to rid herself of the dumbest article of clothing ever invented. "Let me go!"

He pulled on the cape, reeling her in like a fish. "How much did you hear?"

Nikki shook her head. "I didn't hear anything."

He wrenched her arm backward. A scorching pain radiated from her shoulder socket. "Liar."

He dragged her across the room to a tall antique dresser. Pinning her arm behind her back with one hand, he used the other to rummage through what looked like a lingerie drawer and removed a handful of silk scarves. He used one to tie her hands together, then yanked her forward. "Come with me."

Her heart stopped. *Never let an assailant take you to a second location.*

"Oh. I see." She infused her voice with a veneer of bravado about as thick as a piece of Scotch tape. "Now you're gonna add kidnapping to your murder charge?"

Use anything you can find as a weapon.

The hairpins Godiva had given her . . . those could be used as a weapon. If they weren't stuffed in the bottom of her purse back in the Strippermobile.

Sebastian gave her an appraising look, freezing the blood in her veins. "I've already killed once. I'm sure it's easier the second time around."

His words sank deep into her bones, unleashing a string of terrible realizations.

She'd been an adrenaline junkie all her life. Now her desire to chase the big story might actually *end* her life, taking her away from the job that mattered most . . . raising her children.

Who would wrap the Christmas presents? Who would tell the girls how to use tampons? Who would order the corsage for Daniel's prom date? Who would plan the next birthday party? Who would mother her children if this man killed her tonight?

She shook her head to dispel these terrible thoughts.

Focus, Nikki.

"You can't drag me out of here in front of all these people." She'd begun to babble. "Someone will see you."

He grinned. "Servant's staircase. No one will see us. Or hear us."

He stuffed the other scarf into her mouth, and she fought to control her gag reflex. Asphyxiating on her own vomit was not a good survival strategy.

Stall for time.

That's what she'd done in the parking lot that night with Dominic.

She stomped down hard on his foot. He slapped her across the face and continued to drag her from the room.

Use your body as a weapon. Become deadweight.

She went limp and sank to the ground, kicking her feet against the floor to make noise. He grabbed her hair and began to drag her. She moaned as loudly as she could through the gag.

He punched her in the throat. Her eyes began to water as she choked and gasped for breath. The silk scarf in her mouth made it impossible to bring air into her lungs.

She began to hyperventilate as he grabbed her hair again and yanked her to her feet.

Breathe. Don't pass out. Just breathe.

Air entered her windpipe again as he manhandled her down the narrow back stairs, through some kind of servant's entrance, and outside. He tugged a ring of keys from his pocket and pressed a button. In the darkness a few yards from the house, an answering beep pinged from his car.

Never let an assailant take you to a second location.

Panic rose in the back of her mind, threatening to blot out reason and the ability to think clearly.

Focus, Nikki.

She looked down at her bound hands. If she hadn't been gagged, she might have smiled.

He'd made one mistake. It might be enough.

Digging her toes into the dirt, she scuffed her feet across the gravel to slow their progress as he dragged her to the car. He shoved her to the ground and opened the trunk.

He arranged a blanket across the back, then yanked her to her feet and turned to face her.

Now.

She raised her hands and spread her fingers, launching an arsenal of dirt and gravel into his widened eyes.

Chapter Sixty

AINSLEY

Ainsley gnawed on her thumbnail as she squinted up at the house. "Something's wrong. She's been gone for twenty minutes."

If anything happened to Nikki, it would be her fault.

"Text her," Jolene said.

"She doesn't answer."

"Then call her."

"No," Ainsley said. "What if she's hiding?"

Jolene began to pace in front of the Strippermobile. "Text her again."

"Something's wrong," Ainsley repeated, tossing her phone into the van. "I'm going back to find her."

"No way." Jolene grabbed her sister by the arm. "We wait for Detective Chavez."

Ainsley broke away from Jolene's grip and ripped off her sweatpants and sweatshirt, inhaling sharply as the cold air bit into her exposed skin.

"What if it takes her fifteen minutes to get here? Or longer? Do you know what can happen to a woman in a place like this in fifteen minutes?"

Jolene went quiet. "They'll recognize you."

Ainsley reattached her veil. "My face is covered, and I'm in costume. No one recognized me before."

"Maybe we got lucky last time."

Ainsley adjusted her top, trying to cover as much of herself as possible with the limited material available. "Call Detective Chavez again. Tell her Nikki's in danger and she needs to drop whatever she's doing and come *now*."

She took off across the yard, struggling over the grass in high heels, entering through the same door she'd used before.

A cacophony of odors and sounds assaulted her senses as she melted into a forest of tall men. The fruity scent of the vape cartridges favored by the young dancers mingled with the pungent musk of cigars smoked by the donors and middle-aged men, with an earthy undertone of weed and cheese pizza floating beneath it all. The noise level had risen. Aerosmith pounded from speakers in the ceiling, and guttural voices shouted "Drink, drink, drink" from the table in the corner of the kitchen.

Goose bumps sprouted across her naked skin as the party descended like a boulder rolling downhill, faster and faster toward a lawless, feral crescendo. At the club, they had bouncers and rules to protect dancers.

Here, they had nothing. Which was why she'd always refused to work private parties.

Until tonight.

Instinctively, she clutched at the diaphanous material sewn into the straps of her sequined bra top. Every nerve in her body screamed for the exit.

Leave. Right now.

But she couldn't. Not without Nikki. She pushed her way through the crowd, searching for the black ninja costume.

Suddenly giant hands skimmed her waist.

A man who didn't look old enough to shave towered over her with a drunken leer. "Hey, Blondie, take off your veil and gimme a kiss."

Beside him another man-child leered down at her, then raised his enormous hands and squeezed her breasts.

She shuddered and tried to quell her rising panic. "Let me go."

"C'mon, Blondie." Spittle flew from his lips as he slurred his words. "Ditch the veil and gimme a kiss."

"Stop it." An undercurrent of fear pitched her voice higher.

The second man reached for her veil and tore it away, crumpling it in his fist. "Why you wanna cover such a pretty face?"

Disgust rose inside her, laced with dread. Then an instinct from long ago curved her lips into a seductive pout.

"You guys wanna go upstairs?"

A stupid grin crossed their faces. "Um. *Yeah.*"

"I'm gonna grab my friend Jezebel. We'll meet you in the bedroom at the top of the stairs, okay?"

They nodded, speechless.

Casting a coy glance over her shoulder, she ran her tongue over her lips and batted her lashes as she moved away.

Then she wove as quickly as she could through the dense crowd on the main floor, veil gone, face exposed, searching for Nikki.

Frantically, she scanned the rooms on the first floor, but found only strippers and drunk men.

Time to search the basement. Squaring her shoulders, she descended to the place where Harmonee died. At the bottom of the stairs, she became stuck in a logjam of partygoers, unable to move forward or backward. Rising on her toes, she tried to see above the crowd. Her gaze landed on the man in front of her. The back of his neck looked familiar, or maybe it was his ears, which stuck out just a little too far.

She froze in stunned horror as he turned.

Wyatt Jericho.

Every cell in her body screamed at her to run, but she couldn't. The crowd made escape impossible.

Recognition flashed across his face as he reached out and grabbed her wrist. Twisting, she tried to break free but couldn't rupture his grip.

He pulled her through the crowd, tearing a hole in the crush of people, dragging her down a hallway and into a bedroom.

The door slammed shut, filling her ears with sudden silence. As her eyes adjusted to the dim light, he turned the dead bolt, locking them inside.

With rising panic, she took in the odd assortment of equipment arranged around the room.

A giant bed with metal slats at the head and foot sat in the center, surrounded by scaffolding with lights and cameras attached.

"Welcome to the studio," he said.

Her gaze darted around the room. No windows. Only one door. Black soundproofing panels covered the walls.

No one would hear her scream.

He reached for a cardboard box and dumped the contents on the floor. Ropes, blindfolds, handcuffs, sex toys. Then he pulled a black balaclava from the pile. He tugged it over his head, turning him into a creature from a nightmare.

He unbuckled his belt.

She dug her nails into her palms and forced her racing mind to focus.

What could she use as a weapon? Could she somehow handcuff him to the bed?

"This is a new venture for us," he explained as he moved around the room, always staying between her and the door. He flipped on the bright lights surrounding the bed and turned on one of the cameras. "There's a lot of money in porn, the darker the better."

He tossed his belt onto the floor and began unbuttoning his shirt. "The louder you scream, the more money I make."

He removed his shirt and picked up a slender rope. Then he took a step toward her. Suddenly she heard Godiva's voice inside her head.

All my girls wear their hair up for private parties.

She reached up and removed the pins from her hair. Blonde curls tumbled to her shoulders.

The back of her throat filled with bile as his lip curled. "Good girl. You may as well lay back and enjoy it."

He closed the distance between them in one giant stride, shoved her against the wall, crushed his body into hers.

She raised her arm, plunged the hairpin into the side of his neck, and listened to him scream.

Chapter Sixty-One

NIKKI

With her hands still bound in front of her, Nikki tried to run. As she lumbered toward the Strippermobile, Sebastian Hampton's uneven footsteps crunched the gravel behind her.

She glanced back. Even with his eyes pinched almost completely shut, he stumbled after her. Then he lunged. She hit the ground hard, gravel biting into her skin as he took her down in a football tackle.

He straddled her, eyes swollen, oozing tears, and slapped her across the face. "You bitch. Get in the car."

A loud click froze them both in place.

"Don't move, dirt ball."

Nikki dared to look up. Detective Chavez stood over her with a gun pointed at Sebastian's head. A second officer pulled him off Nikki and cuffed him. She rolled onto her side, coughing.

As the night sky filled with the scream of sirens and the strobe of flashing lights, Ainsley stumbled from the house, hair streaming behind her. Nikki rose and ran toward her.

They sank into the dirt, holding each other as they cried.

Chapter Sixty-Two

NIKKI

It was a busy night for Detective Chavez and the officers from neighboring jurisdictions who answered her call for backup. They arrested seventy-eight recruits, current players, donors, and alumni with a wide range of crimes. Nikki roamed the house and yard, taping the arrests with her phone.

With assistance from Lady Godiva, the thirty-seven strippers present at the party vanished into the night. The three underage girls went home with Jolene, who put them up in her condo until they could find a more permanent solution.

Nikki called her old assignment editor and tipped her off to the many men about to descend on the police department for fingerprinting and processing. Channel 9 sent a crew, scooped the competition, and saturated the airwaves with guilty faces. Within minutes, every print and broadcast outlet in the country joined in the coverage.

Wyatt Jericho learned he'd been fired from St. Preston's while handcuffed to a hospital gurney awaiting stitches in his neck. Sebastian Hampton, who'd been charged with murder, sat shackled beside him as a nurse pretended to be gentle while flushing dirt and gravel from his eyes.

By Thanksgiving, the scandal had grown into an FBI investigation accompanied by televised congressional hearings, inevitably known as Strippergate.

After the hearings, and under pressure from the public and Congress, the university freed the former Biltmore players from their nondisclosure agreements. Nikki organized a press conference, where they told their stories publicly for the first time.

When it ended, she sprinted through Target to buy diapers before preschool pickup.

Scarred by the forgotten-phone incident in the mansion, she'd invented a sort of locket-necklace lanyard. She called it the Forget-Me-Not Cell Phone Necklace. When her phone rang in the diaper aisle, she answered with smooth efficiency.

"Hello?"

Gus's voice filled her ear. "How would you like your old job back?"

Nikki froze, effectively blocking the entire aisle. "You're kidding."

"They fired the Cold Brew Kid, and then they fired that woman who replaced you. Fletcher Avery or Avery Fletcher, or whatever her name was."

"Why?" She dug in the diaper bag for a teething ring as Baby Joe tried to devour her grocery list.

"She and Cold Brew were having an affair," Gus explained. "Her husband owns nine Toyota dealerships, and he pulled all his ads in a jealous rage. Sent the station into a financial tailspin. They both got fired, and the owners begged me to come back and fix the mess. I'd like you to be my first hire."

She removed the sodden grocery list from the baby's fist and tried to wrap her mind around everything Gus was saying.

"Things will be tough for a while," he continued. "Cold Brew ran the station into the ground. It's gonna take a lot of work to pull the ratings back up to where they were before."

She traveled to the milk aisle, pulled three cartons from the cooler, and tried to interpret the strange feelings roiling through her mind and body, the prickle of elation and the mantle of dread that simultaneously draped her heart.

It belonged to the same family of feelings created by an impending trip to visit her in-laws in Florida. The anticipation of palm trees and sun mixed with anxiety over her mothers-in-law's questions about why Daniel still ate spaghetti with his fingers.

"I don't know, Gus . . . I need to think about it."

Silence echoed through the phone. "Is it the kids?" he asked gently.

"Yes." She pushed her cart into the bread aisle. "I love reading to them at night. I love picking them up from school. But I also loved you and my job and everything we accomplished. I *want* to work again. But I don't want to work the way I worked before."

There. She grabbed a baguette and flung it into her cart. *I said it.*

She'd thought these words a thousand times, but never dreamed she'd have the courage to say them *out loud*, never considered *asking* for what she wanted, because what if they said no? What if they fired her for asking?

Now she didn't care.

She had skills. Lots of skills, and she could find other ways to earn an income. Best of all, she could survive without her job, because she *wasn't* her job anymore. She was a mother, a wife, a sister, an aunt, a friend, a crusader against human trafficking, an informal adviser to the governor and First Lady, a member of the St. Preston's governing board, and chair of the search committee to replace Wyatt Jericho and Mr. Rupert Smedley Philpott. *And* she was the inventor of the Forget-Me-Not Cell Phone Necklace.

Plus, Josh now made a very healthy income crafting custom furniture with Guzluk and Petru. He even had a three-year waiting list for his new dining tables, thanks to Kenneth.

"Tell me what you want," Gus said.

She pinched the bridge of her nose and spoke quickly, before she lost her nerve. "I want to anchor the ten o'clock show, after my kids are in bed, but I don't want to do the six o'clock show. And I want to work a split shift, so I can work when they're in school, then pick them up and be home for dinner."

"Okay. Anything else?"

"I'd like to do more reporting. And I want to help the First Lady with a special project."

"Project Runaway?"

"Yeah."

"Okay," Gus said. "Done."

Nikki's mouth fell open. "Really?"

"Really. I'll have the lawyers send over the contract. You can start whenever you're ready."

She leaned against the cart, weak with surprise. "Thank you, Gus. For everything."

"No problem. See you back at the ranch."

She hung up the phone and gazed in stunned amazement at Baby Joe's perfect face. He gave her a wide grin, displaying both teeth, as she thanked the creator of the universe for answering her every prayer.

She pushed her cart toward the pharmacy, where one last errand waited. Time to refill her ADD medication.

Chapter Sixty-Three

AINSLEY

Ainsley braced herself as a gaggle of mothers approached at pickup. She had big news to share with Nikki, but first she'd have to deal with her adoring public.

She buttoned an old coat against the November chill and prepared for the usual onslaught. Now she wore clothes she *wanted* to wear, not outfits other people expected her to wear.

After the Wyatt Jericho scandal broke, Tiffany Hastings and her husband were asked to resign from the governing board, and they'd responded by pulling their daughter from the school.

In her absence, Ainsley had inherited Tiffany's posse. This puzzled her at first. Then she realized followers needed someone to follow.

Blonde Jennifer laid a hand on Ainsley's arm, repeating a version of the lie Ainsley had heard multiple times over the last few weeks. "I *tried* to tell Tiffany that Wyatt Jericho was trouble, but she just wouldn't listen."

The other mothers nodded while Also Blonde Jennifer launched into a long story she'd heard about Wyatt Jericho from her husband's dentist's golf partner. Someone else plied Ainsley with questions about her inauguration gown.

"What's your *platform*?" Red Jennifer asked. "I really hope you'll raise awareness about the importance of kale in school lunches. It's a superfood, you know."

She'd heard that Red Jennifer had ditched Big Tobacco and was now lobbying for the Association of American Vegetable Growers.

Ainsley gave a noncommittal reply. After a polite interval, she excused herself and found Nikki, who appeared to be hiding out in her minivan.

Nikki lowered her window. "Has the Hour of Adoration ended already?"

"It's too much," Ainsley said, shaking her head. "I'm starting to miss being the school pariah."

"What's this big news you have?"

"I just talked to Lady Godiva." Ainsley tried and failed to repress an enormous grin. "She decided not to sell her place to the doggie day care people after all."

Nikki frowned. "Who is she selling to?"

"Us!" Ainsley shouted, drawing stares from the parents clustered near the school.

Nikki's mouth dropped open. "For Project Runaway?"

"Yes! We'll have space for bedrooms, classrooms, a family room where the girls can hang out, and office space where we can work. And Jolene is taking a leave of absence from her job to run things until we get staffed up."

Ainsley pulled a leather-bound planner out of her purse and handed it to Nikki.

"What's this?" Nikki asked.

"I made it for you. It's preloaded with dates for all the Project Runaway board meetings, plus early-dismissal days, summer camp dates for the girls, and all the inaugural events we hope you and Josh will attend."

Nikki ran her hands over her initials embossed on the cover. "If we combine this with my ADD meds, I'll be an *organizational weapon*."

“Are the meds helping?” Ainsley asked.

“I always suspected drugs might be the solution to all my problems, and I was right.”

“You’ve been right about a lot of things, Nikki.”

“I still have doubts about my own abilities.” Nikki looked up at her friend. “But I have no doubts about what you and I can accomplish together.”

The school doors opened, and a wave of children streamed across the playground to find their parents. Isabella, Olivia, and Grace ran to their mothers, hair bows bobbing, faces lit with laughter.

Ainsley and Nikki walked forward to meet them, together.

Acknowledgments

This is an incomplete list of the many wonderful people who made this book possible with their love and support:

Michelle Grajkowski of Three Seas Literary. Your expertise, brainstorming, and overall midwestern fabulousness made my dreams come true. Thank you, a thousand times, for everything you do.

Chantelle Aimée Osman, Grace Wynter, and the incredible team at Lake Union. Thank you for taking the best book I could write and making it so much better. I am beyond grateful for your vision and faith.

To altruistic friends who donated time they do not have to read early drafts: Maureen Allen, Brittany Butler, Meghan Campione, Laralyn Doran, Tracey Hewitt Meyer, Nicole Mahon, Kim McCarron, Gibson McMahon, Claire Parker, Christy Simon, and Sharon Wishnow.

To my BSSM ladies: thank you for standing with me in the trenches of motherhood.

To Clay Shields and Sonia Stoszek, for Thanksgiving and Mother's Day, and diplomatically pointing out the underground solar panels in my books.

To the cast of Stale Air: Christine Aliverto, Charlie Klauer, Mary Beth Schultz, and Julie Umstead. Old friends never grow old. :-)

To my Golden Heart Sisters: Tracy Brody, Claire DeWolf, Fenley Grant, Betsy Grey, Melanie McCarthy, Becke Turner, Janet Walden West, Diane Wiggs, and Janet Raye Stevens. Thank you for keeping me accountable and making me laugh while you do it.

To Lisa May, producer extraordinaire, who taught me to write in the chaos of a newsroom.

To Greg Gunderson and Susan Heisler. Thank you for believing in me even when I didn't.

To E, M, and K. You make me laugh, you make me proud, you make me grateful. "I love you more than the sky could be built."

To Brian, the hero of my story and the captain of my heart. You made this possible. Thank you, with all my love.

And finally, to you, the reader. When you purchased and read this book, you made my dream come true. Thank you from the bottom of my heart. I truly hope you enjoyed it.

Friends with Secrets Book Club Discussion Questions

1. Do you think society has unrealistic expectations for women in general and mothers in particular? If so, where do you think those expectations come from?
2. At its core, this is a book about friendship. Do you feel it's more or less difficult to make new friends as we become older?
3. In what ways is making a new friend similar to or different from starting a new romantic relationship?
4. Nikki and Ainsley both have supportive spouses, yet they still have a deep need for a close friend. What needs do friends fill in our lives that spouses or romantic partners do not?
5. Can you think of any recent examples where girls or women were dismissed or not believed when they came forward with allegations of misconduct?
6. Do you feel this book accurately portrays the challenges of modern parenthood? What's accurate? What may be missing?
7. Are you more like Nikki or Ainsley? What are the challenges of disorganization and what are the challenges of perfectionism? Which do you think is harder to

overcome? At what point should we strive to change and "improve," and at what point should we learn to accept ourselves as we are?

8. What do you think of Ainsley's secret? How would you feel if you had a similar secret? How would you or others would react if you found out a friend, colleague, or fellow parent had a similar secret?
9. This book discusses issues of class. Would it be difficult for someone from a lower-income background to "fit" in an upper-middle-class environment? What are the challenges they might face? Do you feel you have contact with people from a variety of socioeconomic backgrounds in your daily life? Or do you feel that our society is becoming increasingly stratified by class, income, and education level?
10. Ainsley is happy at home with her children while Nikki feels trapped. How do their personalities, backgrounds, and occupations make the choice to work or stay home different for these two women? Do you feel women are judged for the decisions they make? Why?

About the Author

Photo © 2023 Renee C. Gage Photography

Christine Gunderson grew up on a fourth-generation family farm in rural North Dakota where she read Laura Ingalls Wilder books in her very own little house on the prairie. She's a former television anchor and reporter and former Capitol Hill aide. She currently lives in the Washington, DC, suburbs with her three children, Star the Wonder Dog, and a very patient husband. When not writing, she's sailing the Chesapeake Bay with her family, playing Star Wars Monopoly, rereading Jane Austen novels in the school pickup line, or unloading the dishwasher.

Christine loves to hear thoughts and ideas from readers or, best of all, delightful emails telling her she succeeded in making you laugh out loud while reading this book.

You can contact her at www.christinegunderson.com.